Dr
STANTON

T L SWAN

AKNOWLEDGEMENTS

I always struggle with this part of the book because there are simply not enough words in the English dictionary to describe my gratitude. Let me try.

To my beautiful mum, your support and friendship means more to me than you could ever imagine. I love you dearly.

To Vicki—the best friend on the face of the Earth. Thank you for all that you do. I can never repay you for your friendship and laughs.

To Am and Rachel M—you two are the reason I can do this gig and stay sane.

You make me laugh every day. Thank you for all that you do. It was a blessing the day you both came into my life.

To Lisa K—my angel from across the water. Your friendship and support is so appreciated. You mean the world to me and are dearly loved.

To Lisa D. Our friendship brightens my day. Thank you so much for all that you do and your encouraging words all the way from Ireland.

To Nadia. Your honesty is adored. I can't wait until the day we finally meet, my friend.

To Linda—you are loved. Thank you so much for all that you do for me.

To my beautiful team: Rachel, Nicole, Brooke, Jodie, and Jane. Thank you for all that you do for me.

To the rocking chicks in my reader group, the Swan Squad.

I love you all and can't wait until the day we get to meet in person. Your support and friendship means the world to me.

To Victoria—you make me better and make me laugh. That's a lethal combination.

To all the bloggers who support indie authors—thank you so much and big hugs.

To every single person who has ever taken the time to read one of my books…

You are the reason I get to live this amazing dream.

Who knew professional Day Dream Believing was possible?

To Ashley and Cameron, you were a dream to write about and I had a smile on my face the whole time. Thank you.

xxx

To my gorgeous hubs. Everything I know about love, I learned from you.
To my three beautiful children—I love you endlessly
Thank you for supporting me.
Xoxoxox

Dr
STANTON

1

Vegas

1OAK Nightclub

I FROWN as the man covered in perspiration tries to cling to me. *Oh, for Heaven's sake.* "Do you mind?" I rip my arm from his grip. The music is pumping and I'm waiting at the bar.

"Not at all," he slurs.

Oh God. My eyes flicker over to my group of friends and I watch as they all smile and raise their glasses to me in jest. Damn them. This bachelorette weekend away is reminding me why I am eternally single. I fake a smile. *Bitches.*

"I mean it, baby. Let's dance."

I roll my eyes. "I can't, I'm waiting for someone so you should probably run along."

"Who?" he asks. Give up, you pushy bastard.

A tall and dark haired, handsome guy walks past, and I quickly grab him by the arm. He frowns as he turns back toward us.

"Erm… This guy. "I smirk.

1

The creepy guy frowns and curls his lip to check out his competition.

My eyes scan up and down the man I've just grabbed.

Oh, he's gorgeous. I timed that well.

The guy raises an eyebrow as his eyes flick between the other guy and me.

"This is my husband." I smile as I link my arm through his. He looks like he could be nice. I'm sure he'll save me.

The tall guy raises an eyebrow in surprise and smiles. "And you are my... wife?" he questions.

I nod. "Uh-huh." Oh boy, don't blow my cover.

Mr. Tall dark and handsome turns his gaze onto the man before us as he snakes his arm around my waist. "I see you've met my gorgeous wife then?"

I narrow my eyes as I listen to his voice. I think he's Australian.

The creepy guy narrows his eyes. "You don't know him." He sneers. "I don't believe you."

Mr. Tall dark and handsome smirks and leans over, grabbing the back of my head before he pulls me towards him. His tongue rims my lips and he sucks on my mouth. His tongue takes no prisoners as it swirls deeper into my mouth.

What the frigging hell?

His hand drops to my behind and he squeezes the cheek in his hand. Oh my God, this was not in the brochure.

He pulls away and licks his lips as his eyes drop to my breasts then back up to my face.

I fake a smile as my mind goes totally blank. "Huh." My eyes glance back at the other guy as I lick my lips. Holy crap. What kind of kiss was that? "Umm."

Mr. Tall dark and handsome takes my hand in his. "Fuck off, mate. She's with me." He then pulls me by the hand through the crowd. What, wait! Where are we going? I look over at my friends who are all high fiving each other over my random kiss with Mr. Holy Hot. Should I just pull out of his grip? What the hell for? This guy is freaking delicious. Oh shit.

We arrive at his group of friends and he puts his arm around my waist to pull my body close to his.

"Boys," he calls to his large group of friends. "You will be pleased to know I just got married on my way back from the bar. Please meet my new wife."

Their eyes meet and they all shake their heads and laugh.

"Hello." They all smile.

"Nice to meet you," one man replies as he shakes my hand.

I smirk as my fake husband's fingers tighten around my waist."

"About time," another guy says as he shakes his hand. "Congratulations, mate. What's your wife's name?"

His eyes flick to me as he thinks before he smiles sexily again. "Blossom."

I laugh out loud. "Blossom?"

His friends all look me up and down, smiling before then going back to their conversation as if this exchange is a common occurrence.

His eyes drop to my breasts again.

"My eyes are up here," I tell him. He can't even pretend not to stare.

He picks up his beer and drinks it. "So?"

I frown, of all the nerve. "So... you keep looking at my boobs."

"You noticed?"

My mouth drops open. "Well, yeah. I'm not imagining it."

He smirks as he sips his beer. "That's exactly what I'm doing."

His friend returns with a tray of drinks. "Murph," he calls. "Come meet Bloss."

His friend raises his eyebrows. "Hello." He smiles as he shakes my hand and passes me a drink.

"Thank you." I smile gratefully. I look between the six men he is with. These guys are all gorgeous... and cultured. Expensive suits and clothes. I glance back at my friends on the other side of the bar and I bite my bottom lip. I'll just have this drink and then go back over to them. It can't possibly hurt to have one drink.

His friend turns back to the other men, while tall dark and handsome's eyes drop to my breasts again.

"What are you doing?" I shake my head.

"Imagining."

I raise a brow. "Imagining what?"

"How those tits are going to look around my cock tonight while I fuck them."

My mouth drops open in shock.

He smiles a slow and sexy smile. "You were safer with the other guy."

My eyes hold his. I have no words.

"Because, unlike him, I will get you to do what I want to do. And tonight I want to fuck those big juicy tits of yours."

My brain misfires as I get a visual of him naked above me, sliding his cock between my...

Woah. It's been too long.

"T-that's not happening," I stammer.

He shuffles around in his suit jacket pocket and pulls out a fifty-dollar note. "Do you want to place a bet on that?"

"What an over confident prick you are." I shake my head. Never have I had such a cheap pick up line used on me. "And yes..." I snatch the fifty dollars from his hand.
"I will bet fifty dollars on you *not* getting your cock between my boobs tonight."

He winks and clinks his glass with mine as he raises a sexy brow. "Thank you. I will take that as a personal challenge."

I shake my head as I sip my drink. "Does that ridiculous pick up line work on many women?"

He smiles and winks cheekily. "You would be surprised."

I smirk. There is something extremely honest about this guy. He isn't pretending to be someone he's not.

It's disarming.

His hand drops to my behind again, and he rubs it as he smiles to himself, looking me up and down.

I raise a brow. "You can stop looking at me like I'm your next fuck. There will be no physical activity between us tonight. I'm not that kind of girl."

He leans over and kisses me again. "Stop talking." He smiles against my lips. "You are only making the challenge so much sweeter for me. I am a goal orientated man, you know."

"Happy wife, happy life," I reply sarcastically.

"Blossom, do you really think I couldn't make you happy as my wife if that were my intention?" He raises his brow.

I laugh out loud. "Shut up, you freak. Who says this shit and gets away with it?"

He laughs out loud as his hands drop to my behind again.

Two hours and six cocktails later...

The sight of his huge cock sliding between my breasts is driving me crazy. We're back in his room, unable to control our mutual attraction, acting like animals. This is casual sex at its absolute finest. This guy is gorgeous, intelligent, funny, and sexy as fuck. Not to mention he's hung like a bloody horse. I've died and gone to Vegas Heaven. His knees are on either side of my body as he kneels over me. Large, dark brown eyes stare down at me, and I arch my back, unable to hold the urge to fuck. How did he get me here, doing this?

I'm not this kind of girl, but holy hell, he makes being bad so much damn fun.

He bends and kisses me, his tongue seductively dancing with mine. "You owe me fifty bucks." He smiles against my lips.

I laugh out loud. "Bastard."

"Time to work off your debt," he whispers as he drives his body forward through my breasts. His eyes close in pleasure as his hands encase my breasts around his cock. "You have the best fucking tits I have ever seen." He growls.

My eyes roll back in my head. God, this is payment enough. What could be better than this visual sensation?

He begins to really pound my chest until the bed starts to rock and my sex clenches in pleasure. Holy fuck, I need this dick inside me *now*.

I laugh out loud. This is unbelievable. How the hell did this guy get me back to his room, having me owe him fifty dollars for the privilege?

He smiles sexily as his mouth hangs slack with arousal. "Arrêter de rire ou je remplirai votre bouche avec ma bite," he whispers as he looks down at me.

Translation: Stop laughing or I will fill your mouth with my cock.

An unexpected thrill runs through me as I reply, "Je pourrais prendre tout cela."

Translation: I could take it all.

His eyebrow rises in surprise. "Tu parle français?" he asks as he rolls a condom on.

Translation: You speak French?

I grab the back of his head bring it to mine. "Je baise en français trop," I whisper against his lips.

Translation: I fuck in French, too.

His mouth ravages mine and I feel his hard cock slide between my wet lips. Back and forth he glides his length. I smile. Let's up the anti.

"Obwohl, wenn ich in Deutsch ficken ist, wenn I'm in meinem besten," I whisper as my arousal hits a fever pitch.

Translation: Although, when I fuck in German is when I'm at my best.

He laughs into my mouth and lifts my legs over his shoulder as he impales me in one hard slam. We stay still and our eyes close in pleasure.

Holy fuck.

This guy is good… and *huge*.

"Sie sollten sehen, was Sie sagen, deutsch meine Bruchstelle ist," he whispers as he pulls out and slides home again.

6

Translation: You should watch what you say, German is my breaking point.

My back arches off the bed. Oh God, this is too good. His brain is as sharp as his body. I don't know anyone else bilingual, and these exchanges are blowing my freaking mind. "Ich wollte deinen Schwanz in den Mund," I breathe.

Translation: I wanted your cock in my mouth.

He pulls out and immediately hovers above me as he feeds his cock into my open mouth. I taste my own salty arousal. Shit. This guy is off the fucking hook.

"Votre souhait est ma commande ma chère femme."

Translation: Your wish is my command, my dear wife.

I smile around the large penis as he slides it down my throat and I feel my sex start to pulse. "Je voudrais que vous souffler dans ma bouche. Si vous étiez vraiment mon mari je boirai vers le bas."

Translation: I wish you could blow in my mouth. If I was really your wife, I would drink it down.

He shakes his head and smiles sexily down at me as he pushes the hair back from my forehead. "Fuck, moi aussi. Vous soufflez mon putain de l'esprit ici," he whispers through his blanket-thick arousal.

Translation: Fuck, so do I. You are blowing my fucking mind here.

I smile as I flick my tongue over the end of him. His knees are on either side of my head, and his body is moving fluently so he slides in and out of my mouth. His dark eyes watch me struggle to take him fully.

This man has the body of a god and the mind of an angel.

I am in Heaven.

"Je dois te goûter."

Translation: I need to taste you.

He growls as he pulls out of my mouth and drops between my legs, his tongue swiping through my swollen flesh.

Fuck. My knees try to close as I struggle to gain control of the sensory overload. He pushes them back to the mattress aggressively as his tongue really takes charge, licking and tasting all that I am.

"How do I taste?" I whisper as my hands drop to the back of his head.

He groans into me as his eyes close in pleasure. His tongue circles and swipes, and I feel myself start to quiver. Oh God, it's been too long. I'm going to come already.

"Come," he breathes into me. "I want you to come on my tongue. Give me some cream, Bloss Bomb."

Holy fuck, this guy is frying my brain. He bites my clitoris and I shudder into him and he groans in pleasure. I grab the back of his head to try and still him.

"Stop," I pant, this is too much. I am too sensitive. He sucks deeper and his eyes roll back in his head. "You are one hot fuck." He growls as he laps it all up. He climbs up and over me and slides home in one swift movement.

I frown at the ceiling as my hand runs through his messy curls. I can hardly breathe. He's so *big*.

He leans back on his knees and holds my legs in the air as his eyes drop to my sex and he watches my body struggle to take his large muscle. His thumb gently circles over my clitoris, knowing full well that will release me and allow his entry.

He's experienced and he knows how to loosen a woman straight up

I watch him as I pant, somewhere in between disbelief, denial, and utter ecstasy. I didn't know that sex could be like this. I haven't had this before. I thought I'd had good sex... but now I've had this...

I realize not.

He gently kisses my ankle next to his ear, and he smiles sexily down at me. My eyes hold his for an extended moment and a frown crosses his face as I hold my breath. His hand gently brushes my hair from my face, his thumb running over my bottom lip

God. I close my eyes to block him out. This fucking guy is ridiculous.

8

"Regarde moi," he whispers.

Translation: Look at me.

I force my eyes to open and drag them up to meet his.

"Vous êtes la plus belle femme putain j'ai jamais été avec," he whispers softly. *Translation: You are the most beautiful fucking woman I have ever been with.*

He drops his body to mine, and his lips dust mine with reverence. We kiss for an extended time, as if forgetting that he's still inside mine. An intimacy that is as beautiful as it is petrifying. Slow, gentle, and tender.

Stop it. You don't even know him and this is a one- night stand.

"Cesser d'être molle et baise-moi," I whisper.

Translation: Stop being mushy and fuck me.

He smiles against my lips. "That's a first." He smirks as he starts to slowly pump me.

"W-what do you... mean?" I pant.

"Nobody has ever said that to me before."

I laugh as he pulls out and slams back into me, knocking the air from my lungs. He pumps me hard again. "And if I want to be mushy with my wife I have every fucking right to be."

I laugh again as he lifts my legs over his shoulders once more and really lets me have it. His knees are wide to give him traction, and I can see every muscle in his stomach ripple as he moves. Strong, punishing hits as the bed smacks the wall with force.

Oh, he won't be easy to forget.

My body starts to quiver again, and he smiles darkly, sensing my orgasm's arrival. He knows his way around a woman's body.

Damn.

Of course he does.

Our bodies are covered in a sheen of perspiration and I close my eyes to try and stop the orgasm. I want this to last.

I need this to last.

"I... don't want... to come," he pants.

9

"Me neither," I breathe as I pull him back to my lips. "Promise me we will do this again in a minute."

He laughs against me. "We can do this all night, Bloss."
I smile as he lifts my behind with his hand to really hit the end of me, and I cry out as my body contracts around his large muscle.

"Fuck, yeah!" he calls as his head rolls forward and he comes in a rush.

We stay still, both gasping for air. Both wet with perspiration.

Jesus Christ…

What the hell was that?

His mouth meets mine and he kisses me softly as he cups my jaw. I smile against his lips and he kisses me tenderly again. "What an excellent wife you are."

I laugh and he rolls us so that I am now on top of his large body. I rest my head against his chest as I try to catch my breath.

His lips dust my forehead. "Don't bother going to sleep." His hand drops between my legs and he spreads them so they hang over each side of his body. He starts to work me again; his three large fingers slide into my wet, swollen flesh. "That was the entrée and this is a ten-course meal."

Four hours and four showers later, I lie in the semi-darkened room with my fake husband. The light is just peeking through the crack in the drapes. My head is on his chest and his large, muscular arms are around me. The night has been unbelievable to say the least.

We have devoured each other, and if he wasn't out of condoms we probably still would be. I think we must have used a whole box.

"Where do you live?" he asks.

"New York," I breathe. I cringe when I hear my husky voice—a symptomatic problem from lasts night's Tequila and giving head activities, no doubt. "Where do you live?" I ask.

"Texas. Originally from Australia."

I gently kiss his chest and smile in contentment. "I had a good wedding night."

He kisses my forehead. "Me, too." I feel his lips smile against my skin. "You probably won't be walking for a while."

I giggle into his chest. "Actually, can you organize a wheel chair to get me back to my room, please?"

"I would, but I think I will be using it myself."

We lie in comfortable silence for a while longer. His hand runs back and forth over my behind, as if he's memorizing every inch.

"Are you using the theorem of calculus to measure my ass?"

He laughs out loud and rolls me onto my back, holding my hands above my head. "Your mind is a fucking turn on," he breathes before his tongue gently explores my mouth.

I just can't get my fill of this guy. "I could say the same thing. I've never had bilingual sex before." I smile. Hell, most guys I've slept with can't even speak English to me when we have sex, let alone drop in and out of three languages.

He smiles as he bites my bottom lip and pulls it toward him. "Moi non plus. Je peux être accro."

Translation: Me neither. I may be addicted.

I have always had a love of languages. They were my stress reliever when I was in high school and my parents were divorcing. I would lock myself in my bedroom and listen to language tapes through headphones so I couldn't hear them fighting. Looking back, all those hours alone in my room spent teaching myself was worth it just to experience the night I had with him.

He challenged me, but I challenged him right back, and I know I surprised him. Hell, I surprised myself.

11

It was empowering to be able to keep up with such an obviously intelligent man. Our eyes lock and something clicks into place as I feel a flutter deep in my stomach.

"What do you do for work?" I ask to change the subject.

He lies naked on his side and rubs his hand over my breast, squeezing it hard. "I'm a mechanic."

I bite my lip to stifle my smile. He has softer hands than me. No way is he a mechanic.

So, we're playing that game, are we?

"What do you do?" he asks.

"I work in an ice cream shop."

He can't hide his smile. "You are a dreadful liar. There is no way in Hell you serve ice cream."

I laugh. "You lied first."

He laughs as his lips drop to my nipple and he takes it in his mouth. "Touché." He smirks.

"What do you think I do?" I ask.

He narrows his eyes as he thinks. "Your body tells me you are a gym instructor, but your mind tells me you're a scientist."

I smile as I bring his lips to meet mine. "I have to go." I sit up.

He frowns and leans up onto his elbow. "What? Where are you going?"

I stand up, and his eyes drop down my body. "New York," I answer.

He frowns, "You're going home? Today?"

I nod as I walk around his room picking up my clothes. "Uh-huh." I pick up my phone and check the time. "I fly out in three hours. I've got to get a move on."

His face drops. "But…"

I pick up my bra and put it on. "But what?"

"I wanted to see you again," he says as he watches me dress.

I smile and lean over the bed to kiss his gorgeous lips. "Hmm." I smile against them. "Sorry. Bachelorette weekend is over."

12

He leans up and grabs me, pulling me back on top of him. "Stay another night."

God, I wish. He kisses me again.

"I already have my plane ticket for today," I breathe.

"I'll buy you another ticket for tomorrow," he offers.

For a brief moment, I consider it.

"*I'm* here until tomorrow," he tells me. "We could spend another night together." He smiles sexily.

Could I?

Who am I kidding? We don't even know each other's names and he just lied straight out and told me he was a mechanic. Besides, I'm totally out of money. I wouldn't even be able to pay for my dinner tonight. Damn it. "Sorry, hubby." I stand and put my black lacy panties on as he watches me. "This is where our marriage ends."

He puts both hands behind his head as he lies back down and smiles broadly.

My face mirrors his. "What?"

"I kind of like being married to you."

I widen my eyes at him in jest.

"I know. Shocking, isn't it?" He smirks.

I pull my dress over my shoulders and slip into it.

"Come back to bed. I'm not finished with you."

I sit on the bed and kiss him once more. "I'm not finished with you, either, but I have to go."

He frowns and begrudgingly gets out of bed. My eyes drop down his naked body. He is one hell of a fine specimen— tall, athletic, muscular broad chest with a scattering of dark hair. His hair is chocolate brown with a little bit of length on the top allowing it to have a *just fucked* messy look. His eyes are dark brown and he has a two-day growth going on. My eyes drop lower to the short, dark, well-kept pubic hair that encases his grand jewels. The man is well endowed and hell… he knows it. I imagine that every woman he sleeps with falls madly in love with him. He has money. He smells of it. plus the clothes he had on last night. The *Rolex* watch. The well dressed large group of men he was with. I think his shoes alone would have cost a couple of grand. This room is luxury, it's not even a room, it's a suite... incomparable to my shitty, shared room with two single beds next to each other that my two girlfriends and me are sharing because we have no money. He pulls on a pair of shorts and a T-shirt. "Can I take you out for breakfast?"

I glance down at myself. Ugh, I look abysmal, but I fake a smile. "No. But thank you."

He frowns as he pulls me against him again. "Are you trying to get away from me?"

I smile. "No, I just got to go."

His lips linger on mine. *Oh to hell with my budget. Stay and fuck this guy stupid.* I pull out of his grip and pick up my handbag.

"Hold on a sec until I get some shoes on and I will walk you to your room." He disappears into the bathroom. I quickly take out fifty dollars and put it on his bedside table, scribbling on the hotel notepad sitting next to his phone.

**Whoever said gambling never pays
has never lost to you**
xx

I needed this money, but a bet is a bet.

He won it fair and square.

He fucked my tits until they were chafe, just like he said he would.

He exits the bathroom. "You ready?"

I nod and smile as I follow him out of the door.

"Morning," he greets the man standing next to his door in a suit.

"Morning," the man replies.

I glance around. All of the doors in the surrounding hallway have men in suits outside them. He takes my hand in his and we start walking down the corridor. "Who are they?" I whisper.

"Security," he answers casually as he strides along.

I nearly have to run to keep up with him. "What for?" I whisper.

"Oh. My brother is here…" He hesitates for a moment. "He has money." He rolls his eyes. "I forget they are even with us, I'm so used to it."

"Oh." I frown. That's random. I turn back and see one of the men following us down the corridor. "He's following us," I whisper.

He smirks as he kisses my hand and keeps walking. "Relax. Ignore him."

I frown as my eyes flash to the man behind us. "Oh, okay."

We get to the elevator and I have to take out my key card to see where my room is again.

"We'll be fine," he tells the security guy before we enter the elevator. The guy nods and stays where he is.

We get into the crowded elevator and stand at the front. I smirk up at him as he holds my hand.

"I can't believe you are ditching me on our first day of marriage," he says loudly so everyone can hear.

My eyes widen in shock. What is he doing?

"So you just used me and abused me all night, is that it?" he asks in an exaggerated voice. I hear a lady behind us gasp in shock while the other people pretend not to listen.

I smirk. Bastard! Two can play this game. "Yeah, well, what happens in Vegas stays in Vegas. And you were totally shit in bed, by the way," I reply dryly.

"What about our kids?" he asks, acting offended.

I drop my head to hide my smile. Oh, this guy is something else.

"Your kids are bastards. One of your other wives can bring them up. I've had enough. I'm going back to prostitution."

"Just don't give anyone anal. You know that asshole is mine." He scowls, acting serious.

15

I widen my eyes at him. He did *not* just say that out loud.

"Oh my God," the lady behind us whispers.

"Shh," her husband hisses.

He drops his head to stop himself from laughing, and he squeezes my hand in his. I squeeze it back as I bite my bottom lip.

The elevator doors open and he walks out, striding down the hall toward my room. "What number?"

"Three Two Two." I smirk.

We continue walking until we get to my room and I turn toward him.

"This is your room?"

"Yep." I smile. Oh, I don't want to go in. I want to stay with him another night.

He takes out his phone. "Can I have your number?"

I raise a brow. "Why?"

"So I can sell it to the highest bidder. Why do you think?" he replies dryly.

"I live in New York, you know..."

"Yes. I'm coming to New York next weekend."

"Since when?" I frown.

"Since now." He smiles as he kisses me. His tongue rims my lips. "Donnez-moi votre numéro avant que je vous traîne retourner dans ma chamber."

Translation: Give me your number before I drag you back to my room.

Could this guy be any more fun?

He takes out his phone and types *Wife* into the contact list.

I laugh. "You can't save me as wife?"

"Who says?"

"Me."

He grabs my behind and pushes me up against the door. "While you're in Vegas, you're my wife, and if I want to fuck you up against the door here, I can." He growls against my neck.

16

I laugh into his shoulder as I push him away. I take his phone and type in my number, and he smiles, his lips lingering on mine.

"I'm coming to New York next weekend and getting a hotel for us. Where do you want to stay?"

I laugh. "You're crazy."

"And you are fucking addictive." He smiles on my cheek as he grips me tight.

We laugh our way into one final lingering kiss before his lips drop softly to my neck.

"Goodbye, my beautiful wife," he whispers as his eyes search mine.

I feel my heart somersault in my chest. "Goodbye." I smile softly.

He starts walking backwards up the hallway as he points at me. "I will see *you* next weekend?"

I smirk as I cross my arms in front of me and watch him go.

"Don't bother packing clothes because you won't be needing any," he calls.

I smirk again and shake my head. God, he's a bona fide sex maniac.

A porter walks past and he calls out to him. "Excuse me, do you have any wheelchairs available?"

I cover my mouth to hide my giggle. He wouldn't?

The porter looks down at his legs, wondering what is wrong with him that requires a wheelchair.

"Oh, its not my legs. I have a very sore dick." He points to his groin. "Hard night."

The porter frowns as he looks at his crotch.

I burst out laughing, and they both turn to look at me. With an embarrassed wave I walk into my room and close the door. I shake my head in disbelief at the crazy events that have panned out over the last twenty-four hours. I lean against the back of the closed door with a broad smile on my face.

Wow.

What an unexpected night.

What an unexpected man.

2

Cameron

I SIP my Scotch to hide my smirk, my eyes meeting my brother Joshua's over the table. It's 3am and we are playing poker in the high roller room in Vegas.

A trace of a smile crosses his face, and he shakes his head, almost to himself, as he lights his cigar. He's just worked out that I'm counting cards.

It's the thrill of not getting caught that enticed me to cheat. It has nothing to do with the financial gain. I don't need the money. But I do thrive on excitement and this is the most fun I have had in years—apart from last night with Bloss. I get a vision of her above me and I feel myself harden slightly under the table.

God, she was so fucking on point.

Mind.

Body.

Mind.

Two men across the table are arguing about something, so I take a moment and glance down at my phone, scrolling through my pictures to find the photo I took of her while she slept. She's naked and on her side with both hands underneath her angelic face. Her long, honey-colored hair is splayed across my pillow, and the white linen is draped over her body. It's weird really—I have never been inspired to take a photo of a woman before then, but she just looked so gorgeous asleep in my bed… I couldn't resist. I send the image to my cloud to save it. My phone beeps, alerting me to a text. It's Joshua.

If you get me barred from this casino
I am going to break your fucking neck.

I'm unable to hide my broad smile, and I glance around the room to see all of the security staff watching on. Joshua, my brother, is a millionaire app developer. His security staff go everywhere with him, and seeing as he is my best friend, they are everywhere with me, too. I'm used to it, but he's completely right. If I get caught cheating here all hell is going to break loose. I smile across the table at him and wink. He raises a sarcastic brow. The round starts again and I start to count.

"He's counting cards!" the man opposite yells.

My mouth drops open in mock horror and Joshua breaks into a smartass grin. Bastard wants me to get caught.

"What are you fucking talking about?" I shuffle through my cards in a fluster.

"He's fucking cheating. I'm telling you!" he snaps.

"I am not." I roll my eyes. "Have another drink, you alcoholic."

The lunatic across the table goes ape-shit, lifting the table and throwing it in the air. Our drinks and cards are sent flying. Next thing I see, he is swinging punches in the air and, thankfully, he can't fight for shit so is missing me every time. The bouncers come running in from every direction.

"I'm going to kill you." He snarls.

"Yeah, well, throwing punches like that means you've got jack shit chance of that happening," I mock as I step to the side to evade his next hit.

Joshua bursts out laughing at this fool. He looks ridiculous doing air swings and not connecting a single hit.

"You shut up or I will kill you, too!" he screams at Joshua.

Joshua raises a brow. "Is that a threat?"

"That's a promise."

"Have a go, prick." Joshua snarls as he steps forward and pushes him hard in the chest.

He launches himself at me, instead, and I hit him once in the face before I am grabbed by the bouncers and ushered to the door with my arms held behind my back. "Take him downstairs to the police," the bouncer yells to his co-worker.

"What?" *Shit,* this could affect my criminal record. "I haven't done anything wrong and I didn't even receive a payout."

"He said you were cheating."

"He's as drunk as a fucking mute. Why would you believe anything that came out of that fool's mouth?" I argue as I am rushed toward the doors, out into the elevator area.

The bouncers exchange looks as they realize they have nothing on me. They push me forward and I go flying. "Go back to your room immediately. You are not to come back on the gambling floor tonight."

I retract my arms from their grip. "I hate your fucking grubby casino anyway." I dust my shirt off.

I glance around at Joshua's two security guards who have followed me out to the foyer, and I wave them back in. "I'm going back to the room. I'm tired. Tell the others I will catch them tomorrow."

"Yeah, okay." They both turn and return to where they came from.

I take the elevator to my floor and smile to myself as I walk along the corridor. That was kind of fun to be honest. Pity I didn't get away with it.

Next time.

God, I'm so fucking tired. That chick wore me out last night. I smile at the memory. I'm going to ring her now and tell her just how much.

I go to grab my phone and realize it's not in my pocket.

What?

I feel all the pockets in my pants. Shit, where is my damn phone?

I think for a moment and my mouth drops open in horror.

Fuck's sake. It was on the table when that idiot tipped it over. It could be anywhere now. I turn and jog back up to the high rollers room and am greeted by the same two security guards again. They step in front of the door, blocking my entrance.

"Hi, I just left my phone inside. I won't be a moment."

The biggest bouncer shakes his head. "You're not coming in."

"Yeah, I know I'm not coming in. I just want to get my phone."

"No."

I screw up my face. "Oh, fuck off. I'm getting my phone." I go to brush past them and they block my entrance once more.

"Get someone else to get it for you."

"If I had my phone, I would fucking ring them and tell them to get it. I don't have my phone!" I snap.

"Too bad."

"This is ridiculous. I want my phone." Fuck, *her* number is on there. If I lose it, I have no way of contacting her. I start to get agitated. "I'm going back in," I announce.

"Like fuck you are."

I go to push through them and we get into a scuffle as they push me back from the door.

"Go back to your room or we are calling the cops to come and arrest you."

Shit.

"Listen, man, I have a really hot chick's number on that phone and it is vital that I find it. Can you go in and get my friends and get them to find it for me?"

The idiot folds his arms in front of him. "Do I look like your slave?"

Something snaps inside of me. "You look like a fucking baboon on steroids."

He pushes me hard in the chest and I push him back. "I need that fucking phone."

"I need to smash your face in. Get out of here or I will."

22

"Try it." I sneer.

The other bouncer picks up the phone and calls someone. "Can you get the police up here immediately?"

Fuck.

I step back as I weigh up my options. If I stay here I'm going to be arrested, and as a doctor, I can't have a criminal record.

I blow out a defeated breath. "Fuck you." I sneer as I turn and leave. Hopefully Joshua, Murph, or someone from the security team find it. It's probably under a bloody table somewhere.

I continue to stride up the hall as I think. I'm sure one of them will have it, although I can't call any of them to look for it. I don't have one person's phone number on me and I don't know any off by heart. All of my phone numbers are on that fucking phone. I head back to the room and, after being severely pissed off with myself, I quickly fall into an exhausted sleep.

"Cabin crew prepare for take-off."

I put my head back onto my headrest in annoyance as the plane rolls down the runway.

The phone is gone. Nobody saw it and when they went back to look for it this morning, it had vanished.

I'm so fucking pissed.

"It might turn up." Murph shrugs as he sips his drink from his seat opposite me.

I look at him deadpan.

Joshua smirks from his seat next to Murph. "It's gone. It isn't coming back."

"You're not helping." Murph sighs.

I roll my eyes. Adrian Murphy—Murph, as we call him—is our best friend. He is the General Manager of Joshua's company, good looking, young, and as gay as all hell. He is forever the optimist and finds a silver lining in every event.

"It's backed to the cloud, though, right?" Joshua asks. "It's not that bad."

"There is only one number on that whole fucking phone that I want. It is not in the cloud."

"That chick from the other night…" he replies flatly.

I stare out the window as the tarmac starts to scream past.

"She might call you," Murph offers.

I shake my head. "She didn't ask for my fucking number," I snap, annoyed.

Their eyes meet and they both smile broadly. "She was probably trying to get out of there as quick as she could." Joshua smirks.

I shake my head. "She could have been Mrs. Stanton, I'm telling you. This chick was out of this world."

"What was her name?" Murph asks.

I roll my eyes. "I don't even know."

They both burst out laughing. "You… You didn't even ask her name?" Murph stammers in shock.

"I was calling her wife and Bloss."

"No wonder the poor bitch ran." Joshua smirks. The two of them clink their drinks. "Who calls a chick their wife on the first night they meet them?" Joshua shakes his head in disgust. "Creepy son of a bitch."

"This isn't funny, assholes. I'm supposed to be going to New York to meet her next weekend and I don't have her fucking number."

Joshua raises his eyebrows in shock. "You were going to fly all the way to New York next weekend, just to see her?"

I nod and blow out a deep breath as I stare out the window. Fuck, I'm so pissed off with myself.

"I would have flown to the moon. She was dropping in and out of languages and had a body to die for. I'm telling you. This chick was the shit." I slam my head back on the headrest. "You fucking idiot," I snap at myself.

"So, let me get this straight. It's taken you twenty-seven years to find a woman you like better than yourself, and then the next day you lose her number?" Murph asks flatly. "This is why you are the stupidest man I know. You make goldfish look smart."

Joshua laughs into his drink. "Snap."

I glare at him. "I'm going to fucking kill you with a smile on my face. Prepare yourself for pain, fucker."

We all fall silent for a moment as the plane launches into the air. "What was the last thing you said to her?" Murph asks.

I narrow my eyes as I think for a moment. "I said I was coming to New York and booking a hotel for us, and don't bother packing any clothes because you won't be needing any."

"Witty," Murph mutters dryly. "I'm glad you lost your phone because if she is as smart as you say she is, she would have dumped you in a week anyway with pickup lines like that."

I roll my eyes. "Just concentrate on sucking dicks, asshole."

Murph throws me a cheeky wink. "Well, it's a lot better than hearing about goldfish pickup lines."

"So, you heading off to Kamala tomorrow?" I ask Joshua to change the subject.

"Yeah, we leave in the morning. Only going for three weeks, though. What are you guys up to?"

"Working," Murph replies. "Somebody's got to hold the company together."

"I'm going to New York next weekend," I announce as I come to an impulsive decision.

"What are you going to do?" Joshua smirks. "Search the whole of New York for some mystery chick you don't even know the name of?"

"Maybe." I stare out the window.

"You fucked it. Just admit it. She's gone."

New York City

Saturday night

I sit at the busy bar in New York named Luco. I've chosen a seat that faces out onto the street and I stare out at the crowd bustling past. This is the craziest thing I have ever done in my life. After thinking on it all week, I got on a plane this morning to come to New York to look for a girl whose name I don't even know.

I had to. She hasn't left my mind since I left her at her hotel room last Sunday morning.

I didn't even tell anyone I was coming. I know how fucked up this must seem, but to me it feels like the only logical thing I could do. I have no idea how to find her.

I take out my new phone and click through to my cloud and stare at the photo I have of the gorgeous creature. I've stared at it every spare moment I've had for six days. This is the only evidence that she even exists.

Who are you?

It's weird. I'm a player. In fact, I'm a player's player. I don't think twice about the women I sleep with most of the time, and I definitely never would have done anything this desperate before.

Maybe I'm going soft in my old age.

An annoying little voice whispers to my subconscious... *Maybe she's different?*

I watch the oncoming crowd in the street and I frown. I don't even know if I would recognize her on sight to be honest. I walk over and take a seat at the bar.

"What will it be?" The bartender smiles.

"Blue label Scotch on the rocks, please." I glance around as I scan the crowd.

She makes my drink, turns back and slides it over the bar. "You here alone tonight?"

I shrug, and for some reason I feel like I need to elaborate. "Believe it or not, I flew in from LA today and am looking for a girl I met in Vegas last weekend. I have no idea of her name."

Her eyes hold mine. "That's crazy romantic."

I shake my head. "I don't do romantic. It's crazy *stupid*."

She serves the man next to me, while I sit and drink my drink. After a few moments she comes back to me. "Why don't you put an ad in the classifieds."

I frown into my drink. "What?"

"Put an ad in the classifieds that only she would understand."

I laugh and run my hand through my hair. "Now that's fucking crazy."

She picks up a cloth and wipes the bar in front of us. "No, that's crazy romantic."

She moves on to the next customer and I sit and think for a moment, and eventually I pick up my drink and return to my table near the window, deep in thought.

Hmm… what would I write in the ad?

A waitress walks by. "Excuse me, do you have a pen I could borrow, please?" I ask.

She feels insides her pockets and hands over a black pen, as well as a napkin.

"Thanks."

I frown as I think. What the hell am I going to write?

To the betting man's wife who works in an ice cream shop.

We met in Vegas last weekend when you needed a stand in husband.

I lost my phone.

Je n'ai aucun moyen de vous contacter.

Translation: I have no way of finding you.

Wer auch immer eine Wette gewinnt mag niemals dasselbe sein.

Translation: Whoever wins a bet to you may never be the same.

I'm in New York looking for you.

Appelle-moin
Translation: Call me
0423788900

I sit and stare at the scratched note on the napkin.
I have officially lost my shit.

Ashley

I smile at the waiter as he puts our Margaritas on the table. It's Saturday night and I'm out with my best friend Jenna for dinner.

"Thank you," we both say as we pick up our much-needed cocktails. "And then what happened?" I frown.

"So, this little shit has put it on her and she rejected him."

"But she was on with him, right?"

Jenna shrugs. "She kissed him."

"And this was at the party?"

She nods as she sips her drink. "Yep and they were drinking."

We are deep in discussion about the little dipshit that is picking on her baby sister who is only fifteen.

"What happened then?"

"She was on with him and then they went for a walk."

I shake my head. "Stupid move."

"I know, right? She reckons she didn't think anything of it."

I roll my eyes and Jenna nods.

"Then they go for the walk and he puts it on her in a park, and she says no. He gets all aggressive and shit."

I frown. "Seriously? How old is this kid?"

"He's only sixteen. They have a fight and he goes back to the party and tells everyone that she didn't want to have sex with him because she has an STD."

My mouth drops open. "You're joking?"

"I fucking wish I was."

My hands go over my mouth in shock. "Bloody hell, what a twat." I sip my drink as I try to process this. "Surely nobody believes him, right?"

28

She shrugs. "You remember what it is like to be fifteen. Any gossip is hurtful. Even if it isn't true."

"Fuck's sake. What is she going to do?"

"I tell you what I'm going to do: I'm going to march into the school and rearrange the fucker's face."

I laugh into my drink. "That will work."

"I'm not even joking. What kind of kid does that to a young girl?"

I shake my head. "If I knew what goes through every man's brain, I would be a millionaire by now." I sigh. All week I have waited by my phone for Vegas guy to call, but, of course, he hasn't. As each day ticked on by so did a little piece of hope that I would be seeing him again.

I really thought we had something.

Jen watches me for a moment. "I can't believe he didn't call you."

"I can," I mutter sadly. "I knew he was too good to be true." I fake a smile. "You know the old saying—what happens in Vegas stays in Vegas." I shrug. "And besides, he lives in Texas."

"Do you think he really lived in Texas, or was that another lie?"

I raise my eyebrows at the depressing thought. "God, probably another lie. He's not a fucking mechanic. I know that for certain. Who knows what else he lied about?"

"You never know… fate may step in and you might see him again."

I smile broadly and roll my eyes. "Will you stop with the fate shit? If we were fated to be together he would have called me, and right at this moment, I would have been staring at him across the table instead of having this conversation with you." Jen shrugs as she grabs my hand over the table. "Yeah, I suppose you're right. Was he really that nice? Surely there was something wrong with him."

I shake my head in disgust. "Jen, I don't even know where to start. He was hotter than hot. Funny. Beyond beautiful and way smarter than me."

She smiles into her drink. "I seriously doubt that, and besides, he must be a fucking idiot not to call you."

We clink our glasses together and I smile with gratitude. I love Jen. She always pulls me out of my funks.

The waitress arrives with our entrée and I snap myself out of my depressive state. "Anyway, I'm making myself forget Vegas guy from here on in. He may have ruined me forever, but I intend to pick myself up and dust myself off," I tell her as I raise my glass in the air. "I shall never give a thought to him again."

"Here, here." She smiles. "Are we going to meet the others at Luco?"

I take a mouthful of my grilled halloumi cheese salad and shake my head. "Hmm, this is good." I gesture to my food. "You know I don't really feel like going to Luco tonight."

"Why not?"

I shrug. "I don't know. It's a dating kind of place and it's not like I am going to see Vegas guy sitting there waiting for me."

Jen giggles around her mouthful of food. "You wish."

I laugh and sip my drink. "Tonight, we are going dancing. Screw bar Luco."

3

Five years later

Ashley

T HE MOVING trucks come to a stop in the wide street, and my eyes flicker over to the back seat. "This is it, baby." I smile.

Owen looks out of the window towards our new house and I feel my nerves flutter deep in my stomach.

It looks okay.

The house is two-story with faded yellow weather-boards. It has a large veranda that wraps around the house. Climbing roses scale the posts, and a cobblestone path leads up to the front steps. It looks welcoming. I glance back and forth up the wide street and the neat manicured lawns of the well-kept surrounding houses.

"It looks so nice, doesn't it?" I smile at him through the rear view mirror.

He nods as he holds his blanket tightly between his little fingers. His angel face is staring out the window in awe.

This will be the new start we need.

The last few years have been hard — harder than hard for me. My big dreams are just a distant memory now.

I met a guy, got engaged, and was happy for a while, until our relationship broke down. All while putting myself through med school.

I had big dreams of being a hotshot surgeon until I fell pregnant. It wasn't planned and I don't know how it happened, but it did and I didn't find out until I was showing. I'd had the contraceptive injection and it should have worked for another twelve months. I never even considered that I would be in the two percent of the female population who it didn't work on. I didn't get a period, so I didn't miss it when it didn't come.

It was shocking, it was devastating, but now, looking at the little boy with the perfect face in the back seat who has taught me how to adult, I count it as the biggest blessing of my life.

He was always meant to come — always meant to be my son.

The timing was just off, that's all.

I'm over it now, over the whole stigma of being a single mom.

The disappointment of shattered dreams.

I'm over the urge to go out and have fun with people my own age. I do grieve the loss of opportunity to fall in love for me. I wanted to marry for passion and true love.

I'm resigned that this is my life and that I made this bed I'm lying in. If I can just scrape through my final year of residency experience at the hospital, Owen and I can move to a quaint little country town where I can open a medical practice, work as a general practitioner, and make enough to pay the bills. Hopefully I can save a deposit and Owen and I can have our own home. I smile at the endless opportunities we have.

Who knows? Maybe in ten years when Owie gets a little older I will meet a nice divorced man with grown children and fall in love. I guess the saddest realisation is that Owen doesn't have a father figure to grow up with. My ex fiancé didn't want to keep up the visits, and now wonders why he's an ex.

We grew apart. The final straw came when I realised I would pretend to do assignments every night, just so I didn't have to go to bed with him. I didn't even want him touching me. How could I have ever contemplated marrying him for life?

I tried to hold on for Owen's sake, but when it became clear to me that he didn't really care if he saw Owen or not, I decided to walk away.

Owen deserves better. I deserve better.

So, here we are in Los Angeles. Our new hometown. Jenna flies in tonight and is staying with me for six months to get me settled so I can find some part time work and childcare. Jenna is my angel. I couldn't have done any of this without her. I park the car and smile broadly as I open the back door.

"Out we get Owie."

He smiles up at me and grabs his little comfort blanket and book from the seat, climbing awkwardly out of the car. I bend down and straighten his shirt and pants. "Are you ready to see our new house?" I whisper with excitement.

He smiles as he looks at the house in awe, and we walk hand-in-hand up the path toward the house.

I shuffle through my bag to find the keys that we have just picked up from the agent. I feel my nerves flutter. This house feels too extravagant for us, but I have a plan as to how I'm going to pay for it.

I didn't want to live hours away from my mom and be unhappy in a dump.

I wanted to come home to a beautiful house each day. I want Owen to be proud to have friends over. I want to make new friends, adult girlfriends, and be able to ask them over for dinner without being ashamed of where I live. I have a job interview tomorrow at a club, working behind the bar. I've never done anything like it before, but with the freedom of moving where nobody knows me, I don't care anymore. For the first time in forever I don't care what people think of me. For so long I refused to work in a nightclub. It was as if I was ashamed of what I had become…

A single mother who worked at night in a club to support her kid.

A failure.

I thought that, down the track, if Jenna moves home and we are short on cash, I could find a young girl from the hospital that may want to board with us. That's the plan anyway.

I slowly open the large front double doors. Owen gasps and I grin.

"Wow," he whispers.

I bite my bottom lip to stifle my broad smile as my eyes scan the large room. There's a grand foyer with high ceilings and a lounge room to the left. I open the door to the right and find a double garage.

He squeals in delight.

I laugh out loud.

We walk through to the end of the hall and find a large, slightly dated kitchen, with a second living area and dining room with a bathroom off of it. A large bedroom with its own entrance is at the side. This will be Jenna's room while she is here, and there's another small bedroom to the left. I put my hands over my mouth in disbelief. Oh my God, this house is fucking fantastic.

I love it.

Owen runs ahead in excitement up the carpeted stairs. "Where's my room? Where's my room?" he calls out.

I run up the stairs after him, and stop dead when I get to the top. Holy shit. This is… are we in the right house? Three bedrooms, a bathroom, and then double doors at the end of a large walkway.

I open the double doors and my mouth drops open. A parents' retreat, a lounge area that opens onto a large bedroom, with its own bathroom and a walk in closet. Double doors open to a balcony that looks out onto the street. Windows and expensive drapes are on every wall. It's slightly dated, but hell, it's the best damn house I have ever seen. I beam at the sound of Owen's squeals of delight.

"This room, I want this room!" he calls.

I run up the hall to the other end of the house and find him in the front room, and take him in my arms. "Do you like it, baby?"

For the first time in a long time, I feel proud of myself.

He nods as he grips my legs, and the sound of the moving truck out front stops us.

He laughs out loud. "I like LA, Mom."

I take him in my arms and squeeze him hard. "Me, too, baby. Me, too."

I sit in the waiting room as my eyes scan the other girls while we all wait for our job interviews. I glance down at my attire and cringe.

I'm overdressed.

I don't mean overdressed as in over the top clothing. I mean I'm literally overdressed — wearing too many clothes. These girls are all gorgeous. Gorgeous hoes.

Cheap looking, busty, gorgeous hoes.

I frown as a disturbing thought runs through my mind. Fuck! What kind of club is this?

I quickly take out my phone and Google:

Club Exotic, LA

My phone takes forever, and I get the ring of death as it thinks. I glance up to the interview office. Thankfully the door is still closed.

Shit, hurry up and load, you stupid thing. I may need to run like the wind to get out of here. In the job applications it didn't say anything questionable... or did it? I quickly open the interview confirmation email and scroll through it in a panic.

Surely not.

I was appalled at being a bartender, but maybe this is normal bartender attire?

I smirk at how different applying for a medical position and a bartender position really is.

Subject: Application
From: Club Exotic
To: Ashley Tucker

Congratulations, Ashley.

You have been successful in securing an interview with Club Exotic. We look forward to meeting you at Club Exotic, 59 Palmer Street, LA at 11am on the 7th of next month.
We pay above average wages, have an excellent career development pathway plan, and we are recruiting ten team members to join our beloved crew.

Please RSVP within seven days of receiving your invitation.

Club Exotic

I frown and scroll to the top of the screen. When was this email sent? The 5th of last month. Hmm, this interview was the reason we had to get here by yesterday. Surely seedy places hire people an hour before their shift, not one month out? I glance back over to the girl sitting across from me. She's wearing cheetah print lycra tights with sky high stilettos, and the words from that selfie song run through my head.

Who wears cheetah?

Who does fucking wear cheetah?

Her huge, droopy boobs are hanging everywhere, and her black roots on her bottle-blonde hair looks like a landing strip.

My stomach rolls and I glance over at the other women waiting for their turn. I feel my *run* instincts kick in a little harder. One is wearing a crop top and I can see the bottom of her bra sticking out from underneath, while the other is wearing a dress that is so small, it looks like a shirt. Although attractive, they are all faked tanned to the max.

Oh, shit.

I need to go. Fucking hell. I wanted thirty-five dollars an hour. I stand and the office door opens.

"Ashley Tucker?" The kind looking lady smiles.

Oh, a lady? I frown. That's unexpected. I was picturing a middle aged bad porn actor.

She raises her eyebrows in question. "Ashley?"

I nod nervously. "Yes, I'm Ashley."

She holds her hand up toward her office. "This way, dear."

I fake a smile and walk nervously into her office. Oh man, two minutes too late.

"Just take a seat, honey, sorry to keep you. I won't be long, girls." She smiles to the others.

"That's okay," they all reply in unison.

I fall into the seat and hold my handbag in my lap. Better keep it close in case I need to run.

She closes the door, sits down and smiles warmly. She is a kind looking lady; a kind cougar looking lady, to be honest. In her late forties, sure, but sexy in a glamorous way. My eyes glance around at her office to see luxurious dark navy walls with silver gilded frames, and on the back wall is a huge mirror. Plants and a large black leather lounge add to the ambience.

She folds her hands in front of her as she assesses me.

She has an inner calm about her—an inner confidence— and I feel a little jealousy sweep over me. I would give anything to have that inner calm and confidence.

It's such a sexy quality to possess.

Her wise eyes scan over my face. "My name is Eliza." She smiles. "So, Ashley, tell me about yourself?"

I swallow the nervous lump in my throat. "I'm twenty-seven and I'm currently studying medicine."

She raises her eyebrows.

"Impressive. What year are you in?"

"I'm in my last year." I smile. It never gets old telling someone that, I'm so freaking proud of myself.

She narrows her eyes. "How long have you lived in LA?"

"I just arrived yesterday… from New York."
"What brings you here?"

"A surgeon."

She frowns.

"I mean… I'm going to be a top surgeon's understudy at LA Memorial hospital. I start in two days."

"How exciting for you." I nod. "How many children do you have?" she asks.

I frown, I never get asked that question. People always assume that, because I'm a med student, I won't have kids. "I have one son."

"What's his name?"

"Owen." I smile. Even saying his name brings out my pride.

She sits back in her chair. "So, you are here for Owen, then?"

"Yes," I breathe.

She picks up her pen and writes something in her diary. "What are you looking for?"

I frown in question. What does she mean? *A job, you fool.* "I'm sorry, what do you mean?" I ask.

Her eyes flash up to me from her notes. "What position are you here for?"

I hesitate. "You have more than one job going? I wasn't aware."

She puts her pen down and smiles. "Do you know what we do here, Ashley?"
I swallow nervously. "You're a club?" I fake a smile. Please be just a club.

"Yes, we are a club."

Oh. I smile broadly.

"We are a gentlemen's club."

My face falls.

"We offer men an escape from their mundane lives — a fantasy, if you please."

I go to say something intelligent, but no words will leave my mouth.

"We have five different positions open at the moment."

I stay silent.

"There's bar work, just normal bar work, and that pays thirty-five dollars an hour."

I nod. "Okay," I murmur.

"Then there is topless waitressing where you don't have to touch or talk to the clients at all. That pays seventy dollars an hour."

I frown and swallow the horror in my mouth.

"We do ten hour shifts, so you can do the math there."

Fuck. That's seven-hundred dollars a shift.

"We have dancing positions available with no contact at all, which we pay one-hundred and twenty-five dollars an hour for."

My eyes widen. Holy shit, that's good money. I do the math again. Twelve-hundred and fifty dollars a shift? *Fuck.*

"We have lap dancing positions."

I raise an eyebrow in question. "That's where you are requested to give our exclusive clients a lap dance. The clients are not allowed to touch you and you have a bouncer with you at all times. Our lap dancers get two-hundred and twenty-five an hour.

My mouth nearly drops open, and she smiles knowingly. "Yes, that's right. With tips, our lap dancers earn over two thousand five hundred dollars a night."

"Oh…" is all I can reply with. I drop my eyes to the floor. Frigging hell, why can't I earn that kind of money serving fucking drinks? "W-what is the other position?" I ask.

She smiles sexily. "Our VIP girls do a full service. They satisfy every fantasy of our clients in a private exclusive part of the club. They are protected with their own bouncers at all times."

My eyes widen. "Prostitution," I whisper.

She smiles again and nods. "Yes, we have some girls that enjoy that kind of work. We pay them a flat rate of five-thousand dollars a night."

I clutch my bag tighter on my lap as my mouth goes dry. I can't even comprehend that kind of money.

She stands and comes around to my side of the desk. "Can you stand, dear?"

Huh?

She smirks. I must appear so damn green. "Just stand up, sweetie, and let me look at you."

"Oh." I frown. I stand cautiously, and her eyes scan up and down my body as she grabs my shoulders and turns me around to check out my behind.

Oh hell. Please, Earth, swallow me up.

"I think you could start out with topless."

I shake my head and fake a smile. "No. I'm not really into my boobs. I can't think of anything worse than walking around with them hanging out…" I hesitate and glance at the door. "In fact, I'm not really into anything here really. I'm sorry I've wasted your time."

"Take a seat, dear."

Oh God, stop calling me dear, you madam from the best little whore house in Texas. I fall into the seat.

She points toward the door. "We have literally hundreds of girls try to get a job here. All those girls out there in the waiting room will be unsuccessful today."

"W-why?" I stammer.

"This is an *exclusive* club. We have memberships that cost a *lot* of money. Our clients are cultured and intelligent, so we only supply them with women who are of the same nature."

I frown.

"This isn't a club that offers slap dash women who have slept with every man in the USA. This is a club where men can come and take pleasure in looking at intelligent, untouched women — women who are putting themselves through college and doing this for their precious children. They know that every single woman here is something special."

I hold my breath.

She tilts her head to the side as she assesses me. "It's very empowering, you know."

"What is?" I ask.

"Turning on powerful men and then walking away."

I swallow the lump in my throat as my eyes hold hers.

"You come here, you make them your bitch so they feel like they may die if they can't have you, and then you go home to your normal life. Nobody knows what you do... except *you*."

I scowl.

"Think about it, Ashley. Two thousand five hundred dollars a *week* for one shift."

I clutch my bag tighter.

She raises a brow. "What holidays could you take your son on? What car would you drive? What designer clothes could you buy?"

"But I can't imagine myself doing any of this," I whisper.

She smiles. "And that's exactly why we want you. I don't want stripper wannabes. I don't want people trying to be discovered to be famous. I want attractive, sexy, and intelligent women who know what they want from life."

The woman does give one hell of a sales pitch.

"We have medical students. Law students, Psychology students." She smiles. "We have girls drive four or five hours to work because they can't get these conditions or this pay anywhere else."

Deflation fills me. I can't do this. Who am I kidding? "Thanks for the opportunity but —"

She cuts me off. "Come tonight. See how the club operates, meet some of the girls and then make up your mind." She takes a credit card thing and swipes it through a machine. "This will get you through security."

I fake a smile and take the card from her. "Thanks." I am so not coming tonight. I stand. "Thanks for the opportunity, though." I smile as I head toward the door.

"Ashley?" she calls.

I turn back to her.

"Take what you want from life. Make it work for you and not the other way round."

My eyes hold hers and I feel like she can see into my soul.

"Just come and see," she urges. "You have nothing to lose."

I nod. "Okay. I'm just looking, though."

She smiles and shakes my hand. "See you tonight."

I sip my *Coke* as I sit at the table in the restaurant with Owie and Jenna. My mind has been in overdrive since my job interview this morning. Owen is playing on his *iPad* and Jenna is sipping her wine.

She looks around excitedly. "I love LA. So many gorgeous men everywhere."

I smile and raise a brow. "Me, too."

"You have been very quiet since your interview this morning. Tell me more about it..." she asks. I haven't had a moment alone with her since I went this morning. Owen has been in ear's distance the whole time.

I blow out a breath and start to stab the ice in my glass with my straw. "It was okay."

"And...?"

I frown and gesture to Owie. She shuffles around in her bag and pulls out some coins. "Owie, can you go and try and win us some chocolates from the vending machine in the kids play area?"

Owen's eyes light up in excitement as he snatches the coins from her and runs.

Jenna's eyes fall to my face. "What happened?"

"Oh, Jenna, what a fucking disaster."

"Why?" She frowns. "It sounded so good."

"It… It was good." I stammer. "Like two and a half thousand dollars a night good."

"What?" She frowns. "Doing what?"

"Lap dancing."

She smirks into her drink.

"Apparently, they are an exclusive gentlemen's club and you get your own bouncer. The man aren't allowed to touch you."

She sips her drink as she listens.

"And the pay is two-hundred and twenty-five dollars an hour over a ten-hour shift."

She frowns as if suddenly interested. "And you don't have to touch them at all?"

I shrug as I stab my ice in my glass again. "Who knows? They probably make you fuck table legs."

She giggles around her drink.

"They asked me to go and check it out tonight."

She frowns. "What time are you leaving?"

I screw up my face. "I'm not going."

"Why not?"

"This is where you are supposed to be the adult and tell me it's a ridiculous idea."

She shrugs. "You should at least check it out. It couldn't hurt? That's a lot of money."

I roll my eyes.

She leans in so nobody can hear us. "Listen, I just want you to have some fun. I don't care if you damn well sleep with them. Nobody knows you here. Get out there and enjoy life."

"Ugh. Can you hear yourself?" I cringe.

"Ashley, since you had Owen, I have watched my positive, strong best friend wither away to become a shadow of the former girl I once knew."

My eyes hold hers.

"Stop punishing yourself for falling pregnant. I don't want to see you stay at home every Saturday night eating mac 'n' cheese and watching Finding Nemo, while struggling to pay every damn bill. You are a fantastic mother, Ash, but please put your needs first for a change."

"I wouldn't change having Owen," I argue.

She grabs my hand over the table. "I know, baby, and I know you tried to make it work with Andrew. I'm just asking you to check it out and give yourself the opportunity to meet new people."

"Who would mind Owen when you go back to New York?" I sigh, defeated.

"That's six months away, and besides..." She shrugs. "I could maybe get a place here. I have nothing dragging me back home. Who knows? Mr. Perfect might come here looking for me?"

I smirk and stab my ice cubes with my straw once more.

"That's ten thousand dollars a month, Ash. Imagine what you could do with that? We could go to Hawaii." She grins.

I blow out a breath. "I can't lap dance for shit." I shake my head.

"Sure you can. You can practice on me."

I laugh into my drink. "I am not practicing lap dancing on my best friend. That's just going too far."

Owie bounces back to the table. "I won a *Snickers* Bar." He shows us excitedly.

Jenna finishes her drink. "Come on, we need to get going."

Owen picks up his *iPad* and book.

"Mom's going to work tonight, kiddo, so it's just you and me. Let's get some ice cream on the way home."

"Yes." He beams.

Jenna's eyes scan me up and down. "We've got to find you something to wear."

I scrub my hands down my face. "Oh God, it gets worse. Shit's getting real."

4

I SIT in my car and watch the large, heavy front doors of Club Exotic across the street. It's 10pm and my nerves are pumping under my surprisingly calm exterior.

"Ashley, what are you doing here?" I whisper to myself.

With each man that arrives, my heart rate goes up another twenty beats per minute. These are no sleazy street guys. They're middle aged, handsome men in expensive suits. My mind goes back to the little sales pitch Madam Whorehouse gave me today.

And that's exactly why we want you. I don't want stripper wannabes. I don't want people trying to be discovered to be famous. I want attractive, sexy, and intelligent women who know what they want from life.

It all sounds too good to be true, but I could never imagine doing this. I get a vision of myself half naked, writhing on a stranger's lap, and I cringe and bring the car engine to life again. I can't do this. Who am I kidding? I steer the car out of the parking lot and pull out into the traffic. Her words run through my mind again:

Think about it, Ashley. Two and a half thousand dollars a week for one shift.

What holidays could you take your son on? What car would you drive? What designer clothes could you buy?

I blow out a deflated breath and pull into *Starbucks*. I need some time alone to think. I would love a cocktail somewhere, but I'm not going to a bar alone. I park the car, get out, and walk in deep thought.

"Welcome to Starbucks. What would you like to order tonight?" the young, chirpy male assistant asks.

I scan the lit up menu board behind him. "I'll take a caramel latte and a chocolate mud cake, please?"

"Sure."

I pay and make my way over to a table. I feel sick — partly because I know what I should do financially, and then what I know I am capable of.

Dancing naked in a whorehouse isn't on either list.

But…

The money would make such a difference to Owen's quality of life… and mine.

My number is called and I go and pick up my coffee and cake, then take a seat back at my table. I wonder what the girls wear for a uniform?

Nothing, you idiot. Half the women don't even have tank tops on. I screw up my face as I imagine the boob fest just hanging out in the open for everyone to see. I wonder what the VIP girls are like. Jeez, I can't imagine going to work and just casually fucking people as if it means nothing. But, five grand a night is insane.

The guys they fuck are probably hot, too. I smirk into my coffee cup. Imagine banging a hot, intelligent man and getting five thousand dollars for the privilege. Hell.

I wonder what they spend their money on? I get a vision of crazy expensive handbags and vacations.

Morals are overrated. I could do with an extra twenty-thousand dollars a month.

If only…

Imagine if I did do the VIP job, and then one day in the future Owen found out.

My eyes widen in horror.

How could you ever explain to your child that you were a prostitute? That you let men fuck you for money. You couldn't. They would never understand and there is no possible excuse you could ever use, because it's inexcusable. I shake my head in disgust that I even contemplated working in a place like that. I eat my cake and drink my coffee alone, and even though I've made the decision not to go in and check out the club, an annoying little voice inside is telling me it's the wrong one.

I need money. I desperately need money. I moved Jenna all the way here to help with Owen and I have to damn well find a job that pays well.

This isn't a club that offers slap dash women who have slept with every man in the USA. This is a club where men can come and take pleasure in looking at intelligent, untouched women – women who are putting themselves through college and doing this for their precious children. They know that every single woman here is something special.

Untouched women. Does that mean that I might meet women who are just like me and trying to make ends meet to get through college? She did say that the women who work there are all young professionals.

Women who want a better life for their kids…

I sip my coffee, deep in thought as I twist the ring on my finger. Maybe she says that to everyone who applies. The girls are probably all druggy smack heads. I can't imagine decent women ever working there. But with that kind of money, I sort of can. I drag myself back out to my car, and then I pull out into the traffic, for some reason finding myself driving straight back to Club Exotic, where I park the car across the road in the darkness. I'll just ring Jenna and tell her I am on my way home soon.

She picks up first ring. "Hey, how's it going?"

"I didn't go in."

"What? Why not?"

I shrug. "I can't work in a brothel, Jen."

She stays silent on the other end of the phone.

"I'll get another job somewhere else."

"You said it was a club."

"It is..." I hesitate. "But there's this VIP section, too, so effectively it's a brothel."

"The VIP section is not where you are working."

"Yes, but some men are there for sex and sex alone."

"Okay, so every nightclub in the United States of America, actually the world, is basically a brothel, too, then."

I frown. "How?" Trust her to be all Devil's advocate on me when I really just need her to agree with my cowardice.

"I guestimate that sixty percent of men in nightclubs are there for sex."

I listen in silence.

"So, do you mean to tell me you won't go to a nightclub because men are just there for sex?"

I roll my eyes. "That's different."

"How? You tell me how? You need a job. You have a babysitter at night. It's one or two nights a week, Ash, and it's behind the bloody bar."

"She wants me to topless waitress."

"Just say no."

I think for a moment.

"Go in, see what it's about, and if you feel uncomfortable walk out and don't go back."

I roll my lips and think as my eyes rise to a group of men disappearing into the club.

"Look, even the bloody bar jobs pay three fifty a night. For two shifts that's seven -hundred a week, Ash. How could you earn that money while working full time for free at the hospital?"

I run my finger over my steering wheel as I think.

"You would have to be stupid to not even check it out. Hell, I'm thinking I might apply there, too."

I smile as I imagine her walking around topless. "Now you are being ridiculous."

"Yes, and you are being a prude."

"What if Owen ever found out?" I sigh.

"Found out what? His mother worked behind a bar while she was studying to be a surgeon. I think Owen would be bloody proud that his mother got a second job to put a roof over his head."

I slide back into my seat. Maybe she's right…

"Just go in and see what they say."

My eyes stay fixed on the door across the road.

"You don't know anyone here, Ash. For the first time ever you can be whoever you want to be… and if that's a part-time nympho, then so be it. It could actually be fun."

I smile softly.

"Go in and make some new friends. Hell, tomorrow morning you will be cooking breakfast, making beds, and scrubbing fucking bathrooms. Enjoy being someone else for the night."

I run my hand through my hair. "Do you think I look okay?" I ask.

"Yes, smoking hot. The guys will all cream their pants when they catch sight of you."

I laugh as I look down at the dress I'm wearing. A camel, woolen ribbed dress, fitted with short-capped sleeves, which falls to my calves. It's tight and sexy without being revealing or cheap. I have high, strappy tan sandals on, and my honey-colored hair is down and full with set curls. Jen did my makeup, I have smoky eyes and a pink gloss on my lips.

I look good, I know I look good, but for a place like this, I have no idea if it is appropriate.

"Are you going in?" she asks.

My heart jumps in my chest. "Yeah, I guess." I pause as I move the rear view mirror to check my makeup. "God, I feel sick. I'm so nervous."

"Just check it out. You may be home in an hour. It could be totally shit. Don't stay if it's seedy."

"Okay." I nod with renewed enthusiasm. "I can do this."

"You can."

"Right, wish me luck."

"Good luck, babe."

I hang up and blow out a deep breath. *Just go in there and check it out, you can leave any time you want to,* I remind myself. I gingerly get out of the car and take out the card that Eliza gave me to get into the club. I hold it in my hand and stare at it for a moment.

I feel like I'm on the precipice of going to Hell. Maybe I'm about to catch on fire.

The good girl in me is begging me to go home and get a job knitting sweaters.

The bad girl in me is daring me to go in and sex it up — show these men exactly what they can't have.

The struggle I feel daily between my conscience and my responsibilities is real.

I put my hand on my stomach as I try to calm my nerves and walk across the road to the large, black double doors.

There are four bouncers in black suits standing around. They all look me up and down as I approach them.

"Hello…" I pause. "Eliza invited me to come tonight."

The tall man smiles sexily as his eyes scan me up and down. "What's your name, miss?"

Ah, shit. What *is* my name? I can't go with my real one. Umm. "Vivienne Jones," I reply calmly.

The doormen all exchange looks and smile warmly. "Welcome, Miss Vivienne." One purrs.

I push out a grateful smile, satisfied that they fell for it. I feel a surge of excitement that nobody questioned my fake name. Vivienne Jones — that's pretty cool to be honest. *I like it.*

"Thank you," I answer nervously. He steps aside, opens the door, and holds his hand out. I tentatively walk in.

I feel the air leave my lungs as the door shuts behind me.

Uh oh.

It looks like something out of a movie. When I was here for my interview, we were taken in the back entrance and didn't see any of this. There's dim lighting with deep coffee coloured walls and big fancy metal cut out lights hanging down from the super high ceilings. The floor is tiered to different levels with large carpeted steps running up the center. It could be an old picture theatre or something that has been converted. Spanning the whole back wall is the most exotic looking bar I have ever seen, and the bottom level has table and chairs which are situated around a catwalk stage. Shit, I wonder what shows go on down there?

The second level has large, luxurious leather armchairs placed singularly, facing toward the stage. The next level up is full of small round high tables with bar stools. My eyes rise up to the top level — the bar and busiest level of all three. My eyes flicker around nervously as I try to get my bearings. There are about fifty men in here, although it feels practically empty. Jeez, it must hold a lot of people when it's full. I stand frozen on the spot as my eyes scan the space. There seems to be about ten women working behind the bar. Gorgeous women, all wearing cream leather skirts that are high waisted and hang just below the knee. Wearing tops made of, what looks like, cream silk that cross over in a drape across the chest and tuck into their high waisted skirts. Every now and then, as they move, you can just see a peek of the caramel-colored lace bra they have on underneath. I swallow my fear as I watch them for a moment. They're all attractive, and I have to admit it, they do look classy... and happy. They're all smiling and laughing with the customers... clients... what the hell do you call these guys?

This isn't what I imagined at all.

My thoughts are interrupted. "You must be Ashley?"

I jump in fright and put my hand on my chest. "Oh, you frightened me." I smile, embarrassed by the kind but hot looking woman that has just approached me. "Yes, I am," I mutter. "But I don't want to use that name here if that's okay?"

She smiles a knowing smile. "Of course. What would you like to be called?"

"Vivienne Jones." I wince. God, this is so wanky.

"Nice." She holds out her hand to shake mine. "I'm Tiffany Smith." She gives me an over-exaggerated wink and I smile, knowing that's her fake name.

"Eliza told me to look out for you."

"Oh." I frown. "Is she here?"

"Not yet, she doesn't start until eleven when the club opens."

I look around. "Isn't it opened now?"

"No, no. This is just the starting crowd. Things don't heat up until 11.30 or so."

"Oh." I wonder what *heat up* means?

"Let's get you a drink and you can hang with me until Elli gets here."

Jeez, I'm like the new kid at school who is assigned a buddy. I fake a smile. This is awkward. "Okay."

She walks over to the bar and I follow her like a child. This place is freaking uncomfortable. She walks to the side of the bar and opens up the black, glossy door into the back of the bar and I stand still. "Come in." She grabs my hand and pulls me behind her.

"Don't be nervous," she whispers over her shoulder.

"This is just so far out of my comfort zone," I whisper back.

She smiles cheekily. "It was for me, too, when I started." She turns and looks me up and down. "You a law student?"

I shake my head. "Med."

She smiles.

"You?" I ask.

"Engineer."

I smile my first real smile. "Is this place really shitty? Should I just run now?"

She laughs out loud as she turns and pulls me along the back of the bar toward the end. "This is the best job I've ever had. It's not what it looks like."

I widen my eyes and glance back at the girls serving drinks behind us. She pulls up a stool and sits me at the end so that I am looking out into the crowd but out of the way. "What do you want to drink?"

Fucking Tequila!

"*Cointreau* and *Coke,* please," I murmur.

She smiles and turns back to make it, while I sit perched on my stool like a freak in an exhibition. The men have started to notice me. Some are making eye contact and giving me a subtle nod. I nervously nod back in acknowledgement. I can't believe the caliber of men in this place.

It's ridiculous.

You just don't see men this handsome out and about, and if they aren't good looking, they are immaculately dressed and scream of success. So even *they* seem attractive.

A bouncer comes to the other side of the bar. He's blonde, big, and muscular.

"Hi, I'm Matt." He grins and shakes my hand.

"Hi. I'm Vivienne." I smile awkwardly.

"You starting tonight?"

He seems nice and friendly and I shake my head. "No, I'm just here to look. I don't think I'm starting at all."

He looks me up and down. "Elli won't let you go. You're too hot."

My confidence gets a much-needed boost. I drop my head to hide my smile and tuck my hair behind my ear. I feel my face flush with heat. "Have you worked here long?" I ask, to change the subject.

"Yeah, about two years. Putting myself through college."

"What are you studying?"

"Environmental science."

"Third year?" I ask.

"Fourth, but good guess."

I smile, relieved that this place isn't half as awful as I imagined.

Tiffany arrives back over. "I have to go back to the door. You okay here for a while?"

"Sure. What do you do on the door?" I ask.

She rolls her eyes. "I'm the greeter tonight."

"Oh." I frown at her expression. "And this is a bad thing?"

"Fuck, yes. It's so dull. I usually lap dance. But the door girl is off tonight."

My eyes widen and she laughs at my expression. "I used to think that, too, but seriously... I get paid a stupid amount of money to turn on gorgeous men."

I bite my bottom lip to stifle my smile. "So, you are topless when you dance?" I ask.

She shrugs. "No, we wear tops." She smiles cheekily. "They are just completely see-through."

"Oh."

She throws me a wink and goes back to her position near the door, and I sit frozen still, hoping nobody will notice the nerdy girl at the end of the bar. Over the next half an hour, I have three more drinks while I watch gorgeous men arrive, one after the other. Some are in groups, others on their own. Although, even the ones who arrive alone seem to know others that are here. How does this work? Do these men come here to socialize? I bet a lot of them are married and this is their dirty little secret. I watch them all standing around the bench tables, down on level two and around the bar. The chatter is loud, and they are all wearing expensive suits and smelling like money. Hmm, it must be expensive to come here. I glance around to make sure nobody is watching and I get out my phone and Google.

Club Exotic Membership.

I wait for it to load and a webpage comes up.

Club Exotic.
Gentleman's Bar.
Club exotic is currently not taking new members. However, please feel free to put your name on the waiting list.

Hmm, God. No new members. That must mean they have their capacity. Matt walks back over to check on me. "You okay Vivienne?"

I smile and suck on my straw. I'm kind of having fun to be honest. "How many members are there here?"

Matt frowns. "I think there are about two thousand five hundred."

My eyes widen. "God, that's a lot. How much is it to join?"

"It varies. I think the basic bronze membership is around fifty thousand."

I frown in horror.

"The silver membership is seventy-five."

My mouth nearly drops open. "A year?" I frown.

He nods. "And the gold is about one-ten.?"

I nearly swallow my tongue. "What's the difference between the memberships?"

"Bronze has access to the facilities."

I frown. "Facilities?"

"Oh, there is an open bar and an award winning restaurant, a gym..."

"So, they don't pay for anything when they are here?"

He shakes his head. "No. Oh, and they get vouchers."

"Vouchers?"

"They get, like, ten lap dances a year, and I think they get a couple of nights in the Escape Lounge." He gestures down the front and I see a door with a lit up sign over it.

ESCAPE CLUB

"What do the silver memberships get?"

"They get the same, but with unlimited lap dances and more vouchers for the Escape Lounge. Those guys have to pay for their drinks, though."

I nod as I sip my drink. This is unbelievable. "What time does it open?"

"There is an 11am till 5pm session on Thursdays and Fridays. And then Tuesdays, Wednesdays, Thursday, and Friday nights."

Shit, so the fuckers can slip in and out of here during work hours. Bring in the weekend with a bang, so to speak. "It's not open weekends?" I ask.

"No, she caters for the business class. They are busy on the weekends."

Yeah... with their wives and kids. Revolting.

"Suits us. We get weekends off." He smirks.

Hmm, that is a big bonus.

My eyes drop to the door down below as I see a beautiful woman use a scanner key to get inside the Escape Club entrance. "What do they get for gold memberships?" I ask.

He smiles. "Anything they want with the comfort of confidentiality. Every member and staff member has to sign a confidentially agreement. An NDA. This place is more guarded than a prison. Not just anyone can join, either. You have to be sponsored by another member."

My eyes widen.

"That's why they pay the big money... To safeguard their reputations."

"Wow," I whisper.

"Some of them just come here to drink, but they know when they are here they are not going to be hassled or photographed, and no silly bimbo is going to go to the press next week for some cash. The girls here are more guarded of their reputations than the men."

I sip my drink deep in thought. "Impressive."

"Do you need another drink?"

I stare at my glass for a moment. I really shouldn't, but I have to admit these are going down nicely. "Okay, one more, maybe." I smirk.

He walks over and orders me a drink from one of the girls. I sit and watch my surroundings. This place has an electric feel to it. It's not at all what I expected. The girls are all classy and the men aren't ogling them like they're a piece of meat.

Hmm, I'm kind of impressed, to be honest.

"Ashley, dear, you came," Eliza interrupts my thoughts as she holds out her hand to shake mine.

I smile awkwardly. "Hello." Wearing a tight black dress, she looks amazing.

Her eyes scan down my body and then back up to my face. "You look divine. Have you had the tour?"

I shake my head nervously. "No."

"What is your name here?" she asks softly.

"Vivienne Jones," I murmur.

She smiles knowingly. "Well, it's lovely to meet you, Vivienne. I am so happy you came." She leads me by the hand through the men, and down the large stairs. I can feel the men's eyes on me as we pass through them, but I keep my eyes focused on her back as she walks in front of me. Hell, this makes me feel sick.

We get to the bottom and walk over to the large, black door where I saw the girls disappearing into earlier. Eliza swipes her security card and we walk in.

My eyes widen. Holy shit.

This looks like backstage of a Victoria Secret show. Small dressing tables line the large space and girls all have hot rollers in their hair and robes on their backs. A few are doing each other's makeup, while others are doing each other's hair.

"Girls, this is Vivienne," Eliza announces proudly.

"Their eyes all flicker to me and they smile. "Hi, Viv," they all chant cheekily. There is a playful air about them, and I can't help but smile.

"I'm hoping Vivienne is going to be starting in the Escape Club." Eliza smiles warmly at me. "I'm just showing her around."

I see a few of the girl's eyes flash to me, as if shocked. *What? Isn't that normal?* Anyway, it doesn't matter because I'm only working behind the bar.

My nerves start to flutter as she pulls me to the other side and through a large archway. "This is our closet." My mouth drops open. Cream leather suits and skirts all lined up on racks, just like in a shop. There are huge baskets filled with cream and caramel colored lingerie, and expensive, gold high heels lined up in pairs. "This is our uniform wardrobe. Everything is dry cleaned daily and hung back up here." Her eyes fall back to me. "The girls don't have to worry about laundering their own uniforms. Leather can be tricky."

I fake a smile. I bet.

She walks to the end and a long rack of cream, sheer, loose tank tops all hang in neat rows.

Unable to help myself, I reach up and touch the fabric.

"Organza," Eliza purrs.

My eyebrows rise. "Oh." Jeez.

"These are the tops our dancers wear with these bottoms." She pulls out the bottom drawer and it is filled with coffee-colored, short, leather hot pants.

I hate to admit it, but with the cream and caramel color palettes mixed with the leather and lace, it really gives off an expensive, sexy feel.

"They don't wear the skirts?" I frown.

"No, it's hard to straddle a seated man, lap dance in a tight leather skirt, and still maintain your dignity."

Not the answer I was expecting, but okay. She leads me through into another room where there is a beauty salon and two European male hairdressers.

"Franco and Merrin, meet Vivienne."

They both look me up and down and smile.

58

I nervously pull my woolen dress down. This is all just so... weird.

"You get all of your beauty and hair needs looked after free of charge when you work here." Eliza's eyes flicker to me. "And the laser hair removal is on the house."

Shit. Well, blow me down. That's a service I never expected to get for free.

"What position are you starting, Vivienne?" Franco asks.

"Oh." I smile awkwardly. "I'm interested in the bar position."

His eyes flash to Eliza and she smiles. "Sweet Vivienne, you will waste away behind the bar. You are way to gorgeous for that."

I shake my head. "Oh, I don't think—"

She cuts me off. "We will talk about that later, dear. Come. I have lots to show you."

"Bye." I wave to the two people I have just met as she drags me by the hand.

We walk out into another large room and I stop on the spot. Rows and rows of designer evening gowns are lined up on racks, and girls are starting to look through the garments. Sequins and feathers are everywhere. Wow, this is something else.

"Hi, Elli," they all call as they keep going through the racks. I frown. What the hell are they doing?

As if reading my mind, Eliza answers me. "They're picking what they want to wear tonight."

Huh?

"Every night, we have a fashion parade displaying new designers."

"I don't understand..."

"Young and upcoming designers bring in their evening wear and the girls do a catwalk show before the cocktail party."

"Cocktail party?" I ask.

She smiles knowingly. Jeez, I should shut my mouth. I look like I am interested in this shit. "I mean... it doesn't matter."

"Do you want to know about the Escape Lounge?"

My eyes hold hers. I do, but only because I want to know what kind of place this is.

"I suppose," I whisper.

She walks off to the left over to two large double doors. "Come, let me show you."

We go through the double doors and it opens onto another bar area private from the rest of the club, and way more exotic. A large water feature is in the middle and the lighting is moody and sexy. Waiters are behind the bar making cocktails. I frown again. The bar staff are all male out here.

Eliza watches me intently, knowing full well that my mind is abuzz with questions.

"Every night, out in the club, we have a fashion parade with twenty-four of the most beautiful woman we have."

I frown.

"Every night, we have twenty-four men who have reserved their Escape night."

My skin prickles.

"At the end of the fashion parade the Escape girls have a private cocktail party out here where they choose their partner for the night."

Goosebumps scatter up my spine.

"Ch-choose?" I stammer, wide eyed.

"Being an Escape girl doesn't mean that you automatically have to sleep with anyone, but you are required to spend the night in one of our suites with the one of your choosing."

The look on my face must be a sight because Eliza laughs out loud. "Don't look so horrified, Vivienne."

I stare at her, dumfounded.

"Would you like to see a suite?"

I nod, because all words have escaped me and I feel like an idiot. She walks over to the large, smoke-mirrored elevator doors and pushes the button. The doors immediately open and we hop in.

"We have twenty-four apartments," she continues.

As the elevator door opens on the first floor, she glides out into a luxury corridor, opening the door to one of the apartments.

"Each Escape girl has an apartment for the night. It's a twelve-hour shift." She holds her arm out to gesture for me.

I gaze at the amazing space. "So, this is the position you get paid five-thousand a night for?" I whisper.

She smiles. "Yes. That's right."

I walk past her into the room as I feel my heart rate quicken. The room is beautiful and exudes luxury. Leather lounges surround a fireplace, and huge bouquets of fresh flowers in crystal vases are scattered throughout the apartment. Champagne and chocolate-coated strawberries are in the glass door refrigerator. I continue into the bedroom and see the most amazing bed I have ever seen, dressed in huge white linen, inviting with big, fancy cushions. The black marble bathroom has a sunken spa bath and a triple headed shower nozzle.

Holy hell. This place is something else. I walk around in awe. I've never been in such a beautiful space in all of my life.

Eliza turns to me.

"You have something special, Vivienne."

I force a nervous smile.

She folds her arms in front of her and leans her behind back against the leather lounge. "Every girl in this club wants this position, but I'm not interested in them. I want you, Vivienne. I want you as an Escape girl." She smiles as she brushes the hair back from my forehead to look at my face.

My breath catches in my throat.

"You can start tonight."

5

I RELEASE a nervous giggle and shake my head. "No, sorry. I'm not." I pause as I look around the room in front of me. "I could never be this person."

Her eyes hold mine and I desperately hope she can't read my mind, because deep down this just may be the most exciting damn escape plan I've ever seen. Five grand a night to get dressed up in designer evening wear, drink cocktails, and then seduce a hot, rich guy in a luxurious penthouse without the fear of anyone ever finding out. No judgement, no boundaries.

I can definitely think of worse ways to go.

"I would like to take the bar position, please," I announce.

Without replying, her eyes stay fixed firmly on mine.

She knows I'm tempted to give it a try.

What if Owen ever found out?

With renewed purpose, I walk toward the door. "Thank you for the offer, though. It was very kind. When would you like me to start on the bar?" I ask confidently.

She hesitates before answering. "Wednesday night?" she finally concedes.

I smile broadly and turn to shake her hand. "You got yourself a deal."

I wake to feel small warm arms around my ribs from behind. My bed partner has stuck to his usual routine. Every night, Owen crawls into bed with me. I never know exactly how or when he comes in. I just know that some time between night and morning I will feel his little arms cuddling my back and he stays there until I wake.

He kisses my back through my pajamas and I smile with my eyes still closed. "Morning, Owie," I whisper sleepily.

"Hi, Mom," his husky little voice replies.

I roll onto my back and put my arm underneath his head, my eyes are still closed. "I thought we were going to try and sleep in your bed all night. Remember, we were going to buy you a new truck if you did?" I murmur. I've stooped to bribery, but at this point I will do whatever it takes.

"I just don't like it in there," he announces.

"Hmm." I sigh with my eyes still closed. I lean and kiss his forehead. "What's on today, buddy?"

"Cornflakes?"

"Yeah. Okay." I doze for a moment. "Momma's tired today?"

"Rise and shine," Jenna's perky voice echoes through the room. She opens the drapes and the sun comes blazing through. "Oh, go away," I moan as I cover my eyes. "What time is it?"

"Wake up time." She smiles as she stands at the end of the bed with her hands on her hips. "This time tomorrow you would have been at the hospital for an hour by now."

I frown. "Don't remind me. I'm trying to forget." I instantly feel my nerves rise in the pit of my stomach.

Owen hops out of bed and disappears up the hall. Jenna lies down next to me on top of the covers. "We have to go shopping and buy you some new work clothes."

"Yeah, I know."

"So?" She leans up onto her elbow to look down at me.

"What?"

"How was it?"

I rub my eyes with my two hands as I yawn. "It was pretty good, actually."

She raises her eyebrows in surprise.

"I start on Wednesday."

She grins.

My eyes meet hers. "Is that okay? I don't have to be there until after Owie goes to bed and I will be home before he wakes up."

"Of course it's okay. I told you already, that's why I moved here — so I can study from home and take care of Owie while you finish your degree."

"I feel like shit that you have to babysit for me." I sigh.

"I feel like shit that I am living with you rent free."

I smirk. "Thank you. You don't know how much I appreciate all that you do for me."

She smiles. "About last night. I want details, all the details."

I shake my head. "Jeez, I don't even know where to start." I pause for a moment as I try to articulate my thoughts. "It kind of looks like an old picture theatre or something that has been converted because it's tiered down to a catwalk at the front."

She sits up. "Okay."

"The stupid fuckwits pay one-hundred and ten-thousand dollars a year."

"What the hell? What are you donating? A fucking organ or something?"

I laugh and shake my head. "Probably. She tried to get me to be an Escape girl."

"Escape girl?" She frowns.

"It sounds weird when I to say it loud, but it didn't sound so bad last night. There are twenty-four men and twenty-four Escape girls. The girls dress up and put on a fashion show in designer clothes—"

"What?" she interrupts. "That sounds fucking stupid."

I rest the back of my forearm over my forehead to block out the sunlight. Those drinks had some punch last night. I feel like shit. "I know. It really is."

"Then what?"

"They dress up in gorgeous clothes and do a catwalk thing and then go into a private area for a cocktail party with the twenty-four men."

Jenna scratches her head. "Sounds like a bad dating television show."

I laugh. "Totally."

"Weird." She frowns.

I remember something else. "Oh my God. Get this: The girls then pick their date for the night and get to go back to this luxury penthouse with the guy for twelve hours."

"Shut up."

I shake my head. "Serious."

Her eyes widen as she imagines it. "Fuck, that's hard core. It would be so bitchy."

"What do you mean?"

"Imagine twenty-four guys and only five are hot. You get paid the same if you bang a hot guy or an ugly guy. All the girls would be going for the same guys."

I frown. "Hmm, true. I didn't think of that, but I suppose they would be. They were all really hot, though. It wouldn't be a hard choice."

"And what happens if you did the deed with one guy and liked him, and then next time some other chick wanted him."

Horror fills me as I imagine the scenario. "Oh, yeah, that's bad. I couldn't deal. I'm taking a shower." I drag myself out of bed, walk into the bathroom, and turn the shower on and I glance at my reflection in the mirror. A stupid thrill of excitement runs through me and I smile goofily at my racoon-eyed reflection. For some reason, last night made me feel alive. It was my very own dirty little secret that only Jenna and me know about. I would never do it. I already know that my morals would never surrender, but damn, it is fun being offered a choice. Dreaming of the impossible, I haven't had any choices to choose from for so long. I undress and hop under the hot water and let it run over my head. Eliza's words run through my mind.

"Every girl in this club wants this position, but I'm not interested in them."

"I want you, Vivienne. You have something special. I want you as an Escape girl."

I soap myself up. Eliza wants me. She thinks I have what it takes to keep her clients happy.

And you know what? If that was what I wanted to do—it's not, but if it was—I reckon I could do a bloody good job of it, too. It's been so long since I had a good night with a man. Years, in fact.

I continue washing my body as I imagine getting my every need met for a change. A powerful man who would do anything to have me in his bed. *What would it be like?*

Maybe it's me who needs an escape.

"What do you have to get today?" Jenna asks, interrupting my daydream. She walks in and sits on the toilet with the lid down.

"Erm." I subtly shake my head to snap my wayward thoughts back to reality, frowning as I think. "A few new outfits. I don't have anything dressy enough. My hospital work stuff is all a bit dated." I think on it. "Oh, and some sensible shoes."

She smiles cheekily.

I smirk. "What?'

"Are you going to wear your sensible shoes on Wednesday night to the Escape Club?" she teases.

I shake my head and laugh. "The Escape Club doesn't do sensible in any way, shape, or form."

"Hello, I'm here to start today," I say nervously through the glass window.

The receptionist looks at me over the top of her glasses. "What are you here for, dear?"

I try to calm the nerves in my stomach. "I have an internship that starts today." I'm nervous as all hell. God, I hope I get a nice doctor.

"What doctor are you with, dear" She smiles kindly.

I shuffle around in my bag and pull out the printed email I have. I quickly scan the document for a name. Oh, there it is. "A Dr. Stanton."

"Oh, yes, Dr Stanton is on level three in the cardiology west wing. His PA will be there, along with the other interns."

I smile. "Thank you."

I stuff the email back into my bag and head to the elevators. My heart is somersaulting in my chest as I ride up to level three and make my way down to the cardiology wing. Eventually, down the track I would love to be a cardiologist, and that's why I applied with Dr. Stanton.

Hearts fascinate me.

They're the center of our very existence. Very few cardiologists take on interns, so it's common for interns to move interstate to take up their positions. I just hope I get a nice crew to work with for the next twelve months. I continue walking up the hall until I get to a staff room where a few younger people are hanging around. This must be it. I tentatively walk in.

"Hello. Is this the cardiology wing? I'm looking for the interns," I ask.

"Yes." The tall man smiles warmly. He stands and immediately shakes my hand. "I'm Mathew."

I smile as we shake hands. "Hello, I'm Ashley."

"Nice to meet you, Ashley." Mathew turns to the other four people with him. "I would introduce you, but I've already forgotten the names." He smiles bashfully.

They all stand. Three men and one woman.

"I'm Steven," one man smiles. He's older, maybe early forties.

"I'm Zane." The good looking guy smiles. He is young and European looking. He looks as if he would only be straight out of med school. Maybe twenty-four or twenty-five.

"I'm Maria," the girl announces as she looks me up and down and makes an internal assessment.

Oh… okay.

I fake a smile and shake her hand. I already know I don't like this bitch. How rude?

"I'm Richard." The last man smiles. He's of a similar age to me. Late twenties and kind looking. I instantly feel comfortable with him.

"Are there just the five of us?" I ask.

"No, apparently there are six of us," Richard replies. "I'm straight out of med school myself."

"Same," I reply.

"Me ,too," chimes in Zane.

"I'm a General Practioner." Steven smiles. "I have my own practice."

"Oh, wow." I smile. "That's exciting."

He smiles warmly. "Does anyone want a coffee while we wait?"

I glance at my watch to see it is 6.45am. We don't start for another fifteen minutes. "Okay, I will."

He gets up and moves over to the coffee urn and starts to make our coffee. "How do you have it?"

"Milk, please."

The others all rise to make their coffees along side of him.

"Another girl walks in and my mouth nearly hits the floor. Has she got the right bloody job? She looks like she belongs in

68

the Escape Lounge with long, dark, straightened hair and a full face of makeup, complete with bright red lipstick. A tight black skirt and a white button up blouse hug her in all the right places. She's got really good tits, too, and she's wearing high patent stilettos and sheer black stockings.

"Hi, I'm Amber." She smiles. Oh, she smells good.

"Hi, Amber." I smile and feel the blood drain from my face as I shake her hand.

I look down at my sensible mom attire. I'm wearing black pants, flat leather shoes, and a light blue, button up blouse that hangs loose.

Shit... why didn't I get something swankier?

I feel like her mom.

"You look so nice," I murmur, embarrassed. "I feel underdressed," I whisper.

"You look lovely. I just couldn't let myself meet him looking frumpy."

I frown. "Meet who?"

"Dr. Stanton."

"What do you mean?"

"My God, haven't you seen him?" she whispers.

"No why?"

"Holy shit. He's ridiculous."

"Huh?" I whisper.

"Here is your coffee." Richard smiles as he hands it over.

"Thank you." I reply as I take it from him. "Richard, this is Amber."

"Hi, Amber." I see a twinkle in his eyes and I drop my head to hide my smirk. I bet she has that affect on all the men.

Bloody hell, even I'm fan-girling here.

A robust, short woman comes in. "Hello, are you Dr. Stanton's group?"

"Yes," we all reply.

"I'm Marci. I'm his personal assistant and his practice manager."

We introduce ourselves one by one with another round of handshakes. She hands us all clipboards with pens attached. "Unfortunately, I have paperwork for you all to fill out and the forms are quite extensive. They will take you about an hour, so please make yourselves comfortable."

We all take a seat.

"Now, Dr. Stanton is the training doctor, and you will be going into surgery with him. He has a partner Dr. Jameson who he works alongside. Three of you will be staying with Dr. Stanton and three of you will be going with Dr. Jameson. The two doctors work together so they are still able to go on holidays and have days off because they cover for each other."

We all nod. That makes sense. I'm going to try and do this when I finally get my own patients.

"I specifically wanted to be with Dr. Stanton." Steven interrupts.

"Me, too," Amber adds.

Hmm, I know why you want to be with him, little Miss Fancy Lipstick.

I bet she's into doctor porn. Is that a thing? I should look it up tonight.

"Now, now. I know that Dr. Stanton's reputation precedes him, but I can assure you that Dr. Jameson is also an amazing doctor. For all operations and procedures, you will be with Dr. Stanton, anyway."

Steven nods. "Okay."

We all nod. Understood.

"So, fill out your paperwork. Dr. Stanton is starting his rounds at 8am and you will be accompanying him."

We all smile excitedly at each other. This is it. Finally, after all these years at med school, we are finally in our last year. This is so freaking exciting.

An hour and a brain explosion later, my paperwork is completed. Dr. Stanton now knows everything about me, from my medical history, to my address, to my work experience and even my GPA. I do feel guilty about the white lie I have told in the forms, though.

Question: Do you have any children?

I thought long and hard before I answered this question, mainly because I don't want to be given any special allowances because I am a single mom. I would hate for anyone to have to pick up any slack because I have to leave early. This is why I'm paying the rent, I remind myself. So Jenna can study from home and take care of Owen without me having to worry about rushing home. I can work without restraints.

They don't need to know if I am a mother, and to be honest, I'm kind of peeved that they asked. Isn't that discriminatory?

Why should it matter if I'm a married or single mother?

Anyway, I lied and said that I don't have kids. They will never know and I can work without the whole 'you go first, I know your kid is waiting' vibe.

"You guys ready?" Marci smiles.

We all stand and follow her out into the corridor where we loiter around the reception as we wait. This really is exciting.

"Oh my God, there he is," Amber whispers.

I turn to look up the corridor and see a male in a navy suit talking to a nurse. His back is to us, and I do have to admit from where I am standing, he does look pretty good. He throws his head back and laughs out loud at something she has said.

Jeez.

"Holy shit," she whispers as she grabs my hand in excitement.

I bite my bottom lip and drop my head to hide my smirk. This Dr. Barbie chick is kind of funny. I can see us being friends.

I glance back up as he turns and my face drops.

What?

Holy fuck.

No... it can't be.

71

That cheeky smile. I would know it anywhere.

Vegas guy.

I frown as the floor moves beneath me. This can't be.

My breath catches as he turns and walks down the corridor towards us. His hair is dark with a bit of length and messy wave on the top, and his muscular physique is framed in his perfectly fitted suit. That square jaw and those dark eyes...

My gaze drops to his feet. Those perfectly clean tan shoes that I remember so well.

He's a cardiologist?

What the fuck? It can't be...

One hand is tucked in his pocket, while the other holds a file. He smiles brightly as he approaches us. "Hello, everyone."

"Hello," they all reply eagerly.

Amber elbows me in the ribs. "See... I told you," she whispers from our place at the back.

I have no words. I never thought I would see him again.

"Please, come into this room for a moment." His deep velvety voice shows off that sexy Australian accent.

We all follow him into an office. He has this air about him — this powerful, confident air.

I remember it.

I remember him.

We all stand in a group and I stay at the back. I look like shit. I want to go home and change immediately. God, why did I fucking wear this?

"My name is Cameron Stanton. Thank you for applying to intern with me. I'm looking forward to spending the year with you all."

Cameron.

"Hi, I'm Amber," Amber announces as she steps forward and shakes his hand. "I can't wait to get to know you." She smiles enthusiastically. I see a trace of amusement cross his face before he disguises it immediately.

"I'm Mathew." They shake hands.

He smiles and nods. "Nice to meet you, Mathew."

72

"I'm Zane."

"Hello." He smiles.

"I'm Maria."

He smiles broadly. "Hello, Maria." They shake hands.

"I'm Steven. It's an honor to meet you," he sings proudly.

Cameron smiles broadly. "The pleasure is all mine."

It's my turn, and I step out from behind the others. He looks up, but his face falls the moment he sees me. My heart stops. "Hello, I'm Ashley," I whisper.

He frowns as his eyes hold mine. "Ashley," he repeats.

I hold out my hand and he takes it in his. I'm jolted with a zap of electricity and I have to stop myself from letting out an audible gasp.

With a subtle shake of his head, he remembers where we are and quickly shakes my hand. "Nice to meet you, Ashley."

Our eyes are locked when a trace of a smile crosses his lips.

I drop my head in dismay. Holy hell.

What are the chances of meeting him here? Like this? I thought he was from Texas.

Oh no.

I'm the loser he never rang.

"Dr. Stanton, you have a phone call," a nurse interrupts.

"Give me ten minutes, please." He smiles to the group before disappearing up the hall.

My heart is hammering. "I'm going to the bathroom," I lie. I walk in the opposite direction to which he went. Crap, I'm so rattled by seeing him. I find a courtyard and I quickly walk out into the fresh air and ring Jenna.

Ring, ring.

"Hey, how's the first day going?" she answers chirpily.

"Oh my fucking God. It's him."

"Huh?"

"It's fucking him."

"What the heck are you talking about?"

"Vegas guy is the doctor I'm interning for."

"Shut the fuck up."

"I'm serious."

There's silence down the line.

"Are you there?" I eventually whisper.

"I can't believe this. Are you sure it's him?"

"It's him!" I snap.

"Jeez." She laughs. "Wow. I told you to wear the skirt today."

I glance down at my daggy attire. "Oh God, Jen, this is a disaster. I'm the fuckwit he never called."

"What are you going to do?"

I close my eyes. "I don't know."

"Where are you now?"

"In the courtyard. "I glance around at my surroundings. "He's taking a call."

"Well go back in. Who cares? Just do it."

"Yeah, I guess."

"Shall I buy wine?"

"Buy a case."

"Bye. Love you." I hear the smile in her voice.

"Yeah, bye." I hang up.

For the next three hours, the group and I follow Dr. Cameron Stanton around as he sees his patients. He is knowledgeable, caring, gentle, and absolutely orgasmic. He has the whole group as well as his patients under his spell. Everyone is hanging off every word that comes out of his mouth with that beautiful Australian accent.

Amber laughs at everything he says, and the boys are trying to become his best friend. Maria is quiet.

Me... well, I'm just plain horrified — horrified that a man I met five years ago for a period of twelve hours still has the ability to make me feel the way I am feeling at this moment.

This is the opposite of professionalism — this is loserism.

We continue to walk around the ward, and for some reason I begin to feel annoyed with him. Everyone in this hospital idolizes him like he's a damn rock star. He's gorgeous, smart, witty... and he didn't fucking call me. En-route to another ward, he stops to talk to another doctor walking in the opposite direction as they cross paths.

"Ten minute break, guys," he says to the group. The doctor he is talking to is also young and good looking, and it is obvious they are friends out of work.

I turn my back to them, but stay in the same spot as Amber starts to talk to me. I can't listen to what she's saying because I'm too busy eavesdropping on Dr. Panty Dropper and his hunky friend.

"Are you going to the conference in Geneva?" The other doctor asks him.

"If I can swing it, I am," Cameron replies.

"Yeah, well try and come and we can make a week of it."

"Okay, I'm on it."

The visiting hours have started and the corridors have people coming and going. One particular woman is on her own with three small children. The two smallest children are throwing tantrums and the youngest one is screaming the place down and she is dragging her along by the arm.

Dr. Stanton turns and smiles in acknowledgment to her before she disappears up the hallway with her screaming kids, then he turns back to his friend. "This is why condoms were the greatest ever invention," he casually whispers.

"Deserves a Nobel prize," the other doctor replies.

What? I frown.

Is he kidding? Who the hell does this twat think he is?

Condoms are the best thing ever invented. Well, he obviously hates kids.

I begin to hear my heart beat in my ears. And to think... I thought he was actually hot. He's an arrogant fucking asshole.

"I'm going to the bathroom," I whisper to Amber.

"Sure thing."

I turn and walk up the hallway.

"Ashley?"

I turn to see Cameron behind me. "Can I talk to you for a minute?"

I swallow my nerves. "Okay."

"In here?" He opens a door into an office.

I follow him into the small space and he closes the door behind me.

His eyes soften and he appears nervous. "I came looking for you."

I frown.

"I came to New York looking for you. I lost my phone with your number on it the day after you left."

What a crock of shit.

"Je vous ai souvent pensé," he whispers.

Translation: I have thought of you often.

My eyes drop to the floor. Oh God, he remembers our bilingual love making. I drag my eyes back up to his.

Why does he have to smell so good?

Every woman in this hospital is in lust with him, and if I let myself go there I will just be another on the list that he didn't call. I can't do it. I'm not going to be that needy girl who pines for Dr. Love.

"I'm sorry?" I reply flatly.

His face falls. "Vegas."

"What about Vegas?" I ask.

He narrows his eyes as if annoyed. "We met in Vegas a few years ago."

I purse my lips. "Did we? I don't think so."

He frowns.

"Vous ne vous souvenez pas de moi?"

Translation: You don't remember me?

My eyes hold his. "I'm sorry. I don't speak German."

Hi lifts his chin defiantly as his ego takes a physical blow. "That was French," he replies sarcastically.

My eyes hold his. "I don't speak French, either. You've got the wrong girl."

He steps back from me. Shock flashes across his face. Hell, I surprised myself. Why did I just say that? His eyes hold mine and he frowns as if processing my lie.

"Please excuse me. I thought you were someone else," he murmurs.

"Who?" I ask as my eyebrows rise. "Who did you think I was?" I don't know why, but I have to know his answer.

He smirks. He's got me. He knows it was me. Why did I bloody ask that question? If it wasn't me, I shouldn't need to know that answer.

He tilts his chin sarcastically. "Just this amazing girl I met five years ago that I haven't been able to forget."

My face falls. *Oh no.*

Anger flares in his eyes. "Never mind. It wasn't you. Sorry to take up your time."

He brushes past me angrily and out the office, and the door bangs with a thud.

I stand in the silence for a moment, the sound of my shallow breaths filling the air.

He seemed hurt that I didn't remember him. I already know that no woman with a pulse has ever forgotten Cameron Stanton.

I tip my head back to the heavens in despair.

Why on earth did I just do that?

6

Cameron

THE SWEAT is running down my torso and the sound of my feet connecting hard on the surface rings loudly through the gym.

The treadmill is flying, but I need to get rid of this fury that's boiling over.

Ten more minutes. Ten more minutes and then I can stop.

She didn't remember me.

I glance up at the music channel playing overhead and wipe the perspiration from my brow as I think back to Vegas when I met her.

How could she have possibly forgotten the night that we had together?

It's seared into my fucking soul.

I've compared every woman since. Nobody has ever measured up. Both physically and mentally, they always fall short.

Until her, I didn't know what I was looking for.

Until I got on the plane empty handed in New York to return home from trying to find her, I didn't know what disappointment was.

Was it even her?

I get a picture of her in my office earlier and trace my mind for the image I have in my head of our time in Vegas.

Yes, it fucking was her!

She has some kind of golden unicorn status in my mind and she was definitely in my office...

Today.

I turn up the speed and run as fast as I can.

"Are you trying to kill yourself?" Murph asks, interrupting my thoughts.

I'm too short of breath to answer him so I shake my head.

"Did someone die today?" he asks, concerned.

I shake my head, still too short of breath to answer.

"What's wrong?"

"Nothing. Fuck... off," I pant. I'm near having a heart attack here. What could possibly be wrong?

"You're a cranky shit, you know that?" Murph frowns.

I continue to concentrate on the belt zooming by beneath my feet.

My brother Joshua—Stan as we call him—walks into the gym dressed to train after finishing work. We are in his office building gym, and it's 5pm in the afternoon. We come here most days, and although he is only in LA a few days a week, Murph and I are here daily. This is the only reliable place where we get to see each other. Obviously, Stan and Murph work together, but with my crazy work schedule and all of us busy on weekends, this sixty minutes a day with my two best friends is sacred. When they are not annoying the fuck out of me, that is.

Stan frowns as he sees me and walks over to the treadmill to watch me for a moment. Murph joins him and they stand in front of me, both smirking.

"Fuck... off," I pant. "I'm not in the mood for your fucking shit today."

"Did someone die?" He frowns. Usually I only get like this if I lose a patient. Thankfully, that's not my reasoning today.

"Nobody died," I grunt, exasperated.

"Then what's up your ass?" Stan asks.

"Nothing. I've had a prick of a day, that's all."

I continue running as they both move on and do their weights together. This is Joshua's second workout for the day. He works out morning and night. He's abnormal, I'm sure.

Why did she say she didn't know me? Could she really have forgotten? A disturbing thought crosses my mind. Fuck, what if she's married? What if I found her too late?

Found who? *She doesn't even know who you are,* I remind myself. Maybe it was all one-sided. Hmm, it could happen, I suppose. I mean, it normally happens to me, only the other way around. The girls fall in love while I look for the closest exit door.

I think back. She *was* very eager to get away from me that morning. Maybe too eager.

Fuck, I shouldn't have let her go. It's the one thing I have regretted over the years, that I didn't push the concierge for more information on her. And that I lost my stupid phone that night. If I had known what affect she was going to have on me, I would have gotten Joshua to hack the security footage, right there and then on the spot.

The treadmill finally comes to a halt and I step off it, my fatigued legs adjusting to the hard floor. I'm panting, covered in perspiration, and exhausted. I walk into the bathroom and get under a burning hot shower. I've never felt so out of control of a situation before.

It's very… unsettling.

I stand under the shower and let the hot water run over my head as I feel my body recover from its exertion.

I think on it for a long time and I know I've got two choices. I can make a fool of myself by trying to make her remember me, even though I know she really already does, or…

I stare into space for a moment as I think. A smile crosses my face as a plan comes to mind.

You want to play mind games, baby?

Let's go!

Ashley

Four hours later, I turn the key in the front door. Exhausted doesn't come close to what I'm experiencing right now. It's 8pm. Nerves, concentration, and the shock of coming face-to-face with — and lying to — an ethereal creature has all taken its toll. I don't think I have ever been so tired in my whole life.

"Momma!" Owen yells excitedly as he jumps from the back of the lounge and runs to meet me at the front door. I scoop him up and squeeze him tight. Coming home to him reminds me why I put myself through this hell: To provide a better life for us. To have stability. I want him to be proud of who I am.

That's the plan, anyway.

"Hi, baby." I smile into his hair. "Sorry I'm late. Did you have a good day?"

He grins. "I got you a present."

My mouth drops open in an over exaggerated gesture, and I place him back down on the floor. "You did?"

He swings back and forth with his hands behind his back and nods proudly. "It's flowers."

I smile broadly. "Why did you buy me flowers?"

"They are first day flowers."

I bend and kiss him.

"But I can't buy them for you tomorrow," he says seriously. "Because it won't be your first day."

"Oh, okay," I reply. "That's a sensible plan."

I catch sight of Jenna hiding in the kitchen as she eavesdrops and I blow her a kiss.

"Do you want to see them?" he asks.

"Yes please." I smile. My little man is so articulate. He grabs my hand and leads me upstairs to my room and sure enough, there on my bedside table is a vase full of beautiful, brightly colored flowers. I bend to inhale their scent. "I love them, thank you, Owen."

He remembers something and runs off to his room. "I did something else," he calls over his shoulder.

I smile and sit on my bed as I wait for his return. Within moments, he is back with me again. He passes me a picture he has drawn. I smile as I try to work out what it is. Hmm. Tricky. It could be anything to be honest. "I love it," I gasp.

He points to it. "Yes, because sometimes you won't have a coat."

I frown. Okay, he's lost me now. I have no idea what he's talking about. "Oh, so this is me?"

He nods. "Yes." He replies as he crawls onto my lap. "Of course it's you. See?" He points to the squiggly lines in a square. "This is the hospital and you are the doctor."
A broad smile crosses my face. "Ah, yes, I see it now."

His proud smile beams up at me. This beautiful child is such a blessing in my life. "Where's Jenna?" I ask.

"In the kitchen."

"Come on, let's go and show her my flowers. She will be so surprised."

Owen frowns as he thinks and then gestures for me to come close so he can tell me a secret. I lean my ear down so I'm closer to his mouth.

"She knows about your flowers," he whispers.

"She does?" I whisper back in surprise.

"She bought them."

I smile. "Oh!" I try to act shocked.

"But I have to pretend I bought them even though I don't have any moneys," he whispers.

"Okay." I kiss his cheek. This kid's honesty kills me. "I won't tell her you told me," I continue. "Your secret is safe and thank you, I love them." I wink to seal the deal.

"Good," he replies as he takes my hand and leads me downstairs to my beloved friend. This is her. This is how she operates. My birthday and Christmas presents from Owen all come from Jenna. She has been the stand-in sensible dad to Owen since he was born because his father was hopeless and my happiness is more important to her than her own. I could never repay her for everything she has done for me. I smile as I walk into the kitchen as she serves up my dinner onto a plate, and I kiss her cheek. "Thank you," I mouth.

She throws the tea towel over her shoulder. "Congratulations on your first day." She smirks, her eyes alive with mischief.

Owen climbs up onto the stool next to me, smiling like the Cheshire Cat.

"Owen bought me flowers," I reply.

"I saw them." She smiles. "You are so lucky to have a son like him."

Owen smiles a proud of himself smile.

I put my arm around his shoulders and kiss the top of his head. "I know. My little prince." I begin to press kisses all over his face until he swats me away, laughing.

"Stop it, Mom," he squeals. "Stop it."

Jenna pushes my plate over to me and I look down at the casserole and mashed potatoes she has made.

"Thank you." I grab her hand over the table as emotion overcomes me. "I can't tell you how much it means to me that you do all you do."

She smiles warmly. "I know."

Her eyes glance to Owen as he sits beside me, and then she pours me a glass of wine. "I can't wait to hear all about your day and your new boss." She widens her eyes in jest. I shovel the first fork full of food into my mouth. "My new boss is nice." I gesture to the food. "This is delicious."

"And?"

I smirk around my mouthful, not wanting to elaborate in front of Owie. "And I will tell you later when I have drunk this bottle of wine."

Two hours later I am trying my hardest to explain my predicament.

"The forms were really long and I was doing them for an hour. I don't know why I wrote it, I just did."

We are on our second bottle of wine at the kitchen table with Owen safely tucked up in bed.

Jenna frowns. "I just don't understand why you lied. There is nothing wrong with having kids Ashley."

I blow out a defeated breath. "I know, but I didn't know I was going to know him when I filled it out, did I?"

Her eyes hold mine.

"I don't want to be judged and given special treatment because I'm a single mom."

"You won't be."

"I will be. I will get the whole 'you go first, your kid is waiting' bullshit. 'You can't do overtime because you have a kid at home'."

Jenna watches me sadly. "But what happens if you like this guy and he asks you out on a date?"

"He won't."

"He might. He remembered you. That's something." She smiles hopefully.

I roll my eyes as I drain my glass. "Trust me, as soon as he finds out I have a kid he will lose interest instantly and I will become someone's mom who is not needed anymore."

Jenna purses her lips as she thinks. "You need to tell him, so if there's a chance, you can rekindle what you had."

My eyes hold hers.

"You've talked about this guy for years, compared everyone to him, and now he's come back to you in a weird twist of fate and you've started it all with lies. What's wrong with you?"

I drop my head into my hands. "Oh God, I don't know. I was flustered, he's all gorgeous, and the women swoon over him. I just felt so bloody old."

"Go in there tomorrow and tell him everything. Tell him you remember him, tell him you had a son, and tell him you want to explore anything there might be between you."

"I'm not saying that." I screw up my face in disgust. "I want to explore things with you." I shake my head. "Sounds like bloody David Attenborough."

She laughs. "What did he look like?"

I throw my head backwards. "I have never seen a man so hot. He could do me some damage, that's for sure." I shake my head in disgust. "I'm practically a virgin again."

"Did you take a photo of him?"

I screw up my face again. "Are you a freak? I am not taking a fucking photo of him." I shake my head. "Oh, my friend wants to see what you look like. Mind if I get a shot?"

She laughs and we both fall silent, deep in thought. "What are you going to do?" she eventually asks.

I narrow my eyes. "Well, first things first, I'm going to ace up the work clothes and look hot. Second of all, I'm going to drag him into an office and 'fess up about my lie."

"You should kiss him."

"What?" I smirk.

"Can you imagine? You look really sexy and then you ask him to come into the office and you kiss him all seductive like."

I look at her, deadpan. "This is my job and there are rules that I can't break."

She smiles and raises her glass. "I would like to propose a toast."

I sip my wine and raise my glass.

"To breaking rules in French, in offices, on desks with doctors."

I laugh and snort my wine up my nose the wrong way. I begin to cough uncontrollably. "Shut up, I am not seducing a doctor in French on a desk." I cough. "I will get fired."

"Or fucked hard."

I continue to cough as I laugh.

"Oh, we we mouser, we shall see," she retorts in a fake French accent.

I wait for the boom gate to rise in the car park. Its 6.40am and I am preened to the nines. After today I will be wearing scrubs while I'm working, and then there is zero chance of impressing anyone. Least of all Dr. Vegas.

Black fitted dress? Check.

Hair out and straightened? Check.

Makeup? Check.

Sheer black stockings and heels? Check.

Absolutely no sleep and running on empty? Check, check, and double check.

I blow out a frustrated breath. Go up, you stupid thing. The boom gate is not going up. *Why?* I put on the parking brake and get out of my car. My card got me through the first gate, but then stopped me at the second. Now I can't go back because I have to get back through the second boom gate.

For fuck's sake.

I glance at my watch. 6.45 am. I'm already late because I was thinking dirty thoughts about a certain doctor all night and hardly slept right up until an hour before my alarm went off. I push the little red help button and wait while it rings.

"Hello, can I help you?" The male voice comes through the speaker.

"Hello, I'm through the first boom gate, but now it won't let me through the second."

"Have you used the card before?"

"No, I'm new. I'm a doctor intern."

"The card must be faulty. You will have to come to level two in the car park and get it swiped through the machine."

I frown and look at my watch again. I don't have time for this shit.

"I'm sorry, I don't have time. I'm due at work. Can you just lift the gate and I will sort it tonight?"

"No. It's against policy."

"Are you kidding me? I'm blocking traffic. If anyone tries to get in behind me, they will get stuck, too."

"Most of the staff park in B block," he replies sarcastically.

I narrow my eyes. "Well, not this staff member, so can you open the gate?" I snap.

I glance back down to my watch. Fuck, it is 6.50am.

"Nope, come down to level two."

Oh God. "How do I get there?"

Leave your car, walk down the stairs, and up the other end is an office.

"I'm... I'm going to be late for work," I stammer in a panic.

"Seems so," he replies sarcastically.

Shit!

I hang up, lock my car, and half run to the stairs, taking them two at a time. I get to level two, take my heels off, and bolt to the other end of the parking lot with my heels in my hand, with only my stockings hitting the bare ground. I arrive panting and a skinny guy who couldn't care less looks up at me.

"Oh, are you the lady whose parking ticket isn't working?"

"That... would... be me," I pant. Oh, man, I'm out of shape.

I give him the ticket. He scans it and then opens the gate with a button. I watch on his security camera as it rises.

"You couldn't do this for me when I was up there?" I snap. Honestly... *some people*.

"No. I don't want to get into trouble." He smiles sarcastically as he hands over my card.

I snatch it from him and turn to run back to the stairs and up to my level, and then over to my car. I'm out of breath when I glance at my watch. 6.58am.

Oh, man. I'm late!

I drive like a maniac into the car park. I get out, lock the car, and run. I don't even know where I will come out in the hospital, but I hope it's close to where I'm going. I push open the heavy door and come out into an area I haven't seen before. Where the heck am I? I look around in a panic.

I see a janitor. "Excuse me, where... is... cardiology?" I pant. So much for me looking good today. I look like hell on a stick now.

He frowns. "Down the other end of the hospital and up two levels."

My face falls. "What?" Crap. I start to run and catch an elevator. I pant as I try to fix my hair in the mirror, and just before the doors open I glance down to see a huge ladder in my stockings that runs up the whole length of my leg.

"Ah. Fuck it!" I snap.

The doors open and I scramble out. I need to find a bathroom to take my stockings off. I glance at my watch. 7.10am.

Oh my God. Oh my fucking God!

I'm never late.

I don't do late.

I finally see a restroom sign and run into the cubicle and rip off my stockings like a crazy person.

This day is starting out really fucking bad. I throw them into the trash and scramble out, finally arriving at the cardiology wing. I open the double doors to see all of the interns standing in a group with Dr. Stanton.

Cool, calm, and on bloody time.

I'm panting, my hair is all over the place, and they all turn to look at me together.

Oh crap.

"I'm sorry I'm late," I whisper, embarrassed as I slide over the where they are standing.

Dr. Stanton's dark eyes meet mine. I feel myself wither under his glare.

"Nice of you to finally join us." He sneers.

My face falls. "I'm sorry, Dr. Stanton. I had a parking incident."

His angry eyes hold mine. "The reasoning is irrelevant. You're late."

My eyes hold his. *Oh my God.*

The other interns all look away. This is uncomfortable.

"I… I know," I stammer nervously. "I'm sorry." I drop my head in shame.

"I don't tolerate late. You need to pick up your act or you won't last two minutes around here." He growls angrily. "I don't deal with incompetent people."

"I'm sorry. It won't happen again."

"Give your lame excuses to someone else," he mutters before he turns and walks up the corridor.

The other interns and I all stand still on the spot in shock. *What the actual fuck was that?*

He turns. "Are you coming?" he snaps.

The interns all take off after him into a patient's room, while I drift along at the back, hearing my furious pulse in my ears.

"Ashley, don't make us wait any longer," he calls from inside the room.

Dr. Vegas might need a fucking doctor himself soon.

How dare he?

7

YOU KNOW the thing that annoys me about sexual chemistry? It doesn't turn off when you want it to. Cameron Stanton is openly furious with me, and here I am, following his cranky ass around all day, imagining how he would look naked. I mean, the suit is nice… perfect, in fact. That messy dark hair that looks like he has just been fucked hard is inspiring. The spotless shoes are designer, and the watch probably cost more than my car, but nope… it's naked that's working for me. We walk up the corridor as a group following Dr. Stanton on his rounds. This is the worse kind of torture to watch. He is so gentle and caring with his patients that I can feel myself melt more and more as the day goes on. We stop out the front of the room so he can give us our usual briefing, and he opens the client chart.

"This is Gloria Hernandez. Gloria is ninety-two and in need of a triple heart bypass." He pauses. "Although at her age, she likely wouldn't survive the surgery, as she isn't well enough." His eyes rise to meet ours. "She will be staying on here so that I can keep an eye on her and make sure she is as comfortable as possible. She has no surviving family left."

The group falls silent. We know that's code for Gloria is dying... alone.

Dr. Stanton fakes a smile and heads into the room. He smiles broadly as he sees the frail, little old lady in her bed.

"How is my favorite patient today?" He smiles as he picks up her hand affectionately in his.

Gloria is little, old, and frail. Her hair is completely white with a pretty curl to it and her small hand is covered in dark purple veins. She is wearing a pretty pink nightdress and has a pink clip in her hair holding her bangs back. Her face lights up when she sees him and she smiles excitedly as she takes his hand. "Hello, Dr. Stanton," she gushes. "I've been waiting for you."

He gives her a cheeky grin and squeezes her hand. "Gloria, this is my new group of interns. They are here for the next twelve months."

Her eyes flick around to all of us and she smiles politely. "Hello."

"Hello." We all smile.

"How are you feeling?" he asks.

"I'm okay." She pauses. "I would like to go home, though, please."

He smiles harder as he pats her hand, still held firmly in his. "We have this conversation every day, Gloria. You won't be going home anytime soon." He picks up her chart and starts to read it.

"It's just so boring in here, doctor."

"Just try and relax." He flicks the chart up to the next page as he reads on.

"Can you do something about my sight?" she pleads. "If only I could read. This is a cruel end, not being able to read."

His eyes meet hers and he nods sadly. "Unfortunately, I can't restore sight, Gloria. If only I could."

A lump in my throat forms as I watch on. As an avid reader I can't imagine anything worse than the day when my sight will no longer allow me to read. Dr. Stanton continues to read the chart. Unable to help myself, I speak up.

"What is your favorite book, Gloria?"

She looks over at us, surprised by my question.

"I'm Ashley." I smile as I hold my hand out and gently shake her little hand.

She smiles. "Hello, Ashley." She reaches up and cups my face in her hand. "God blessed you, my love."

I frown. "I'm sorry?"

"You are so beautiful."

I smile bashfully, embarrassed by her attention.

"Pride and Prejudice." She smiles a soft, far away smile. 'If only I could read it one more time."

I smile as I try to block out the emotion. "That's my favorite book, too, Gloria."

"It's a classic." She rubs my cheek, and suddenly aware that eight people are looking on, I step back from the limelight. Dr. Stanton's eyes hold mine for an extended time.

"Doctor?" Gloria interrupts.

His eyes flash to her. "Yes, Gloria."

"I would like custard today, and not that hideous yogurt that they try to make me suffer through."

He throws her a cheeky wink. "Are you going to be a good girl?"

She laughs mischievously. "Oh, Dr. Stanton, if only I met you sixty years ago."

He smiles as he hands the waiting nurse her chart. "Can you please order custard today instead of yogurt?"

The nurse practically melts at his feet. "Yes, doctor."

With one last smile at Gloria he leaves the room.

It's just before lunch and I am famished. "Is it this way?" Amber asks.

I frown as I look around the parking lot. "I don't know." I'm walking in front of her as we search the parking lot for Dr. Stanton's car. We are picking up some files from his trunk that he brought over from the private hospital. "Who does he think he is asking us to get things for him from his car anyway? I'm not a damn slave," I snap.

His gorgeousness is seriously pissing me off.

Everyone loves Dr. Stanton. *Why does he have to be so fucking perfect?*

Ugh, it's so annoying.

I'm glad I told him I didn't remember him because we are going to be mortal enemies, I can just tell. I have to watch him be pathetically nice to everyone around me, but then he totally ignores me like I don't even exist.

Every nurse at every opportunity flirts up a storm with him. And what's more infuriating is that he flirts back. I can only imagine how many women he must sleep with around here.

"Why are you complaining? He actually asked the guys, remember? But we wanted to hide for ten minutes, so we offered." Amber replies.

"Oh, yeah, we did."

"I'll be his slave. Seriously, how fucking gorgeous is he?" Amber sighs.

I roll my eyes. "He's okay, I suppose," I murmur. "I haven't really noticed. He's too busy being an asshole."

"Are you kidding me? He's a lot better than okay," she continues from behind me as we weave through the cars. "I think he likes you."

I turn to face her. "Why do you say that?"

"He is checking you out every chance he gets."

I narrow my eyes. "Is not."

"Is too."

That shouldn't excite me, but it does. "Like when?"

"Like when you bent down to get all the things out of the filing cabinet, he was checking out your behind."

I screw up my face. "Oh, please, he so wasn't."

"You should ask him out."

"What?" I shriek. "Ask him out? Have you been sniffing the gas in theatre?"

"If he was checking me out, I would ask him out." She widens her eyes to accentuate her point.

I smile wide. "Amber, you're crazy. Do you know that?"

"Well, he couldn't ask me out, so I would have to ask him."

I frown. "Why couldn't he ask you out?"

"Hospital policy. The doctors are not allowed to have..." She puts her fingers up to air quote. "Liaisons with interns."

"Why? Last time I looked we were all adults."

She shrugs. "I don't know, but I'm seriously breaking that rule if I get the chance."

I smile as we keep walking.

"Tell me if you see him checking me out so I can pull the trigger," she continues.

I burst out laughing. "Pull the trigger?" I repeat.

"Yes, you know. Seize the day. Mow that fucker down."

I laugh as we walk. "Mow that fucker down." I snicker. I glance around the parking lot. "What car is it again?"

She frowns. "I don't know. He said it was in the farthest B block in the secured parking and the number plates were 777." She changes direction and I follow her across the parking bay.

I frown. "What kind of wanky plates are 777 anyway?" Ugh, this guy is an idiot.

She stops still and I nearly run into the back of her. "Oh... my... fuck," she stammers.

"What?"

"Look at his fucking car."

I glance around. "Huh, where?"

"I swear I need to marry this guy," Amber whispers.

"What?" I snap. "What are we looking at here?"

She points to a black, super shiny, flashy car and I frown. It's so fancy, I don't think I have ever seen one like it before. "What kind of car is that?"

"An Aston Martin."

My face falls. "How… much do they cost?" I stammer.

"Like, two-hundred thousand dollars."

I stand still on the spot. "Oh," I whisper. My mind goes back to Vegas and the guards he had. Who is this guy? Not many doctors are at this level of wealth at his age. She clicks the button and the lights go on as it unlocks. She climbs into the driver's seat.

"What are you doing?" I frown.

"Let's go for a spin." She smiles mischievously as she turns the engine on. It purrs like a kitten.

"Are you fucking crazy?" I whisper as I glance around guiltily. "Get out! I have already been in trouble once today."

She grabs his black playboy sunglasses from the console and puts them on as she pretends to drive and turn the wheel. "Oh, Amber, I want to fuck you so hard," she mimics in a fake Australian accent.

"Oh, Amber, I want to section you in a mental institution," I hit back in a better Australian accent than hers.

She smiles up at me. "Get in."

"Are you crazy? No."

"Nobody is here. Just get in and sit in it for a minute."

I glance around. The parking lot is empty, I suppose. I walk around to the passenger side, get in, and close the door.

Amber's loud laugh is contagious and I find myself giggling like a schoolgirl as she pretends to drive fast and turn the wheel back and forth. "Oh, Amber, suck my dick while I drive you to my castle," she mimics again in her bad Aussie accent.

I burst out laughing. She is the most refreshing fool I have met in a long time. Med school people are usually so boring.

She turns to me, all serious. "You know what this means, don't you?"

"No. What does this mean?"

"It means I need to bag myself Dr. Stanton."

I smirk.

"And if he doesn't want me... then you have to bag him."

"He doesn't want me," I reply.

"He might."

"He might want Henry." I smirk. "He could bat for the other side."

"Fuck." She thinks for a moment as she falls serious. "Then there is only one solution to that problem."

"What is it?" I smirk.

"You will have to give me a gender realignment."

My eyes widen. "And where am I getting your new penis from?"

She twitches her lips as she thinks for a moment. "Got any old boyfriends we can cut up?"

We struggle up the corridor with a box of files each to find Dr. Stanton standing in the door of his office. "Where do you want these?" Amber asks him.

His eyes fall to the boxes in our hands. "Amber, your box has to go down to archives on level one, and Ashley, your box comes into my office."

Amber frowns. "So, do I just take it down to the office?"

Distracted as his eyes hold mine, he answers, "Yes, just go down. The receptionist will guide you." He holds out his arm. "Come into my office, Ashley."

My stomach flips. Could he sound any more seductive? I walk past him into his office and he closes the door behind me. I stand with my back to him for a moment, too scared to turn and face him. Surely he will be able to read my mind.

Stop it, stop it, stop it.

I nervously turn to face him. "Where do you want me?" I whisper. *What the fuck?* "I... I mean. Where do you want the box?" I correct myself, embarrassed.

He steps toward me as a trace of a smile crosses his face. His big brown eyes are fixed on mine. "I know what you meant, Ashley."

Oh, the way he says my name is just so…

He leans forward and takes the box from my hands, placing it on top of his desk before he turns back to me. The gentle aroma of his aftershave surrounds me. I have never met a man who smells so damn good. We stay still, only a meter apart as the air crackles between us.

It's still there.

The chemistry is still there. I felt the fireworks all those years ago, only now it's nuclear energy.

His eyes roam all over my face and then fall to my lips.

I can hardly breathe. Holy hell, this is insane. I watch as his tongue slowly licks his bottom lip.

I remember that tongue.

My eyes flicker to his desk and I remember Jenna's words from last night. Have French sex on the doctor's desk were her exact words.

She was onto something because that's exactly what I want to do. I catch myself and I smirk.

"Something funny?" He frowns.

"Where do you want the files, doctor?" I ask innocently. Does he feel it?

He regains his composure and nods. "They will need to be filed into the bottom drawer, please."

"Do you want me to do it now?" I whisper as I feel my arousal start to pump deep inside of me.

His eyes hold mine. "Yes."

My breath catches.

"You will have to get on your knees." His eyes darken.

Wait, what? Are we talking about the same thing here? Our eyes are locked firmly. "Sure," I reply without hesitation.

I can feel his arousal. He's baiting me. He wants to know if he is doing it for me, and holy fuck, he so is.

Unable to help it, I walk to the filing cabinet and drop to my knees on the carpet. He stands above me, his hands clenching at his sides as if he's stopping himself from doing something.

Oh, he wants it, alright.

I could give it to you so good, Dr. Vegas.

"You going to give it to me?" I breathe.

He stands tall, looking down at me on my knees, clearly aroused and dominant, and I know we are supposed to be talking about patient files right now but in my mind we are talking about unzipping those expensive suit pants he's wearing.

"You want the whole lot?" He raises an eyebrow.

I nod. "Yes."

He turns and picks up the box, and then places it on the floor next to me, our faces only a few inches away from each other.

So close I can nearly taste him.

Holy shit, it's been way too long.

Knock, knock.

He stands abruptly, as if remembering where he is. "Yes?" he snaps, annoyed at the interruption.

I quickly grab two files out of the box as I pull out the bottom drawer in a fluster.

A tall, handsome man sticks his head around the door and his eyes glance between the two of us. "Am I interrupting?"

Dr. Stanton scratches his head in frustration. "Come in, please." He gestures to me. "Ashley, this is William Jameson, my partner."

Oh shit, my other boss. I scramble to my feet. "Hello." I shake his hand. "Nice to meet you." I smile.

"Ashley Tucker?" he asks.

I nod. "Yes."

"Oh, you are with me then." He smiles broadly.

"No. She's with me." Dr. Stanton replies curtly.

Dr. Jameson's eyes flicker between us. "But I thought —"

98

"Change of plans," Cameron interrupts.

Jameson fakes a smile. "Well, I will leave you in his capable hands then."

I nod nervously as I glance over to Dr. Stanton. This is awkward.

"Cameron, can I see you for a moment outside, please?"

"Sure." His eyes fall to me.

"Do you want me to keep filing?" I ask.

He frowns. "Actually, just leave that and come back to it later. Will, take a seat. We will talk in here."

I stand and head to the door.

"Ashley?" Dr. Jameson calls.

I turn back to face the two men. "Yes?"

"We are having a welcome reception for coffee on level two this afternoon. You will join us?" He smiles warmly.

"Thank you, that would be lovely."

"See you at two."

I nod, and without looking back at my dreamboat Dr. Vegas, I leave the room.

That was close.

I glance at my watch as the cashier rings up my purchase. I chew the last of my sandwich as I wait. I was starving and I couldn't have waited a minute longer. I ducked out in my lunch hour to a store to pick something up. I couldn't help myself. I can't imagine not being able to do my most favorite thing in the whole world.

She hands me my brown paper bag. "Here you go. Enjoy." She smiles.

I take my package from her. "I will, thank you. Have a great day." I exit the shop and quickly get back to my car.

Fifteen minutes later I find myself at Gloria's room.

Her little face lights up when she sees me. "Hello, Ashley." She smiles.

She's as sharp as a tack. "Hello, you remember my name?"

I smile. "I brought you something."

Her face lights up. "You did?"

I smile and pass her the little brown paper bag.

Her eyes lift to meet mine. "What is it, dear?'

"Open it."

She smiles as her little frail hands struggle to open up the tape and I stand patiently, I wonder how long it has been since she had a present. She finally gets it open and pulls it out of the bag. Her face drops and she gasps. "Oh…" She puts her little hand over her mouth. "You remembered?" She opens the hard cover edition of Pride and Prejudice that I have just bought her.

I smile proudly. "I told you, it's my favorite book, too. I wanted you to have a copy with you in hospital."

Her eyes fill with tears. "Thank you," she whispers as she looks down at the book. "That's the most thoughtful thing anyone has done for me in… I can't remember how long."

"You're welcome." I take her hand and sit next to her in the chair. Dr. Stanton said she has no surviving relatives. How long has she been on her own?

"Do you have time to read me a page, dear?" she asks. "It's okay if you don't, it's rude of me to ask."

I glance at my watch. I have fifteen minutes before I have to get back. "Yes, but only ten minutes, okay?"

Gloria smiles excitedly and lies back as I open the book with a huge smile on my face. This is the most fun I have had in a long time, too. I curl my legs up underneath me on the chair and I begin to read.

It is a truth universally acknowledged that a single man in possession of a good fortune must be in want of a wife.
However little known the feelings or views of such a man may be on his first entering the neighborhood.

I smile as I read, and on a few occasions I blink back the tears. I feel like I'm having an out of body experience, gifting an elderly woman time with her favorite book before she dies. Suddenly, this is the most important job I have ever had.

Gloria lies in her bed with her hands clasped tightly in front of her, a huge smile covering her face as she listens attentively.

"His pride," said Miss Lucas, "does not offend me so much as pride often does, because there is an excuse for it. One cannot wonder that so very find a young man, with family, fortune, everything in his favour, should think highly of himself. If I may express it, he has a right to be proud.

"I had my own Mr. Darcy." Gloria smiles softly.

I place my book down onto my lap as I watch her. "Did you?"

"I did."

I smile.

"He swept me off my feet and we were married for seventy-four years. Happy until the day he died."

"How wonderful, Gloria."

Her face falls solemn. "We were never gifted with children."

"Oh." Is all I can muster because I'm not sure what to say.

Her eyes flicker up to me. "What about you? Have you found your Mr. Darcy?"

I laugh and shake my head. "They don't make men like they used to, Gloria." I stop for a moment as I try to articulate my thoughts. "We only seem to breed one dimensional men these days."

Her wise eyes hold mine. "And you want a three dimensional man?"

I nod as I smile softly. "Yes. I want mind, body, *and* soul."

"And you just find the men who want the body?"

I nod sadly. "Seems so."

She holds out her hand and I take it in mine.

"Your Mr. Darcy will come for you," she whispers.

I smile and squeeze her hand in mine. "Maybe."

I glance at my watch. I have five more minutes.

"That is very true," replied Elizabeth, "and I could easily forgive his pride, if he had not mortified mine."

"Pride," observed Mary. "Is a very common failing I believe."

From the corner of my eye, I see something move, and I glance up to find Dr. Stanton leaning on the door frame listening to us both.

How long has he been there?

I sit up nervously and close the book. "I'm... I'm just reading to Gloria," I stammer.

He smiles softly. "So I heard." His eyes hold mine with a glow I haven't seen in them before.

What is that look?

"Gloria, can we pick this up tomorrow?" I ask as my eyes find her.

"Yes, dear, thank you so much. You have made me so happy."

I smile, place the book on her nightstand, and she holds her hand out. "Can you pass the book to me please, Ashley?"

"You are going to try and read it?" I ask.

She shakes her head. "No, I just want to sleep with it."

Emotion overcomes me and I quickly hand her the book. I keep my eyes on the floor and scurry out of the room before Cameron sees my tears.

I don't want to die alone.

The sound of the music echoes through the space, and I struggle to hear what the clients are ordering.

"Scotch on the rocks," he announces. I swear I'm getting good at lip reading.

I'm on my third shift behind the bar at Club Exotic. It's so busy. Men are everywhere and, even though I would never admit it, I look forward to coming here now. The girls are really nice and the members are all so polite and friendly. The money is amazing and I don't start until Owen is in bed tucked up safe. I couldn't ask for a better part-time job.

Never once have I felt cheap.

We're short staffed tonight. The Barr exam is on tomorrow for all of our Law students, so we are all working that bit harder to cover for them.

"Vivienne, can you do the door for me for a minute while I run this order down to the Escape Lounge?" Ebony asks me.

I frown. "I've never done the door before. What do I have to do?" I ask.

"Come, I will show you."

I follow her over to the little desk near the front entrance and she swipes on the touch screen computer. "So, when they come through, you swipe the barcode on their card with this gun." She picks up a little laser gun thingy and shows me how to use it.

"Okay."

"And then all the names will come up on the screen of the men who are in the club tonight."

"Aha."

"Just welcome them with *Welcome to Club Exotic* and then check the screen to make sure that their name adds to the bottom of the list."

"Got it." I frown. "Wait, do I ask them their name?"

"No. They don't ever tell you their name, but their real names come up on the screen. But you never acknowledge that you know it. That's a big deal. Never let them know that you know who they are."

My eyes widen. "Oh, okay."

"If someone is going to the Escape Lounge tonight, you will have to wait until I get back, so just let them in, but tell them they have to come back to see me."

I nod. "Got it. How will I know if they are going to the Escape Lounge?" I ask.

"Their name will be red on the screen."

"Okay."

She disappears into the darkness and I stand and wait at my position by the door. I'm wearing my little leather cream outfit. My hair is down and the girls put my makeup on tonight in the staff room. I'm feeling a bit sexy, to be honest. I watch as Simone, one of my new friends, walks past me in her sheer top and her little leather hotpants. She's about to give someone a lap dance. The song *Naughty Girl* by Beyoncé comes on, and I watch her slowly walk up to the guy sitting in the chair like she is going to eat him alive. His eyes hold hers and he sits back as he waits for her private show.

The sexual tension between them is thick and I hold my breath. The hypnotic beat pumps all around and I watch as she drops to her knees on the carpet in front of him. He sits back dominantly as she places both her hands on his upper thighs and crawls over the top of him.

A broad smile crosses my face. Holy hell, this is like another world here. My private peepshow is soon interrupted by a man walking through the door. He hands his card over to me. "Hello." He smiles.

"Welcome." I smile. I pretend to know what I am doing and swipe the barcode on his card with my little gun and he walks through. That wasn't too hard. I actually like being on the door, I get to see what's going on. Oh shit, I didn't check the screen to see if his name got added. I touch the screen and it lights back up and I glance to the list of names. I go through them from the bottom up.

Jack Hammond

Brandon Miller
James Holland
Stuart Miles
Carson Archer
Cameron Stanton

My eyes widen when I get to a name that is all too familiar.

Holy fuck.
He's here.

8

OH MY God. Oh my God. He's here. What if he sees me? Oh no! He can't see me.

Hang on a minute. He comes here by choice?

He's a member?

What a cock!

My blood starts to boil. I'm so glad I didn't tell him I remember him. He's one of those players that comes here behind the backs of his girlfriends, wives, or whatever the hell they are.

Ugh... I'm so off men. This is bloody typical.

I keep my head down and face the front as I hear my angry pulse in my ears. Damn it. I don't want him to see me. Should I just go home? I swallow the nervous lump in my throat as I glance around the club trying to locate him. My entire professional career will be out the window if he knows I work here. Fucking hell, I can hardly breathe.

Ebony reappears through the crowd smiling and her face falls when she sees the worry on mine. "What's wrong?" she asks.

"There is a guy here... from my work," I stammer.

"Shit," she curses.

"What do I do?" I whisper as I look around nervously.

"Go out the back and get a wig, glasses, and a hat."

I screw up my face. "What? That won't work."

She shrugs. "We all do it and nobody has been caught yet."

I run my hands through my hair. This is a disaster.

"Well, you can't go home. We have no staff already."

I look around as I weigh up my options and, seeing as there are no others, I ask the question. "Where are the wigs and stuff kept?"

Another girl walks past us and Ebony grabs her hand. "You need to cover the door for a minute while we deal with an emergency."

"I can't. I'm on drinks," the girl replies flatly.

Ebony grabs my hand and pulls me behind her, totally ignoring what she just said.

"Thank you. We will only be a minute," she calls over her shoulder.

The girl puts her hands up. "Hey!" she calls behind us.

We walk along the back, into the staff area and down a long corridor. I'm in a near panic now. "I have to go home, Ebony. If he sees me here I'm totally screwed."

"Who is he?" She frowns

"My boss."

She grimaces. "Oh shit." She continues to drag me along until we get to the hairdressing salon and the male stylist Franco is in there doing two of the Escape girls' hair.

"Vivienne needs a disguise. Her boss is here," she announces.

Everyone's eyes fall to me, and they all screw up their faces in sympathy. I throw my hands over my eyes. "I can't get caught. Maybe I should just leave this job right now?"

The stylist turns his attention to me. "It's okay, calm down. We can work wonders in here." He sits me down in a chair and opens a large cupboard door revealing drawers. He bends and pulls out the second from the bottom. "Brunette?" he asks the girls.

"Yes, and long," replies Ebony.

He takes out a long, dark chocolate wig and places it on the chair, and then he ties my hair back in a tight bun and puts the wig on my head. Long, dark, luscious thick hair hangs just below my breast.

I stifle a smile. "This wig is…" It's kind of cool to be honest.

"It's high quality," he replies, distracted as he straightens and pins it on. "If you come in here every shift, I will wig you up."

I nod gratefully. "Okay. Thank you"

One of the other girls disappears and comes back with a sexy pink sailor cap, placing it on my head as Ebony hands me a pair of pink-tinted glasses.

"There." She smiles as she puts her hands on her hips and stands back to admire her handy work. "No one would ever know it's you."

"You need lipstick," the stylist says as he fluffs around with my wig.

One of the other girls shuffles around in the drawer in front of where she is sitting and pulls out hot pink lipstick, passing it to me.

I screw up my face. "Really?" I frown. That looks very clowny.

"Really," they all reply in unison.

I put on the hot pink lipstick and stare at my reflection in the mirror. I'm wearing a tight leather skirt and a skimpy tie around leather top, gold high heels, long dark hair with a sailor's cap, pink glasses and pink lipstick. I do hate to admit it, but I don't even recognize myself.

"Thank you." I smile. "Shall I just go back out?" I ask.

"Yes, go and find a job where he won't see you," Ebony replies.

Find a job. What job? "Should I go back to the bar?"

"Maybe collect glasses from the tables until you see where he is and then decide where he will least likely see you."

I nod. "Good idea." I think on it for a minute. "Will I get into trouble for not going back to the bar, though?"

"No, it's cool. The glasses need collecting from the table anyways." She gives me a smile and runs her fingers through my long dark hair. "You make a pretty hot brunette, Viv."

I look at her over the top of my rose-colored glasses and smirk. "Thanks." I turn and walk back out into the club feeling a little braver. My eyes roam the club at the hundreds of well-dressed men in suits. It's like looking for a needle in a haystack

Right. Cameron Stanton?

Where are you?

It's been over an hour and I have walked what feels like five thousand miles around this club in the search of my Dr. Vegas. Where is he? My eyes scan the bottom level as I walk along with my tray, picking up empty glasses from the tables. Group after group of gorgeous men surround me, but I can't seem to find mine. Well, he's not mine, but you know what I mean. The music comes to a crescendo and the lights dim. Shit. The fashion show is starting. The spotlight comes on the catwalk and I stand still for a moment as I watch the first model glide down the runway. Gosh, she's breathtaking. A natural redhead with porcelain skin—she has this confident, sexy walk going on, and to be honest, I think she is the most beautiful girl I have ever seen in real life. Wearing a cream sequin dress that is backless, her hair is down and set in Hollywood curls. She has sky-high, strappy gold stilettos on. I stand still for a moment as I watch her command the room with her beauty. The men on the bottom level all watch her, captivated, and they exchange looks with a smirk.

What must it be like to be her? She gets to pick from these men.

Who will she choose?

Transfixed, I watch her make eye contact with some of the men in the front row as she comes to the end of the runway and puts her hand on her hip, throwing them a sexy wink. I bite my bottom lip to stifle my smile. She's playing with them.

The men all glance at each other and size each other up. Suddenly the penny drops. These are powerful men... they could have any woman they want on their own merits in the real world, but in here they are just a number... and *she* gets to choose.

It's the powerful man's ultimate game.

Suddenly I'm frantic to find Cameron Stanton. What if she wants him?

No, she can't have him. I want him. I begin to look around nervously. Of course she'll want him. Any woman would pick him over the rest of these idiots. The models all start to file out in their fashion parade, but I'm focused on my task. I continue to pick up the glasses and weave in between the men. I bend over a table and I feel a hand on my behind and then slide down to the back of my thigh. I look over my shoulder to see a distinguished looking man with dark hair standing behind me.

He's in his late thirties and handsome in a sophisticated, naughty way.

"Hello." He smiles sexily as he raises his brow.

I smile nervously, relieved that it isn't Dr. Stanton. Or maybe I do wish it was him. No, I don't! He can't find out that I work here. Oh jeez, I'm confusing myself here.

"Hello." I smirk.

His eyes drop to my feet and back up to meet my eyes. I can feel the heat from his gaze. This man is hot. "What's your name?" he asks.

"Vivienne."

He holds out his hand and I stare down at it. He wants to shake my hand. Even in a place like this, his manners overrule his desire.

I nervously shake his hand.

"You're new?"

I smile softly. "Yes."

His eyes drop back to my feet and then back up as he licks his bottom lip. "Are you going to be working in the Escape Lounge?"

I glance down at the models floating up and down the catwalk and shake my head. "No." I glance around nervously. "I'm just behind the bar."

His dark eyes hold mine. "Pity." His hand drops to my hipbone and he gives it a dominant squeeze. "Do you give lap dances?"

The heat from his hand is burning hot. I feel arousal begin to swirl between us. It's been way too long since I've been touched by a man—nearly two years, to be exact.

"No." I look around nervously. "I wouldn't know how to give a lap dance," I murmur

He bends and puts his lips to my ear. "I could teach you," he whispers so close that I feel his breath on my skin. Goosebumps scatter, and he gently runs his hand up my forearm to feel them.

My scared eyes hold his and he smirks triumphantly.

He bends to my ear again. "I could turn you into my Escape girl." He gently kisses my ear.

I frown and step back from him abruptly. Okay, this guy is freaking me out. He is gorgeous and tempting and fucking dangerous to my morals.

"I don't think so," I murmur.

"Could be fun." He smirks.

A smile crosses my face. "I have no doubt, but I'm nobody's Escape girl."

"Maybe I could be your Escape man?" He raises a sexy brow.

Now… there's a proposition worth thinking about. I smile and grab his hand and squeeze it in mine. "Keep dreaming." I pick up my tray and turn and walk off through the crowd. I hate to admit it, but I feel ten-feet tall. He was gorgeous and he wanted me. I can hardly wipe the stupid smile from my face. My tray is full and I have to return it to the kitchen, which is in the restaurant at the back of the club. I walk up the three steps into the industrial trendy looking bar. The floor is polished cement and the furnishings are all recycled expensive timber. The chairs are all a funky tan leather, and the dropped light fittings are huge copper pendants. The music is different in here. It's more of a relaxed vibe. This place must have cost an absolute fortune to furnish. I've never been up here before and I glance around as I look for the door into the kitchen. There it is at the back. As I walk through, I hear a familiar laugh, and I glance up at a table of six men sitting in the corner having dinner.

Cameron.

He's with five other men and they are all around a table eating and laughing, paying no attention at all to the women in the fashion parade. I drop my head and continue walking into the kitchen to place the tray in the line up for the dishwasher. A waitress is in the kitchen running the food.

"Hi." I smile as I watch him through the peephole.

"Hello." She smiles. "God, it's hectic tonight."

"I know." I grin as an idea runs through my mind. "Hey, see that table of men up the back?"

She glances over at them. "Yes."

"How long have they been here?"

"A few hours."

I nod. "Okay..." I hesitate. "Thank you."

I drop my head and walk back out of the restaurant. Please don't see me, please don't see me. I pick up another tray and begin to collect my empty glasses again. After another hour of restaurant door stalking, I glance up and see Cameron and his group of friends walking out of the restaurant.

Shit. I drop my head and scurry into the darkness between the crowd. I watch on as he and his friends head down to the front of the club where the Escape girls are.

Oh no...

I follow him through the crowd as I pick up glasses. He and his friends stand in a group and begin to talk again, and it's all I can do not to run up and scream *get out of here before you scar me for life.*

I continue to pick up my glasses in the shadows as I watch on and one of the Escape girls walks up the stairs, over to their group of men. She has long black hair and a body to die for. She's wearing a skimpy orange dress that leaves nothing to the imagination. I frown in horror. Oh no...

"Hey," a man yells. "That glass is still full."

"Oh, I'm sorry." I quickly put his glass back down on the table. God, this is multitasking at its absolute worst. How the hell can I concentrate on glasses when this shit is gong on? The girl walks straight over to Cameron and says something to him. He gives her a smirk as his hand drops to her behind. I watch him squeeze her cheek in his hand and then pat her ass.

My stomach rolls.

He says something else through that cheeky grin and she laughs out loud.

Fuck, he knows her. He's been in the Escape lounge with her.

How many nights has he spent with her?

Stop it. It doesn't fucking matter anyway.

I watch on for another thirty minutes as he and his friends talk, drink, and check out the occasional girl who walks past them.

He's a player. His friends are players, and even though I knew this all along, it kind of sucks to have proof. He shakes everyone's hand and heads toward the door.

Is he meeting her out the front?

Shit.

Unable to stop myself, I put my tray down on the nearest table and follow him out. Luckily, the bouncers are talking to a group of men and are distracted, leaving me to walk around the corner and into the shadows without being noticed.

I stand in the silence and watch him walk across the road alone. The lights flash on his luxury car as he unlocks it and hops in.

I stand in the silence as I watch his *Aston Martin* pull out of the parking lot and drive away down the deserted, dark street.

I look down at myself in shame. I'm dressed in next to nothing, wearing a wig and pink sunglasses. Reality sets in. There will never be anything between us. He lives the fast life and I live the life of a married woman... only, there is no husband.

Who was I kidding?

"Cameron," I whisper softly into the darkness. "I wanted you to be my escape man."

I sit with my elbows on the kitchen table as I try to focus my eyes. I'm so tired after only four hours sleep. To make matters worse, I'm in surgery all morning. Well, I'm not actually in surgery. I'm in the watch room, which is boring because you can't actually see anything.

Owie sits on my lap as he eats his breakfast. I'm missing my little man, working all these hours. I have to keep reminding myself that this is for him and his future. Jenna is up, dressed, and acting all perky. She even has makeup on and her hair done. I frown as I watch her flit merrily around the kitchen.

"What's wrong with you?"

She smirks. "What?"

I glance at the clock. "It's 7am and you are up." I frown as I try to articulate my thoughts. "And you're ready."

She smiles. "So?"

I frown. "It's weird, isn't it Owie?" I kiss the top of his little head.

He nods as he keeps eating.

She stands on her tiptoes to look through the kitchen window, out to the house next door. I rub my eyes as I try to wake up, and put Owie down on the chair. I go and stand next to her at the window and look out to see what, exactly, she is looking at.

A handsome blonde man is working on the fence.

I look at her and raise my eyebrows. "And who is he?"

"He's our new neighbor."

"Is he?"

We both watch him through the window.

"And what is our new neighbor's name?" I ask.

"Elliot."

"Elliot," I repeat. "And where did you meet Elliot?"

"At the park," Owie interrupts.

"Owie, eat your breakfast," Jenna replies.

My mouth drops open. "You're going to the park to meet neighbors now?"

She shakes her head. "No, he was just there with his niece. It was a coincidence."

I smile as I turn my attention back to him sitting on top of the fence. He really is kind of hot.

"How convenient," I mutter.

Jenna sips her coffee as she watches him. "It was a bit."

"And what's Elliot's story?" I ask as I flick the kettle on. "Apart from being all rugged mountain-man like and a fence fixer."

"He's just bought the house next door and is renovating it."

I dunk my teabag in the cup. "And?"

Her eyes hold mine and she smirks. "And he's single."

I smile broadly and raise a brow. "Once again, very convenient."

She raises her eyebrow. "That's what I thought."

We both turn our attention back to him. He's wearing a red and black flannel shirt, has a few-days growth, and his blonde hair is shaggy. He's hammering something into the fence. We watch him for a minute.

"You should probably be a good neighbor and take him out a cup of coffee."

She smiles into her cup. "I really should, shouldn't I? It would be rude not to."

"And cookies," Owie interrupts.

Jenna smiles and I get out another cup.

"How did last night go?" she asks.

I roll my eyes. "Guess who's a member?"

She frowns. "Who?"

I raise an eyebrow.

Her mouth drops open. "Fuck off," she mouths.

"Nope."

"Did he see you?"

I shake my head again and glance at Owie eating his breakfast as he watches the morning cartoons on television.

"Oh my God," she whispers as she leans in so Owie can't hear her. "Was he with anyone?"

"Not last night, but obviously he's been before."

Jenna's eyes widen as she bites her bottom lip. "I have no words."

"I have one," I whisper, deadpan.

"Hmm." We both stay silent as I make the cup of coffee for Elliot.

She shrugs. "Maybe he goes there for the articles?"

I look at her, unblinking. "Maybe."

"What are you going to do?"

I sip my coffee. "I have no idea." I pause. "Nothing."

I hand her the coffee and grin. "Go get him, tiger."

I stand in the corridor, outside the operating room. Amber and Scott are suited up in scrubs while the rest of us are waiting for Dr. Stanton.

"Hey, we should go out tomorrow night to celebrate our first week," Nick says.

Amber's eyes light up. "Oh my God. Yes!" She grabs my hand in excitement.

"Ah." I pause, I don't really want to leave Owie with Jenna again. She has him all week. It's just not fair. "Let me see if I can get out of another arrangement," I reply sadly. I would love to go, but I already know I can't.

Amber smiles. "You're coming. We are all going to go — the six of us. It will be so much fun, and we can ask Dr. Stanton and Dr. Jameson is they want to come, too."

"Go where?" Dr. Stanton asks from behind us. I turn to see him standing behind us wearing navy scrubs, a navy cap and shoe covers. My mouth goes dry. I don't think I've ever seen anyone look so beautiful in my whole life. My body instantly craves his and I have to bite my lip to stop my mouth from hanging open. His eyes find mine across the group as my stomach starts to swirl with nerves.

"We're all going out tomorrow night. Do you want to come?" Amber asks.

He smiles politely. "We'll see." He turns his attention to the rest of the group. "Good morning, everyone," he announces in his husky, deep voice, and that hot Australian accent. He sounds like bloody Liam Hemsworth, only ten times better.

"Good morning," everyone replies. If I could speak, I would, but I'm too busy with my 'doctor throwing me on the operating table' fantasy. When that man touched me last night at the club he awakened something that has been dormant for a long, long time.

A fire — a fire with only one effective extinguisher who looks fucking edible in scrubs. His eyes hold mine for a moment longer than they should, only this time I stare back. I want him to see me. I want him to know that he still does it for me. Does he remember me the way I remember him?

The group all make small talk and Cameron goes through the procedure he's doing today, but his eyes keep coming back to me.

I feel like I'm the only one in the room. Like I'm the only one he is speaking to.

Am I imagining this?

"Okay, Ashley," he says.

I raise my brows as I'm snapped from my daydream. "Oh. Erm. I'm sorry. I missed that part."

"I said that we're all meeting for a welcome coffee in the cafeteria this afternoon at 2pm, if I don't see you all before then."

"Oh." I nod and fake a smile, feeling foolish.

The group moves to their positions, but he stays standing in front of me. "Will you be coming?"

That could happen just by watching you, you sexy beast of a sleazy man.

He seems to be waiting for my answer. Huh?

"Oh. To… to coffee, you mean?" I stammer.

A trace of a smile crosses his lips. "Yes." His eyes darken. "Where else would you be coming?"

I feel my cheeks heat in embarrassment and I blurt out the first thing that comes to my mind. "I'll be there with bells on." His eyes continue to hold mine. "Bells are a personal favorite." He smirks sarcastically. I just want the floor to swallow me up. I watch as he disappears into the operating room, and I drop my eyes to my feet in disgust. I've really got to work on my flirting game. I will be there with bells on may just be the most ridiculous thing that has ever left my mouth.

I need to find my old, witty self, and I need to find her quick.

We all sit together in a group in the hospital cafeteria. There are six interns and the two doctors. Amber is taking center stage with her quirky sense of humor, and everyone is hanging on her every word. Dr. Stanton, however, seems to have fixed his attention firmly on me. But, once again, that could be all in my head because I think I'm becoming delusional. Even though I have no idea what's going through that head of his, I do know he's attracted to me. But then, maybe he keeps looking at me because he is trying to work out whether it really was me he met in Vegas?

Maybe.

The sexual tension between us is like nothing I've ever felt before.

It's undeniable and I know he feels it, too.

All week, sparks have been flying between us.

"Oh, give me yours," Steven says as he Facebook friend requests everyone in the group.

I glance around the table to see everyone busily adding each other. Shit, this is why I have two accounts.

"I'm Ashley T." I smile. I hardly use this account and only have work friends on it.

They all friend request me and to be polite. I go around the table and add everyone,

"Do you have a Facebook account, Dr. Stanton and Dr. Jameson?" Amber asks.

God, she's so forward. It's bloody embarrassing.

They both shake their heads and I smirk. As if they would want to be friends with a bunch of interns.

Dr. Jameson is the first to stand. "I have an appointment. Once again, welcome to our team. We are so happy with everyone so far."

The group all smile.

"Oh." Amber replies. "We're going out tomorrow night for drinks. Do you want to come with your wife?"

Dr. Jameson smiles. "Thank you for the invitation, but no. We're unable to make it. My wife is heavily pregnant with our fourth child."

"Oh." The group gush.

He smiles, and with a courteous nod, he leaves the cafeteria.

"Are you going to come, Dr. Stanton?" Amber asks.

"Please, call me Cameron."

"Oh." She lets out a fake laugh. "Cameron is such a nice name," she gushes and I feel myself cringe. Just shut up, stupid.

"Who is going?" he asks as his eyes flicker to me.

"We all are."

His eyes hold mine. "Sure. Why not?"

Shit. Over my dead body is Amber getting her claws into him. This day is getting worse by the minute.

What would I wear if I did go?

"Tomorrow morning, Ashley, I'm going over to the children's hospital. You will be coming with me," Cameron suddenly tells me.

"Oh." I smile. That's exciting. "Okay."

He sips his coffee, and as I watch him, I practically melt in my chair. "Do you want me to meet you there?" I ask nervously.

"No, you can come in my car." *I bet I could.* "If that's alright?" he adds.

"Of course." I smile. "Shall I meet you here?"

He nods. "Yes, I will pick you up by the front doors at 7am."

I smile hopefully. "Okay, great." I glance at my watch. "I have to go."

Ambers face falls. "Where are you going? We don't have to be back for another twenty minutes."

"Oh. Erm." I pause, because I know I sound like a weirdo. "I just wanted to read to Gloria for a little bit."

The group all laugh and I feel silly. I glance over at Cameron and his eyes have that sexy glow in them again.

"See you later."

It's 10pm and I am in bed with a book that I just can't get into. The room is dimly lit. Everyone is asleep. I've been tossing and turning, wondering if I've done the right thing by not 'fessing up to having a child. I lied in my enrollment form for my job, and now it seems like I'm going to get caught. What is the punishment for this sort of thing? Is it really so bad if I don't tell them for a week or two that I have a child? If I tell Cameron now he will just see me as someone's mother. He will always see me as someone's mother. I want him to get to know me for me first.

I know he's attracted to me. I can feel it. But I also know he's not the type of guy to take on a woman with a kid.

He hates kids. God, why did he say that? How can anyone hate kids?

Maybe I could just leave it for a week before I tell him. A week won't hurt in the grand scheme of things.

Will it?

I pick up my phone and scroll through Facebook as I think. I click onto the other account that I gave them today and scroll through a few of their pages. I smile when I look through Amber's page. She is wearing hardly anything in any of her pictures.

A message pops up and I click on it.

Hello

I frown and click on the name. Mechanic.

I smirk as my heart rate picks up, and I quickly click on the profile picture—a picture of an *Aston Martin*. A white one, though. His is black.

Is it him?

Fuck.

I message back.

Hello

I hold my breath as I wait for a reply. Oh my God. Is this him? I wait for a moment and message again.

Do I know you?

A message bounces back immediately.

I don't know. Do you?

My eyes widen. Oh my God. It is him... isn't it? I sit up in bed, suddenly wide-awake.

A message comes in.

I can't stop thinking about you.

My smile grows as my heart starts to somersault in my chest, and I stand and wave my arms around in the air in excitement. Oh my God, it's him.

I think for a moment. What will I write? What will I write? Shit.

I text back my reply.

Why?

I hit send and then scrunch up my face. Oh hell, that was lame. Why did I write that?

He responds.

Why is grass green?

I smile, knowing this is a test.

**Grass produces a bright pigment called chlorophyll.
Chlorophyll absorbs blue light and red light, but mostly
reflects green light, which accounts for its color.
Are you going to continue to answer my questions with
rhetorical questions?**

I bite my bottom lip and wait for his reply.

There she is.

I smile broadly as my heart rate picks up.
I type back.

When you think of me, what do you think about?

I wait and an answer bounces straight back.

I want to know how you taste.

My eyebrows rise. Holy fuck. That is a great answer. I respond.

And?

An answer comes back.

I want your taste on my tongue.

I frown as I feel my arousal start to rise.
Holy fuck.

Are you still tight?

My eyes widen and I walk into my bathroom to stare at myself in the mirror. Is this really happening? I eventually go back into the bedroom and type a response with shaky fingers.

I'm just going to give it to him straight. Oh man. I hope I'm talking to the right guy here?

You have no idea.
I haven't had sex in two years.

There's no response straight away. Oh no. Why did I say that? Finally, after about five minutes, a message bounces back.

You sure know how to drive a man insane.
I'm so fucking hard right now.

Holy crap. I'm about to have a heart attack here. I message him back.

Where are you?
What are you doing?

A response bounces straight back.

I'm naked, in bed.
On my back with my legs spread.
My hard cock in my hand.

My eyes widen and I hear Owie call out from the other room. Ah, damn it!
I quickly reply.

Lucky hand!

I put my phone down and quickly walk up the hall to Owie's room to see he is tossing and turning in bed. "Are you okay, baby?" I ask.
"I feel sick." He sighs.

"You had too much ice cream." I sit with him for a moment until he settles. "It's okay. You're okay. Go back to sleep now," I whisper as I tuck him back in.

He rolls over and closes his eyes, and I sprint back up the hall to my phone to read his latest message.

Touch yourself.

Oh hell. He wants a sexting orgasm. Fuck, so do I. I smile deviously as I message him back.

I've been touching myself every night thinking about you. I want the real thing…

A response bounces back immediately.

Fucking hell! Get your ass over here now!

9

OH GOD, I wish…

I can't.

He answers.

**I'm coming to you.
What's your address?**

"Mom," Owie calls from his bedroom. Oh, fucking hell. Perfect timing.

I throw my phone down and run up the hall just in time to see Owen vomit all over his bed.

"Oh, baby."

He starts to cry as he vomits again. I pick him up and carry him into the bathroom.

"It's okay, sweetheart."

He cries.

"It's alright. It's just a vomiting bug or something. You will be okay." I take off his clothes and put him under the shower. He finally settles and now I've got to go clean the sheets.

So much for my sexting session.

Arousal level... instant zero.

Cameron

I sit at my desk as I roll the pen between my fingers. It's 6am and I'm at the hospital early. No use me staying in bed. I can't fucking sleep anyway.

I jacked off three times last night and still I can't stop thinking about her now.

What's it going to take to rid myself of this uncontrollable urge to have Ashley Tucker beneath me?

Why did she disappear last night? I thought we were getting somewhere and then... gone.

Maybe I'm reading this all wrong? Maybe it isn't her? I stare into space for a while as I try to gain some perspective on the situation. I blow out a deep breath because there is no perspective.

This is just fucked up.

She's my intern. I'm her boss and I have the uncontrollable urge to bend her over every hard surface in the hospital. I rub my eyes and shake my head. Jameson walks past the office and glances in, and then doubles back.

"Hey, you're in early?" He smiles.

"Morning. I had some reports to get done."

"Do you want a coffee? I'm going down now."

"Yeah, that would be great. How's Hanna?" I ask.

"She's good. Any day, I think. She's due on Thursday."

I smirk. "Four kids, man."

"Fuck, don't remind me. I feel old enough as it is."

He narrows his eyes and I get the feeling he has something to say, so I raise an eyebrow in question.

"Can I ask you something... off the record?" he asks.

I nod. "Of course." He glances around and then shuts the office door.

What's this about?

He takes a seat and hesitates for a moment "So... what's the deal with Ashley Tucker?"

I frown. Fuck. "What do you mean?"

"I've seen the way you look at her."

I shake my head and sit up, acting guilty while perching on my chair. "No, Ashley and I are strictly business."

His knowing eyes hold mine and my stomach drops with more guilt. He knows I'm lying though my teeth. "You do know our whole professional image depends on how you handle these interns."

I bite my bottom lip to stop myself saying something I'll regret.

"The board is watching. Fuck around with the nurses all you want Cameron, but don't touch the interns."

I nod once, annoyed that I'm being pulled in line for the first time ever.

He stands and smiles. "I knew you would agree with me on this."

Half an hour later, I'm at the entrance of the hospital, watching her standing out on the curb as she waits for me.

Her thick, honey blonde hair hangs around her shoulders and she's wearing a black dress with heels with stockings. My eyes scan her body and I feel myself harden. She's on her phone while she waits for me to pick her up.

She's breathtaking.

Whenever I see her, I have this overwhelming urge to wrap her in my arms.

What is this connection?

Why can't I stop thinking about her for even a minute?

I need to get a fucking handle on it right now.

Ashley

I wait nervously on the curb of the hospital for my ride to the children's hospital. I glance down at myself in my black dress. I'm as nervous as hell. It was two hours before I got Owen settled last night, and when I finally got back to my sexter, he wasn't online — obviously pissed, thinking I had ditched him.

God, what a mess. My life is like a bad sitcom.

"The car is this way," a voice mumbles from behind me.

Huh?

I turn to see Cameron walking past me with his briefcase in his hand. What the hell? I follow him through the parking lot, but he doesn't say a word. My heart hammers in my chest. His car beeps as he opens it and we climb into the low luxury seats.

"Hello." I smile nervously.

He checks the mirrors as I watch him. Isn't he going to say anything to me at all?

"Hello," he replies emotionlessly as he pulls out into the traffic.

He has his playboy sunglasses on and a dark charcoal suit with a crisp, light blue shirt and tie. His dark hair is messy perfection, and his day old growth is darkening his square jaw.

This man is the epitome of gorgeous. The way he smells. The way he looks. His mind. His beautiful, filthy mind.

I watch him.

His eyes stay glued to the road in front.

"Thanks for picking me up."

He continues to drive and I turn to watch the road in front of us with my mind in overdrive. Was that even him messaging me last night?

What if it wasn't?

"Did you have a nice night?" I ask nervously.

He glances over at me. "I did." He raises a brow and I can tell he's pissed off.

It was him!

"Did you?" he asks.

I clasp my hands so tight in my lap. "It started out well, but my Internet dropped out and it didn't come back on until this morning," I lie.

His eyes meet mine and he lifts his chin defiantly, as if not believing it for a minute.

I wonder did he go out last night after we spoke. For all I know he could have been at the Escape Lounge fucking some model all night.

Stop it!

His phone rings, connecting through the Bluetooth of the car. "Hello, Cameron Stanton," he answers.

"Hello, Dr. Stanton. This is Pauline from Pediatric records at the children's hospital."

"Hello, Pauline."

"Sorry to bother you, sir. We have a small problem."

He exhales. "What's that?"

"We have a new staff member and, unfortunately, when she was scanning the reports into the patient files, the latest report you did for Sasha Mills is not in there, and we're unable to locate the original one."

He rolls his eyes. "That's fine. I will call in and resend it over to you."

"Thank you. I just knew you wouldn't be happy if it wasn't here when you arrive."

"Thank you for your call." He hangs up.

He drives for a minute more and then turns abruptly. "We just have to make a quick detour."

"Okay."

He flies down the road and we sit in silence. I'm not sure what to say and he is clearly ignoring me. Finally, he pulls into a swanky suburb and pushes a code into a gated community security gate. The doors swing open and I frown. "Are we going to your office?" I ask.

"My office in my house."

My eyes widen. He lives here? We turn a few corners down a long road, and he pulls into a large driveway with huge gates. He pushes another security code in and the gates swing open to reveal the most horrifying thing I think I have ever seen.

He's rich.

This house is a mansion — like, an over the top mansion. He pulls up in the circular driveway. "Can you come in for just a minute?"

I nod, distracted by the luxury I'm surrounded by. "Is this your house?" I whisper.

"Yes," he answers as he climbs out of the car and opens the front door with his fingerprint in some space-age key system. I get out of the car and slowly walk up the front steps as my eyes stare up at the high ceilings.

"I won't be a minute," he calls out from a room up the hall. "Actually, can you put the coffee machine on and I will make us one?"

"Okay," I whisper as I look around. I don't even know where the kitchen is.

"Kitchen is toward the back wing," he calls, as if reading my mind.

"Okay." I walk down a grand hallway to find the kitchen and my jaw nearly hits the floor. Beautiful and spotless — not a dirty cup or dish in sight. I look around as I feel my dread start to creep in. This is the most beautiful house I have ever been in, and the cleanest.

I glance out into the yard. The pool area looks like a resort pool.

Fuck off.

This is stupid rich.

I turn the coffee machine on and walk up the hall where I heard his voice come from before. "Hello?"

"In here," he calls.

I continue up the hall until I come to the room he's in. It's an office—a huge, swanky office. He's sitting behind a large mahogany desk which faces the door, printing out a report. I stand nervously in front of him.

"Is this your house?" I ask meekly.

His eyes meet mine. "Yes."

"W-who do you live here with?" I stammer.

He sits back in his chair and swings side to side as he assesses me. "I live here alone."

I look around at the opulent surroundings. "You're not married?"

His eyes darken and he stands abruptly. "Not married."

"Girlfriend?" I whisper.

He shakes his head. "No."

My eyes hold his as he walks toward me. "Do you want the tour of my house?"

I nod because all the words have left my brain.

I follow him out of the office and down the hall. "This is the party room."

I peer into the room that opens out onto a pool area and I fake a smile.

"This is a guest bedroom." He gestures to a bedroom to the left.

We keep walking down. "Gym." He gestures to a room filled with gym equipment. We get to a door and he walks past it.

"What's in there?" I ask.

He turns to face me. "Laundry room." He opens the door and I peer in. The room is smaller and darkened, the blind pulled down. For some reason, I like this small room and I walk past him and head into it. He follows me and then closes the door behind him.

Shit. My breath catches.

Suddenly alone together in such a small space, the energy between us starts to zap, and he steps forward to look down at me.

My heart starts to race.

My eyes drop to his large lips and he stands still for a moment as our arousal rises between us. He steps forward again until I am effectively wedged between the washing machine and his hard body.

"I like your laundry room," I whisper up at him.

He towers above me. "I like you," he whispers back.

My eyebrows rise. "You do?"

He nods as he steps toward me again.

"But, I have a problem," he murmurs as he pushes his hips forward against mine.

Oh man. He's hard. I can feel him through his pants.

"What?" I breathe.

"I'm unable to act on it."

Holy crap.

"Why?" I whisper.

"I'm not allowed to ask interns out." His eyes drop to my lips and his hips pin me to the washing machine. He pumps them forward and I nearly combust.

"Nobody has to know what happens between us," I breathe.

In slow motion, he bends and kisses my neck, and my eyes close by themselves. "Can you keep a secret?" he breathes against my skin.

I nod. I'm unable to answer. This is the best damn laundry room I've ever seen. His hands snake around my behind and he pulls me to him, and then his lips are on me. His tongue tentatively brushes against mine as he goes deeper and deeper. His body has me pinned in place so hard, it's almost painful. His hands move to hold my jaw, positioning me the way he wants me. Holy fucking shit. I have never been kissed like this before.

He's desperate to have me.

Suddenly we are frantic, as if all the sexual tension we've been feeling for the last week is set free in this room. He aggressively lifts me, sitting me on the washing machine and ripping my legs apart so he can move between them. My hands go to the back of his head and he starts to drag me onto his waiting hard cock.

Oh dear God.

His mouth is ravaging my neck, while his hands are roaming up and down my body.

"You feel so fucking good, Bloss," he growls into my open mouth.

He remembered. He remembered what he called me that night, all those years ago.

He suddenly lifts my legs around his waist, and his hand slips under my blouse to skim my ribcage and cup my breast.

Holy... shit! I'm going to come, right here, right now.

His hand grabs the back of my hair and he pulls it aggressively so that my head tips back and our eyes meet.

"Do you know how badly I want you?" he breathes. Unable to answer, I nod.

"My bed. Now." He growls as he grinds me through his pants.

"Cameron," I whisper. "Work," I breathe. God, we are supposed to be at an appointment in twenty minutes.

"I can't wait."

"You... have to," I pant.

"I want you now." He grinds against me hard again as he bites my neck painfully.

Holy crap. This man.

"Tonight," I breathe. "Tonight, you can have me." He kisses me again, slower, as if slightly satisfied with that answer "I want *all* of you tonight."

I smile against his lips. Unable to pretend anymore, I whisper the words, "C'est moi qui veut tous vous.

Translation: It's me that wants all of you.

He smirks as he kisses me. "I fucking knew it was you." He pulls back to look at me. "Why did you say you didn't know me?"

I rub my fingers through his stubble as my eyes search his. "Why didn't you call me?"

"I lost my phone." Suddenly, his passion turns to regret, and he kisses me softly as he runs his fingers through my hair to straighten it back out. "You're a bad influence, Ashley Tucker." He smiles sexily. "Seducing me in my laundry room on my way to work."

As if a weight has been lifted from my shoulders, I see the fun, carefree man I met in Vegas standing in front of me, and I feel like I can finally be myself with him, once again, as we kiss tenderly.

Oh, it's still there. That feeling between us is still there.

"What are you going to do when I suck your dick under the desk in your office, Dr. Stanton?" I smile up at him.
His eyes widen. "That can't happen, Ashley."

"It might. This tongue gets pretty crazy." I stick it out and wave it around.

He smirks. "No, I'm serious. I can't..." He stops, all flustered. "You can't ever do that. I will lose my job. I'm not supposed to be going anywhere near you. Nobody can know about this. Ever!"

I stand on my tiptoes and run my tongue over his lips. "What if I swallowed?"

He smiles and grabs me roughly as he half tackles me up against the wall. "You're still a fucking great wife." He turns me and pushes me in the direction of door and slaps my behind hard.

I stumble as I reach the hallway, and he falls back into his role-play. He gestures to the laundry. "And that's the laundry room, where dirty things go to be cleaned."

I laugh and he leans in to kiss me. "I'm going to have to punish you for accidently forgetting me on purpose," he whispers against my lips.

I bite his bottom lip and drag it out. "That was my plan all along."

He grabs me hard, and our eyes lock. "You're going to fucking get it tonight."

A thrill of excitement runs through me. "And you better have your blue pills ready."

It's 3pm and I am sitting in our hospital's cafeteria with Amber and the other interns. Cameron and I spent the morning at the children's hospital, and I practically floated around the corridor watching him with the children, mesmerized by everything that came out of his perfect mouth. He was focused on his job, but when we left he stole a kiss in the car and promised me more carnal things. I'm hardly able to wipe the goofy grin from my face. He kissed me. He's still here — the beautiful, witty guy I met in Vegas is still alive, he just hides himself at work under this serious exterior. It's a requirement of being in the medical profession, but I'm so glad that I'm the one getting to peek behind his mask. I'm bursting to ring Jenna and tell her of the latest development.

"I'm just going to go to the bathroom."

"Okay," they all reply, distracted.

I walk up the hall and dial her number. She answers on the first ring. "Hello? Oh my God. Guess what?" she cries out.

"What?"

"Elliot asked me out tomorrow night."

I smile broadly. "Great." I bite my bottom lip. "Holy shit. I have news, too."

"What?"

"We kissed. I 'fessed up to knowing him."

"What?"

"I know. He's still the same. He hasn't changed at all and he wants to see me tonight," I whisper as I screw up my face. That means she has to babysit again. "Is that okay?"

"Oh my God, yes, of course." She laughs. "Oh hang on, aren't you working at Exotic tonight?"

"No."

"Yes, remember that girl asked you to swap the shift."

"Oh fuck. Is... Is that tonight?" I stammer.

"Yes, hang on. Let me check the diary on my phone." She disappears for a minute and then comes back. "Yes, you start at nine."

"Fuck's sake," I whisper. I rub my hand through my hair in despair. I want to see him tonight. Damn it.

"Just make it tomorrow night."

I frown. "No, you have your date with Elliot tomorrow night." I pause as I think of a solution. "Doesn't matter. Maybe the next night." I smile sadly.

"Sounds good. Woohoo, look at us go." She laughs. "Elliot called me twice today already."

"It's been a great day. See you tonight, babe."
"Bye."

I hang up and blow out a defeated breath. Maybe I should call in sick tonight. But then I won't get paid and I really need the money.

Damn it, why do I have to have this shitty fucking job? I drag my feet back to the cafeteria feeling very sorry for myself, only to find that Cameron is sitting with the other interns. This day just got a little better. I take a seat opposite him. "Hello." I smile.

"Hello, Ashley." Our eyes linger on each other. Amber is already deep in flirtation mode with him. "So, Dr. Stanton, what do you do to unwind?" she asks as she runs her fingers through her long, dark hair

"I like Vegas and ice cream shops," he answers without hesitation.

I smirk at the floor. His memory is spot on, I click into my Facebook account on my phone to message him.

"What are you doing over there?" Amber asks as her eyes flash to me.

"Just downloading the Find My Phone app," I reply. Amber frowns. "I would hate to ever have to give a lame excuse to someone about losing my phone."

Cameron's eyes hold mine and he tries his hardest to hide his sarcastic grin. He fails miserably. I flick onto Facebook and message him.

Change of plans.

He keeps talking to Amber and I roll my eyes.
I continue my one-sided conversation.

My mother is flying in unannounced and I can't do tonight. Can we do Friday instead?

He laughs at something Amber has said and I frown as I keep typing.

Sorry, it's annoying.
I really wanted to see you tonight
xxx

I fake a smile as I act like I know what they are talking about, and I hold my phone up to him as he glances over at me. *Look at your phone, stupid.* He takes the hint and opens his Facebook. I start talking to Scott who is on the other side of me. A message bounces back.

No.

I read it and frown. He glares at me, and I type back.

What do you mean *no*?

He responds.

**I'm seeing you tonight.
Tell your mother she can see you on Friday.**

I fake a smile and reply. Somebody is horny.

**Don't be a baby.
I will see you Friday.**

A message fires back immediately.

I mean it. Stop pissing me off.

I fake a smile as I start to become infuriated.

**Friday.
Take it or leave it!**

He answers.

Leave it!

Oh… this guy is something else. Hasn't he ever been told no before?
    I reply.

Stop being so high maintenance.

He reads the message and his eyes bulge in fury. I can't hide my smirk. God, he's like a two-year-old. He types his message with so much force, I'm surprised he doesn't crack the screen.

**I'm not high maintenance.
Although you may soon be no maintenance.**

I smile sweetly at him across the group and he purses his lips in anger. I reply sweetly.

When you are finished being a spoilt brat…
Call me.
xx

I stand and smile at the group. "I'm getting back to it, guys. See you later."

He narrows his eyes and I walk up the hall to visit Gloria.

Club Exotic

10pm

I walk along the back of the club wearing my long, dark wig and my next to nothing cream leather outfit. My mind is on Cameron Stanton and what I could be doing tonight. I'm collecting drinks again. I think this is my favorite job here at Club Exotic. I get to see what is going on and walk around without making a million drinks for a million men.

"Vivienne."

I turn to see the man from the other night. "Hello."

He grabs my hand. "Have you come looking for me?" He smiles sexily.

I laugh. "No." I take my hand out of his and bend to pick up a glass from a table. "I'm collecting glasses."

His hand drops to my behind as his eyes travel to my breasts. "I will get you into the Escape Lounge." He raises a sexy eyebrow. "You do know that, right?"

I shake my head and smirk. "Keep dreaming."

He bends and kisses my cheek. "Very soon, Vivienne." He then brushes by me before he heads down to the Escape

Lounge. I smirk as my eyes follow him. He is one sexy son of a bitch.

"Ashley," a familiar voice snaps, and I turn to see Cameron standing behind me. He's furious. I can practically see the red glow around him.

My eyes widen. Oh no.

"Or should I call you Vivienne?" He sneers.

10

"C-CAMERON." I stammer.

"What the fuck are you doing here?" He growls.

I step back, shocked at his venom. "I'm working." I glance around nervously.

"You work in a brothel?" he yells.

"Is everything okay here?" My boss Eliza interrupts.

Oh no. I've hardly seen her out on the floor since I started and she chooses now to show up. She glances between the two of us in question.

Cameron regains his composure. "I was just asking Vivienne to give me a lap dance." He fakes a smile.

My mouth drops open in horror. What the hell is he doing?

Eliza smiles warmly. "I'm sorry, Vivienne doesn't work in that part of the club, although I'm trying to persuade her." She puts her arm around me affectionately.

Cameron narrows his eyes at me in contempt.

"I just work at the bar…" I interrupt.

"I can get someone else to give you a lap dance, sir?" Eliza smiles warmly.

Cameron's eyes meet mine. "Yeah. That would be fantastic."

I glare at him.

"I'll make sure you are well looked after tonight, sir." Eliza smiles. "Take a seat down in chair two and I will have one of our best girls on your lap in just a moment."

His eyes hold mine for a moment before he smirks and disappears down the stairs.

My anger starts to boil. So he expects *me* to watch *him* get a lap dance from another woman?

Like hell.

"I will do his lap dance, Eliza."

She frowns. "Are you sure?"

"Yep."

"Do you know what to do?"

"Yes, I sat in on Ebony's class the other night before my shift." Thankfully Ebony teaches lap dancing classes once a month for the new girls, and I just happened to arrive early.

She smiles and grabs my hand in hers. "You're going to love it. I can't tell you how excited I am for you." She glances down at me. "You will have to go and get the correct uniform on."

I nod. "Okay." I turn my attention back to Cameron as I watch him down on the level below, talking to a girl as she gets his drink. He listens attentively to something she says and then he smiles sexily before he falls into the large, leather chair and makes himself comfortable as he waits for his private dance.

Asshole.

I'm raging mad. I couldn't see him tonight, so he comes here to fuck an Escape girl on the sly.

Oh, he's something else.

He may not survive this. He may bleed to death when I bite off his dick mid dance.

I march to the dressing room where the assistant is folding clothes.

"I need a lap dancing uniform," I snap.

She frowns.

"Please," I add. Oh hell, this isn't her fault. What's wrong with me? "Sorry for being rude."

She is in her fifties and kind looking, curvy, with a perfect silver bob hairstyle. She's also very well dressed. "Are you okay, dear?" she asks.

I nod as I try to calm my anger. "Yes…" I pause. "I'm just having a really shitty night, you know?"

She smiles. "Oh, I know."

I smile back. She's nice.

"What size are you?"

I look up to the clothes hanging perfectly on the rack and I blow out a breath. "I don't know."

"Undress and put this on." She hands me the cream, sheer, small organza top, and I stare down at it.

"I don't think I can do this…" I sigh.

"Sure you can." She hands me a pair of skimpy leather shorts and I glance around, looking for a change room.

"Just dress here darling, I've seen it all."

Oh man. Okay. I slide my leather skirt down my legs and stand before her in my lace panties before I slide the short hot pants up and into place. I turn and glance at my behind in the mirror. "Oh jeez. These are skimpy."

"That's the plan, love." She laughs. "Take your top off."

I close my eyes. I can't believe I'm taking my clothes off in front of this woman. I glance around nervously and slide my leather, lace up top off over my shoulders. I stand before her, topless and vulnerable. No other woman has ever seen my boobs before. Not even my mom, I don't think.

She smiles. "You are lovely and have nothing to be ashamed of." She hands the top to me and I take it, sliding it on. It's so short that the bottom of my breasts are peeking out from underneath it. She straightens my wig and passes me a lip-gloss. I turn to the mirror and reapply.

I blow out a breath.

"Any man would be lucky to lay eyes on you in that," She says softly.

I smirk.

"Go out there and show him what he can't have."

I grin. I needed to hear that. "Wish me luck."

"Good luck."

I walk out the door and into the alcove where three bouncers wait. My friend Matt is there and he turns to face me. "Hey." He smiles as his eyes scan my scantily dressed body. "Look at you."

I cringe. "Oh God. Do I look okay?" I whisper.

"You look fucking hot."

I smile, grateful.

"You dancing tonight, babe?" he asks.

I nod. "Just one."

"Let's go." He gestures to the door.

"Huh?" I frown.

"I will come with you. You won't be anywhere alone out there."

"Oh." My eyes widen in horror. Oh no, he can't watch me. I'll get stage fright.

"Matt, can you do me a favor?"

"What's that?"

"Can you just watch me from over near the wall. I won't be able to do it if I see you right there."

He smiles and nods before we walk out into the club. The lights are dimmed, and scantily dressed girls weave between the mass of powerful men. The mood in the room is sexy. It's forbidden desire at its best. How many of these men are married, here to quench their thirst for new flesh?

I look over and I see Cameron. Wearing his expensive suit, he is seated in the large, leather chair, drink in his hand as he waits for his own pound of flesh. His dark hair is wavy on top and he has a growth shadow over his square jaw.

I slowly walk over to stand in front of him. His eyes rise to meet mine and a sexy smile crosses his face.

He won.

"You wanted a lap dance, sir?"

He sits back and readjusts the obvious erection in his pants. Fuck, he's hot.

"I did," he replies as his eyes hold mine and he slowly sips his drink.

I walk toward him and slowly drop to my knees between his legs, he inhales sharply.

"Your wish is my command," I whisper.

His eyes are locked on mine and his jaw hangs slack. Electricity zaps between us.

"What do you want?" I breathe as my tongue darts out to lick my bottom lip.

His hungry eyes watch me. "You," he whispers. "I want you."

The music starts. Rude boy from Rihanna and I smirk. This song is very fitting.

Come here rude boy, boy,
Can you get it up?
Come here rude boy, boy,
Is you big enough?
Take it, take it.
Baby, baby.

I seductively slide my hands up his shins and rest them on his inner thighs to push his legs apart and pull him forward in his chair. He inhales sharply and places his drink down on the side table. His eyes never leave mine. I drop my head between his legs and blow hot air through his pants, onto his thigh. I hear him moan softly and I nip his thigh with my teeth. His hands instinctively go to the back of my head, and he holds me tenderly between his palms. My eyes close in pleasure.

This man…

I move my ass in time to the beat as I focus my attention on his hard cock, placing my mouth over it. His hand tightens on the back of my head.

"Jesus Christ," he whispers.

I look up at him and smirk from my position between his legs. "My name is Ashley," I whisper.

His eyes hold mine. His face falls as something changes between us. He brings his hand up and tenderly cups my cheek, and I turn my head to kiss the palm of his hand. Dear God.

What is this? What is this feeling between us?

I remember where I am and continue to move to the beat as I climb onto his lap. My knees rest on either side of his legs, my body only inches above his crotch. I lean closer so that my breasts are only inches away from his mouth, and arch my back.

"Fuck." He growls as he reaches up and grabs my hips to slam me down onto his hard cock.

My head rolls back in pleasure and Matt suddenly appears out of nowhere. "Hands off," he orders Cameron.

I put my hand up in a stop signal. "Go away, Matt," I snap. I need Cameron to touch me.

Hell, I really need him to touch me.

Matt backs off to his corner and my attention goes back to the hard man beneath me. With his hands planted firmly on my hips, he drags me over his hard cock, and my body shudders in approval.

His eyes flicker with a dangerous level of arousal, and it's all I can do not to slide my shorts to the side and mount him.

Fuck... I need this. He sways my hips and grinds me onto his hard body. His mouth opens and he takes my nipple between his teeth and bites down.

I shudder as an orgasm teeters dangerously close.

Holy fucking hell.

"Ride me," he whispers. "Ride my cock."

I circle my hips and begin to rock back and forth, round and round, and he grips my hips with a bruising strength.

His eyes search mine. "Kiss me," he breathes.

I can't help it. I know I'm not supposed to do this. Hell, he isn't even allowed to touch me, but those are rules that I have no chance of obeying when I'm on top of him.

"Cameron," I breathe as he rocks me back and forth. Holy fuck... I'm going to come.

His lips take mine, aggressively, passionately.

Perfectly.

His eyes are closed, his cock is hard, and this is the most amazing thing I have ever experienced. We lose control and our kiss turns desperate as he grinds me harder and harder and hell... I can't hold it. I shudder as an orgasm rips through me. Satisfaction flashes across his face, but it's short lived as he pulls me down with pressure and I feel the telling jerk of his cock. His breath catches as his orgasm steals his ability to speak. We kiss and we pant until, finally, I can't ignore where we are any longer. As my orgasm fog lifts, I look up to see I am in a club... and he is just another client. As if having the same epiphany as me, he pushes me off his lap and stands abruptly. His haunted eyes hold mine for an extended moment and then he strides toward the door. Oh God.

I hold my hand up to Matt, asking him to give me five minutes before I take off after Cameron. I catch him as he reaches his car in the parking lot, his back to me.

"Cameron."

He turns. "Go back inside," he growls.

"Cameron..."

"Get away from me, Ashley, before I fucking lose my shit with you."

"Don't be angry with me," I plead.

"Don't be angry with you!" he yells, outraged. "I have thought of nothing else but you all week, and then I find you here practically naked for other men after lying to me about where you're supposed to be!"

"If you have thought of nothing else but me for the week, why are you here, Cameron?" I cry. "Are you here to have sex with somebody else while you think of me? Is that it? Is that how your fucked up, high flying world works?"

He narrows his eyes in contempt.

"You don't know what it's like to struggle," I cry.

"So you work in a brothel?" he yells.

My face falls in disappointment and my tears break free. I swipe them away angrily. "Don't you dare judge me! I don't have a castle and a two-hundred-thousand-dollar car like you. I can't even pay my fucking phone bill this week, Cameron."

His nostrils flare in anger and he points to his *Aston Martin*. "Get in the car."

I frown. "What?" I glance back at the door across the road. "I can't just leave, I'm in the middle of a shift." I can't leave. We've only kissed twice, and he may not even be around next week, and I will have no job.

"So help me God, if you don't get in the fucking car..." he yells so loud that they could probably hear it in the next suburb.

"I will lose my job."

"You will lose me if you don't," he yells.

"Cameron. Please..."

"Last chance."

"Cameron," I plead.

With one last look, he gets into his car and starts the engine. I step back as he revs the shit out of it before he tears off down the road.

I stand in the darkness, listening to his tires screeching in the distance.

"You alright, Ash?" Matt voice calls from across the road.

I nod and drop my head as I let the disappointment sink in. Matt walks across the road and stands next to me silently, staring up the road where Cameron has disappeared.

"Was that your boyfriend?" he asks quietly.

I shake my head. "No."

"Then why was he losing his shit?"

"It's... complicated."

"Want to go back inside?"

149

I blow out a deep breath. "Yeah, I guess." I frown. "Matt, have you ever had the feeling that you may have just made the biggest mistake of your life?"

He smiles sarcastically. "Every hour, on the hour."

Timing can make you or break you, and tonight I learned just how true that statement is.

It's 4am when I slowly pull into my driveway. That was the longest shift in history. I had to stop myself from walking out at least ten times. Why did he have to come tonight, and why couldn't he have handled it better?

Fuck. I'm so full of regrets right now, I can hardly see straight.

I hate that I need this crappy job, and my mind is weighing heavily on Cameron Stanton. I know I did the right thing by not leaving with him, but it doesn't make me feel any better about it. The cold, hard truth is… he was there. He was there when he said he had been thinking about me all week, and after we made out yesterday. I know that, even if we did have any chance of working out, a long-term future with him is not on the cards. My first instinct was right. Once a player, always a player. He never lost his fucking phone in Vegas all those years ago and he probably slept with someone he picked up in the casino the very next night. Who was I kidding? I frown as I see the lights in our house are all on. What's happening? Why is everything lit up? I quickly climb out of the car and head to the front door, but it opens before I put my key in. It's Jenna. She's been crying.

My face falls. "What's wrong?"

She screws up her face. "Mom's had a heart attack."

"What? Oh, Jenna."

She nods, unable to speak through her tears. I wrap her in my arms and hold her as she sobs. "Where is she?" I ask.

150

"At the hospital."

"You need to go to her."

She nods as she wipes her nose with a tissue. "Is that alright?"

"Of course it's alright."

"What will you do with Owie?" she whispers.

"It doesn't matter. I'll work something out." I lead her into the kitchen, put the kettle on, and sit her at the table.

"What if she dies?" Jenna whispers.

I take her hand in mine and watch her for a minute. "Everything is going to be okay. Heart attacks aren't always as bad as they sound."

She puts her head into her hands and really starts to cry. What can I do to help her? I grab my laptop and go online in search of an airline ticket for her to fly home to Iowa. "There's one here for tomorrow at ten in the morning. Will that be okay? That's in about five hours from now."

She shrugs.

"Let me check the other airlines to see if I can get one cheaper." I continue to search, but eventually end up going back to the first flight I found.

Jenna finally falls into an exhausted sleep on the sofa, and I sit quietly at the

kitchen table as I try to work out what to do with the disaster that is my life.

I've lost Cameron, even though I never had him to begin with.

I now have no babysitter, which means I can't work, which means I may now lose my internship.

The house is silent and dark, just like my options. I know I got myself into this life, but hell, it doesn't make it any easier to cope with. It's 6am and I plan to wait up to call work in an hour to tell them I won't be in. I guess the worst thing of all is that it looks to Cameron that I am not going into work because of my fight with him last night. This timing sucks so badly.

What the hell am I going to say?

Oh, I can't come in because I have no babysitter for a child that doesn't exist. Or how about *I can't come in because I gave my boss a lap dance last night when I told him I was seeing my mother after we dry humped on his washing machine.* Or maybe *I made my boss blow in his pants last night and I refuse to pay for the dry-cleaning bill.*

I put my head into my hands. This is a fucking disaster.

"Hey." Jenna smiles from the door.

I smile back. "There she is." I stand and wrap her in my arms. "How are you feeling?"

"I'm okay. Thank you for last night."

"We should go and get you packed."

She nods. "Did you ring your mom?"

I shake my head. "No."

"Why not?"

I shrug. "It's all a bit too hard. I'll have a couple of days off and then work something out from there."

She watches me for a moment. "Why don't you just ring your mom and offer to fly her out here for a week or two. I'm sure I will be back by then."

I exhale slowly. I want to tell Jenna about Cameron and our fight, but now is not the time.

"Maybe." I sigh.

"She won't mind, and she can stay in my room."

"Yeah, I guess."

She watches me for a moment. "You okay?"

I smile sadly. "Yes. Of course. I'm just really tired." I grab her hand in mine and squeeze it. "You should go pack. Owie and I will take you to the airport."

She smiles, nods, and disappears up the stairs. I pick up the phone and stare at it for a moment. I love my mom with all of my heart. I love my mom, but things are a little strained between us — because of me, not her.

I guess I never got over the disappointment I saw in her eyes when I fell pregnant out of wedlock. She didn't want me to have the baby and, although she has been amazing since

Owen was born, it was like a fire in my belly was lit and I vowed to never rely on her for anything.

I especially don't want to now.

I put the phone back down onto the kitchen table and head up to shower as I run over my options in my head. I'm so tired that the tears are just running out of my eyes as the hot water runs over my head. I keep seeing Cameron's beautiful eyes looking up at me as I sat on his lap. The regret runs deep through my soul.

What could we have been if our timing had been different?

If we had met up after that weekend in Vegas five years ago, things could have been so different between us. I put my head in my hands as the tears flow. I need them to stop. I'm a mother now. With that, I lost the right for any romantic notions I ever had for myself.

But I can't help it.

I feel it. I feel that pull towards him, and I so badly wanted to see where it could go.

I allow myself to cry for ten minutes and then I pick myself up and dust myself off.

That's it now. Get on with it. I wipe my eyes and mentally prepare myself to toughen up. I need to stop with this sappy shit.

He's gone.

I shower, dry, dress, and then go downstairs and dial Mom's number. She answers on the first ring.

"Hello, Ash. What's wrong?"

I smile and roll my eyes. "Hi, Mom."

"Is Owie okay?"

"Yes, Owie is fine," I reply. "Sorry to ring you so early."

"Oh gosh, Ash, you scared me. I never hear from you at this hour."

"I know, I'm sorry. Jenna's mom had a heart attack."

"Oh no." She gasps. "Is she okay?"

I nod. "Hopefully." I shrug. "They are doing more testing to today."

"Is Jenna going home?"

"Yeah." I hesitate, this is the part I hate — the asking for help bit.

"What are you going to do with Owie while you work Ash?" she asks.

"I'm kind of stuck, Mom."

"Oh—"

I cut her off. "I was wondering, if I bought you an airline ticket, would you be able to come over here for a week or two and help me out with Owen?"

"Of course, love."

I smile. "Really?"

"Of course I can. I would love to get to spend some time with the both of you."

I close my eyes as they fill with tears again. "Thank you, Mom. It means so much."

"I'm going to the doctors first thing this morning for my blood tests and then I will call you later and we can arrange flights."

For the first time in ten hours I feel optimistic. "That's great. Thanks, Mom. Love you."

"I love you, too, Ash. Speak soon."

At 7am sharp, I ring the hospital. I know Cameron does his hospital rounds at seven on the dot and that there is absolutely no chance at all that he will be the one to answer the phone.

"Hello, surgery," the female voice answers. I frown as I try to remember the girl's name. Shit, what is it?

"Hello, this is Ashley Tucker. I'm one of Dr. Stanton's interns."

"Yes, hello, Ashley," the kind voice replies.

I scrunch up my face. I really don't want to do this. "There's been a family emergency and I won't be in for a few days."

"Oh dear. I hope everything is okay."

I nod. "Me, too." I pause for a moment. "Would you please be able to give Dr. Stanton a message for me?"

"Yes, of course."

I think quickly. It's Wednesday now, so if I fly Mom in on Thursday or Friday, I will be good to go again on Monday. "Can you just tell him that I had an emergency and I won't be in until Monday?"

"Sure."

"Can you please tell him that I will be taking the days without pay?"

"Ashley, that won't be necessary. You're entitled to sick days."

"I'm not sick," I reply. "I'm just unable to help it that's all, but I want him to know that I am not sick."

"Okay," she answers. I know what she's thinking: *This chick is wacko.*

"Just… tell him that I will definitely be in on Monday."

"Okay. Good luck. I hope everything works out well."

"Thank you."

I let out a sigh of relief. I did it.

We've parked the car at the airport and are walking across the parking lot towards the terminal. Jenna and Owen are in front of me holding hands and I'm dragging the suitcase on wheels. "Look at that big plane, Owie," I call from behind.

A plane takes off over us and we all stand still as we watch it zoom past.

"Awesome!" he yells, and we all laugh.

My phone rings. It's Mom. "Hey." I smile as I struggle with the heavy suitcase.

"Hello, love. We have a problem."

I freeze. "We do?"

"My bloods came back, and remember how I stopped taking the blood thinners for the thrombosis I had last year?"

"Yes." I frown.

"The doctor said I am unable to fly for a month."

"What?" Shit.

"He said I can't fly until I take another course and it will take a month until my blood is safe enough for me to travel."

I close my eyes and pinch the bridge of my nose. Fuck's sake.

"But that's okay. Why don't you fly Owen here and he can stay with me for a week or two, and then you can fly back and get him?"

"Oh no. That's okay. I've never been away from him before. I couldn't do that."

"Ashley, he will be fine."

"No, Mom. It's too long. We've never been apart for more than one night. Never mind, I will try and think of something else."

Jenna has overheard our conversation and is standing watching me with a frown on her face. "What?" she mouths.

I shake my head. This is just my luck.

"Can I speak to Owen for a moment, please?" Mom asks.

"Sure." I hand the phone to Owen. "Say hello to Grandma."

He jumps excitedly on the spot and takes the phone from me. "Hello, Grandma."

"What's going on?" Jenna frowns.

"Mom can't fly for a month because of her thrombosis."

"Shit."

"I know, bloody hell. She offered for me to fly him there, but that's impossible."

Jenna frowns. "Why?"

"I can't be without him for that long."

"He'll be fine."

"I won't."

"Like you have another choice. Do it."

I shake my head. "Nope, not happening. I would rather lose my job than be without him. I can work it out."

"It's his grandmother. He will be safe."

"I can't do it."

Owen holds the phone down. "I want to go to Grandma's for a vacation." He beams.

I look at him, deadpan. "We will go later. Give me the phone."

He gets back on the phone. "I'm coming, Grandma. Mom said it's okay," he tells her excitedly, his eyes flickering to mine. "Yes, tomorrow." He smiles cheekily and nods. "Yes, I will bring my swimming things."

I roll my eyes and Jenna smiles. I snatch the phone from him. "Hi, Mom."

"So I will see you tomorrow?" she asks hopefully.

"Mom, I love you, but no. Thanks for the offer, though."

"Ashley." She sighs.

"Bye." I hang up.

Jenna puts her hands on her hips in disgust. "Ashley!"

"What?" I snap as I start to pull the heavy suitcase across the parking lot again.

"You don't have a choice, Ash, and it will do the two of them good to spend some quality time together."

I shake my head. "I can't be away from him for two weeks, Jen. I would die not seeing him for that long."

She smiles sadly and takes the suitcase from me. "Fine. We will work something else out then."

Tears fill my eyes as I hold my little boy in my arms at the airport. It's Friday morning and I am about to fly home to LA without him for the first time. After agonizing over it for a whole eight hours, I had to concede that I had no other choice

157

but to fly Owen to my mom's. Yesterday we made the trek here, and today I fly home without him. This is my worst nightmare.

"You be a good boy for mommy," I whisper.

He smiles excitedly and I turn to Mom. "Please ring me the instant he needs anything."

"I will."

"I can be on the next flight."

"I know, darling."

I bend to Owen. "I will call you every morning and every night, and if you want to speak to me, you just tell Grandma and she will call me straight away."

He smiles excitedly. He couldn't care less. He's just excited to be at Grandma's.

"You better go, love." Mom smiles.

I frown and bend to squeeze Owen in my arms. Maybe this isn't a good idea. I don't care about work. "Oh, I don't know," I whisper to Mom.

"Go," she mouths. "We are *fine*."

I nod, and through tear-filled eyes, I watch her lead my son away as he waves happily. I walk through security on autopilot and take a seat at the bar while I wait for my flight.

This is the worst week of all time. To save my job, I've had to leave the most important person in my life. What kind of a parent am I?

"What will it be?" The cute bartender asks.

"Can I have a vodka, lime, and soda, please?"

"Sure."

My phone dances on the table and I pick it up. "Hello."

"Hello, Ashley."

I frown as I try to place the voice. "Hello."

"This is Eliza from the club."

My eyes widen. "Oh, h-hey," I stammer. Shit, am I in trouble?

"Darling, I am just ringing because I have had a special request and I thought you may be interested."

I frown. "Okay?"

"A gentleman has requested you for an Escape night."

"Eliza, you know I don't do that."

"I know and I told him that, but he was very insistent."

I shake my head. "I'm not interested, thank you."

"He said to tell you that it was the man you gave the lap dance to the other night."

Wait, what?

"Wait a minute." I pause as my brain tries to catch up. "It was the man I was talking to when I saw you?" I ask.

"Yes."

I stay silent.

"It's very weird, actually, because he specifically asked me to tell you his name. Which I have never had before from a client."

"What is it?" I whisper.

"His name is Cameron Stanton."

"What does he want?"

"He wants a night with you… alone."

My heart starts to race. "When?"

"Tonight."

11

I FROWN. "What?"

"I said, he wants a night alone with you… tonight."

"Where?"

"In one of our Escape apartments."

What the hell?

I don't know whether to be flattered or horrified. Does he want to see me because he wants to *see* me, or does he want to pay to have sex with me so he can treat me like the hooker he obviously thinks I am?

"I'm sorry, Eliza, but can you tell him that I'm not a prostitute for sale, and make sure you tell him in those exact words."

"I'll give him the message, but you know you don't have to sleep with him, and he knows that, too."

I think for a moment. What should I do? I want to see him tonight, but not under these circumstances.

"No. I'm sorry."

"Okay. I'll pass on the message."

"Thank you." I hang up as the bartender puts my drink on the counter. I pick it up and drink it down. Shit, what fucking next? I would have loved to have had a chance to talk to Cameron, but who in the hell does he think he is?

I sit and stare as I think about the night we could have had if he wasn't such an asshole. Eventually, I click into Facebook and scroll through my feed. A message pops up from 'Mechanic'.

I narrow my eyes and open it.

Why don't you want to see me?

I roll my eyes and I reply.

For a smart man, you really are quite stupid.

He responds.

I want a night with you.

I shake my head and drink my drink as I think of something to reply with. Who the hell does he think he is? I text back.

And I want respect.

A reply arrives quickly.

**I do respect you.
What are you talking about?**

I shake my head and reply.

**No. You demanded I leave my job.
AND
You told me that you couldn't stop thinking about me, and then you went to a strip club to sleep with someone else!**

I imagine him reading my response, and the angry look no doubt on his face.

You told me you were having dinner with your mother…
And then I find you working half naked at the same strip club.
You're not exactly innocent here.
GIVE ME A BETTER ARGUMENT!

I smirk. He *is* kind of cute when he's throwing a tantrum. I bite my thumbnail as I think, what will I write. I text.

Why haven't you called me?

I wait for his reply.

I don't have your phone number.
Your file is kept in Jameson's office.
I can't exactly go and ask him for it.

I sip my drink and write back.

Whose fault is that?
Oh, that's right. Yours. You lost your phone.
Oopsie.

I laugh into my glass as I imagine his face.

Don't make me come over there.
I am so angry with you right now.
Stop fucking with my head.

I think for a moment. He is making an effort, so what should I do? I write back.

I've been thinking about you.

"Would you like another drink?" the bartender asks.

I nod. "Yes, please."

A reply comes in.

I can guarantee you that you haven't been thinking about me as much as I've been thinking about you. Spend the night with me, Ashley.

My breath catches and I frown as I write back.

I'm not a prostitute, Cameron. You can't buy me.

A reply comes in.

I know that. If I could take you out for dinner, I would. I can't, so... think of this as a date in a protected environment.

I smile. A date in a protected environment. I think on it for a while, This could either be really, really stupid, or it could be really, really good. I don't know what to do. I sip my drink while I sit and think. He messages me again.

So... I will meet you in the Exotic lounge at 9pm?

I inhale sharply as nerves flutter in my stomach. Why am I even contemplating this? I take out my phone and ring Eliza.

"Hello."

"Hello, Eliza. It's Ashley..." I murmur.

"Hey, Ashley."

I swallow the lump in my throat. "I've been thinking about your offer."

"Yes."

"Is it too late to accept?"

"I'll call him back right away and let him know you've changed your mind."

I smile. "Thank you."

"Come in two hours earlier tonight and I'll be here. We can go through everything then."

I nod. "That would be great. I'm very nervous."

"Don't be nervous, dear. He clearly had his heart set on you. He'll be a very happy man."

I smile as I imagine the night we're going to have together. "Thank you. See you tonight."

"Just turn right there, darling."

I close my eyes in horror and turn to face Eliza. "I don't think I can do this."

Why in the hell didn't I remember the stupid fashion parade? I've been walking up and down this damn catwalk for twenty minutes now and I still can't get it. I'm wobbling all over the place in these ridiculously high shoes.

"Of course you can. You're a natural." She smiles calmly.

I look at her, deadpan.

"We're just perfecting the delivery, that's all."

It's 9.30 and the Escape Lounge is just about to open. Quite clearly, I didn't think this through at all. I have to do a fashion parade before I get to see him, and now I wish I'd paid more attention to what the girls do in this stupid line up.

"Ashley, come with me." Eliza holds her hand out. I nervously take it and follow her out the back where she takes me into a room filled with mirrors. She stands behind me and smiles. "Look at yourself. Take a *good* look at yourself."

My eyes rise to the mirror and I stare at my reflection. My honey colored hair is loose and full from my earlier hair appointment. They applied my makeup model style, and because I was so early to arrive here, I got to choose my dress first. It's amazing—white spaghetti strapped, fitted with tiny crystals that are embedded around the neckline, before it then drops softly to the floor with crystals scattered all over.

It's super sexy without being cheap. In fact, it kind of looks like a dress you'd see at The Grammy Awards. I have sky-high, silver, strappy heels on. Underneath, I'm wearing a white, lace suspender belt and sheer white stockings with a sexy, matching strapless bra.

"Look at how beautiful you look?" Eliza smiles. "Do you know how blessed the man is going to be who gets you tonight?"

I smile.

"Now, as this is your first night, the men may be quite aggressive in securing your company. I want you to prepare yourself for that."

I frown. "What do you mean?"

"New blood—new *beautiful* blood—means the men will be circling and competing against one another. This is a power game to them, but it's you who gets to chose who you want."

I frown.

"You don't have to pick the man who invited you here. You can choose anyone you want."

My eyes hold hers. *I only want him.*

"So, how does it work?" I ask.

"Well, you now can go in and have a few cocktails with the girls, half strength cocktails, of course. You're not permitted to get drunk while working, but you are expected to drink for pleasure and to relax. Then the fashion show will begin."

I nod. "Okay."

"Once that's finished, the Escape men are invited into the private lounge area for cocktails and that's when it becomes interesting."

"What do you mean?"

"You get to choose, and they know that, so they will be asserting their power over you."

I feel a nervous flutter in my stomach.

"Some men won't compete for you at all because they have their favorite girl and will be too busy pursuing her. Some men will be breaking their neck to be with you on your first night."

I blow out a deep breath. This is hectic. What if nobody competes for me at all?

Oh my God. Horror dawns. What if Cameron doesn't show up at all and I have to choose someone else?

Holy fuck.

"I don't want you to be rattled. Just take your time and choose who you want." She smiles calmly. Is she kidding? This is just a walk in the park for her.

"What happens then?" I ask nervously. The thought that Cameron might not be here sets my heart into overdrive.

"It happens quite quickly from there. You will leave alone with him and go to your room."

I swallow the lump in my throat.

"You will have champagne and canapés, and you may order dinner, cocktails, or anything you want from room service. We have butlers at your service."

I watch her intently as my mind goes wild.

"You don't have to have sex with him. You don't even have to kiss him, but you are expected to be good company, make him laugh, make him feel sexy. Give him intelligent conversation."

"How many of the women end up having sex with the clients?" I ask.

Her eyes hold mine. "To be honest… all of them. The men are gorgeous and powerful. This is a gift that our girls are given—a night with a beautiful man without consequence or judgement. A night where they can leave their morals at the door and enjoy being a virile woman and have their sexual fantasies met for a change. But, Ashley, beware and listen to this very carefully: these men, if you let them, will have you under their spell in a minute. Don't ever fall in love. It's dangerous to your sanity."

I frown, because I'm already under his spell.

166

"There's a spa bath and a pool on the rooftop. Whoever you choose is yours to do what you wish with," she continues.

I swallow nervously.

She turns me back to face the mirror. "Now look at yourself, Ashley."

I stare at the girl in front of me, and I hate to admit it, but I'm kind of excited. This is so far from anything I could have ever imagined, and I look good. I know I look good... but this catwalk thing is freaking me out.

"I'm just nervous, Eliza. Do I really have to do the walk?"

She thinks for a moment. "What if you come out on stage, but don't actually do the catwalk?"

"Could I?" I ask hopefully. "It's just these shoes. I'm not used to them and I don't want to wobble and make a fool of myself."

"Fine," she concedes. "But you will have to learn how to walk properly before the next time."

I smile. "Okay. Deal." There won't be a next time, but she doesn't have to know that.

She smiles warmly. "Let's go and get those cocktails."

I stand at the side of the stage as I watch the girls float up and down the catwalk. Club Exotic has come to a stand still as the crowd watch the Escape Girl show in awe. The bottom level of the club is filled with men, and as I glance out behind the curtain, I realize I can't see mine.

What if he's not here?

What if I have to choose someone else?

I glance around nervously as I try to calm down.

He will come... stop it. Of course he will come.

The second track comes on, and I know at the end of this song, on track three, I have to show myself to the men. My heart starts to pound and I close my eyes as I try to block out the fear.

How the fuck did he talk me into this?

Protected environment. How the fuck is this a protected environment?

Oh my God. Oh my God. I'm about to hyperventilate.

"You're up."

I glance around to the girl who just tapped me on the shoulder. "What?"

"It's your turn."

I close my eyes in horror as the song changes. Candy Shop The sexy beat blasts through the club.

I'll take you to the candy shop
I'll let you lick the lollipop
Go 'head girl don't you stop
Keep going 'til you hit the spot

I walk out onto the stage to find all of the girls lined up on the catwalk, and I stand as I put both of my hands on my hips in the center of them.

The men's eyes hungrily scan my body, and then I see their chins all lift as if accepting the challenge they've just been issued. The girls smile sexily as they face me, and in a well-rehearsed move, they all gift me with a welcoming round of applause.

I smile and nod in thanks. Two girls on the end of the catwalk walk up and take my hand to lead me to the end of the catwalk, and the sexy beat blares out as I stand still. Finally, after what seems like an hour, I'm lead from the stage.

"Holy shit," I whisper. "That was bizarre." I shake my head in disbelief that I actually went through with it.

"You did great." They all laugh.

"Oh my God, he's here," one girl gushes as she peeks around the curtain. "I knew it was him."

"I didn't see him," another girl says.

"Who?" I frown.

168

"Blake Stevens," another whispers as she takes her place to spy through the crack of the black velvet curtain.

My eyes widen. "Blake Stevens. The formula one driver?" What the hell? This guy is one of the most eligible bachelors in the world. What in the world is he doing here?

He's gorgeous, too.

"Yes. Oh my God!" The girls all chatter excitedly and practically run back to makeup to reapply their lip gloss.

I didn't see Cameron, and I'm feeling like I want to run out of here as fast as I can.

"Vivienne," Eliza calls me from the other room. "You're needed in here, please?"

I close my eyes as I try to mentally prepare myself. "Okay," I call.

I walk into the adjoining room to see the girls all in a group near the large, black double doors that go out into the Escape Lounge. They are laughing and jovial, like this is the most fun they have ever had in their lives.

I suppose it would be if you weren't so nervous that you felt like you were going to throw up.

You can do this, but you need to get over yourself, Ashley.

The double doors are soon opened, and the girls all breeze out into the lounge. I hear the men's jovial chatter float through from the other room. I stand quietly at the back of the group.

Eliza notices my trepidation and walks up to me. "You doing okay?"

"I'm not sure I can do this," I whisper. "I don't know what I was thinking."

She smiles warmly. "Of course you can and you picked exactly the right night to debut. We have some very powerful men here tonight."

I swallow the lump in my throat. "The race car driver?" I whisper.

She leans into me. "We have the president of one of USA's allies."

My eyes widen.

"We have two men who are in the wealthiest list." She smiles knowingly. "We have two famous actors, three well known football players, and we have the head of the United States Marine Corps." She winks sexily. "All gorgeous. All experienced at bestowing pleasure upon our lucky ladies."

Holy crap. What about a doctor? Do you have any doctors?

"You get first choice, Vivienne. Decide on the man you want to please you tonight."

I swallow nervously.

"Come on, dear." She smiles as she takes my hand in hers and leads me into the other room where I am handed a Margarita. The men's eyes all fall to me and I nearly slide down onto the floor to hide. I feel like I'm the newest exhibit in a zoo.

I can feel the hungry eyes roam over my body as they imagine what they could do with me.

"Gentlemen." Eliza smiles as she holds her hands up to me. "I'm sure you have all noticed that we have someone debuting tonight. May I introduce you to the delectable Vivienne Jones." I smile and drop my eyes to the ground in embarrassment.

"As you all know, she will be picking first tonight, and will be making her choice in five minutes." She smiles and tucks a piece of my hair behind my ear. "It will be quite a night for one of you. She has something very special."

The men fall silent and, without making eye contact with any of them, I sip my drink.

Where's Cameron? Why can't I see him?

I down my drink and grab another from a passing tray.

Eliza smiles and the group go silent. "Gentlemen, make your intentions known."

What does that mean?

Most of the men come and stand in front of me and I instantly feel myself frown. What the hell are they doing? And then, one by one, they introduce themselves. The first two are older, distinguished, and handsome. The next man has longish dark hair and doesn't take my fancy at all.

The next man is blonde and gorgeous. He picks up my hand and kisses the back of it.

"My name is Blake Stevens." His lips linger on the back of my hand, and I feel myself flutter. Oh my... *I know who* you *are.*

"Nice to meet you, Blake," I whisper.

The next two men are obviously the gridiron players and are huge and muscular. Holy crap... they could do some damage. Those are some lucky girls who get them tonight.

The next group of men are all gorgeous and well mannered... but where is *he*? Why isn't *he* here?

I start to hear my heartbeat in my ears as I begin to panic.

The next man is a face I know. It's the man who has followed me around out in the lounge a few times.

Oh no. He picks up my hand and kisses it. "Miss Vivienne, I'm looking forward to our night together."

"I don't think so," a voice snaps, and I turn to see Cameron standing behind me.

I smile with relief. I don't think I've ever been so happy to see someone in my life.

"Hello," he whispers as our eyes hold each other's.

I smile softly. "Hello," I breathe.

He came.

Oh, he's so beautiful, he's wearing a dark grey suit, a light blue shirt, and a tie. He looks orgasmic. Standing taller than the other men, I instantly feel myself drawn to him.

"Who will it be, Vivienne?" Eliza smiles.

What... *now*? I have to choose now? "Oh —" I'm cut off by the man I sort of know from outside in the club.

"I would like to offer a twenty-five thousand dollar tip to Vivienne if she picks me," he announces.

My face falls. What? Twenty-five thousand dollars?

The girls around me gasp and my eyes flicker to Eliza. She smirks knowingly.

"Fifty thousand," one of the other men snaps.

My eyes widen as the girls begin to gasp. Is this uncommon? What the hell is going on here? Fifty thousand dollars to spend a night with me? Is this a joke?

"One-hundred thousand," Blake Steven's adds.

"One twenty," the first bidder bites back.

I swallow the lump in my throat as the room begins to spin. That is so much money.

The room falls silent as they all wait for my reply.

"Who will it be, Vivienne?" Eliza asks. "The gentleman are all more than willing to pay a hefty tip to you for your company."

I look around the room and my eyes find Cameron's. "What's your offer, sir?" I ask softly.

"No tip." A trace of amusement crosses his face. "And no sex."

The men who have been bidding all burst into laughter. "No sex," one calls. "Are you fucking mad?"

My heart starts to beat harder and harder.

He gets it.

This isn't about the sex or the money.

I slowly walk closer and stand before him as the room falls silent again.

"Are you a betting man, sir?" I ask him.

He raises a brow. "I am."

I pick up his tie and gently run it between my fingers. "I would like to bet you fifty dollars that I can get you to do whatever I want tonight."

He smirks. "I think we both know that that's a bet you have already won."

I smile softly as emotion overcomes me. "I pick you," I whisper

"I pick you, too." He carefully lifts my hand and kisses the back of it. Our eyes are locked on each other and I can hardly breathe. Suddenly, we remember where we are and he takes my hand in his before he leads me out of the room, while the other men move their attention to the next girl. We stand and wait in silence for the elevator to arrive to take us to our room. The electricity running between us is like nothing I have ever experienced before. I look up at him and he smiles softly down on me.

"You look beautiful," he whispers as his eyes drop to my lips.

"So do you," I breathe.

The elevator doors open and he leads me in. I turn to face the door and he stands behind me. The door slowly shuts and he pushes my hair to one side as his lips drop to my neck. My eyes close instantly. The feel of his lips gently kissing my skin is so damn good.

He kisses my neck, softly at first, again and again and then, as if losing control, he bites me hard and I whimper. He grabs my hipbone and pulls me back so I can feel how hard he is behind me.

"You have no idea how badly I want you," he whispers in my ear causing goosebumps to erupt, and whether it's his breath on my skin or the sound of his words that nearly make me convulse, I will never know.

He sucks my skin as my knees nearly buckle from underneath me. "Cameron," I whimper.

I've never had this—had a man that is so in tune with my body before. It's as if he knows exactly what to do, exactly where to touch me, and exactly what to say.

The door of the elevator opens and he snaps out of his daydream, takes my hand, and retrieves the key to the room from his pocket.

I frown as a sense of sadness swipes through me that he knows the drill here.

How many times has he done this before? Has he slept with any women that were downstairs with me?

"What's wrong?" he asks, sensing my disapproval.

Get a grip of yourself. He doesn't need to explain his past. God knows you haven't even scratched the surface of yours, I remind myself.

I fake a smile. "Nothing."

He watches me for a moment. "Just say it."

I shrug, embarrassed.

"What?"

"How many times have you been here before, Cameron?"

He shrugs and rolls his lips as he contemplates his answer.

"It doesn't matter," I whisper. "Sorry for asking. I know it doesn't matter."

"Does it matter to you?"

I drop my eyes to the carpet in front of me. "It shouldn't."

"That's not what I asked."

He's got me. I nod softly.

He cups my face with his hand and lifts it so that our eyes meet. "I only wanted to meet you here because I knew you needed the money."

I frown.

"This is the last place on Earth I want to see you."

A lump forms in my throat.

"You belong in my home." He pauses and kisses me gently. "In my bed."

Of all the things he could have said, that's what I needed to hear the most.

"I don't want you to judge me because I work here," I murmur.

"I won't."

"I'm not here for the money tonight," I whisper as he kisses me softly. "I'm here for you."

He stills for a moment and looks up the hall toward our room, and then back down on me. "I don't want you staying here."

I frown.

"Come home with me."

"What? I can't. I'll get into trouble." I frown.

"Nobody will know. There's a separate exit."

"Cam…"

"If we stay here..." He frowns as he thinks. "This is always where our first date will be."

I smile softly. Why does he insist on getting better and better? I put both of my arms around his neck and lean in to kiss him gently. "I like how you think," I whisper through a smile.

He smirks against my lips and drops his hand to my ass. "I like you more. Now let's get out of here."

12

C AMERON SITS behind the wheel of his luxury car and pulls into the wide circular driveway of his mansion. I sit quietly in the passenger seat and I think I may have just done the stupidest thing in my life so far. I've let him make me hope for something more.

The club was safe. The club was just fucking.

This feels raw, intimate, and very much like he'll soon have the ability to hurt me.

Run. Now.

He appeared to be deep in thought all the way to his home.

Cameron parks the car and we sit in the darkness for a moment, as if lost in our own thoughts while my heart hammers in my chest.

Eventually, he climbs out and opens my door to help me out. He takes my hand in his as we walk in silence to his front door.

"Is that you, Mr. Stanton?" a male voice calls from around the side of the house. I can hear the gravel crunching under his feet as he approaches us.

"Yes, Steve," he replies.

A man appears from around the side of the house with a flashlight in his hand, and his eyes flicker between us. Upon realizing it is, in fact, Cameron, he smiles and disappears back to where he came from.

"Who's that?'

"My security guard."

"Why do you have a security guard?" I whisper.

"Joshua's insistence."

"Who's Joshua?"

"My brother."

"Oh." That's weird. "Is this a bad neighborhood?" I ask.

He lets out a deep, permeating, perfect chuckle, and I find myself smiling broadly.

"Does it look like a bad neighborhood?"

I glance around at the opulence and wealth around me. "Sort of." I smirk. "Rich people are creepy sometimes."

He laughs again as he opens the door, and we are quickly transported into his luxurious world. The foyer is dimly lit and he takes my hand to lead me toward the kitchen, turning the lights on as we walk past them.

"Would you like a glass of wine or champagne?" he asks.

"Whatever, I'm easy," I answer as I look around. I can't believe this is his house.

He walks me out to a room that has a large bar, and he glances through the glass door of the drink fridge. He frowns. "I wasn't expecting company and haven't got any good stuff chilled. Hang on a sec, I'll go get some."

He takes off toward the kitchen and I follow him without thinking. Where is he going? He opens a door and disappears down a set of stairs. What the hell? A wine cellar? He has a fucking wine cellar? I frown as I follow him, and my eyes widen as I approach the bottom of the stairs.

It's a huge room lined with shelves creating aisles, and the walls and floors are sandstone. The air is crisp and cold down here. Wow. This is something else.

He walks along the aisle looking for the wine he wants. "Champagne or wine?"

I shake my head and his eyes rise to meet mine. "What?" he asks.

"You have a wine cellar..." I frown, this is just ridiculous.

"Yes." He smirks. "I have a wine cellar."

I shake my head and blow out a breath.

"What?" He frowns.

"Where did you get all this money, Cameron?"

"Champagne?" he asks, distracted.

I nod.

He takes two bottles of champagne from a rack and comes back to me. "Well, that's a hard question to answer."

"Why?"

He shrugs. "I had a trust fund from my father, and then my brother became an app developer and hit it big," he replies nonchalantly.

I frown. "Who is your brother again?"

"Joshua Stanton."

I nod. That name sounds familiar somehow. "So, this is their money?" I ask.

"Yes and no."

I raise my eyebrows. "No?"

"I have an extensive property portfolio from my own investments, so what started out as their money is now money I make for myself. I could probably pay them back now."

"And this house...?" I ask.

"... was a thirtieth birthday present from my brother."

I roll my eyes, unimpressed. A birthday present? Are you fucking kidding me? I glance around again. This house must be worth an absolute bomb.

"What's with the eye roll?" he asks

"Money doesn't do it for me, Cameron."

"Money doesn't do it for me, either. Why do you think I'm a doctor? Just so I can have the title before my name?" He pauses for a moment. "But, I'm accustomed to a certain lifestyle now and I'm not going to apologize for that." He smiles sexily. "And besides, having no money limits your choices."

I smirk. That's true. "Don't I know it..."

He takes my hand and leads me back up the stairs, and we sit at the kitchen counter. He takes out two crystal champagne flutes and pops the cork of the bottle before he fills our glasses.

He hands me one then holds his glass in the air. I smile and clink it against mine.

"No toast?" I ask.

His eyes hold mine. "I have no toast. Do you have a toast?" he asks.

"Perdre des paris."

Translation. To losing bets."

He smiles sexily as the pull starts to swirl between us again. "Perdre des paris."

Translation. To losing bets," he replies.

We clink glasses and sip our champagne.

His eyes drop to my mouth and I smirk as I roll my lips.

"So, you placed a bet that you could get me to do anything you wanted me to do..." he says.

I smile. "I did."

"And what exactly is it that you want me to do?"

I like this game. "I'd like you to kiss me."

He smirks and rises from his stool. He comes around to stand between my legs. He drops his hands to the counter on either side of me, holds his weight, leans in, and gently kisses me. His lips are firm and soft, and he uses just the right amount of suction. Holy hell, he's such a good kisser. "It's nice to have you in my home," he whispers against my lips.

I smile as his tongue gently sweeps mine, silently promising me carnal things.

"I'm glad we came here," I whisper, although it's hard to know what I'm saying because my brain has stopped functioning altogether.

He smiles as he lifts and sits me on the kitchen counter, pulling my dress up so he can stand between my legs.

His lips drop to my neck and he bites my skin softly. "Why is that?"

"I'm not an Escape girl," I whisper and my eyes close at his sucking and nibbling.

Dear God.

"You're my Escape girl," he breathes on my neck.

Oh… he feels so fucking good.

The crystal beads underneath my behind hurt pressed against the hard counter, and I shuffle around to try and get comfortable.

"Is that dress uncomfortable?" he asks as he wraps his arms around me and holds me close.

"Yes," I breathe.

"Let me take it off you."

My eyes search his.

He lifts me down and turns me away from him. My heart begins to dance as he slowly releases the zipper. The dress drops. I slowly step out of it and turn to face him. Wearing my white lace panties and bra with suspender belt and stockings, I know I look like an Escape girl right now. His eyes drop down my body and then back up to meet mine.

"You're as beautiful as I remember you." He kisses me softly.

"What else do you remember about me?" I breathe.

"Everything." He kisses me again as he holds my jaw. "I remember the way you smell. The way you kiss."

My heart stops as he kisses me again.

"Your smart ass personality and your perfect mind."

My hands rise to his broad shoulders that are covered in that suit. He's wearing way too many clothes.

"More than anything, I remember the way you made me feel," he murmurs against my neck.

Oh God. His open lips run from my jaw to my neck, back to my jaw, and then to my mouth. "How did I make you feel?" I breathe as his lips drop to my collarbone. Oh hell. How am I supposed to hold an intelligent conversation with this man while he is doing this to me?

"Something."

"Something?" I repeat.

He stands and I look up into his eyes. "You made me feel something I'd never felt before."

"Like what?"

He shakes his head softly. "I don't know." He narrows his eyes. "I haven't put my finger on it yet. I only know that I've thought about you over the years… a lot."

I smile softly. "Is that so strange?" I ask as I raise my brows.

He smiles sexily. "For me? Yes."

"You usually forget women you've been with?" I frown.

He shrugs. "Perhaps." He picks up his glass and sips his champagne. "I never forgot you, though."

I watch him for a moment as the pull to him increases at an alarming pace. "You getting soppy on me Stanton?"

He smirks. "You prefer dirty?'

Our eyes hold each other's and the electricity swirls between us.

"I prefer filthy dirty," I whisper.

He raises his eyebrow sexily. "This may be your lucky night then, Bloss, because filthy dirty happens to be my specialty."

He picks up his glass and holds it high. "I would like to propose a new toast, actually."

"My name is Ashley, not actually." I smirk.

He narrows his eyes and winks sexily. I smile and hold my glass up to his.

My eyes drop to his tongue as it darts out to lick his bottom lip, and I feel it all the way down there.

"To sop-free, filthy, dirty fucking," he announces.

I laugh and repeat. "To sop-free, filthy, dirty fucking."

He puts his glass down and his eyes darken. "Get in my bed now before I pummel that fucking ass of yours on the counter."

I laugh. "There he is." My eyes dance with delight. "I thought you'd gone all soft on me."

He shakes his head and pulls on a drawer to retrieve a wooden spoon. My eyes widen as excitement shoots through me. He points toward the stairs with the spoon. "Upstairs," he mouths.

"Make me," I breathe.

His eyes flicker with arousal. "You're going to fucking cop it, Bloss."

I laugh into my champagne flute.

"Now!" he barks.

I stand as I bite my bottom lip to try and stop myself from smiling like a goon.

"Upstairs."

"Is that where I get to suck your dick, sir?" I ask sweetly.

He laughs, enjoying this game as much as me. He turns me and marches me up the split staircase.

"If you behave." He swats me hard across the behind with the wooden spoon and I yelp.

"Ouch," I half laugh, half cry out. That fucking hurt. My hands go to my behind to sooth the smarting.

"What do I get if I misbehave?" I ask cheekily.

"You get driven into the mattress by my cock."

I laugh out loud and he swats me again.

Oh man, option two sounds like the winner.

I yelp again. We get to the top of the stairs and, once again, the luxury of it all steals my breath. This house is so stupid rich, it's like a resort. Bench seats are outside each room and the hallway veers off in every direction as far as I can see. Sensing my trepidation, he grabs my hand, leads me to his room, and I stop at the doorway.

Holy fuck.

This bedroom is ridiculous. It's as big as most suburban houses. A large four-poster bed sits in the middle of the room with luxury furnishings. The walls are covered in a dark, textured fabric, charcoal wallpaper, and the bed linen is all different shades of grey, while the pillow cases and sheets are a crisp white. There's a room to the left that has a leather lounger and ottoman, and three doors sit around the bedroom. I turn my attention back to him as he waits for me to take in my surroundings.

"I need you naked," he purrs.

I smile shyly. This is it — the moment I've been both looking forward to and dreading at the same time. It's been a long time for me. Too long.

He steps forward and kisses my lips softly as he reaches around and undoes my bra with one hand.

Like a pro… he's done that many times before.

Stop it.

His eyes drop to my breasts as his hand comes up to cup them. "Perfect," he mutters as his thumb dusts back and forth over my nipple.

Our eyes lock and he drops to his knees in front of me. I hold my breath as he leans forward and inhales deeply. "You smell so fucking good." He growls against my panties.

Oh hell…

He slowly slides them down my legs, slips them off, and then nuzzles into me, his lips kissing my inner thigh as his eyes close in pleasure.

"I need to taste you. I want you on my tongue," he mutters to himself as he stands. He meticulously unclips my suspender belt and then slides it off over my hips, bending to roll my stockings down each leg… and there I stand completely naked and vulnerable. He kisses me as he pushes me back until my legs are touching the bed. He lays me down and then spreads my legs open. His eyes drop to my open sex and he smiles darkly. "That's the angle I was looking for," he whispers.

I giggle as I look up at him, standing at the end of the bed still dressed in his full suit and tie, and here I am naked and spread eagle on his bed.

I don't want to lie here like this for him while he's fully dressed. "Cameron," I plead.

His dark eyes hold mine. "What do you want?" he asks.

"I want you." I wriggle around on the bed to try and relieve some of the pressure between my legs. "I want all of you."

With his eyes still burning a hole in mine, he takes his suit jacket off and then rips his tie to loosen it. My sex clenches in appreciation. I watch as he undoes the tie, slides it off, and then unbuttons his shirt.

My heart starts to hammer at the first glimpse of his naked skin. His broad chest has a scattering of dark hair and his stomach is rippled with a distinct V that disappears into his pants. I lick my lips in anticipation. This is going to be so good. He kicks his shoes off then slowly unzips his suit pants and slides them down his legs. He's wearing tight black *Calvin Klein* briefs; his hard cock is just peeking above the waistband.

With his eyes fixed firmly on mine, he slides them down his legs, revealing the biggest damn dick I have ever seen. His dark pubic hair is short and well kept.

I have no words. Yes, I do.

Holy fuck.

My mouth goes dry. He's so beautiful. He's the perfect male specimen.

I had remembered this about him. I remembered that he was hung like a horse, but until you see it in the flesh you can't quite put it into perspective. I thought maybe my memory had exaggerated it somehow.

Not in the least. In fact, I'm not quite sure I can take him without it tearing me in half.

My insides start to liquefy and that dull ache makes itself known. His hand drops to his cock and he gives himself three long, hard strokes. I can see every vein in its thick length and the pre-ejaculate is beading on the head. With each stroke, my insides clench.

"Do you know how fucking good you look in my bed?" he whispers as he crawls over my body.

"Not as good as you look crawling over me like that," I breathe.

Our lips connect and he holds himself over me, resting on his elbows. His hips push forward and he grinds his cock up against my stomach. Oh dear God. My eyes close in pleasure. His lips drop to my breasts when he bites and, as if not being able to get enough, he sucks his way down my body. He nips my hipbone and I jump, but he grabs my legs and pins them to the mattress.

His dark eyes hold mine, ablaze with desire. I can honestly say I've never seen a man more aroused. This is off the hook.

"Dinner time," he whispers as his tongue swipes through my flesh.

Holy shit! I convulse with pleasure and he smiles against me. His tongue laps at me, softly at first, and then deeper and deeper until I begin to lift off the bed to meet his mouth.

His eyes close in pleasure.

"Fuck, you taste good," he purrs.

"Oh." I sigh as my body shudders and I grab the back of his head with both hands. *Please don't come... please don't come already. Show some restraint, for God's sake.*

What chance do I have? He only has to look at me and I nearly orgasm on the spot.

His tongue dives deeper and deeper, and the grip he has on my thighs is almost painful. His eyes are closed and I watch him with my hands tenderly on the back of his head. He nibbles and sucks in a rhythm that can only be called practised technique, and I begin to grind underneath him.

Oh God. I writhe beneath him, and my body starts to really work on his face.

Fuck, this feels so good. His hips begin to circle against the mattress to try and relieve some of the tension he's feeling.

"Cam..." I breathe. My hips grind into his face and I can feel the stubble burn between my legs.

He pushes a finger in and we both groan in pleasure.

"You're so tight," he whispers.

My eyes roll back in my head as he adds another two fingers.

Ouch! I jump and my legs close around his head on autopilot.

"Open." He growls as he rips my legs apart and pins them again. He sits up and really starts to work me with three large fingers. He works me so hard that the bed begins to rock.

My body begins to lurch forward. "*Cameron...*" I whimper.

He pumps again.

My body lurches forward as an almighty orgasm rips through me. He drops his mouth again and licks me, and I nearly jump off the bed.

"Give me some cream, baby. Show me how you taste when you come?" he whispers into me.

Holy fucking dirty talking Heaven.

I writhe on the bed as I try to push him off me. "Cameron, no, stop." I hold his forehead and try to push him off, and then he slowly rises above me.

Dear God, help me.

His dark eyes are locked on mine and my arousal glistens on his lips. The muscle between his legs is so hard. I've no doubt I'll need to be hospitalised after this.

"Spread your legs, Bloss," he whispers.

I pry my legs apart as far as I can, and he gets up and walks around, opens his bedside drawer and retrieves a box of condoms, as well as a bottle of lube.

I swallow the lump in my throat. Lube... he thinks he needs *lube*.

Fuck.

He walks back around to the side of the bed and kneels next to me before he pours some lube onto his fingertips and watches intently as he glides it through my flesh.

Arousal dances like fire in his eyes and I hold my breath as he concentrates on the task at hand.

"How long has it been?" he asks with a raised brow.

"Two years," I whisper.

He smiles a satisfied smile, bends, and gently kisses my inner thigh. "I'll behave," he whispers darkly.

Oh man. That's his way of saying he will try not to hurt me. I watch on intently as he removes a condom from the box and carefully rolls it on. His eyes then rise to meet mine and he licks his lips as his fingers drop to my sex again, and he glides them in and out of my body.

"Fuck. I want you," he whispers, deep in concentration, and I feel grateful for this break in passion to give me a moment of clarity.

This is special. He is special and he makes *me* feel special.

I smile up at him.

"Do you know how beautiful you look all messed up with an orgasm afterglow?" he breathes.

"Why don't you show me?" I whisper.

"Excellent idea." He crawls over me and kisses me softly as his cock slides up against my stomach. "Open your legs, Bloss. Let me in."

I smile against his lips and his tip nudges my opening.

His kiss turns desperate and he lurches forward.

Pain shoots through me and I tense instantly. *Fuck!*

"Shh, Bloss. Relax, baby," he whispers into my mouth. We kiss again and he slowly pushes forward with force. My eyes close as I try deal to with him. God, he's everywhere. The way his body is overtaking mine is overwhelming and I whimper.

"Here we go, Bloss. Relax, baby," He whispers again as he kisses me and drives home hard. I cling to his back tightly and he stays deep and still to let me adjust around him

"Kiss me," he breathes, and our lips crash together as he slides out and pushes back into me slowly. I smile against his lips as the first glimmer of enjoyment flickers through the pain. As if sensing the opening, he circles slowly to stretch me out and my mouth hangs open in pleasure as I moan softly.

Fuck, I can't even pretend to act cool when he is doing this to me. He kisses me again and again, and I am so grateful for his patience. I can hear his breath quiver as he holds back from going hard. He's stalling. He doesn't want to hurt me. He pulls out, then pushes back in, and I smile. "When did you get so fucking big, Mr. Stanton?" I whisper.

He smiles down at me. "When I turned fifteen. My father and brothers all suffer from the same affliction."

I laugh and he pumps me hard and steals my breath. "Well, I like it," I whisper.

He fucks me hard again and I cry out. "I know you do. I can feel you clenching around me."

He starts to lose control quickly. His mouth hangs slack as he pumps me harder and harder, and it's all I can do to hold on.

Holy shit.

"Lift your legs." He growls.

I lift my legs and he really lets me have it with deep punishing pumps that make the bed rock and hit the wall. His mouth is ravaging my neck, his cock is ravaging my body, and I have absolutely no idea how to deal with this level of possession.

He completely steals my body as he takes it as his own. He lifts one of my legs and I cry out as he hits the exact spot. Holy hell. I pant and I scrunch my eyes shut as I try to stop it, but I can't, and after only a few hits, another orgasm rips through me and I scream out.

Cameron sees that as a green light, and that's when he starts to really fuck me hard.

And this *is* fucking. Unbridled, animalistic fucking. He starts to moan, his mouth hanging slack as he picks it up to piston pace, and I don't think I can take any more.

God help me.

He pushes deep and then shudders as he comes silently inside my body.

His eyes are closed and he breathes heavily. I wrap my arms around his perspiring body and he holds me close. He kisses me softly and we pant as we try to catch our breath. Eventually, he rolls over and reaches down, takes off his condom and drops it onto the floor.

I sit up and smile broadly, suddenly aware that I have a sex god naked in bed with me. His tanned body is rippled with muscle and his dick is still hard. Semen is leaking out and, unable to help it, I bend down to lick it off.

Hmm, tastes salty. Tastes good. His eyes hold mine and I lick him again. His hand drops to the back of my head tenderly and suddenly this becomes the most intimate thing I have ever done. His dark eyes watch me as I take him completely in my mouth and smile around him.

"You owe me fifty bucks," I whisper.

He smiles sexily. "Best fifty bucks I've ever spent."

13

I GLANCE around the luxury bathroom as I sit on the toilet. It's early morning and the sun is peeking through the side of the drapes. My eyes roam from the oval stone bathtub sitting in the center of the room, then over to the three-nozzle shower with the bench seat. I have never been in a bathroom like this before. In fact, I don't think I've even seen one this exotic in movies. The more time I spend in this house, the more uncomfortable I become. I don't know rich. I've never had money. So how could I ever fit in to Cameron's cultured lifestyle? I blow out a deflated breath. This is a lot to take in. My body is tired. Cameron and I stripped each other bare last night. We couldn't get enough and finally fell asleep with our arms wrapped around each other. The last time we made love in the shower was surprisingly intimate, and to be honest, I kind of wish it hadn't happened. I now have a super high bar of what lovemaking should really be like. He was tender, soft and loving, and kept whispering beautiful things in my ear as his body slowly brought mine to orgasm. It was great. It was better than great. It was mind-blowing

But now I'm ruined forever.

I finish up, wash my hands, and stare at my fucked-all-night reflection in the mirror, a goofy smile crossing my face.

I look a total mess and Cameron Stanton is frigging perfect. From his body to his mind, to his... I look around at my surroundings... to this house. There isn't a thing I would change about him. How many men have I met in the past and thought to myself, *he would be perfect if only he was funnier?* Or *he would be perfect if he was smarter?* Never have I had a guy who ticked every damn box. I blow out a deflated breath. All this box-ticking is freaking me the hell out, and I know that this is one high that's going to be hard to come down from.

I don't want to rain on my own parade, but I really do need go out there and tell him I have a son.

"It's no big deal," I murmur to my reflection. But I know it *is* a big deal. Who am I kidding?

Just go out there, say it and be done with it. *The longer I leave it the harder it's going to get,* I remind myself.

Maybe he won't care and things will just be the same? But I have this annoying, nagging voice in my gut, warning me that he could be so disgusted, he'll cut all ties with me immediately.

The problem is that I'm not going to know how he's going to handle it until I actually get it over with, and it scares the hell out of me that he will end it. I should have told him before I slept with him. I brush my fingers through my just-fucked, rat's nest hair as I contemplate his reaction. It could be the best thing I ever do, or it could turn sour instantly. I blow out another deep breath. I guess I'm about to find out.

"Just go out there and tell him," I mouth to my reflection in the mirror. *Just do it.* I drop my shoulders as I prepare myself.

Just fucking do it.

Right.

I open the door and walk back into the bedroom to find Cameron lying on his back with his hands folded behind his head. His dark skin and rippled abdomen are contrasted against the crisp white sheets. He smiles sexily and holds his arm out to me. I smile and drop down to sit next to him on the bed.

He pulls me down and kisses me softly. "Good morning, Blossom." He smiles as his dark curls hang down over his forehead.

My stomach flutters at the sight of him naked and smiling up at me.

"Good morning, Dr. Stanton." I smirk. His hand snakes around to cup my ass and I notice a book opened upside down on his bedside table. "What are you reading?" I ask as I pick it up.

He puts the back of his forearm over his eyes as if embarrassed.

I read the cover and my mouth drops open as my eyes meet his. "Pride and Prejudice?" I gasp. "You're reading Pride and Prejudice?"

He shakes his head. "You weren't supposed to see that."

I smile broadly.

He takes the book from me and places it back down. "I was carrying out some market research."

My eyebrows rise.

"I wanted to see what was so special about this three dimensional man you were so enamoured with."

"Mr. Darcy..." I smile broadly, this is without a doubt the best news I have ever heard.

He purses his lips. "Don't see what the fuss is about to be honest. He definitely wouldn't sweep me off my feet."

"Mr. Darcy could sweep anybody off their feet. If he can't do it, who can?" I smirk.

He smirks. "Ashley Tucker is doing a pretty good job of it," he answers.

"Is she?" I murmur with a raised eyebrow.

"She is."

"Well, Ashley Tucker told me that it's her feet being swept off the ground," I add.

He smiles as he pulls me down and kisses me softly. "You tell Ashley Tucker that I haven't even started to sweep her off her feet yet. She should probably prepare herself."

"Ashley Tucker has her force field on to protect her from such things," I whisper as I smile against his lips. We kiss, and he flips me so that I am on my back and he has my two hands pinned above my head. I smile up at him.

"Let's go to New York."

My face drops. "What?"

"I want my date."

I frown.

"I want the weekend we arranged all those years ago. We can leave this morning and spend the weekend there, maybe catch the red eye home for work on Monday."

"What do you mean?" I pause for a moment. "I mean... I can't."

"Why not?"

I stare at him blankly. Why couldn't I go? My mind begins to race. I mean... Owen *is* away. This would be the perfect opportunity if ever there was going to be one. Holy crap, I haven't been spontaneous for so long, I think I've forgotten how to be.

"I can book us some tickets now." He smiles hopefully.

Oh shit, I have no money. "I'm sorry, I can't," I murmur through my disappointment. Fuck, I hate having no money.

"My treat."

I frown. "Cam, I'm not letting you pay for me. It's not fair."

He sits up abruptly. "Why isn't it fair? I have the money. You know I have the money."

I stand and blow out a breath. "Cam. No."

He stands abruptly, too, and pulls his boxer shorts on. "If it wasn't for the money, would you want to go?" He wraps his arms around me, his lips taking mine in his.

I smile up at him. "I would, but why can't we just hang here for the weekend?"

He shakes his head as if it's a no brainer. "I can't take you out here? How am I supposed to sweep you off your feet when we can't leave the fucking house?"

"We don't need to go out. You live in a castle."

"Can we go?" He smiles playfully as he starts to walk me backward while biting my neck.

I laugh up at the ceiling while he attacks my senses. "I said no."

"I said yes." He bites me hard and I laugh as I try to push him away.

"No."

"Yes." He growls into my neck as he picks me up and throws me back onto the bed and crawls over me.

"Stop it. My vagina is a very tired girl." I giggle.

His eyes dance with mischief. "It's lucky I know mouth to mouth resuscitation. I reckon I could bring her back to life so she's ready to party."

I laugh out loud. Oh Lord, this man kills me. "I have no doubt about it."

"I'm booking a flight." He bends and takes my nipple into his mouth and bites me.

"No." I laugh.

"Say yes or I am biting this nipple off."

"Yes or I am biting this nipple off," I repeat.

He bites me hard and I giggle. "Smart Alec," he snaps. He bends and bites me again and I squeal. "Cameron. Stop it!" I yell.

"Come to New York with me…"

"No."

"Yes."

"Alright." I laugh.

"Alright?" he asks, half surprised as he pulls back to look at my face.

I narrow my eyes as I stare up at him leaning over my body. "Just tell me why do you want to go to New York so much?"

He pauses. "I want to go back to the weekend we were supposed to be meeting—"

"Before you lost your phone," I interrupt.

He looks at me, deadpan. "How many times are you going to bring that up?"

I shrug. "As many as it takes to annoy you."

"You already reached that quota ten times ago." He frowns.

"Really? Oh, I had no idea." I act shocked.

He rolls his eyes. "I want to go back to the people we were when we met in Vegas."

My heart drops. I don't even know where to find the girl he met in Vegas.

She is long gone, replaced with responsibilities and debt.

He wraps me in his arms and kisses my forehead. "Let's go away and forget everything but each other."

I smile into his shoulder. I could nearly tear up at the thought—a weekend of just us, not worrying about the future would be so nice.

What should I do?

I frown into his shoulder and he kisses my temple softly. "Lets go," he whispers.

I smile and, unable to stop myself, I whisper the word, "Okay." I lean up and kiss his soft lips. "Deal. Mr. Stanton. Nothing but us."

"You're going to have to take my car and drop me at yours," Cameron replies casually as we walk out the front door, towards the garage.

"What?" I frown. This morning he has fussed over me, booked our flights and accommodation, and made me breakfast. I feel like Lady Diana with all this attention.

"Well, you can't be seen going back to get your car on the security cameras. They'll know you didn't stay in the apartments last night," he replies.

I stare at him blankly. Shit, I didn't think of that.

"Do you want to get paid for last night or not?" he asks sarcastically as he gets into the passenger seat of his *Aston Martin*.

I stand still as stare at the car door he has just sunk into. "I suppose so." *I hate this*. I'm calling Eliza and telling her I'm not accepting payment.

Shit, my car is a mess. I don't want him to see it. I troll my brain to try and remember the state of it. I know I haven't washed it since I moved here. I'm pretty sure it's filled with empty coffee cups.

Fuck's sake, why am I such a slob? Damn it!

I climb into the driver's seat and he passes me the keys. I glance around. "Why don't you just drive and we will swap when we get there," I murmur, distracted.

"I want to be sure you can drive it." He points to the ignition and I frown. I start the engine. It purrs like a kitten.

"Why do you have such a stupidly expensive car anyway?" I ask as the seat automatically moves forward and all the mirrors move into position. "Oh wow," I whisper, impressed.

He smirks, places his hand on my thigh and grips firmly. "Because I can."

"Hmm." I turn and glance over my shoulder as I slowly reverse the car out and turn slowly.

"Just go this way." He points to another driveway disappearing down the side of the house.

"Where does that go?" I frown.

"Willy Wonka's Chocolate Factory, where do you think?"

I fake a smile. "You're so witty, you should be locked up." I drive the car down the driveway slowly.

"Yeah, I know. It's dangerous letting me loose in society," he replies, amused. "Other guys don't stand a chance."

I giggle, not because of what he said, but because it's completely true.

Where the hell do you go after Cameron Stanton? Dick of a god, wit of a champion, house of a mogul. I'm totally screwed in the worst way.

We reach the end of the long driveway and the automatic gates open. "Turn left." He points to the left and without thinking I turn right.

"I said left." He frowns.

"And I said I'm driving the car, so you better shut up."

"Excuse me, this is the long way."

I smirk as I turn down the street. The truth is that I have no idea where I'm going, but it's just so much fun disobeying him. He has control freak tendencies that I like to push.

We eventually come into view of Club Exotic and I drive up the road slowly.

"Just pull up here. Which is your car?"

"The white one in the back row."

A frown crosses his face before he remembers to hide it.

I smile anyway. "She's no *Aston Martin*."

He smirks, but wisely holds his tongue. "Be back at my house in an hour?"

Um, that won't work. I need to race to the shops to get myself a sexy date dress for tonight. I have no idea what the hell I'm going to wear all weekend. I'm going to do a smash and grab at the shops. "I'll be a few hours," I reply.

He frowns. "No, just get your stuff and come straight back. Pack your clothes for Monday work because we won't get home until late on Sunday night."

"I will be going back to my house on Sunday night," I tell him as I pull the car to the side of the road and glance over at him. "I'll probably be well and truly sick of you by then."

"You have an hour," he answers, unimpressed.

"Stop bossing me around."

"Stop behaving like an errant teenager," he fires back.

I lean in for a kiss. "You have to pump the clutch a few times to get the gas to come through." I smile against his lips.

He pulls back and looks at me flatly

"And don't go around the corners too quick because the driver's door is faulty and it flies open sometimes," I add.

His face drops in horror. "You're joking?"

I smile as I kiss him again. "Yes, I am."

He shakes his head. "Seriously, though, is this car going to kill me?"

I giggle. "I hope not. I'm not written in the will yet."

He chuckles and shakes his head as he climbs out of the car. He leans down through the window. "Don't be late, our flight leaves in five hours."

"Okay, boss." I smile and, unable to help it, I step on the gas and do a burn out up the street. I glance at the rear view mirror to see the horror on his face, and I laugh to myself. Oh man... he's so fun to antagonize.

I pull the car into the shopping parking lot and dial Mom's number. I've been waiting to make this call.

Owen answers on the first ring. "Hi, Momma."

A broad smile crosses my face. "Hey, baby." I laugh. "How's my little man this morning?'

"Good."

"Watcha doing?"

"Baking cookies."

"Oh, what type?"

He puts the phone down. "What type are they, Grandma?" he calls.

"Chocolate chip," I hear my mom say in the background.

"What are you doing?" he asks.

"I'm just..." I pause for a moment. "I'm cleaning the house. Are you being a good boy and helping Grandma?"

"Yep. We're going to the playground after lunch, too."

"Oh, that's fun." I smile and my heart breaks a little. I miss him.

He starts talking to my mom as though forgetting he's on the phone to me.

"Owen?" I call.

"Yeh?"

"I'm going to go, darling, but I'll call you later tonight. I love you." I smile.

"Love you, Mom. Grandma she wants you," he says.

"Hello, dear." Mom says through an obvious smile.

"Is everything okay?" I ask.

"Everything is fine."

"Did Owen sleep alright?"

"Perfect."

I smirk. "In your bed?"

Mom laughs. "Perhaps."

"Thank you so much, Mom. I can't tell you how grateful I am to you for you doing this for us both."

"Ash, stop worrying about us and have a nice peaceful week."

My phone alerts me to a text before the name Cameron flashes across the screen.

"Okay, I'll call you tonight."

"Speak then. Have a great day."

I hang up and click on my message.

You are grounded without wifi, young lady.

I laugh out loud and text him back.

Your car was made to be driven like that.

A reply pings back.

That's a whole different punishment.
I'm talking about the state of your car.
It's a health hazard, Ashley!

I bite my bottom lip to stifle my over the top smile. I write back.

Quit nagging me.

I glance around at people walking by the car. I must look crazy laughing to myself while I sit in the car alone. A reply bounces back.

You have fifty minutes!

I get out of that car and press the fancy car lock. Everything bleeps and as I walk across the parking lot, I call Jenna. It goes to voicemail and I leave a message.

"Hi, babe. I hope everything is going alright. Call me as soon as you get a chance."

I hang up and straighten my shoulders.

Right. Sexy hot date dress, coming right up.

The thing about shopping that annoys the crap out of me is this: When you have no money and nowhere to go, you see every damn hot outfit ever created. But, when you have no time and a specific target in mind, there is absolutely nothing to be found anywhere. I'm in a near panic. I have ten minutes left to find a dress for tonight and I'm starting to sweat.

Why is it so fucking hard to find a sexy, non-slutty dress?

I flick through the clothing rack, annoyed. Everything here screams that I'm a two dollar whore, or come grab a granny. There's nothing in between. My phone rings and I glance at the screen to see one of my favorite names light up. Jenna.

"Hey." I smile. "Are you okay?"

"Hi, Ash. Yes, it's not as bad as they first thought. She's going to be alright."

I put my hand on my chest in relief. "Oh, thank God, Jen."

"I know. She had us all scared for a while there but they think she's going to make a full recovery."

"That's great." I smile.

"I'm so relieved. What are you doing?"

I shake my head and smirk. "I have news."

"What kind of news?"

"Mr. Stanton news," I whisper as I continue to flick through the dresses.

"Oh my fucking God. What?"

"He came to the club and I was busted. He knew it was me, despite the wig. We had this *huge* fight and then he demanded a lap dance."

"What?"

"And then two days later he requested a night in the Escape Lounge with me."

"What the fuck?" she screeches.

"I know. But he didn't want me to sleep there, so he took me back to his house, which is like crazy rich, and we had awesome sex all night and now I can hardly walk. He's taking me to New York for the weekend, but I'm going to look like a potato because I can't find anything to wear," I blow out through my last breath. Jeez, that was a mouthful.

"What the heck" She pauses for a moment. "Did you tell him about Owen?"

I scrunch my face up. "Erm. No, not yet." I wince.

"Ashley, what the hell are you doing?"

"Oh, Jen, I just want him to get to know me before I tell him I have a son."

"Why?"

"Because it's going to change the whole dynamic and I will become someone's mom to him. I won't matter anymore."

"You don't know that."

"I kind of do," I mutter sadly. "Look, I'll tell him as soon as we get back on Monday. Jen, when have I ever had the opportunity to go away with a dreamy guy for a fun weekend with no strings attached?"

"This is true," she mutters, distracted.

"Do you think it's bad if I hold out until Monday? I mean... who knows, we might not even hit it off and it won't matter anyway."

"Again, true."

I blow out a deflated breath as I turn a full circle, looking at the dresses on the racks. "I've got to find a date dress and there is literally nothing anywhere." I sigh.

"Hmm, look at that little dress shop near the coffee place we go to."

I frown. "Which one?"

"You know... It has the rocking horse in the window?"

"What? Near the coffee shop?"

"Yes, across the road. I saw about fifty things in there to die for."

I shrug. "Okay, it can't hurt."

"Send me some photos from the changing room."

I fake a smile and give the attendant a wave as I exit her shop. "I have approximately..." I look at my watch. "Eight minutes to find a dress that is going to drive him wild."

She giggles. "Piece of cake. Get off the phone and start running, bitch."

I fall into the seat as Cameron fusses about in the overhead luggage compartment.

I've never flown first class before. I glance around at everyone who all look like its their God given right to fly in such luxury. Cameron is wearing blue jeans and a navy sports suit jacket with a white T-shirt. His dark hair is in messy curls and he looks like he probably owns this frigging plane. He exudes money. My eyes roam down to my thirty-dollar dress and shoes, and I cringe. Do I look like I have no money? Because that's sure how I feel. He pushes our bags around and rearranges them in the overhead, and a broad smile crosses my face as I watch him. Cameron has to have things just as he likes them or it annoys the hell out of him. When I got to his house earlier, I found him in the throes of hoovering and cleaning my car. He said it would have bothered him all weekend if he didn't do it. My little baby is now sparkling clean, like a diamond. Cameron finally falls into the seat beside me and, without thinking, picks up my hand and places it on his thigh. I've noticed he does this a lot — he wants my hands on him. In bed he wants me to cuddle his back. In the car he picks up my hand and puts it on his thigh. He turns his attention to me now and squeezes my hand in his before he throws me a sexy wink and flashes a swoony smile.

"We didn't have to fly first class, you know," I whisper.

His head leans back against the headrest. "Yeah, we did."

I lean in so nobody else can hear. "You waste a lot of money."

He smirks. "And you talk too much."

Cameron

I tap my pen as I think before I write the words Mount Everest.

"That's not it," Ashley interrupts from over my shoulder. I smirk. "Know it all. Yes, it is."

I'm doing the crossword in the paper and we are just about to land in New York.

"Try Mauna Kea in Hawaii," she tells me.

"I'm looking for the highest."

"Yes, and while Mount Everest is the highest above sea level, it's not the actual tallest mountain."

I frown. "Everest stands at nearly thirty-thousand feet. Mauna is only at thirteen."

"Yes, but twenty-thousand feet of Mauna is submerged in the pacific ocean."

"Therefore not being the tallest," I say softly.

She shakes her head. "You have no idea what you're talking about."

"I know more than you do," I add.

She smirks. "I doubt that and it won't fit, big shot. Trust me, I know my shit."

I go to write it down and, low and behold, it doesn't fit. I purse my lips and she smiles smugly. This woman will be the death of me. I have never been with someone smarter than me before. Can't say I like it to be honest.

Next question: The chemical element of the atomic number two. I frown and glance over at Ashley.

"Helium." She smirks without hesitation.

I fake a smile. "Smart ass," I mouth.

"Dumbass," she mouths back.

I lean over so that nobody else can hear us. "You should probably start worrying about what I'm going to do to your ass in our hotel room."

"Nothing I couldn't handle." She smirks and I instantly raise a brow in question. She shakes her head. "That's off limits."

I smirk. "Why is that?"

"I would like to have something to give to my husband when I finally meet him," she whispers.

I feign shock. "You wound me. I thought I was your future husband."

She laughs. "Oh Lord, no. You're too dumb for me."

I smirk as I lean in and kiss her softly. I feel myself harden. "Don't set me a challenge, Bloss. You know I'm a goal-orientated man."

She smiles against my lips. "Tell me what you want to do to me," she whispers.

I bring my hand up to cup the back of her head and kiss her again. "Well, right now I would like you naked and riding my cock." I grab her hand and bring it over the bulge in my jeans, watching as her eyes light up with excitement. She subtly squeezes and I kiss her again.

"Mile high club," she whispers.

"Damn it, I should have brought my brother's jet and we could have joined that club for real."

She cringes. "Your brother has a jet?"

"Yeah, I would normally take it, but then if I told him I was taking a girl somewhere it would have become a *thing*."

"A thing?" She frowns.

"They would all want to meet you."

"Who's *all*?" she asks.

"My brother Joshua. His wife Natasha. Then Murph, although Adrian is his real name."

"Oh good, don't tell them anything. I don't want to meet them."

I frown. "What's wrong with my family? Why wouldn't you want to meet them?"

I'm horrified. She should want to meet my family. Most girls would cut their right arm off to meet them.

"Well, we're not like that, are we?" she says casually.

"Well... we could be," I stammer.

She grins as she picks up my hand and kisses the back of it. "Cam, it's fine. You don't have to pretend this is something it isn't. I'm not."

I stare at her for a moment as my brain freezes. Is she using fucking reverse psychology on me right now? I've never been given the cold shoulder by a woman before, and she seems to do it on an hourly basis. "Are you blowing me off?" I ask.

She leans over and licks my ear. "No, but I will be blowing your dick very soon."

I half-smile, mollified for the moment. "That's more like it."

I open the hotel door with my lips locked on hers, walking her backwards into the room as I throw the bags down. I tear my jacket off my shoulders and she laughs in excitement.

This woman is driving me insane.

I can't get enough and it was hard to control myself for the duration of the flight.

"Clothes off." I growl.

Ashley laughs as I lift my T-shirt over my head. "I said clothes *off*," I repeat.

She bends and starts to undo her sandals. I kick off my shoes and slide my jeans down my legs, revealing my hard cock.

Her eyes dance with delight. "You're one hell of a man, Cameron," she mutters sexily.

I grin and lie on my back on the bed.

"No time for small talk, Bloss. Get the fuck on me now."

She smiles sexily as she slides her dress down her legs, and my breath catches. She's wearing pretty pink matching lace underwear. Unable to help it, my eyes scan her body and my tongue darts out to lick my bottom lip. She is utterly fucking beautiful, curvy, and feminine, and the way she looks at me drives me wild.

I don't know what she's done, but somehow she has tapped into something inside of me. She has me washing her fucking car, for Christ's sake. I'm like her pathetic little puppet waiting for my next fix.

This is new.

I watch her as she slowly removes her bra, letting her breasts fall free. She's got big tits—big, juicy, fucking perfect tits. I grab my dick and hold it so it doesn't explode on the spot.

God, she's so hot.

She slowly slides her panties down and I'm blessed with the sight of the tiny patch of Heaven.

My Heaven.

She slowly crawls over me, smiling as she waits on her hands and knees. "What do you want, Dr. Stanton?" she whispers darkly.

"I want you to suck my dick."

She smiles sexily and disappears down my body. I inhale deeply as she licks me on the upstroke.

"Oh… you taste good," she breathes onto me.

My eyes close in pleasure and my legs open. She takes me in her mouth and I feel a hard pulse begin to grow. My breath quivers in anticipation. She takes me deeper and deeper, and I lift off the bed as I hold my breath. My hands rest softly on the back of her head.

Don't fucking come, I start to chant in my head. *Don't fucking come.*

She moans around me and I scrunch my eyes shut to try and block her out. "Ash," I whisper. God, she's too perfect. I can't hold it. "Get on me." I growl.

"Where are the condoms?" she asks.

"What." I frown. "Are you on birth control?"

"Yes."

"Fuck the condoms. Let me come inside of you."

"No."

I lift my head to look at her. "I'm clean. I've never not worn a condom in my life."

Her eyes search mine.

"I promise," I whisper.

"This would be your first time?" she asks, clearly surprised.

I nod.

She smiles shyly and climbs over the top of me as the sound of my heartbeat rings in my head.

Holy fuck. I'm going to blow so hard.

She kisses me and my hands roam up and down her body, from her full breasts to her tight ass. I slide my hand underneath and run my fingers through her wet flesh.

My cock thumps in approval. She starts to slide up and over my body as we kiss, and I'm unable to open my eyes. "Now." I growl. "I need you now."

She rises onto her knees, and I hold the base up and she moves it into position before I pull her hips down.

We both moan in pleasure and she stops midway down. "Give me a minute," she begs.

We haven't done this position before. I've had to take her how I wanted her—my body wouldn't have given me the choice.

I watch her struggle to take me, and honestly, I think it's the hottest thing I have ever seen in my life. She moves from side to side to loosen herself up.

I get to come inside her.

Soon.

Suddenly, I'm near frantic. I need her now. "Ash... Come on." I growl. "You're killing me."

She giggles and leans forward, allowing her body to open up, and I slide home. Our eyes lock as our bodies become one without anything in between us, and something changes for me.

I want her to meet my family.

For the first time in my life, I want all the strings attached.

I lift her slowly and circle her hips onto me. She groans and I bring her back to rub her pubic bone over mine. Her dark eyes hold mine.

"Fuck me," I whisper.

She smiles and starts to slowly pump me. I grab her hips to hang on for the ride. Up, down, in and out—the burn and the pleasure is off the charts.

"Cam, you feel so good, baby," she whispers.

Hearing her call me baby sets me into overdrive and I start to slam her onto me without thinking about the consequences.

"Ahh," she cries out.

We get into a rhythm and I watch her perspiring breasts bounce up and down as she rides me. What a beautiful fucking sight. I can feel every muscle deep inside of her. This tight thing she has going on is driving me wild.

"Cam, I'm going to come. I can't hold it, baby," she whimpers.

That's my green light. I can go. I start to lift and really hit her hard, and she screams out as her orgasm rips through her. I lift her at a racer's pace, and holy fuck, I can't get deep enough.

I can't get close enough.

I want more, so much more.

The orgasm rips though me and I cry out. For the first time in my life I actually come inside of a woman...and it's perfect. Just like she is.

"What will it be?" The bartender asks.

"Bloss?" I ask.

"Erm..." She peruses the cocktail menu. "I'll have a Margarita, please."

"And I'll have a Blue Label Scotch on the rocks."

I smile at the beautiful woman sitting opposite me. After spending the afternoon in bed we've been out for dinner and now we're having drinks. The conversation flows easy and she makes me laugh. I feel like I'm hanging out with a good friend. There's no bullshit at all between us. We are seated in the corner of a trendy club. The decor is dark and moody, and the copper bar is large. Huge, black, metal pendant lights hang down from the center of the ceiling.

Our drinks are delivered and Ash sips hers and smiles at the bartender. "Bravo."

He throws her a satisfied wink and I smile as he walks away.

She sips her drink again. "Tell me why you've never had unprotected sex before," She says quietly.

I shrug. "It's never been something that's bothered me before."

She raises her eyebrows. "And it bothers you with me?"

I nod. "Strangely enough, it does."

"What abut your past girlfriends?'

"Only ever had one girlfriend and that was in college."

She screws up her face in shock. "What?"

I shrug and smile.

"So, you're just like a huge sleazebag who sleeps with everyone?"

I laugh out loud. Trust her to say it how it is. "I have fun," I reply. "And I don't sleep with everyone. I've never had a girlfriend because I couldn't ever be a cheater."

"Why not?'

"Its not who I am. I love women too much to go out of my way to hurt them."

"So, you just break their bodies instead of their hearts?" she asks.

I smirk. "Something like that. I usually get in about five dates before I have to end it."

She frowns. "So five dates is the expiry date?"

"No. It usually takes about five dates before they start stating wanting more and I end it."

She bites her bottom lip. "Right, so what date are we on?"

"Date twelve."

She laughs into her drink. "How do you work that out?"

I count on my fingers. "Well… Vegas."

She smirks.

"Then the five days at work count for five dates."

"We didn't touch each other at work."

"But I couldn't take my eyes off you, so that counts as a date for each day because that was, like, extended torture."

She laughs and holds her drink up to me in approval.

"Then the club."

"The lap dance?" she murmurs in horror.

I smile. "Yes. Then the night at my house."

"Which was last night, so that only comes to eight."

"But we had sex four times today."

"Are you counting?"

"Yes." I keep counting on my fingers. "Really, I say that makes it ten dates and tonight will be worth another two."

Her eyes hold mine. "I guess the end is near for me then." She puts the back of her hand over her forehead to fake distress. "Oh no, what ever will I do?"

"You better watch your step and be a good girl. I might keep you around for another few dates yet." I smirk

She grins and sips her drink.

"What about you?" I ask.

She raises her eyebrows, as though surprised by my question. "Erm, a few boyfriends in college." She pauses as if thinking. "After I met you, I got engaged."

My face falls. What? That shouldn't bother me as much as it does.

"What happened?" I ask.

She sips her drink as if uncomfortable. "He wasn't the one."

I raise an eyebrow in question. "The one?"

"He wasn't the man I met in Vegas, that's for sure."

Our eyes lock as the electricity zaps between us. "You getting sappy on me, Tucker?"

She rolls her lips. "Temporary slip up. I'll stop drinking immediately."

I raise my hand to the bartender. "Four more, please," I ask and she bursts out laughing.

"Have you ever dated anyone who had children?" she asks.

I screw up my face. "Fuck no. I could think of nothing worse."

14

Ashley

I BLINK, in shock, I think. "You could think of nothing worse than a child in your life?" What a stupid thing to say. Well, I wanted my answer and there it is.

We're doomed.

"Hello, Ashley," a voice echoes from behind me. Cameron and I turn to see Andrew, my ex fiancé standing there.

My eyes widen. "A-Andrew?" I stammer. My eyes flicker between the two men. "Hey. Erm. Andrew this is Cameron. Cameron this is Andrew," I mutter nervously.

Cameron smiles warmly. "Hello."

Andrew nods and shakes Cameron's hand. "Hello."

Are you freaking kidding me? Of all the people to see tonight, it had to be him.

"I thought you moved to LA?" he asks flatly.

Oh God. Don't start being snarky now. "I did."

Cameron interrupts, looking happy with a cheeky grin. "I stole her away for the weekend so she could show me her home town."

Andrew looks between Cameron and I, while I hold my breath. *Don't say anything. Please don't say anything.*

"So... you just met this week?" Andrew sneers.

A frown crosses Cameron's face as he sums up the situation.

"Cameron and I are old friends, Andrew. No need to be snarky. Now, if you don't mind leaving us to it..." I turn back to my drink. I don't need his shit tonight. Why the hell is he here?

"Yes. I do mind, actually. Why haven't you returned my calls."

"Listen, mate, I don't know what your problem is..." Cameron starts.

"My problem is that my mother has cancer and she wants to see Ashley before she dies, but Ashley has gone missing and isn't replying to any of my messages."

My face falls in horror. "Oh, Andrew, I'm so sorry. I thought you were messaging me about us."

"No." He screws up his face.

"I'm taking it you are the ex?" Cameron asks.

"Ex fiancé," Andrew snaps, annoyed.

Cameron's eyes meet mine and I swallow the lump in my throat. "Andrew, is it alright if I come and see her tomorrow?" I ask as I turn to Andrew.

His eyes hold mine for a moment. "Tomorrow isn't a good day."

"When is a good day?"

He shrugs. "I'll let you know."

I stand and give him a hug. "Thank you, that would be great. It will be really nice to see her again."

He holds both of my hands in his and looks at me. "You look really well, Ash." A sad smile crosses his face.

I smile in return as my eyes flash to Cameron. He seems unimpressed with Andrew's hands on me, but he's keeping his mouth shut. "Thank you." I give Andrew a peck on the cheek and with a last lingering look, he walks away through the crowd without saying goodbye to Cameron. Rude.

I sit down, rattled by what's just happened. Marie has cancer. Fuck. She's only young, too—maybe fifty-five at the most.

"So… he's the ex?" Cameron smirks.

I smile as I sip my drink. "Yes."

He rolls his lips to hide his emotions.

"And?" I smirk.

"And what?" he asks.

I raise my brows. "What's your verdict?"

He shrugs as he sips his Scotch. "He's not good enough for you."

"And you are?"

He purses his lips. "Probably not."

Our eyes lock as the chemistry swirls between us. "I think I'll be the judge of that."

"How am I'm doing so far?"

I smile broadly as I tap my fingers on my chin. "Hmm. Rankings could be dangerous."

He chuckles at the challenge.

"I wish I had some paper and a pen. I would do a full tally of the scores," I add.

Cameron's eyes dance with delight and a waitress walks past. "Excuse me, do you have a pen and a napkin we could use, please?"

"Sure." She shuffles about in her pockets and pulls out a pencil and then grabs a napkin from a nearby table.

"Thank you." Cameron smiles, before he then gets to work. "What are the categories?"

He starts to rule lines and I laugh.

"The categories?" I ask.

"Yes, you know. Like different categories you can judge me on. Let's call it a performance appraisal."

I burst out laughing and choke on my drink. "A performance appraisal?" I repeat.

Oh Lord. This man kills me.

I smile, though. I like this game. "Okay, so there's conversation."

He scribbles down the word conversation.

"Brain power." I smirk.

He adds it to the list with a broad smile, he likes this game too.

"Swoon factor."

He looks up with a frown. "Swoon factor? Is that a thing?"

I widen my eyes. "Oh my God, yes. Swoon factor is the most important one." He cocks a sarcastic brow in question. "Well, not *the* most important thing," I add.

He writes the word sex.

I narrow my eyes. "Hmm, what else?"

He frowns as he thinks.

"Romantic." I smile.

He grimaces. "Do we have to put that one down?"

I laugh. "Yes."

He rolls his eyes and scribbles it on the paper.

"Body," I add.

His eyes rise to meet mine again and he licks his lips. I feel it all the way down there. I already know he's getting a hundred out of ten for that one.

He smiles broadly and points the pen at me. "Occupation."

He already knows he's a ten in that category, too.

He sips his drink. "Okay, conversation…"

I bite my bottom lip. "Probably a six."

"A six?" he gasps. "How am I only a six?"

I smirk. He's totally not, but I have to bring him down to earth a bit.

"Fine, you're a seven," I concede.

He shakes his head in disgust and writes a seven next to the word conversation. "Brain power is a ten," he tells me as he writes a ten next to the words brain power.

"You are not a ten." I laugh.

He screws up his face. "Oh, please. Your stupid mountain and helium questions prove nothing. I'm a ten and you know it."

I smile. He's right, he's probably a hundred, if I'm honest.

"Swoon factor?" he asks.

I frown as I think. "Hmm, I don't know what you are in that category."

He sips his drink. "What is swoon factor, anyway?"

"Oh, you know… like how dreamy someone is."

"So how dreamy am I?"

I smile and lean over to cup his face in my hand. He looks at me attentively, and I stare at his dark hair with his day old growth on that square jaw, and his big beautiful eyes and lips. He's the definition of swoon worthy, but I can't let him know I think that. I narrow my eyes. "I would think maybe a six."

His mouth drops open in fake horror and the waitress walks back over to collect our glasses. "Do you think I'm a six?" he asks her in disgust.

I burst out laughing and the poor girl looks between us.

He points the pen at me. "She thinks I'm only a six out of ten in the swoon factor category."

The girl looks over at me and frowns. "You must be drunk. He's totally a ten."

We all burst out laughing and he gives her a tip before she walks away with our empty glasses.

He goes back to his list. "Sex?"

"Ten," I reply without hesitation.

He raises his eyebrow in question. "I don't think we are at a ten level yet."

"Really?" I frown. Jeez.

He shakes his head. "Nope. I've had to be too gentle with you so far."

I widen my eyes. "Hasn't felt very gentle."

"It has been." His dark eyes drop to my lips and I feel the alcohol start to heat my body.

"How rough can it get?" I whisper.

"Rough." His hand goes under the table and he slides it up my thigh, trailing beneath my dress. He slips his finger into the side of my panties, and slides it though my flesh.

My eyes close. Jesus. Public place, hot man, inebriated, and getting fingered in public. What fucking next?

"I haven't introduced you to my kink yet." He smiles as he slides a finger in, and I clench in appreciation.

"What would that be?" I whisper as his fingers gently probe my lips.

"Public fucking and bondage."

He pushes another finger in and I clench. "Does this count as an initiation?" I breathe.

I start to feel my body pulse as his fingers work my flesh.

"Maybe," he breathes, and his eyes begin to glaze over. He gets this look in his eye when he's aroused. It's a no turning back look — kind of like he'll die if he doesn't get to fuck me.

It's hot, and damn, I'm addicted.

I want to just go over there and straddle him on the stool. His finger becomes almost violent and I close my eyes to deal with the pleasure. I glance around. Luckily, we are in a darkened corner. "This list..." I breathe.

The bartender arrives with a tray of our drinks and he slips out and sits up straight.

"Here we go. A Margarita and a Blue Label Scotch." The bartender smiles casually.

"Thank you." I smile in return. I glance over to see Cameron sucking his two fingers with his dark eyes firmly on me, and I nearly convulse.

Holy fuck he's hot.

Blazing tower, inferno hot!

The bar tender leaves us alone and Cameron slowly licks his lips. "You taste good."

I feel like I can hardly breathe with all these clothes on.

"Better than good," he whispers.

"The list..." I whisper. It's only early. We can't go home to fuck yet or there will be no walking for a month.

He glances down at the list as he tries to refocus. "Romantic." He raises a brow in question.

I screw up my face. He's not very romantic, I do have to admit. "A three."

He smirks and then breaks out in to a deep chuckle.

"What?" I laugh.

He shakes his head as he sips his drink. "You got me. I'm totally a three."

I smile around my glass.

"Body?" he asks.

"One hundred."

He smirks and raises a brow in question. "One hundred?"

"I've never been with a man so physically perfect."

He raises his glass and clinks it with mine. "Let's just hope the body counteracts the romance factor then shall we?"

I laugh and shake my head.

"Occupation?"

"Ten." I smile. "But you already knew that."

"I did." He smiles. "I do have the best job in the world. I'm very grateful."

"I never asked, but why did you become a cardiologist anyway?"

His face falls solemn. "The first patient I ever lost was because of a heart attack."

"Oh no—"

"It was my uncle," he interrupts.

I watch him as he struggles with the painful memory.

"I was just out of med school and we were at his house when he had a heart attack." He frowns and I know he is right back there. "The ambulance came, but I had to use the defibrillators in the back of the ambulance to try and save him. I was the most experienced there and, looking back now, I was nowhere near prepared for it."

I watch him. I dread the day I lose someone.

He shrugs as he sips his drink. "I couldn't do it. He died despite my efforts."

I reach over and take his hand in mine.

"I vowed I would learn more about hearts, and in the end I came to love everything about cardiology. It fascinates me."

I smile softly. "Just like you fascinate me."

He smirks and returns to his sheet, and I watch him as he tallies up the scores. I don't know if it's the alcohol or the fact that I know that as soon as I tell him my secret, this will all be over, but I'm feeling very attached and needy. I need to snap the hell out of it.

I deserve to have a nice week with him. Hell, I know its going to end and that's okay. I hold no grudges as to how he will feel when he finds out I have a son. I already know his stance on children.

And I know it's selfish, but I want the week.

I deserve the week. I'm going to tell him when Owen gets back. Then I will deal with it.

"So I got..." He scratches his head for a moment. "I got a score of a hundred and forty-six out of sixty."

"How did you work that out?"

"Well, basically my body counteracted all other negative aspects out."

I laugh. It's true. It totally does.

A song comes on and he stands. "Let's dance." He takes my hand as he guides me off my stool.

"What?"

"I have to work on that swoony thing." He leads me to the dance floor and wraps his large arms around me, and I laugh into his shoulder.

"You don't have to work on anything, Cameron."

He spins me hard and we nearly lose our footing. We stumble to the left sharply and run into another couple.

"Sorry," he mouths before grimacing at me.

"What are you doing, you idiot?" I chuckle.

"Hitting these appraisal targets could be dangerous, Bloss." He spins me again and I laugh out loud. "Hold on to your hat."

I wake to the feel of gentle kissing of my shoulder blade from behind. I smile and turn my head as he kisses me softly.

"Good morning, Blossom," he whispers huskily.

"Good morning, baby." I smile as I reach behind my head to cup his face.

He pulls me closer to him and I lie in his arms. I inhale deeply in happiness. Now, this is the way to wake up to a new day. Encased in Cameron's safe arms.

What an amazing night with an amazing man.

He's perfect.

Every single thing about him is perfect. We laughed our way around New York City last night. He is the funniest man, maybe person, I have ever met. Witty, intelligent, sexy. I didn't know men like him even existed and I knew I didn't imagine it all those years ago. This is the ultimate male species.

"What do you want to do today?" he asks.

"Just stay in bed." I try and swallow. My mouth is dry from all those drinks last night. "I need a drink," I murmur groggily.

He gets up and goes to the mini bar before he turns and hands a bottle of water to me. Then he goes to the bathroom.

I nearly drink the whole bottle in one go. This is taking dehydration to a new level.

He returns with new enthusiasm. "I know what we can do today." He smiles excitedly as he stands there, butt naked.

"You do?" I frown. Oh God, please don't let it be jumping out of a plane or some extreme bullshit. "What's that?"

He points at me. "We're going to go out to breakfast and then I am taking you to the New York Library."

"Huh?"

He widens his eyes in excitement and turns the television on. "Do you want a cup of tea?" he asks chirpily.

220

I watch him for a moment. He's super energised while I feel like a complete train wreck.

"You weren't tipping those drinks of yours into pot plants last night, were you?" I ask dryly.

He laughs and crawls over the bed on his hands and knees to pin me beneath him. "Not feeling so good today, huh?"

I shake my head. "No."

"You shouldn't have drunk so much," he murmurs against my stomach as he bends to kiss me.

"It was the company I was keeping. Peer pressure."

He bends and bites my hipbone and I squirm underneath him. "Perk up, old girl, we have a full itinerary."

I close my eyes as a wave of nausea rolls through me. "That's what I'm afraid of."

We walk into the library hand in hand and Cameron smiles like the cat that got the cream.

"What's wrong with you? You're acting creepy." I smirk.

He winks. "I am creepy." He walks up to the reception desk. "Hello, I want to search for some records. How do I do that?" he asks the lady.

"Just go to computer twenty-two, type into the search bar what records you are looking up, and it will search for you."

"Thank you." He smiles and we walk to the station where all the computers are.

"What are we doing here?" I frown as I look around at all the people reading intently as I drop into the seat next to him. "Is this part of your brain power plan?" I ask as I rub my hand up his muscular thigh. I smile. I like being able to touch him whenever I want to.

"You'll see." We've just been out for breakfast where we sat in the sun in a park and read the morning newspapers.

It was unfussed and easy, and God, I don't want it to ever end. He makes me feel so alive and so… I don't even know the right word to describe it.

Complete?

He types in a few things and frowns. I take the opportunity to look around. "What are you looking for?" I whisper.

This is annoying. He's wasting my date time in a frigging library.

"Have some patience, woman," he replies, distracted.

I roll my eyes, sit back in my chair, and fold my arms. Come to think of it, I'm hungry again or is just that the hangover reappearing?

I don't know, but I think I need cake. "Can we have cake and coffee when we finish?" I ask.

"The only cake you will be eating is cream pie," he murmurs with a raised brow.

I lean in. "You're a sex maniac, Stanton."

"I know," he replies casually as he concentrates.

"I want banoffee pie," I whisper.

He smirks and keeps typing. "You're going to look like a banoffee pie soon."

I giggle. "Lucky, I'm going out with a sex maniac who will like me anyway."

"True. I prefer cream pie to banoffee, though." He smirks, distracted.

I roll my eyes. "We already established that, Einstein. This isn't helping your brain power score."

He grins. "I'm trying to raise another score out here." He stands abruptly. "Switch seats with me."

I frown up at him before I switch seats.

He points to the screen and I focus on what I'm meant to be looking at. "Huh? What's this?" I ask.

"Classifieds."

I look over at him. "Why am I looking at old classifieds?"

He widens his eyes in exasperation. "Just read them."

"Fine," I breathe, half annoyed. Why the hell we are wasting time here, I have no idea.

I read down the list and then at the bottom I see it.

To the betting man's wife who works in an ice cream shop. We met in Vegas last weekend when you needed a stand in husband.
I lost my phone.
Je n'ai aucun moyen de vous contacter.
Translation: I have no way of finding you.
Wer auch immer eine Wette gewinnt, mag niemals dasselbe sein.
Translation: Whoever wins a bet to you, may never be the same.
I'm in New York looking for you.

Appelle-moin.
Translation: Call me.
0423788900

Oh my God. My eyes rise to search his. "You *did* try to find me?"

He smiles softly. "I told you I did."

I look back to the computer and read it again so I know I'm not imagining this.

Nope. It's definitely still there.

"Cam," I whisper, and for some reason I get a really big lump in my throat and my eyes tear up.

What a horrible case of sliding doors. If only we'd met back then things, could be so different between us.

His face falls. "What's wrong?"

I shake my head as I try to pull myself together.

He picks up my hand and kisses the back of it. Overcome with emotion, I lean in and kiss him softly. He looks down at me as he brushes the hair back from my forehead. "Are you getting soppy on me, Tucker."

I nod and smile through my tears. "Most definitely." I pause as I reread the ad.

"I think I just found another dimension," I whisper.

He smiles softly and kisses me. "Two down, one to go."

15

I WALK down the aisle of the plane as I head back to our seat. We're midway through our flight back to Los Angeles. Cameron is sitting with his head against the seat, and he smiles sexily as I approach, patting his knee.

I feel my heart flutter. Lately, that seems to be a common occurrence. Just one look from him sets me into schoolgirl raptures. As I approach our seat, he pats his knee again and I bend to kiss him gently. "I can't sit on your knee," I whisper as I look around.

"Who says?" he grumbles as he pulls me down. "This isn't coach. We can do what we want here."

He lays me across lap with my feet on my seat, and then he shakes out the blanket and covers us both. I smile as I curl into him and his warm arms come around me before he softly kisses my temple. "That's better," he whispers.

I smile against his chest and snuggle into him. He smells so damn good, and he's right, being this close is much better.

We laughed, we danced, we made love, and we fucked like animals in New York. I have never felt so fulfilled in my entire life.

If happiness is a gift, Cameron Stanton is my Santa Claus.

I'm falling in love.

With every glance, with every touch, with the air that he breathes every second.

Cameron Stanton is his own kind of magical drug and the high he gives is as good as it gets.

The longer I'm on it, the harder the withdrawal will be.

Unfortunately, I already know our fate, but I'm trying to put it to the back of my mind and enjoy the time we have together.

"Thank you for a beautiful weekend, Cam." I smile up at him.

He kisses my forehead and he smiles in return. "Thank *you*," he whispers against my hair. "It *was* a great weekend and I don't want to go home. Can't we just run away?"

I smile and listen to the drone of the engine while sitting on top of my beautiful traveling companion, his lips pressed to my forehead. I somehow drift into a peaceful sleep.

First class really is the only way to travel.

The car pulls up in Cameron's driveway at 11pm and we both climb out of the car on sleepy feet. We're tired. After drinking copious amounts of alcohol and engaging in a million sex sessions over the last forty-eight hours, our bodies have literally given up. The driver retrieves our bags from the trunk and Cam takes them. "Thank you." He smiles as the driver hands his credit card back.

We walk up the driveway. "I'm going to go home, babe." I yawn.

He frowns. "I thought you were staying…"

"I didn't bring any of my stuff for work."

His eyes hold mine. "Don't go." He bends and takes my lips with his and brushes the hair back from my face. "Stay with me again."

I smile. I know I should go home, and I know I should tell him everything because my sanity and my job depend on it. But I just can't bring myself to do it. With a heavy heart, I turn toward the house. "I'm going to get sick of you," I reply dryly.

He smacks me on the behind and I laugh as I jump. "I'm already sick of you. This is a sympathy sleepover." He fires back.

I smirk as he opens the door. "Good, I thought you were getting needy on me."

He flicks the light on. "I don't do needy." He turns to face me. "Ashley Tucker, my all night fucker."

What the hell? My eyebrows rise by themselves and I burst out laughing. "Ashley Tucker, your all night fucker?" I gasp.

He smiles a proud-of-himself smile and raises a brow. "Has a ring to it, doesn't it? You should think yourself lucky to be spending time with someone as romantic as me."

I widen my eyes in jest. "Should I, now?" I mouth, I smile as I watch him put our bags down. His cheeky personality is addictive and really, he shouldn't worry—I'm needy enough for both of us.

"Why don't you go and take a shower while I fix us a snack?"

"Do you want me to do anything?" I ask.

"Just get naked and clean."

"I'm just telling you now…" I point at him. "There is zero chance of you getting laid tonight."

He laughs as he walks into the kitchen. "I'll bet you fifty bucks I do," he calls after me.

"You need to get a referral to gamblers anonymous," I call back as I walk up the stairs. "You have a serious addiction."

I walk up the stairs and down the corridor towards Cameron's bedroom. I call it a corridor because it is way too long to be a hallway and it seems to go on forever. I turn the light on and stand at the doorway. It doesn't seem real that I should sleep in a bedroom like this. It's huge, exotic and luxurious. From the thirty-foot ceiling to the carpet that is so plush that you sink into it, not a detail has been missed. The furnishings are straight out of a magazine. Black drapes hang over the huge windows in that little bit too long trend. I walk around the room with my arms folded in front of me as I stare at my surroundings. This has to have been decorated by a stylist. In fact, the whole house must have been. I frown as a thought crosses my mind, and I walk back down the hallway until I get to the next bedroom, walk in and turn the light on. Another room filled with cream, caramel, and coffee furnishings. There's a large bay window with a window seat overlooking the exotic pool, too. I smile as I walk around. What a beautiful tranquil space. I open the first door that leads off it and find a full bathroom, all white marble. I open the next door and find a walk in robe. I stalk back into the room and smooth out the velvet coffee-colored quilt as I look around. If everything did work out — and I know its not going to, but if it did — Owen would love this room.

My heart constricts. I miss my little man desperately. Even having spoken to him morning and night hasn't lessened the ache I feel for not having him around and I'm counting the days until I see him again. Just over seven to go now.

I need him here. I need him here with Cameron and me.

Will Cameron ever accept him?

I close my eyes as the sharp sting of reality bites.

I walk back into Cameron's room and turn on the shower in disgust at myself. How did I get myself here, in this position?

Why didn't I just tell him on that first day?

I've fallen in love with a man who doesn't even know about the biggest part of me.

I blow out a deep breath as I realize I've left my bag downstairs. I walk back into the bedroom and into the closet and I stop dead in my tracks, my eyes widening.

Holy fuck! Are you kidding me? His closet isn't a closet. It looks like an upscale

store lined with hanging space and shelves. Suits and business shirts all hang in color code. Expensive shoes are all neatly in rows, too. Dear God. For a while, I'd forgotten he was rich. I feel my apprehension rise and I go to the large set of drawers. I slide the top drawer out and frown. There's at least thirty expensive brand name watches all laid out on display. Why would you need that many watches? I pull out the next drawer in a rush and find at least a hundred ties all neatly rolled up in perfect rows. I shake my head and go to the third drawer. I take out two pairs of boxer shorts and two T-shirts. I walk out of the closet, close the door and I notice another door next to it. What's in here? I open it to find a closet, a mirror of his, but empty. This is the wardrobe of Cameron's future wife. I frown and walk in and look around. It has the same beautiful shelving, wall-to-wall mirrors and drawers, a plush carpet... but no wife.

Sadness overwhelms me and I think back to the ad in the classifieds — how different things could have been... if only...

I walk back into the bathroom feeling very rejected, and hop under the hot water, lost in my thoughts. I don't know if it's because I'm so exhausted or because I have realized just how much I stand to lose when the truth comes out, but I feel like the weight of the world is on my shoulders.

This isn't how it was supposed to go.

A strip club, me working for him, and risking my job just by being here, falling in love...

I'm acting happy and carefree when all I want to do is beg on my hands and knees for him to accept Owen and for the three of us to make a go of it. What seems like a long time later, I feel Cam get in the shower behind me. He takes me in his large arms and holds me close, his large muscular body cradling mine. "You tired, Bloss?" he asks as he starts to soap up my body.

Unable to think through my fragile mind, I nod as I put my head on his chest and he washes my back.

"It's okay. We're home now, baby," he whispers above me with a gentle kiss.

With his arms around me and the hot water running over the two of us, I feel myself fall further into the abyss of Heaven. Unfortunately, with it comes a sense of dread.

There is a lot at stake here.

I fear it's more than my poor heart can survive.

"Good morning, Dr. Stanton." The surgery nurse smiles.

"Good morning," he replies chirpily to everyone as he approaches the group. Wearing navy scrubs and a hat, this is still most definitely my favorite outfit that Cameron wears.

It's surgery day and the interns are watching from the station. I'm in the operating room as an assistant. We've all taken turns and today it just happens to be mine. We are in the changeover room where patients say goodbye to their loved ones. I left Cameron's in darkness during the early hours of this morning when he got up to go to the gym. Now at work, I'm feeling very jumpy indeed. What if someone discovers we went away with each other?

What if someone saw us?

Would I get sacked from my job if they did? I glance around at the other people in the room. Can they tell that we are sleeping together from our body language? My heart is hammering in my chest.

God, what a fuckup my life is. Don't talk to him at all. Just say nothing. It's safer.

The patient—an overweight man in his early fifties—is wheeled in with his wife walking behind.

"The big day is finally here. This is John, everyone." Cameron tells us through a smile.

"Hello, John," we all reply. Cameron takes the man's hand in his. John coughs, as though short of breath. He looks up at Cameron, his fear evident. "Just make sure I wake up, hey, doc?" he says roughly.

Cameron smiles warmly. "Everything's going to be fine, John. I do this operation all the time. We'll have you back on that golf course in no time." Cameron's eyes flicker to the man's wife as she wipes her tears with a tissue. The poor woman is frantic with fear. "He's going to be okay," Cameron reassures her. "Say your goodbyes and he will be back with you in approximately eight hours."

"Eight hours?" she gasps.

He smiles sympathetically. "It takes a long time to repair hearts, Elsie. We can't rush these things."

Elsie bends and holds her husband in what she fears will be their last embrace. Cameron moves back to give them space and finally, she gives him one last kiss and is shown from the room, unable to hide her tears. The anaesthetist moves in and explains the procedure and puts the cannula in, while Cameron goes back to holding the man's hand and making small talk about football to take the terrified man's mind off what is about to happen.

This is life or death surgery.

If I didn't love him before.

I most definitively do now.

He was born to be a doctor — to save lives. His purpose is greater than the average human's. That cheeky, playful personality is a mask for a man who is very in tune with the people around him, a man who has a gift to save lives. The empathy he has for his patient has torn a huge hole in my defences.

I will tell him tonight.

With tears in my eyes, I watch Cameron walk up the hospital corridor toward Elsie, his patient's wife. The lump in my throat is making it hard to breathe as I try to remain professional. John didn't survive the operation. On the seventh hour of surgery, after Cameron had done everything he could, John's heart gave way. In what can only be described as the most traumatic experience of my life, I watched Cameron fight for forty minutes to save him. The entire operating surgery was in tears as we watched him fight and fight.

He wouldn't give up.

In the end there was nothing he could do, and it was the nurses who urged him to stop.

With his gloves in his hand, he approaches Elsie and hangs his head. He says something and then her hands fly over her mouth in shock. She drops her head and burst into tears. Cameron takes her into his arms and holds her for an extended time. My tears break the dam and roll down my face. I glance around to see Amber and Scott in tears as they watch, also.

This isn't how it is supposed to go.

This isn't how things are supposed to go.

Two senior nurses, who had been waiting in the wings, approach them and pry her from Cameron's arms to take over and usher her down to an office.

Cameron falls into a seat in the corridor, and with his elbows in his knees and still dressed in his scrubs, he hangs his head.

Oh God. He's devastated.

His pain is palpable.

His partner, the other surgeon, walks around the corner after obviously hearing what has happened. He puts his hand on Cameron's shoulder in sympathy and sits down next to him.

They both sit in silence and say nothing.

What is there to say?

I didn't see Cameron for the rest of the day today. He went home not long after John died. He didn't answer his phone when I called him, either. It's after eight when I pull into his driveway. At the security gates, the guard approaches the car. Oh shit, I forgot about this nonsense.

"Hello?"

"Hey, I'm here to see Cameron," I say nervously. He probably won't even let me in.

"Is he expecting you?" he asks.

"No. I came to see if he's alright."

The security guard frowns, puzzled. "What's your name?"

"Ashley Tucker."

He disappears into the watch house and I see him pick up the phone. A moment later the huge gates open and he waves me through. I park the car and walk nervously up to the front door. My heart is beating so hard in my chest. I open the door and walk in.

"Hello?" I call out.

I glance around and don't see anyone, so I walk into the kitchen. Where is he? I see the lights on in the backyard, so I open the door and walk out into the resort-like pool area.

Cameron is sitting in the dark on a deckchair with a glass of scotch in his hand.

"Hey." I smile sadly as I walk toward him.

"Hi," he replies flatly.

I sit next to him. "You okay?"

He nods.

We sit for a while in the silence. I'm unsure what to say because everything is the wrong thing at this point.

Finally, I ask, "Do you want me to make you something to eat?"

"Not hungry," he whispers, almost to himself.

I watch him struggle to contain his emotion. "How many patients have you lost in surgery?"

"Five," he replies, emotionless.

I nod.

"Five too many," he adds softly.

I stare out at the pool in front of us. I wish there was something I could do to take away his hurt. "Do you want me to go?"

He shakes his head.

I bite my bottom lip as I watch him. "How can I help you?" I whisper.

His eyes stay focused on the pool in front of us.

"Can you make me forget the day I've just had?" he whispers sadly.

I stare out at the pool. "I think I can."

A trace of a smile crosses his lips as he sips his drink.

"Do you want to show me what this bondage thing you like is all about?"

His eyes flicker to me.

"I've never done it." I smile shyly. "But… would that take your mind off things?"

Arousal flickers like fire in his eyes, and suddenly, I don't know if that was a good suggestion.

"It would," he whispers darkly. Without another word, he stands and takes me by the hand, leading me into the house and slowly up the stairs to his bedroom.

We get to his room and he slides my shirt over my head, and then slides my pants down my legs until I stand before him completely naked. He bends and takes my nipple into his mouth, biting me hard until my head throws back in pain.

Ah shit, I think I'm about to find out what rough fucking is really like.

"Lie on the bed," he orders.

I kneel down on the bed.

"On your back," he commands.

Oh shit. I roll over and lie on my back.

"Starfish."

I spread my legs and arms, and he walks into his wardrobe, returning with silk, navy tassel ropes.

Hell. Here we go. This is not what I had in mind when I came here to comfort him. He's not going to try anal is he? Fucking hell, what have I got myself into? I swallow the fear in my throat, and he ties one arm to one bed post, and the other to the other post. He pulls me tight so I can hardly move.

"Legs open." He growls.

Oh shit. I spread my legs and he ties one leg to one bedpost and the other leg to the other bedpost. I'm spread out as far as I can stretch.

His eyes scan down my naked, spread body, and he smiles as he licks his lips. I watch him circle me on the bed as he lifts his shirt over his head and then drops his pants.

Naked and beautiful, he gives himself three long strokes, and I feel my insides clench in appreciation. I never imagined doing anything like this... but if I can distract him and give him just an hour of relief from his pain, it will be worth it. He leans down and kisses me — all tongue, all suction — and my head lifts off the pillow to try and get more of him. His lips drop to my neck, and I turn my head in time for him to see my eyes close with pleasure. With him kneeling on the bed next to me, I can see every vein and the pre-ejaculate that drips from the end of his thick cock.

I start to melt.

"I can't get enough of you," he whispers before he bites me hard. "Even when I'm deep inside your body, it isn't close enough, Ash."

He starts to really bite me and it borders on too painful as his stubble burns my skin.

Holy hell, I've never seen him like this.

His lips drop to my collarbone, down to my breasts, where he bites my nipple. "You drive me fucking crazy, Ashley."

He sucks deep and I cry out in pain, "Ouch, Cam."

"Don't *Ouch Cam* me." He growls as he bends and bites my hipbone hard. "You're about to find out how ouchy it can get."

I buck and feel the bite of the ties. Jesus, what have I got myself into here? He bites my hipbone again and I pull on the ties as I struggle. He drops his head lower and lower until he's between my legs. I hold my breath. He stills and spreads my flesh wide for him to gaze at.

"You are so fucking beautiful," he whispers. Goosebumps scatter across my skin. This seems too intimate for where we are supposed to be. His mouth moves over me and he sucks as his eyes close in pleasure. He sucks harder and harder, and I buck up, earning a smirk from him as he pushes me back to the mattress. "You're going to come, Bloss. You're going to come so fucking hard, it's going to hurt."

I watch him, half petrified because I'm in a state of pain already, yet half aroused and intrigued. He starts to lap at me, lick me, bite me, and it's all I can do not to break the ropes that bind me. He almost brings me to orgasm, and then doesn't let me have it, pulling back at the last second again and again.

"Cameron," I cry. "Give… it to… me," I pant as I struggle with the ties. I need to break free. He starts to flick his tongue over my clit in what I can only describe as the most amazing feeling I have ever experienced, and I shudder as I pull on the ties and let the orgasm fill my body. I pant as I battle with the overwhelming urge to close my legs.

"Cameron…" I plead. "Untie me."

He rises up to his knees and pushes three fingers into me hard, and my body shudders. Oh God. He starts to work me. In, out, hard, hard pumps with his fingers, and I'm so sensitive from the orgasm, I don't think I can take it. I need to bring my legs together and I struggle with the ties.

"Cameron…" I pant as I struggle.

He pushes four fingers in and I cry out. "Ouch!" I yell. He's deep inside me, up to his knuckles.

"Oh, this beautiful cunt needs a good workout. I can't wait to fuck it." He growls as he works me. I can see every muscle flex in his upper body as he moves.

He hits my g-spot and really starts to pump. I start to convulse. Holy fucking shit. Another orgasm rips through me and my legs beg me to slam them shut. "Cameron, please..." I whisper. "Untie me."

He kisses my stomach tenderly with an open mouth. "We haven't even started yet, baby." He smiles against my skin as his finger softly plays with my hypersensitive clit. I'm so wet, and this just seems too intimate, giving him complete control over my body like this.

My eyebrows rise. Haven't even started yet? What the hell? Oh God, this is torture... in the best possible way.

He rises above me and straddles my stomach, his hard cock resting just above my navel until he starts to rock himself on me. I watch him, his tanned body, his muscles rippling as he moves, his dark, wanting eyes watching me as he pumps higher and higher... until he's over my face, teasing my mouth with his dick.

"What do you want, Ashley?" he purrs.

The sight of him above me and the throb of my sex starts a fire deep inside me — a fire I didn't know I had the ability to bring to life. I struggle with the ropes and I lift my head to lick him, but he pulls away from me.

"No licking." He growls. "You'll take it all."

I frown as he feeds his cock into my mouth and slides it down my throat until I gag.

He slides out with a dark smile and I can't help but frown as he does it again. I gag once more.

"Cameron," I whisper. "You're too big."

"If you can take me vaginally, you can take me orally." He pushes forward. "Open your goddamn throat." He growls.

I close my eyes and struggle with the ropes as I try to calm myself down. He's right. I can do this. I open my mouth and try to calm down, and he smiles as he senses my submission.

"Good girl," he whispers as he slowly starts to work my mouth. "Do you know how fucking perfect you look from up here?"

We get into a rhythm, and the sight of him above me with a sheen of perspiration on his skin is too much. I want to touch him. I want to hold him.

"I'm going to come?" he whispers as he watches me.

My eyes widen. Holy hell. If I wasn't choking before, I know I'm about to now. I nod around him and he puts his hands onto his headboard and really starts to ride my mouth. I close my eyes to deal with him. In, out, deeper and deeper. I knew he was a lot of man to take, but this is reaching a whole new level. He cries out as he comes in a rush... and, surprisingly enough, the head job gods bless me with the ability to take it all. I lick my lips and smile up at him as he slowly empties himself into me.

His eyes go darker and he crawls back down my body, sliding himself into my sex. My head falls back onto the pillow and I moan as I tug on the ropes.

He's everywhere — in my mouth, pulsing in my sex, my neck still burning from his whiskers.

This is the hottest sex I've ever had in my life.

Oh... I need this.

He spreads his knees and slowly starts to work me. I need to be fucked.

"Fuck me," I beg.

He smiles and picks up the pace, and starts to hit me full on. Hard punishing hits that leave me with no option but to lie here and take it. I can't move, I can't clench. I can't hold it.

I scream out and he pants as he hammers my body. Suddenly, he pulls out and is untying me in a rush. I pant as I try to get my bearings, but he flips me over and pulls me onto my knees, pushes my head down to the mattress, and slams into me from behind as he stands at the side of the bed.

And then it happens. I feel like I'm having an out of body experience as my body hands complete control to him. He takes me over as he holds my hips and fucks me like an animal.

I'm wet with perspiration, still with semen in my mouth when he slaps me hard on my behind and pushes his thumb into my behind.

Holy fucking fuck.

I scream into the mattress as an orgasm rips through me. Cameron moans a deep guttural sound as his own climax tears him apart.

We stay still and silent for a moment. I'm in shock.

What was that?

He bends and kisses my shoulder softly, and then he turns my head and takes my lips in his over my shoulder. "Now *that...* was a ten..." he pants. "Good girl, baby."

I laugh against his lips as my body starts to thump in pain. Rough sex with Cameron Stanton is a where the term pleasure and pain came from.

There's not a doubt in my mind.

The day has been long as I stand in my lounge room like a child waiting to be picked up for her first party. I didn't see Cameron all day today. He was in appointments at his surgery. But he texted me at three this afternoon and asked if he could take me out to dinner tonight. He said he knew a place that was completely private. I'm going to tell him about Owen tonight over dinner... and I think it's going to be okay. I rushed out this afternoon and bought a new dress. I even had time to do my hair and makeup. Last night after we had animal sex, and he was so tender and loving, we laid in bed in each other's arms and talked for hours after.

He's a beautiful man and I'm in love with him. There isn't a doubt in my mind.

He knocks on the door and my nerves somersault in my stomach. I open it in a rush.

"Hello." I smile.

His eyes drop to my feet and back up to my face, and he smiles sexily. "You look fucking hot." In one quick step he has me in his arms and is pushing me backwards as he kisses me.

I giggle up against his lips as I walk backwards. "I like this greeting"

He sits down on the sofa and pulls me down onto his lap. "How has my girl's day been?" he asks.

His girl. If only. "It was good." I smile. "How was yours?"

"Good. Average." He smiles cheekily. "It's about to get better."

His smile is contagious. "Why's that?" I smirk.

"Because I..." He stops and slips the spaghetti strap off my shoulder. "I get to take this off you when we get back here tonight."

I smile. "You're staying here tonight?"

"I have my work stuff in the car."

I bite my bottom lip to stifle my goofy smile. He's acting very boyfriendly tonight.

I kiss him softly. "Well, I'll just have to make it worth your while, won't I?"

"You will." He stands and pulls me by the hand. "We have to get going or we'll be late."

"Are you sure nobody is going to see us?" I ask.

"No. But I've decided that I'm going to talk to Jameson tomorrow and tell him I'm seeing you."

"What?" I frown. "No, Cam, I don't want to get in trouble."

"You won't, but I'm not walking away from you because you're an intern."

Hope blooms in my chest. "You're not?" I ask.

He shakes his head. "Nope. Let's go."

The car trip is made with my hand on Cam's thigh as he drives, while I'm having a silent freak out about Jameson. Is this the right thing to do? *He doesn't want to walk away from me.* I'm excited that he doesn't want to end this, but I'm petrified that I'm going to get into trouble. Worse than that, I know I have to tell him in the next half hour.

We pull up at a set of fancy stone gates. A security guard comes out, bends, and peers into the car, smiling warmly. "Hey, Cam. Go through."

The gates open to reveal the biggest mansion I've ever seen and I frown. "What's this restaurant?" I ask.

"This isn't a restaurant." His eyes flash to me. "This is my brother's house. Tonight you're meeting my family."

My eyes widen in horror.

Oh no.

16

ALARM BELLS start to ring. Oh my God. Oh my fucking God. Up until now, I haven't told Cameron about my son. Bringing his family into this as well is the worst possible scenario I could ever have imagined. What if they ask me if I have children? What if they ask me anything about my life?

I can't lie. I'll have to tell them. My eyes widen in horror as I imagine the night ahead of me. This is not the way I wanted to tell Cameron.

He's going to hate me. He's going to fucking hate me.

"Cameron..." I splutter. "I thought we weren't at the meeting family stage yet." My eyes widen with fear. "Why didn't you tell me that you wanted to come here?"

He smiles sexily and squeezes my thigh. "Because I knew you would freak out."

I stare at him as my brain misfires. Freaking out doesn't come close.

I feel sick to my stomach as we drive up a large, circular driveway and Cameron parks the car. My heart is hammering hard in my chest. I'm lying to his family now, not just him... it's a thing now.

What kind of a person am I? Oh my God. I just want to go home.

Two men approach us and Cameron smiles broadly.

"Max and Parker, this is Ashley. Ashley, this is Max and Parker, my brother's and his family's security."

The men both smile and shake my hand and my heart starts to thump. Security? Who are these people?

Parker steps forward. "Ashley, as house policy you will leave your phone here in the security office."

I glance at Cameron.

Cameron shakes his head. "No, she's good."

"Nope," Parker replies. "I'm not breaking protocol."

I nervously take my phone from my bag. "It's okay." I hold it out to him.

"That won't be necessary," a male voice asserts from behind us.

We all turn to see a tall man walking towards us with a little girl in his arms. He smiles. "Thanks, Parker, but we have it from here."

Cameron smiles and shakes the man's hand. "This is Ashley." He presents me proudly. "And Ashley, this is my brother Joshua, and this is Ellie."

Joshua smiles and I see him do a quick assessment of me before he hides it and shakes my hand. "Hello Ashley. Say hello Ashley," he prompts the shy little girl.

I smile as I watch her. She's timid like Owen.

"Hello." She smiles sweetly.

Joshua is tall—about six-foot four like Cam with crew cut, dark hair and a muscular physic. I swallow the lump in my throat. He has a square Jaw, two-day shadow, and piercing blue eyes, and he's wearing a pair of cargo pants with a white T-shirt. He's gorgeous like Cameron, but in a different, rugged way. Jeez, these two as brothers would have been trouble when they were younger. Holy crap.

Joshua gently kisses his daughter on her forehead as she sits comfortably on his hip, and I feel myself melt. What is it about super alpha men and the softness that their children bring out in them that makes all women go gooey?

My heart starts to really pump with nerves. For fuck's sake, and I'm here with my beautiful doctor and his gorgeous, rich brother, and I am nothing but a fucking lying bitch.

Oh please, Earth, swallow me up. I can't deal with this.

I stare at Joshua as I search my brain for something intelligent to say. Nope, I got nothing.

The gene pool these two come from is insane.

Joshua smiles warmly and his eyes flicker to Cameron whose smile is beaming off his face.

I frown. Have I missed a part of their conversation? Could have. I can hardly hear anything over my heart going into cardiac arrest over here. Good thing I have a resident cardiologist present.

"It's nice to finally meet you Ashley." Joshua smiles.

I fake a smile. "You too."

He gestures to the house. "Please, come inside and meet my wife and family." He walks toward the house.

I should tell Cam right now, I should do it before I lie to his family. Cameron pulls me by the hand to follow his brother, but I stand still on the spot.

"Cam," I whisper.

He turns to face me and cups my face with his two hands. "What is it, Bloss?"

My eyes search his. "We don't even know each other yet. Isn't it too soon to be meeting families?" I whisper.

He smiles and kisses me softly. "No Ash. It's not. And seeing as you are the first girl I've ever brought here to meet my family, I thought you'd be happy."

My face falls. "First time?" I frown. "Cam... we need to talk."

He smiles as he takes my lips in his. "We need to fuck, too."

"Cam." Oh God, he's a bona fide sex maniac. "Haven't you had enough sex?"

"I will never have enough of you," he whispers as he kisses me softly.

"Well, that's the last thing on my mind." It honestly is, I'm not lying.

He winks. "Let's go in. You have nothing to worry about. They're going to love you. What's not to love?"

I smile softly as I watch him. He's excited to have me here meeting his family. My guilt runs through me like a freight train.

He deserves better.

I give him a nervous nod and he leads me up the path to the house. Two more security men are at the front door and they wave us through.

"What's with all the security?" I ask.

"They've had some issues in the past."

"What kind of issues?"

He turns to me and frowns. "You've honestly never heard of the names Joshua or Natasha Stanton before?"

I shake my head.

"Have you lived under a rock?"

I shrug. "Maybe." Shit, I'll have to Google this when I get home. What the hell is he talking about?

We walk through a grand foyer and across to the back of the house before we enter the kitchen. Oh my God, and I thought Cameron's house was swanky.

A beautiful girl with long dark hair comes into view. She smiles broadly and kisses Cam. "This is Ashley." Cam smiles proudly. "This is Natasha," he introduces.

She turns to me and hugs me. "I'm so happy you're here, Ashley. Please... come in."

I smile in relief. Oh, she's normal and not at all what I expected with all of this money. She's wearing ripped, faded, tight jeans with a black T-shirt, and her hair is plaited down her back. She's wearing hardly any makeup. I follow her into the kitchen. It's huge with four ovens and a large stone island bench that has ten stools around it. Sitting at the end of the bench is a man—blonde, good looking, and wearing a suit. Hell… yet another beautiful person. I can't cope.

Natasha walks around and puts her hand on both of his shoulders from behind him. "This is Adrian."

I smile and nod. "Hello."

He smiles and stands to kiss me on the cheek, and then takes both of my hands in his as he inspects me. "You're beautiful, Ashley." He smiles warmly.

"She is, isn't she?" Cameron says from behind us.

Oh no. They're nice. This gets worse. They're fucking nice. I turn to face Cameron and he smiles sexily. He gives me that look and I feel myself melt. Natasha and Adrian smile at each other and Adrian winks. I feel like a bit of a freak as they all do their assessment of me. This is so awkward.

"When you two are through being creepy, how about you offer the poor girl a drink?" Joshua asks as he walks into the kitchen and wraps his arms around Natasha from behind.

Natasha smiles. "Would you like a drink, Ashley?"

I nod as I wring my hands nervously in front of me. "Thank you, that would be nice."

"What would you like? Red, white?"

Adrian stands. "I think this is a champagne kind of occasion."

My face falls. This just keeps getting worse. I nod. "Or there's that," I whisper.

Suddenly, three children come running into the room, two girls followed by a boy who is chasing them with a tennis ball. He throws it hard and it hits the eldest girl. She squeals, picks it up, and throws it back at him.

"Dad!" she screams. "Blake is hitting us with the ball."

"Blake," Joshua snaps. "Cut it out."

I smile broadly. I love it when other people's children misbehave.

"Come and meet our new friend," Natasha calls to the kids.

They seem to remember where they are and all file over. "This is Jordana."

I smile and she shakes my hand. She's a pretty girl aged about nine or ten with long, dark hair like her mom, and matching blue eyes. "Hello. Are you Uncle Cameron's friend?"

I'm taken aback with her forwardness. "I am. It's nice to meet you, Jordana."

"This is Ellie." Joshua announces proudly and Ellie shyly shakes my hand. Oh, this one is a little sweetie.

"And this is the crazy Blake man." Cameron picks up Blake and throws him onto the sofa. They begin to wrestle. Blake is around seven years old, I think.

"You have three children? You must be very busy," I say to Natasha as the three kids run back to their chasing game.

"Ha." She smirks. "I have five children." She raises her wine glass to Adrian and he lifts his in return with a broad smile. "This is why we drink the good stuff," she adds.

My eyes widen. "Five?" I gasp.

"The two youngest in two years." She replies dryly. "Three-year-old and a two-year-old, boys. They're in bed, thankfully."

Joshua shakes his head and rolls his eyes. "If you ever want to lose your mind, have two children that close," he grumbles.

I laugh as Adrian hands me a glass of champagne and holds his up until we all clink his glass. "To Ashley the doctor." He smiles softly

"You know that I'm a doctor?" I frown. Has Cameron been talking about me?

"I know all about you, Ashley." Adrian smiles.

"You're fucking creepy, Murph," Joshua says, and we all laugh. "Ignore him, Ashley. He knows nothing."

My eyes linger on Joshua, and I can't believe just how good looking he and Cameron are. How do two brothers seem so different, yet so similar?

Cameron is tall, broad and dark like Joshua, but where Joshua is rugged, Cameron is cultured. Cameron has the whole rich playboy look mastered to perfection.

Cameron walks over and picks up his glass. He grabs my hand, our eyes meet, and I feel myself melt. As long as he is with me, everything is okay.

Adrian

I watch Cameron watching Ashley and I smile. He's absolutely smitten and hangs off every word that comes out of her mouth.

I like this girl. She's different to anyone he's ever dated before. Naturally beautiful, intelligent, and witty, and she gives it back to him. I haven't seen Cameron like this with anyone, ever.

The conversation has been light and natural. She's very easy to get along with and I'm getting flashbacks of when I first met Natasha and the hold she had over Joshua. Dinner is nearly ready and Natasha is fussing in the kitchen. Joshua is doing as he's told and helping her. Cameron is next to me and Ashley is on the other side of him. We're sitting at the kitchen counter still drinking champagne.

"Can I help with anything, Natasha?" Ashley asks.

"No thanks. We got it." She smiles as she bends to get something out of the oven and Joshua's hand drops to her behind, only for her to swat him away with the tea towel.

"Behave." She smirks and he grabs her again just to show her who's the boss.

I smile. He can't keep his hands off her.

"Adrian, shall we have pie or cake for dessert?" Natasha asks me.

"Pie," I reply, distracted by Ashley and Cameron. I can't take my eyes off them.

The sexual energy between them is palpable.

A text beeps through Ashley's phone and she picks it up to read it, immediately frowning.

"That's weird," she mutters to herself. I don't think they can tell I'm listening.

"What's weird?" Cam asks as he slides his hand up her thigh.

"I just got a text to say thanks for my phone bill payment today, but I didn't pay it yet," she whispers.

"Oh, I paid it this afternoon," Cameron replies nonchalantly.

What? Cameron is super conscious with his money. *He is serious about this girl.*

Her face falls. "Why would you do that?" she whispers angrily.

"Because I know you didn't have the money to pay for it," he whispers back.

"How fucking dare you?" she hisses.

I bite my bottom lip to stifle my smile and I sip my drink as I listen.

"Don't how fucking dare me. A simple thank you is all that's needed," he snaps back.

I shouldn't be listening, but I really can't help myself.

"Just because you have money, it doesn't mean I fucking want it," she whispers angrily.

He taps her on the leg and signals to us. I try and act as though I'm not listening. "Yes, pie would be great, Tash. Do you want me to whip the cream or anything?" I ask.

"No, it's good. Joshua can do it."

Joshua shakes his head, smiling with a curled lip. "Whip the cream, Murph," he mouths.

"Can you show me the back yard, Cameron?" Ashley asks as she stands abruptly.

Cameron purses his lips and I want to hoot with laughter. He's going out the back to get blasted.

I really, really like this girl.

"Sure." He picks up his glass and leads her out the back, and I watch as they close the door behind them.

"Oh my God," I whisper to Natasha and Joshua. "She's gone out there to give it to him."

Natasha's face falls. "What? Why?"

"He paid her phone bill and she just found out."

Joshua frowns. "How do you know that?"

"I was eavesdropping."

Joshua rolls his eyes. "Why am I not surprised?" he mutters with a shake of his head.

Natasha comes over to the counter. "Cameron really likes this girl. I haven't seen him like this before."

"You know who it is, don't you?" I whisper.

"Who?" She frowns.

"This is Mrs. Stanton."

Natasha screws up her face. "Who?"

"Remember the girl that Cameron met in Vegas years ago when he lost his phone and couldn't contact her," I reply. "He called her Mrs. Stanton."

Natasha's eyes widen and they flicker between Joshua and me. "That's *her*?" She gasps. "He was obsessed with that girl."

"Still is by the looks of it," Joshua adds.

Her mouth drops open. "And fate has brought them back together." Natasha grabs my hand. "Oh my God, this is it Adrian. She's the one."

I smile broadly and lift my glass. Natasha clinks her glass with mine as excitement fills us both.

Joshua rolls his eyes. "Don't get excited with your fairy tale bullshit. I don't think Cameron has a 'the one'. He'll probably be sick of her in two dates like the rest of them." He sips his drink. "They only just met," he adds.

Natasha whips him with the tea towel. "Will you be nice for once?"

"I am being nice. She's in my fucking house, isn't she?"

Natasha's eyes come back to me. "So, wait, why is Cameron in trouble?"

"Apparently he paid her phone bill."

Joshua looks at me deadpan. "And that's a problem because?"

"Oh no, he can't pay her phone bill. Doesn't he have any idea?" Natasha whispers, horrified.

"I know, right," I reply.

Joshua frowns. "Why can't he pay her fucking phone bill? He has the money."

Natasha rolls her eyes. "Oh God, Joshua, you have no idea, either, do you?"

He grabs her ass and drags her against his hips. "I'll pay your phone bill in a minute." He gives her a pump. "With my dick."

"Whip the cream," she snaps as she pries herself from his clutches.

"You should invite her this weekend," I add.

Natasha smiles broadly and points the spoon at me. "Yes, I will."

"I wouldn't," Joshua adds.

"Why not?" Natasha frowns.

"Are you forgetting that our mother is going to be there, and Cameron will probably be over this chick by the weekend?"

Natasha smiles. "I think she could handle your mother." She starts to serve the dinner onto the plates

Joshua smirks. "I pity the poor girl who tries to take Mom's beloved Cameron away."

Natasha rolls her eyes and then looks to me. "Shall I ask her or not?"

I shrug. "I think so. If he asked her here he's serious—"

"He's not serious," Joshua interrupts. "Calm the fuck down, you two."

Ashley

The children have gone to bed and we are just finishing dinner. It was delicious. "Thank you, that was beautiful, Natasha. You're a really great cook."

"Call me Tash." She smiles. "And this is all a façade."

I frown as I watch her. I don't think I have ever seen such perfect dimples and white teeth.

"Façade?" I frown.

She rolls her eyes. "I'm a hot mess. I'm lucky enough that Joshua earns enough so that we can have a cleaner, a gardener and all that."

I smile gratefully. She obviously doesn't come from money and she knows how lucky she is.

"The house would be pure chaos without them."

I smile into my glass and nod.

"What about you, Ashley. Tell us about yourself." Adrian smiles.

My heart drops and I hesitate. "I'm in my final year of medicine." My eyes flicker to Cameron. "I'm one of Cameron's interns, so I'm really not supposed to be seeing him at all."

Joshua winks at Cameron who grins in return.

"Vous serez le stagiaire le plus chanceux au monde pour me rendre visite"

Translation: You will be the luckiest intern in the world to date me.

I laugh and fire back, "Ou le plus stupide, je ne suis pas encore terminé avec vous. Voyons ce que vous avez chanceux ce soir."

Translation: Or the stupidest. I'm not finished with you yet. Let's see how lucky you get tonight.

Adrian's and Natasha's eyes meet across the table. "German?" Adrian asks.

"French." Joshua smirks. Oh shit. He speaks French, too. I drop my head embarrassed that Joshua has understood what I just said.

"So, you two met years ago?" Natasha smiles as she puts her hands under chin dreamily.

"Yeah." I smile, embarrassed.

"She fucked my brains out," Cameron adds as he shovels a mouthful of food into his mouth.

Natasha and Joshua choke on their drinks, and the table bursts into laughter.

My mouth drops open in horror. "I did not. I'm a virgin!" I chuckle. "C-Cameron," I splutter. "Please use your table manners." I shake my head. "You are uncouth."

Cameron smirks. "You love it, Bloss."

Our eyes lock. He's right, I do love it. I love everything about him. Even his family are beautiful.

"But then..." I hesitate and sip my champagne and narrow my eyes. "Cameron." I bring my hands up to accentuate the word. "Lost..." I smile broadly. "His phone."

"I did lose my fucking phone that night." He fires back. "Back me up here Stan. Did I lose my phone that night?" he asks.

Joshua smiles and nods. "Affirmative. He did."

He points at me across the table. "And I was pissed that I lost your number."

"I was kind of glad to be honest. I think I dodged a bullet." I smile cheekily. The table erupts into laughter again.

This is a fun night. I can be myself and I feel comfortable.

"You won't be dodging anything when we get home," Cameron fires back.

"Ash, I have a charity ball on the weekend. You must come." Natasha smiles.

My face falls. "Oh. Um..." I glance at Cameron.

His face lights up. "Yes! We can go away again."

"You went away at the weekend?" Adrian asks, clearly surprised.

"I took Ash to New York."

Natasha and Adrian's eyes meet across the table in some kind of unspoken acknowledgement.

"Why didn't you take the plane?" Joshua asks.

Cameron frowns. "Because then it would have been a thing and I would have had to explain who Ashley was."

Joshua looks at Cameron, deadpan. "Then you bring her to my house three days later?" He raises his eyebrows. "That makes perfect sense."

I burst out laughing. I like this guy. He's dry as all hell. I clink my glass with Joshua's and he smirks.

"He didn't tell me we were coming here tonight," I add.

Cameron sips his drink and smiles across the table.

"Why didn't you tell her you were coming here?" Natasha asks.

"Because she probably wouldn't have come."

The table's attention turns back to me. "Why wouldn't you have come?" Adrian asks, surprised again.

"Honestly?" I smile bashfully.

"Yes, honestly?" Joshua replies, and I get the feeling that they are all really interested in my answer.

"Because Cameron hardly knows me and I didn't want to be in the position of letting anyone down. Especially him. I think it was a bit too soon for me to be meeting the family."

Joshua frowns, intrigued by my answer.

Cameron smiles softly across the table. "You're refreshingly honest, Bloss."

Our eyes lock and I feel a pull to him that can only be explained as magnetic.

"So will you come?" Natasha smiles. "At the weekend?"

My eyes flicker between her and Adrian. "What's the dress code?" I ask.

"Black tie—"

"But you don't need to worry about that. I'll buy you a dress," Cameron interrupts.

"No, that's fine." I smile softly. "Maybe I'll give it a miss and come to the next one, if that's okay. Thank you so much for the invitation, though."

Cameron's face falls. "Why don't you want to come?"

God. Why is he so pushy? "You go with your family and I'll just see you when you get back." I smile.

"No. I want you to come. I'll buy you a dress," he asserts.

I frown. "Not now, Cameron." God, he's so annoying.

"Don't *not now* me," he snaps.

I glare at him. This money thing is really starting to piss me off. "You're not buying me a dress. I'm fine without one."

"What's the big deal. He has the money. Let him buy you a dress," Joshua intervenes as he sips his wine.

I turn my attention to him with a frown. "With all due respect, Joshua, butt out. This is none of your business."

Joshua's face falls in shock, and Natasha and Adrian burst out laughing. Adrian grabs my hand over the table. "Oh, I love you, Ashley."

"Don't worry about them, they have no idea." Natasha smiles. "They have no idea how it feels to have a man buy you things. You feel owned," she adds.

I smile, grateful that she gets it.

"This was really hard for me to get used to in the beginning."

My eyes hold hers.

"We're about the same size, aren't we?" she asks.

I shrug, embarrassed that I just snapped at Joshua. My eyes flick to him and I can see he's just as shocked as I am. God, I'm a rude bitch. I drain my champagne glass in one gulp.

"Adrian, I have lots of dresses that would fit Ashley, don't I?"

Adrian smiles broadly. "Of course."

I frown as my eyes find Adrian. "Adrian is the family stylist." Natasha laughs. "He's the only one around here with any taste."

I smile, my cheeks still ablaze.

"Borrow one of my dresses and then you can pay for the dry cleaning bill." Natasha smiles with a wink.

I fake a smile in return. "We'll see," I murmur.

Somehow it's now Thursday and I still haven't told Cameron about Owen. It's getting harder and harder every day.

Cameron has stayed at my house all week and, although I have had Owen's door closed, I kind of thought he would catch on at some point. He hasn't.

Today, Natasha and Adrian picked me up from work. I had the afternoon off and we went to Natasha's and picked out a dress. It's weird that I feel so comfortable with the two of them. They sat on the bed while I tried on dress after dress and they worked out what I was going to wear with which shoes and bag. They're normal. Refreshingly normal.

Then we went out to lunch and we laughed like old friends. It was strange having Max, Natasha's security guard, with us. Even Adrian has a guard. It turns out Adrian is gay and beautiful, and I can see him and I becoming good friends. And Natasha... well, she is just so lovely and genuine — the kind of girl I would be friends with even if we didn't know the Stanton boys. I'm still not sure about Joshua. Only time will tell what happens there.

The pressure is amped up, though. Not only have I lied to Cameron, but his family seem to be making such an effort to make me feel welcome, and I really like them, so now I'm effectively lying to them too.

This is a big fucking mess.

I hold the phone in my hand. I'm working tonight and I haven't told Cameron yet. He sent me a text asking me to come over because he was making dinner. We've spent every night together since we hooked up. I dial his number and he answers on the first ring.

"Hey, Bloss. How did the dress shopping go?" His voice is happy and jovial.

My heart flips in my chest at the sound of his voice. I adore him. "Hi, babe. Tash's wardrobe shopping was good. We went out for lunch afterwards."

"It seems you have them wrapped around your finger."

I giggle.

"Natasha rang me this afternoon and told me not to fuck things up with you."

My stomach drops. I'm the only one who is going to fuck this up.

"Cam, I can't come over tonight."

"Why not?"

"I'm working."

"What?" He hesitates as he puts the puzzle together. "At the club?" he snaps.

I swallow my nerves. "Yes, I start at ten."

"No!" He pauses for a moment. "I don't want you going there at all."

"Cam."

"Ashley, I fucking mean it. You do not go there. Call in with your resignation right now." He snarls.

"Cameron, I need the money."

"You are not working there. I'm not having my fucking girlfriend working in a brothel."

My heart somersaults in my chest. "Girlfriend?" I whisper.

"Yes, you are my fucking girlfriend, so get used to it."

"Cam, listen to me. I can't just leave."

"Ashley, so help me fucking God, if you go there tonight we are through."

"Is that a threat?" I snap.

"That's a fucking promise." He growls.

His anger has gone from zero to ten in a second.

"Cameron, you can't tell me what to do. It's bar work and nothing else."

"I don't want those sleazy men looking at you. You're mine to look at. Ring in with your resignation."

My anger bursts. "Need I remind you that you *are* one of those sleazy men, Cameron? I can't give up a job for a man who has a membership at the same club. I'm not that stupid," I yell.

He stays silent for a moment as he thinks.

"Hand in your resignation and I will cancel my membership."

I close my eyes as tears fill them. Why is he making everything so hard?

I need this job.

"Cameron, I can't do that," I whisper. "I need this job. Why don't you come with me and sit at the bar?"

"I'm not sitting at the fucking bar watching other men drool over you. I will end up killing someone."

"Cameron..." I beg.

"Resign." Then he hangs up.

The rain pours down as I stand at the door and knock. It's 10.30pm.

Cameron opens the door, his face falls in relief and he takes me into his arms, holding me close. "I resigned," I whisper. "I'm not going back baby." I cling to him like my life depends on it.

He kisses me and it's the most beautiful kiss he has ever gifted me with. My eyes instantly fill with tears.

Tonight Cameron showed me that I have absolutely no control over my emotions with him. The thought of him leaving me was unbearable.

He kisses me again and I melt into his arms.

He's driving this ship and all I can do is hang on and hope to survive the ride.

17

I LIE on my side and smile at the beautiful man facing me. We're naked and in his bed after a couple of rounds of lovemaking.

This is special.

Every moment with him is sacred.

I couldn't go to work tonight knowing it may cause us to end. I could never purposely end what we have because I know what a gift it is.

His eyes watch me and I smile softly as I run my fingers through his stubble. "What are you thinking about?" I ask.

He swallows and his eyes don't leave mine. "You," he eventually answers.

I smile as I push his hair back from his forehead and kiss him gently on the lips. "What about me?"

"That soft fucking thing that you do messes with my head," he murmurs.

I smile broadly. "That's called intimate lovemaking, Cam." His eyes search mine. "It's new to me."

My heart explodes. "It's new to me, too," I whisper as my lips brush his.

He holds me tight and the emotion between us is so strong — so strong it feels like love, even though we have only known each other for two minutes.

But what a perfect two minutes they have been.

"I don't know what I'm doing here," he whispers.

I frown and push the hair back from his forehead as I watch him battle with some kind of internal struggle.

"What do you mean?" I ask.

He pauses before he answers. "Something is going on with me. I'm acting crazy and demanding that you do things the way I want you to do them."

"And?"

"And that's not who I am. I don't usually give a fuck what girls do."

I kiss him softly. "Why does it scare you to feel close to someone?"

"Because I don't have any control."

"You have a lot more control of us than you think Cameron."

"I can't even stand the thought of one night without you," he whispers as he holds me close.

My eyes tear up. "I can't, either. Why do you think I resigned tonight? I don't want this to end."

He pulls back to look at me. "I'm sorry. I didn't want to tell you to leave, but I just can't handle you working there."

I blow out a breath and roll onto my back. "It's okay." I think for a moment. "To be honest, it's kind of a relief that you didn't want me to go back." I sigh.

He leans up onto his elbow and places his hand over my stomach. "What do you mean?"

I run my hand up over his shoulder and up the back of his neck. "If you didn't mind me working there then you it would mean you don't really care."

His eyes hold mine as his brain catches up with my thoughts. "I'm probably going to fuck this up between us, you know…" he whispers.

"Will you stop being such a chicken?" I smirk.

260

He watches me for a moment and eventually he smiles. "You're right. You'll probably fuck this up way before I do."

Oh man, if only he knew how true that statement is. I giggle as he rolls on top of me.

"I've got an idea." I smile against his lips.

"What's that?" he asks as his mouth drops to my neck.

"How about you show me that animal fucking thing that you do so well."

His eyes widen in delight and he slides his hard cock up my stomach. "That *is* a good idea, Tucker."

I laugh and he slides into me with a sharp snap.

"Legs up." He growls.

I laugh as I wrap my legs around his waist and he withdraws before he slides home deep. My eyes close from the pleasure.

"This is much better than pouring drinks, right?" he whispers as he pumps me hard.

I giggle as I clench and he moans in pleasure.

"Fuck, yeah," he whispers up against my ear.

"You need to fuck me, Cameron Stanton. Really hard. Right now."

He laughs and lifts his body off mine and with straightened arms, he does as he's told.

It's Friday night and we're boarding the Stanton private jet bound for San Francisco for Natasha's charity ball tomorrow night. I feel like we are in some Mission Impossible spy film. There's people everywhere and the children are boarding the plane first with Natasha and Joshua. There are the five children, two nannies, three guards who are apparently the children's guards. Adrian, Cam and me, and a man I haven't met before called Jarvis. Then there are another six security guards, Max, and the other man I met the other night. The children are all playing quietly on their *iPads* and I watch on in wonder. They're so accustomed to flying that they don't even flinch and are paying absolutely no attention to their exciting surroundings.

"Do the kids always come?" I ask Cameron as I watch them all get onto the plane.

"Yes, always. They would never leave them in another city."

"Oh." I frown, distracted.

"Do they always have the nannies?" I ask. They seemed so normal the other night. I would never have imagined all this carry on.

"They are employed, but they only come away on things like this. Tash doesn't like to have people in the house, but sometimes they're needed."

I frown at him. "Would you have a nanny for your children?"

He shrugs. "Depends."

"On what?"

"On whether their mother worked or not."

"Hmm," I mutter distracted.

"I was brought up with nannies," he replies.

My eyes widen. This is news. "Really?"

He nods and picks up my hand to kiss the back of it. "My father travelled a lot and my mother... well, she was always distracted."

"Oh. So... you come from this kind of money, too?" I ask.

He shrugs. "Not this much, no. But yes, I come from money. You knew that."

I nod as another piece of the Cameron puzzle fits into place.

"You will meet my parent's tomorrow night, actually." He smiles.

"Really?" I feel a nervous flutter in my stomach at the thought.

He smiles, puts his arm around me and kisses my forehead. "Yes, really."

I wrap my jacket around my shoulders as I curl into him. I just want my Owen home. I'm missing him so much with these kids around. These last few days have been horrendous without him. Three days to go.

The guards move to the side and we are ushered onto the plane boarding from the back. We take a seat in the middle. The children, Natasha and Joshua sit at the front, and the children's chairs are already laid back with blankets over them as they play their games quietly.

This is another world. "Tell me about this charity?" I whisper.

"Natasha and Nicholas run a charity for mental health."

"Oh." I think for a moment. "Who is Nicholas?"

"He's one of our friends."

"They have raised over thirty-million dollars to date."

"Wow, that's amazing." I smile. "Impressive."

"Tash works really hard on it. This is her thing."

"What does she have to do with mental health?" I ask.

"She's a psychologist."

My eyes widen. "You didn't tell me that?"

Cameron shrugs. "You didn't ask."

"Where does she work?"

"She has her own private practice near their home."

"In LA, where we were the other night?"

"No, near Willowvale, their property. They live there most of the time. LA is just, like, their holiday house. They only live there a few days a week and even less now that the children are at school."

"What?" I whisper. "Are you kidding me?" That mansion is a frigging holiday house.

"Joshua works out of LA one day a week and then the other days from home. Adrian is his CEO."

What the hell? "So Adrian runs the company?" I frown.

"Pretty much."

I shake my head in disbelief. Jeez, this is full on. I knew Adrian seemed intelligent, but a CEO of a billion-dollar company... I had no idea. Natasha is a psychologist and Joshua a pioneer app developer. Cameron's a doctor. I wonder what Jarvis does? The plane takes flight into the sky as my mind tries to catch up on the dynamics of the of the Stanton clan.

Well educated and beautiful.

This money runs deep.

The sun peeks through the blinds we didn't shut properly last night. We're in the Four Seasons on the top floor. I would call it the Stanton floor because the whole floor was booked just for us for security reasons.

I can't believe how the other half live. And what seems unbelievable is that they are really, really nice people. We had dinner last night in Natasha and Joshua's suite after the kids went to bed with Adrian, Nicholas, and Jarvis. We drank expensive wine and laughed. I haven't had so much fun in a long time. The conversation is natural, intelligent, and funny, and I feel like I've finally found my people... just as I'm on the precipice of fucking it up.

Cameron is sleeping and I sit up and watch him for a moment. What a beautiful man he is. He's different to his brother. I can tell by the way he is with Adrian and the others, he seems more in tune, but then I suppose that's a doctor thing. It's his job to be in tune with people.

And he is so in tune with me.

I've never had this. I've never had a man who dotes on me — and he does. My wish is his command. I know it's not his normal behavior by the way the others are all shocked at how he treats me. We got back here late last night and had a hot bath together. We drank tea and I can feel myself slipping deeper and deeper into his abyss. Unfortunately, now I know what kind of a loss I really face. I've never had this happiness, never even dreamed of it. I didn't know it existed, to be honest. I get up and go to the bathroom, and when I come back and open the blinds just a little, I peer out at the street below. It's early morning and a truck is unloading across the street as the sun comes up. I watch the workers unload presumably their first job of the day. On the surface, I'm so happy and ecstatic, yet underneath my nerves are simmering in a boiling pot.

I miss Owen.

Owen is my priority. I have to do what's best for him and if Cameron doesn't accept him then I will walk away… and I will die a little inside because I know how happy we could have been. Of course, I know that I probably won't have to walk away because Cameron will walk away from me. Pain slices through me at the thought. How could I go on knowing what it feels like to be with 'the one' and then not have him in my life? I close my eyes as the horror sinks in.

"Morning, my beautiful Bloss," his sleepy voice murmurs.

I turn and see Cam lying on his side facing me, and I immediately go and sit beside him and kiss him softly. "You sure know how to make a girl's day with a morning greeting like that?" I smile. I run my fingers through his messy curls and try to tame them. "You have just-fucked hair." I smirk.

"Hmm," he murmurs. "That's because I am in a constant state of just fucked with you."

I giggle and lie down next to him. He wraps me in his arms and inhales deeply with happiness and contentment.

"Thank you for introducing me to your family. It means a lot."

He smiles sleepily as he grabs my behind.

"What's on today?" I ask.

He frowns. "I don't know, whatever you want. Tash and Adrian will be organizing stuff for tonight and Joshua will be with the kids, so we can do anything."

"What will Natasha be doing?" I ask.

He shrugs. "Venue shit, I don't know."

"I should help her."

He groans with his eyes closed.

"Yeah, I want to help them. Can you ring her and find out what I can do?"

"No, babe. Stay with me today."

I sit up. "No, you hang with Joshua. I want to help." I get up and get Cameron's phone and scroll through. I dial Natasha's number.

"Hey, Cam," she answers chirpily.

"Oh, hi Natasha. It's Ash."

"Oh, hey Ash."

"I was wondering if I could help you today."

"Oh, that's so nice of you, but not necessary. It's a shitty job. We just set tables and crap."

"No, honestly. I would love to help."

"Really?" She thinks for a moment. "Okay, fantastic. We can pick you up in hour."

"Great, see you then." I hang up and smile.

"Are you really ditching me today?" Cameron frowns.

I smile as I get up and flick the kettle on. "Sure looks like it."

Natasha, Adrian and I sit on the floor at the back of the ballroom. Natasha has her shoes off and we're each having a much-deserved soft drink. It's four in the afternoon, and we have worked our asses off all day long. The stupid coordinator called in sick and then the girl who took her place knew nothing, so we ended up doing the lot. We set one hundred tables, each with ten places. Full cutlery, full table arrangements... you name it, we did it. Adrian had about five meltdowns at the incompetent staff missing butter knives and cutlery. The table flower arrangements were nothing like what Natasha ordered, so her and I did them all again. We both have about a thousand rose thorn pricks on our fingers and have established that we can swear like sailors when forced to.

"I'm too tired to come tonight." Natasha sighs. "Bed sounds really, really good."

I laugh and nod. "Same."

"I'm exhausted. This function coordinating is over the top," Adrian replies dryly.

I lean my head back on the wall behind me. "If I don't eat soon, I may faint," I grumble.

Natasha burst out laughing. "Way to chase you away." She elbows Adrian as if this is his fault. "Don't tell Cam we didn't even feed you."

I smile. "There was food. I just didn't get time to eat it."

"Thank you so much, Ash. We wouldn't have got it done without you." Adrian smiles as he takes my hand in his.

We sit for another ten minutes as we try to get the energy to go home and get ready.

"If I fall asleep at the table tonight, it's that stupid fucking coordinators fault," Tash sighs as she stands.

I smile as Adrian pulls me to my feet.

Natasha looks at her watch. "Ash, I'll send my hairdresser and makeup girl down to your room when she's finished. Should be there about six, is that okay?"

"Oh." I frown. "That's not necessary. I can do it myself, but thanks so much anyway."

"Nonsense," Adrian snaps. He throws his arm around mine and Natasha's shoulders as we walk toward the exit. "Both my girls need good hair."

I stare at the mirror as the makeup girl paints on the last of my gloss red lips. I feel like a movie star. I'm wearing a gold sequin designer dress that is fitted and backless with spaghetti straps. My hair is down and set in Hollywood curls, and my makeup is out of this world. When I knew I was wearing this dress, I even bought matching sexy cream underwear. I'm buzzing with nerves. I'm tired, yet excited, and I've missed Cameron today. I've seen him for all of ten minutes.

"So, this is your lipstick and then this is the lacquer to put over the top. And here is the powder if you get a bit shiny to reapply throughout the night." The trendy makeup girl smiles as she hands everything over.

"Okay." I look around for my purse. "How much do I owe you for this?"

She smiles warmly. "It's all been taken care of. Nothing to pay."

"Oh." I frown. This seems so weird. "Are you sure?"

She nods. "Have fun." And with one last look at me she smiles and leaves the bathroom. I blow out a breath as I turn and check out my behind, once more. I walk out into the bedroom and then into the lounge area where Cameron is standing at the window in a black dinner suit and tie, a glass of Scotch in his hand. He turns and smiles sexily as his eyes drop down my body.

"You look fucking beautiful," he growls in that come-fuck-me voice he uses so well.

I try to stifle my goofy smile.

He circles me as he does his inspection, and I wipe my hands nervously on my thighs as I feel the heat from his gaze.

"You know what that dress would look great with?" he purrs.

"What?" I whisper.

"My cock in your mouth."

I giggle. "Sex maniac."

He brushes my hair back over my shoulder and kisses my collarbone softly. "I'm an Ashley maniac." His mouth trails up and over my neck and then kisses my ear. "You look beautiful, Bloss," he whispers. "I'm so proud to have you on my arm tonight."

Tears instantly fill my eyes, and he frowns. "What's wrong?"

I swallow the lump in my throat. *Stop it.* "I'm just really happy Cam, and I'm scared this is going to end," I whisper.

He smiles as he takes my lips in his and kisses me softly. "It's not. Don't be scared."

"Promise me if something comes up between us, you won't walk away," I whisper against his lips.

His tongue dives deeper and I feel his cock harden against my thigh. "Stop being so fucking gorgeous or you going to be bent over this bed and fucked hard." I smile as he wipes my tears and he seems to suddenly remember something. "Oh, I got you something today."

I frown.

He disappears into the other room and reappears with a small, navy blue, velvet box and hands it to me.

I stare at the box for a moment. "What? Why? I—"
"Just open it," he interrupts.

I open the box to find a pair of gold, filigree-drop earrings with a teardrop shaped gold stone. My eyes widen. "Cam, I don't need fancy earrings."

"I know, but I want you to have fancy earrings."

My eyes hold his. "You're spoiling me," I whisper.

He smiles. "For the first time in my life, I have someone I want to spoil. Let me do it."

I want to blurt out that I love him... but it's too soon and I have to tell him about Owen before I can even think of doing that.

"Thank you," I whisper.

I walk to the dressing mirror and begin to put them on. He walks up behind me and, with his hands on my hips, starts to kiss my neck from behind. I watch us in the mirror and I know that this is my Cinderella moment—dressed to the nines with a beautiful prince worshipping me. I'm going to keep this moment in my memory bank forever.

This is how I want to remember us... just like this.
Knock, knock.

Cameron smiles, and with one last peck on the side of my face, he goes to answer the door.

It's Max. "Time to roll."

"You ready, Bloss?" Cam asks.

I nod, smile, and walk out into the corridor to see guards on every door and exit of the floor. My eyes flash to Cameron in question. "The children will be here alone with the nannies tonight. Security around them is high," he murmurs as he takes my hand.

"Oh." I frown. God, having money is not worth this.

Natasha comes out of the room with Joshua trailing behind her. She's wearing a navy lace evening gown and she looks amazing.

She smiles broadly as she approaches me. "Ashley, you look fucking awesome."

I burst out laughing. How is she so normal? Here we are, flanked by security guards and she is just dropping F-bombs in front of everyone.

"You look amazing too," I whisper as she takes both of my hands in hers to inspect me.

Joshua approaches us, smiles and nods. "Joshua. Look how beautiful Ashley is," Tash coos.

"Gorgeous." He smiles as he gives me the once over.

"And all mine," Cameron interjects with a cheeky smile.

I laugh and Natasha links my arm with hers. We walk down the corridor with the boys behind us, talking.

"How do you deal with all this security?" I whisper.

She shrugs. "It is annoying, but you kind of get used to it."

"It's really necessary?"

"Unfortunately, yes. Joshua has some crazies out there and we've had incidents in the past. He's obsessed with the children's safety."

I frown in question.

She shakes her head. "God, that's a whole other Stanton story. I'll tell you one day."

We get into the elevator and Cameron takes my hand in his. Joshua is in conversation with the security guard who is staying at the hotel. We walk out into the foyer of the hotel and three photographers appear from nowhere. Suddenly the cameras start flashing and we are shown to a waiting black fancy rented car.

Natasha and Joshua are ushered in first and then I climb into the car as the security push back the photographers. Cameron dives in and slams the door shut.

"Fuckers." He growls.

"What the hell was that?" I frown.

Joshua rolls his eyes and Natasha smiles. "Photographers."

"What on earth for? That's just bizarre. And they were so pushy."

Joshua and Cameron start to chuckle, while Natasha smiles sympathetically. "Do you have any idea how refreshing you are, Ashley?" She takes my hand in hers.

I smirk as I realize there's a bigger picture going on here that I don't know about. "No, not really." I definitely need to Google these two when I get home.

What *is* their story?

As the car speeds into the night, I put my hand up to check I haven't lost my beautiful earrings and Cameron smiles as he gently kisses my face.

Cameron

We walk into the ballroom and the atmosphere is electric. Tash knows her stuff and these balls are an amazing achievement. Tash and Ashley have clicked and are getting along famously. Even Murph loves her.

"What do you want to drink?" Joshua asks us.

"I'll have a Margarita," Tash replies.

"Me, too." Ash smiles. "My favorite drink. Great picking."

"Scotch for me," I murmur.

Natasha smiles and her and Ash begin to chatter. I'm distracted. I need to find my mother before she gets to Ashley.

"Back in a minute," I whisper in Ash's ear.

"Okay." She smiles and gives me a squeeze of my hand.

I follow Joshua to the bar. "Have you seen mother?"

He glances around. "No." His eyes hold mine in a silent acknowledgment. "Good idea," he says.

My father comes into view as he walks through the crowd toward us. I laugh and shake his hand and pull him into an embrace. I love my father. He's travelled from Australia to be here tonight. He never misses a function. His flight only landed a few hours ago.

"Hey, Dad." I smile.

"How's my son?" He grins.

"Good. Great, actually."

Joshua turns when he sees our father and grabs him in a headlock. The two of them laugh together.

"Dad, I have someone I want you to meet." I smile.

His eyebrows rise in surprise. I think that's the first time I've ever said that to him.

I lead him through the crowd to the most beautiful girl in the room, and I wrap my arm around her from behind until she turns. "Ashley, this is my father, Robert."

Her face falls in surprise. "Hello, lovely to meet you." He kisses her on each cheek and smiles and then turns to take Natasha in his arms as he says hello to her. I glance around as the three of them make small talk.

Where is my mother?

Suddenly, I see her approach us through the crowd. Fuck it. I wanted to get her alone before she met Ashley.

"Cameron." She smiles as she approaches and I wrap her in my arms.

I love my mother but I know she's an acquired taste with zero tact.

She kisses Natasha and my father.

I smile. "I have someone I want you to meet."

She turns in surprise.

"This is Ashley, my girlfriend." I take Ashley's hand in mine and my mother raises a brow.

"Girlfriend," she repeats with surprise. "And when were you going to tell me this, Cameron?"

"I'm telling you now. Ashley, this is Margaret, my mother."

My mother's eyes drop to Ashley and she looks her up and down.

Ashley shrivels under her glare and I feel my protective instincts kick in.

"Hello, nice to meet you." Ashley smiles.

Mother puts her hand out and shakes Ash's hand with a fake smile. "Likewise."

A frown crosses Ashley's face and my father interjects, sensing my mother's lack of manners.

"Ashley, what do you do for work?" he asks politely.

"I'm a final year med student," she replies meekly as her eyes find mine across the group.

I smile and nod as my fury begins to rise.

I bend down. "A word, Mother," I whisper in her ear as I pull her over to the wall.

"What is it?" she snaps.

"What was with that greeting to Ashley?" I snap.

She frowns in disgust. "You introduce someone to me as your girlfriend and expect me to play happy families? Forget it. How dare you not tell me you were seeing someone? It's the height of rudeness. I should know everything that is going on with you." She sneers.

"Let me make something very clear to you: Ashley is important to me and you will be fucking nice to her."

"I'll do nothing of the sort. She looks cheap. Where did you meet her? In a trailer park?" She looks around the room to escape my penetrating glare.

"Listen here… I mean it. You better behave yourself." I growl.

Joshua walks over and my mother smiles and kisses him. "Oh, Joshua, talk to your brother. He's picked up God knows who."

Joshua rolls his eyes. "Cut the shit, Mom. Ashley's nice."

"You don't even fucking know her." I sneer. I swear to God, if she's rude one more time, I'm going to lose it.

"Mind your language, Cameron," she snaps. "How long have you known her?"

"I met her years ago and we lost touch. She's only just came back to me."

She smiles slyly. "Well, let's just see how long she lasts, shall we?" She walks back through the crowd to Ashley. "We do know your track record with women."

Joshua rolls his eyes.

"I swear to God, if she ruins Ashley's night, it's fucking go time."

Joshua smirks. "Look at you getting all protective."

I clench my jaw as I watch my mother's fangs come out as she talks to Ashley across the room.

"You really like her don't you?" he asks.

I nod once. I don't even know how to verbalize how I feel about her.

He pats me on the shoulder. "This could be it, mate."

I raise a sarcastic brow.

"Maybe she's the one." He smirks sarcastically.

"Fuck off, will you?" I reply flatly. He walks back to the group and I stand and watch them all talk.

She's the one, alright. I knew it five years ago.

I know it more than ever now.

The night has been fun, but it's coming to an end. Ashley, Natasha, and Adrian are dancing and laughing like they have known each other forever. I stand and watch them from my spot near the bar.

"You can't take your eyes off her, can you?" Joshua asks.

"Hardly."

"She's beautiful."

"I know." I smile as I sip my drink.

He watches her for a moment. "It's a weird feeling, isn't it?"

I nod, knowing that he knows exactly how I'm feeling.

He's obsessed with Natasha and always has been.

"How can you be with so many women and feel nothing, only to then meet one woman who makes you feel everything?" I ask.

"I don't know." He thinks for a moment. "Wait till you have kids one day, mate. Then you're totally fucked. Your heart doesn't even beat inside your body anymore. It belongs to them."

I frown. It doesn't feel like it is now.

Ashley turns and sees me, and her face breaks into a broad smile. She wiggles her finger for me to go to her. I down my drink, put my glass on the bar and walk over to take her in my arms. We sway to the music in a slow waltz. She leans up and kisses me. "What an amazing night." She smiles.

"It has been."

"Your mother hates me."

"My mother hates everyone. Pay her no attention."

"That's what Tash said." She smiles hopefully.

Joshua comes and joins the group. He takes Natasha in his arms and they kiss tenderly.

Ashley smiles as she watches them. "God, those two are so in love, aren't they?"

I smile as I watch them. "Since they were kids."

Her face falls in surprise. "They fell in love when they were kids?"

I nod as I watch them laugh together. "They fell in love as kids and then couldn't be together. They reconnected in their late twenties."

Ashely smiles in wonder as she watches them. "Sounds so romantic."

"They've got one of the most incredible love stories. They've been to Hell and back. They adore each other."

She frowns and then looks up at me, smiling softly. "I adore you."

I bend and take her lips in mine. "You ready to go home, Ashley Tucker, my all night fucker?"

She laughs out loud and I spin her around.

"With a romantic line like that, how can I resist?" she replies.

"Well, I am a three in the romance category, remember?" I raise a brow.

"Five." She smirks.

We continue to sway to the music. "I've been upgraded to a five?"

She kisses me and then smiles softly, pulling my ear down to her mouth. "Maybe a seven, but don't tell anyone," she whispers. "I don't want it to get out on the street."

I laugh. This woman kills me. "How about I take you home where I know I can give you a ten?"

She licks her lips and smiles up at me, with those big beautiful eyes shining.

I need to bury myself deep inside this woman tonight.

Fuck. I can't get enough.

I can't get close enough.

I push my hips forward so she can feel how hard I am for her.

"Do you want to fuck me, Cam?" she whispers sexily.

"You know I do."

She smiles as her eyes drop to my lips. "My body is yours. You just have to take it."

I raise an eyebrow. I want her body. I want all of her body. That beautiful fucking ass is on my hit list.

"We're going home, Bloss. I need me some supper."

I stand at the end of the bed. My cock is thumping at the sight of her lying naked and spread waiting for me. Only a small lamp lights the room. Ashley's writhing around with arousal as she watches me slowly take my suit off. I undressed her first. I've been waiting to do it all night. I undo my bowtie as my eyes hold hers and she smiles

276

sexily as I throw it aside. Then I open my shirt button by button, and then slide off my pants. I've never been so hard, so hot for one woman in my life.

This is as much mental as it is physical.

I drop to my knees at the side of the bed. I need to worship every inch of this woman who can make me feel this way. I open her legs and spread her pink flesh in front of me.

Perfection.

Unable to help it, I slide I finger in and feel her clench around me. My cock pumps in appreciation.

"Cameron," she whimpers.

Our eyes lock, and in some unspoken way, I know she feels the same. "I know, baby," I whisper. "I know."

I drop my head and inhale her scent deeply, my eyes closing in ecstasy. My tongue darts out for a taste, just a taste of Heaven that only she can give me.

I lick deeper and then I have to suck. I can't help it. I become almost violent as I take her hard. Her hands drop to the back of my head and she moans in pleasure.

I smile against her. It's going to be one hell of a long, hard night.

Ashley

I sit at the table at my house with my heart hammering in my chest. It's Monday night. We're at my house and Cameron has just cooked us dinner. Owen gets home in the morning and I have to tell Cam now. We're inseparable and I've never felt closer to anyone before. We flew in late last night, and then today we worked. He was in his surgery today, so I didn't see him. The days are long without him. It's just assumed now that we will spend every night together. It's what feels natural — what feels right. My heart is about to escape my chest as I watch him over the table.

"Cam, I have to talk to you."

"What about?"

I pause as I watch him. *Please handle this well. Please, please handle this well.*

"There's something I haven't told you about me."

He frowns. "Go on."

My mouth is suddenly as dry as sandpaper and I can't speak. How do I say this?

"I want you to know that it doesn't change who I am. Who... who we are?" I stammer.

"What are you going on about?"

"I have a son."

His face drops. "What?"

"I said I have a son."

His eyes widen in horror and he stands violently with his glass in his hand. "What the hell do you mean you have a son?" He growls. "Where is he?"

"He's been at his grandmother's for twelve days. He gets back tomorrow," I push out in a rush.

He runs his hand though his hair. "How old is he?"

My eyes tear up. "He's four."

Fury fills his face. "You had a fucking child after we were together?"

I nod.

He throws his wineglass at the wall and it smashes everywhere.

"Cameron, calm down," I whisper through tears. I've never seen anyone so furious.

He storms toward the door.

"Cameron, wait!" I cry.

"I don't do kids, Ashley. How could you not tell me this?"

"This doesn't change anything between us..."

He stops on the spot and screws his face up, as if I'm an idiot. "This changes every fucking thing." He grabs his coat and rushes out the front door, slamming it behind him.

The tears run down my face in shock.

278

"Cameron," I whisper in the silence. "Come back."

18

P URPOSE IS a funny thing. Last week I spent my time with a man and it felt like it was exactly what I was supposed to be doing — as if fate had stepped in and taken care of everything for me.

Yet this week, I will be spending my time with a little man who is the reason I am here.

He's my purpose.

He's my world. The make believe world I had up until yesterday was just a smoke screen, an optical illusion of happiness.

Cameron doesn't even know who I really am.

Last week I arranged to take the day off work today. Now I sit in the crowded arrival lounge at LAX airport, deep in thought. I'm an hour early. I couldn't sit still at home. Cameron didn't come back last night and he didn't answer his phone when I called him after a few hours, either.

The more I think about it, the angrier I become. He has no right to judge me the way he did.

He had no fucking right to smash a wine glass in anger because he wasn't getting his way.

Distraught, disappointed, and unable to go to sleep in the coldest bed of all, I stayed up and cleaned my house from top to bottom in celebration for my two favorite people arriving home today.

My people.

My real people.

"Coffee for Ashley," the girl calls.

I smile and step forward as I take my coffee, and then I go and sit near the window and stare out over the runway.

I need to talk to him. There's so much to say. I take out my phone and stare at it for a moment. I'm not playing games. I was in the wrong and I know it. I should have told him, but I didn't expect to fall in love, or that he would return my feelings. I didn't know the connection we had would escalate at the rate it did. We were together for a total of ten days, for Heaven's sake. Every day I knew I had to tell him and every day I chickened out.

I deserve this.

I click on his name and hit call. It rings and then goes to voicemail. I close my eyes, knowing he rejected the call.

I leave a message anyway. "Cameron, it's me." I pause for a moment as I look around. "I need to talk to you, Cam. I need to explain a few things." My eyes tear up. "Call me back... please," I push out over the lump in my throat. "Can you come over tonight after work?" I glance around and then realize where I am and swipe my tears away angrily. "See you later, I hope." I hang up. I blow out a deflated breath.

I did it. I just hope he comes over tonight before I have to see him at work tomorrow.

"Mommy!" Owen calls as he runs and jumps into my arms. I laugh as he nearly knocks me off my feet, and I squeeze him tight.

"Oh, baby. I missed you so much," I whisper as I start to kiss him all over his face and hold him close.

I feel myself instantly relax and I know I'm going to be alright... because the only man that matters in my life is Owen.

I stand and grab Jenna in an embrace. "Oh, I've missed you, Jen." I smile through tears.

She stands back and cups my face as she studies me. "Are you okay?" she asks.

I smile through my tears. "I will be."

She frowns.

I take Owen's bag from him and sling it over my shoulder. "We got a lot to talk about, kiddo." I smile as I take his hand. "Let's go get your suitcase."

It's 3pm and I lick my ice cream as I walk down the street holding hands with Owen. I've just dropped off Natasha's dress at the drycleaners she told me she uses. I may as well get that out of the way.

Owen and I are eating our way through the city this afternoon, and I can't stop smiling.

He's home. My little man is home.

"Ashley?" I hear a woman's voice call.

I turn and see Margaret, Cameron's mother standing behind me.

Fuck.

My face drops. "Oh, hello, Margaret."

She fakes a smile as her eyes drop to Owen and then back up to me, and then back to Owen. Oh damn it. Of all the people to see.

"I thought that was you." She smiles. "What are you doing in this neck of the woods?"

"Ah..." I hesitate. "I just dropped the dress from the weekend at the drycleaners."

She smiles as she studies Owen, her calculating eyes rising back up to me. "Yes, that's where I am heading, too."

"Nice to see you, Margaret," I lie. I've got to get away from this bitch. She gives mother-in-law from hell a whole new meaning.

"And who is this?" She smiles down at Owen.

I swallow the lump in my throat. "This is Owen." I hesitate. "My son."

Her mouth drops open as she frowns. "I didn't realize you had a son."

I fake a smile. "Yes." I look down at the little angel looking up at me. "I have the best son in the whole world."

Owen beams as he looks between us and swings our linked hands in glee.

"How lovely," she replies falsely.

"Nice to see you, Margaret, but I'm in a rush. Sorry." I smile and I nearly pull Owen's arm out its socket.

She stands still on the spot as she watches me walk away. I get around the corner and practically run to the car with my heartbeat ringing in my ears.

That woman is pure evil.

Cameron

I sit in my parked car at the hospital. I'm just getting back from the children's hospital. I click on the voice message I rejected this morning and listen.

It's Ashley. The sound of her voice brings with it a heavy feeling. "Cameron, it's me." There's a pause. "I need to talk to you Cam. I need to explain a few things." I blow out a breath as I listen. "Call me back please." She's crying, I can hear it in her voice. "Can you come over tonight after work please?" I listen as I pinch the bridge of my nose. I can't stand to hear her upset. "See you later… I hope." The line goes dead.

I blow out a deep breath and drag my hand down my face. I'm gutted.

I had plans for us. Plans for us to have a future… and then she just throws it in that she's done it all already with someone else and there's a kid as evidence.

I shake my head and with renewed determination, I get out and slam my door shut.

I've had a shit day. I had to work with Amber who is now openly flirting and laughing at everything I say in front of patients. I'm about to grab her in a chokehold. I'm not in the mood for her shit. I'm her fucking boss for Christ's sake.

I walk through reception and see Mia. I quickly turn to go into the elevator, but she sees me.

"Cameron?" she calls.

Shit. I stop and turn to face her. "Hi."

She's all flushed with big tits in my face wearing that tight nurse uniform. "Where have you been? I haven't heard from you in a couple of weeks."

I scratch my head awkwardly. "I've been busy."

"Too busy for your favorite girl?" She smirks.

I smile. Mia is the most uncomplicated woman I know. We fuck. We've fucked for a long time. No strings. No feelings… just as it should be. "Never." I smirk.

"Do you want to catch up later?"

I purse my lips as I consider her offer. "I'm not in the mood, Moo," I reply.

She frowns. "Since when are you not in the mood?"

"Since today." I sigh.

"I can put you in the mood. I'm an excellent stress reliever."

I smile as my eyes drop to the floor. Maybe that's just what I need?

"We'll see. I might call you later," I reply as I walk into the elevator.

She smiles and goes up onto her toes with excitement. "I'll look forward to it," she calls after me.

I get into the elevator and I'm grateful when the doors close on her. At the back of the elevator an elderly couple holding hands smile, and I nod in acknowledgement. Great. Old people. Happy, in love old people. Just what I fucking need.

I want to go home and get to the gym. This day can't end soon enough. Now I know why Ashley had to have today off. She had to pick up her son from the airport. I feel the fury boil in my gut.

I'm so angry with her, I can't see straight. I don't even know her. I haven't the slightest idea who she really is. There I was being all soppy and honest and fucking pathetic, and she's been lying to me through her teeth.

The elevator opens and I walk down the hall to my office. Well, I gave the relationship thing a crack for the first time and got burned and that's it. I'm not doing that again.

Sex is a lot easier than this bullshit.

I walk into my office and sit down. My phone rings and I glance at the screen. Joshua.

I answer. "Hey."

"Hey, mate. Can you swing past my office on your way home?"

I frown. "Why?"

"I got some shit I need you to sign for the settlement."

"Fuck, man. I've had a prick of a day. Can't it wait until tomorrow?" Joshua and I are co-investing in some property.

"What's up your ass?" he asks.

"Nothing. I'm tired," I snap.

"Just come in for two minutes. I'll have the paperwork ready."

I roll my eyes. "Fine." I hang up.

Two hours later, I walk into Joshua's office on the top floor.

It's just after six and most of the staff have gone home for the day. He's sitting at his desk when I walk in.

"Where's this document that couldn't wait a fucking day?" I roll my eyes as I sit at his desk.

Joshua fakes a smile and holds his pen in his hand as he gestures to the leather sofa in the corner. My mother is sitting there. I didn't see her as I walked in.

"Mom?" I frown. "Sorry, I didn't see you there."

She stands, walks over and kisses my cheek. "Hello, darling." She puts her hands on both of my cheeks and looks at me. "Are you alright, dear?"

My stomach drops. I never could hide my emotions from her. "Yes, fine." I sigh.

She walks over and stands near the window and looks out. I frown at Joshua. *What's she doing?*

He shrugs.

"I ran into Ashley today, Cameron."

My jaw clenches and my eyes flicker to Joshua. "Did you?" I reply flatly.

"Yes. She was dropping off Natasha's dress at the dry cleaners."

I stay silent as my eyes drop to the floor.

"She had a child with her. Her son."

I roll my eyes. Here we go.

Joshua frowns in question. "Ashley has a son?"

"Yes. I only found out last night," I reply.

He widens his eyes. "Fuck," he whispers to himself.

"How well do you know Ashley?" she asks.

"Not as well as I thought, clearly. I didn't know she had a son." I walk over and look out the window at the street way below.

"The child is yours, Cameron."

I turn to her. "What?" I frown.

She raises her chin defiantly. "I'll bet my life on it."

"He's not. No way. That's ridiculous—" I huff.

"What the hell are you on about, Mother?" Joshua interrupts.

"You met her before?" she asks.

"Yes, but..."

"The child would be four or five then? And he just so happens to be the spitting image of you at his age."

I frown as the room starts to spin beneath me.

"It's… it's not possible," I stutter.

"I'm telling you. He is the spitting image of Blake."

"Well, then maybe he's Joshua's, because I wore a condom," I yell.

She withers and folds her arms. "You're upset."

"And why the hell do you think that would be?" I yell. "You trick me over here to tell me I have a son I don't know about." I shake my head and throw my hands in the air. "I'm fucking thrilled."

I turn to Joshua. "Do you have something for me to sign or not?"

Joshua shakes his head as he stares at the floor, stunned. He's as rattled as I am.

I shake my head in disgust. "See you both later." I walk out and head down to my car in the underground parking lot. The sound of furious blood pumping hard throughout my body is deafening and I rest my head in my hands as I sit in the darkened car, trying desperately to calm down.

When did I meet her in Vegas exactly?

I try to do the math and work backwards. I've no idea how long ago it was. Years, I know that much. How will I find out? I think for a moment, but my brain is so rattled, I can't think straight. I get out my phone and flick through to the advertisement in the classifieds when I was searching for her. The date was 2012. Nearly five years ago, exactly.

I frown. Mother said Ashley's son was four or five.

I stare into the darkness for a while as I think.

Fuck.

I start my car and slowly drive from the parking lot to end up sitting at the end of the driveway.

What now?

Ashley

I pace in the lounge room as I glance out at the street. Owen, Jenna, and I have just had dinner and I'm wondering if I should call Cameron again. My son is playing *Lego* in the lounge room and Jenna is reading a book beside him. I feel sick to my stomach.

Why won't Cameron just call me?

A car pulls up outside the front of the house, and I peer through the sheer curtains to see the familiar *Aston Martin* parking.

My heart beats faster. Holy hell.

I quickly walk out the back to the lounge room and I tap Jenna on the foot. She looks up from her book.

"He's here," I mouth.

Her eyes widen and she bites her bottom lip.

I put my hands over my mouth and walk back out to the front of the house where I peer out through the curtains. Cameron's just sitting in his car.

Shit, what should I do?

I stand for a moment as I try to calm down, only for him to climb out of the car, slamming the door as he does. Before I know it, I've opened the front door and he is standing at the bottom of the steps.

Our eyes meet and regret kicks me hard.

He frowns in pain. "Is he mine?" he whispers.

I nod as tears fill my eyes. "Yes."

He stares at me blankly.

"We need to talk, Cam," I whisper.

"I have nothing to say to you."

My breath catches, and the screen door slams shut behind me. I turn to see Owen walk out. My eyes turn to Cameron and his face drops in horror.

Owen is the image of his father. The same dark hair with a curl. Same eyes. Same skin.

I rub the top of Owen's head. "Owen, baby. I'd like you to meet my friend." Owen smiles up at Cameron. "This is Cameron."

"Hello, Cameron." Owen smiles happily and reaches up to shake Cameron's hand, Cameron fights tears as he takes his hand and shakes it.

"Hello, Owen," he whispers.

The lump in my throat nearly chokes me.

The door slams again and Jenna appears with the car keys in her hand. "I'm going to take Owen for an ice cream," she announces.

Cameron's eyes are fixed firmly on the steps in front of him, he's in shock.

"Jenna, this is Cameron," I murmur.

"Hi, Cameron." She smiles sympathetically.

"Hello," he answers robotically without looking up.

I kiss Owen before he and Jenna get into the car and drive away.

"Come in. Please. We need to talk."

His eyes finally rise to meet mine, but this time they flash with fury and I'm a little scared to be alone with him.

He walks into the house and I follow as he takes his place in the lounge room.

"Start fucking talking," he orders quietly.

I shake my head as tears of despair fill my eyes. "I don't even know where to start," I whisper.

"How about at the beginning?" He growls.

I jump at his tone. "Don't be angry," I whisper.

"Don't be angry? Don't be fucking angry?" He cries out as he kicks the sofa.

"I didn't know how to tell you, I lied and said I didn't have children on the paperwork. I... I didn't want to get in trouble," I stammer in a rush.

He closes his eyes and shakes his head in disgust.

"This isn't about us anymore, Cam. We don't matter in this equation," I whisper.

His eyes rise to meet mine.

"I knew that once you found out that we had a son, I would become your child's mother and nothing more—the psycho that turned up with your kid." I scrunch up my face, tears still falling. "I'd no longer be the woman desperately in love with you."

"Don't you dare," he shouts as he points at me. "Don't you fucking dare tell me you love me like this!"

"But I do Cameron," I cry.

"Stop messing with my head! He's not mine, he can't be. I wore a condom. I was there, remember?"

"I know," I sob. "One of them must have broke. I was on the injection too. I didn't even find out about him until I was sixteen weeks pregnant."

He frowns, staring at the floor as he listens.

"Do you have any idea of the shame I've carried for five years? I didn't even know my child's father's name," I whisper.

His eyes rise to meet mine.

"I had no way of contacting you. I didn't know anything about you." I shake my head. "My parents were distraught that I was pregnant to a man whose name I didn't even know."

He swallows the lump in his throat.

"Cameron, I didn't tell you because I wanted you to myself for a week." I sob. "Just one week. And I know it was selfish, but it was the happiest ten days I have ever had."

"Don't." He growls.

"This isn't about us anymore. This is about Owen."

He drops his head. "I can't do this."

"You have to."

"I don't have to do anything."

"Yes, you do. Owen needs a father, so you are going to step the hell up and be one."

"Go to hell!" he yells.

"It's time to grow up, Cameron."

His dark eyes hold mine. "I will never forgive you for this as long as I live."

My face screws up. "I love you, too," I whisper.

With one last look, he leaves in a rush and slams the door, my heart physically hurts my chest.

I hear the car start outside and screech off down the street.

Dear God, help me.

It's just gone light when something wakes me from my sleep.

Bang, bang, bang.

What the hell is that?

I'm delirious and feel like I've only just fallen asleep. It's been a rough night. I grab my robe and head downstairs to whoever is banging on the door.

Is it Cameron?

I open the door in a rush to find a sheriff in front of me. My face falls.

"Can I help you?" I ask.

"Are you Ashley Tucker?"

"Yes."

"Can I see some identification, please?"

I frown. "What's this about?" I go to the table and retrieve my wallet and hand over my licence.

"Sign here, please." He points to the signatory line.

I sign and he hands me over the envelope and leaves.

I tear the envelope open and pull out the document.

A court injunction for paternity and DNA testing.

My eyes rise as a cold shiver runs through me.

He's about to get nasty.

19

I SIT at the kitchen table and blow into my coffee cup, deep in thought.

"What are you going to do?" Jen asks.

I shrug. "Go to work, do my job." I pause for a moment. "Ring Eliza and beg for my bar job back. Carry on as usual."

She picks up the letter for the DNA testing and rereads it for the tenth time. "So you have to go to this medical centre tonight?"

I nod. "He's meeting us there."

She blows out a deflated breath and shakes her head. "Shit, this is horrible."

I smirk. "This isn't horrible. This is a relief. What's horrible is not being able to tell your son who his father is." I widen my eyes. "That's horrible."

"What's going to happen when you see him at work today?"

I shrug. "He'll probably carry on acting like a spoiled brat, as usual."

"What about you and him?"

I swallow the lump in my throat. "That's over. He screwed any chance of that last night when I told him I loved him and he threw it back in my face."

Jen frowns and grabs my hand over the table. "He's just in shock, Ash."

"I don't care." I sip my coffee. "I may be a lot of things, Jen, but weak isn't one of them."

She smiles sadly.

"I didn't get myself through med school being a single parent just by fluke. I can do this on my own. I don't want anything from him. He can go fuck himself."

"Far out, Ash," she whispers as she runs her hands through her hair.

"Owen starts preschool tomorrow, remember?" I smile. "That means you'll get some more time to yourself."

"God, that's the last thing on my mind," she mutters into her tea.

"Did you speak to our neighbor while you were away?"

She smiles. "I did actually. We messaged each other every day."

My eyes widen. "Really?"

She giggles. "Yeah, but he kind of wrecked it last night."

"Why?"

"He sent me a cock shot. Why do guys assume we want to see their junk?"

I smile broadly. "Because they're idiots and they think dicks are pretty." I shake my head. "Can I see it?" I ask.

She widens her eyes. "No. For my eyes only."

I smirk and raise an eyebrow. "How was it?"

"Fucking awesome," she whispers and I laugh.

"Why don't you go over there tonight and get an action shot?" I smile.

She smiles excitedly. "Maybe." She bites her bottom lip in thought. "I need some serious laser on my bits, though."

"Try and get an appointment today."

"Yeah, I will." She looks over at me and takes my hand again in hers. "Are you sure you're okay?"

I nod and fake a smile. I'm not. I'm so not okay, but I can't fall in a heap. This is about Owen now and what *he* needs.

My needs don't matter anymore.

I wait in the corridor with the other interns as we wait for Dr. Stanton to arrive. There's a fire in my belly, a simmering ember that is starting to burn. When he served me with those papers this morning, he lit a match inside of me.

How dare he question me saying he's the father? Does he really think I'm stupid enough to try and trick him? He obviously thinks I'm loose and fuck around. I've slept with two damn men in six years, and then he questions if I'm lying about my own son's paternity.

He must think I'm stupid.

More fool him.

The only thing questionable here is his character.

He's a good man, a little voice screams from deep within, and I know it's true. I just hope that one day we can become amicable, but at the moment I'm just so damn disappointed. In fact, I don't think I've ever felt this let down by anyone in my life.

He comes into view around the corner, and I drop my head so I don't have to look at him.

"Good morning, everyone." He smiles casually.

"Hello," I murmur along everyone, without making eye contact.

"I trust you all had a good night?" he asks.

My nostrils flare. Just shut the fuck up and start the rounds, asshole.

"I'm a bit tired from my hot date last night." Amber smiles stupidly.

Oh God, cringe. *Shut up.* Her open flirting with Cameron is really grating on my nerves.

A trace of a smile crosses Cameron's face before he hides it. "Excellent." He smirks. "At least someone around here is having hot dates," he adds.

The group laughs.

Don't look at him. Do not look at him. Don't fucking look at him.

How about I put a hot poker up your ass, dipshit? Does that count as a hot date?

Because it's totally doable.

He starts his rounds and I follow at the back of the group. He's being his usual, witty, fun self, while I'm over here internally drowning in blood from my broken, furious heart.

We get to Gloria's room and Cameron smiles cheekily. "How is my favorite girl today?" He smiles.

She frowns and fake coughs. "Not too good today, doctor."

He picks up her chart and reads it as he softly takes her hand in his. Gloria smiles up at him. I snap my eyes away in disgust.

Watching him here being so kind and fun with everyone while he totally ignores me is hard to take. Maybe I should ask for a transfer to Jameson's team?

Yeah, maybe that's a good idea. I'm going to have to think on that one. The morning rounds seem to take forever and we stop at the café for the usual midmorning coffee where we all sit together. I glance at the spare tables around us and consider sitting somewhere else, but I know it will stand out to the others that something is wrong.

I stand behind Cameron as he waits in line. Amber is beside him, and if she isn't careful, I'm going to king hit this bitch.

"Where do you like to go out Dr. Stanton?" She smiles. "I'm new to town and you know… it's so hard to find descent places to go?"

"Yeah," he replies, distracted. "I mostly go to friends' houses and private parties."

"Oh, really. Are there any parties coming up?" she asks as she runs her fingers through her hair.

The hairs on the back of my neck prickle and I roll my eyes. Please, give me a break.

She's as subtle as a Mac Truck. I order my coffee and see some of the nurses from reception sitting over in the courtyard. I wave and smile.

Thank God, I'm saved. I'll go and make conversation with them. I wait for my coffee and head over.

"Hello, Ashley," they all chirp happily.

"Hi." I smile. I love these four girls. They're older, probably mid forties, and really nice. They're all married with kids and have been around the hospital for years. "How have you all been?" I smile as I take a seat.

"Oh, good," Tracey replies. "The damn plumbing is playing up, though, and a hot shower is hit and miss."

"Oh no." I frown. "That sucks."

"Did you call that plumber I told you about?" Christine asks her.

I glance over and see Cameron deep in conversation with Amber. I come back to the plumbing conversation.

"He didn't turn up and he spent all that time quoting. I just found it bizzare." Tracey shakes her head.

Cameron laughs and I bite my lip so hard I taste blood. I swear to God, I'm going to lose my shit any second.

"Oh, man, will you look at him?" Tracey whispers.

The women all glance over and pretend not to look.

"Who?" I frown.

"Dr. Love." Christine rolls her eyes and points to Cameron with her chin.

My stomach sinks and I glance back at them only to see Amber throw her had back and release the fakest laugh I've ever heard.

"Don't you ever get involved with him, Ashley. He's trouble," Christine tells me.

I fake a smile and sip my coffee. I can't help myself. I have to ask. "Why is that?"

"He breaks more hearts than he mends."

"Bit of a player is he?" I ask.

"The worst kind. He sees more nurses in this hospital than patients. Every unmarried nurse in this hospital is in love with him, and he picks and chooses between them to use as his latest play toy."

My heartbeat thuds.

"He treats them like crap, too," Tracey whispers. "I don't know why they put up with it," she whispers.

I glance back over and right on cue, Amber and he laugh again.

"Treats them like crap?" I frown.

"Yes, tells them straight up that it's just sex so don't get any ideas about trying to snag him as their own."

My heart runs out the bottom of my scrubs and onto the floor in a puddle.

How many women has he slept with?

How many women feel like I do about him?

I was just a number.

I sip my coffee, but I don't taste it. My taste buds are dying by the second along with my pride.

Oh God, this is a mess. I can't sit here any longer. I can't take watching him over there with her, so I stand in a rush. "Catch you later, girls, I have to go make a call."

I rush out of the cafeteria and down to the courtyard. I need to take back some control. I can feel my life slipping through my fingers. I take out my phone and dial Eliza's number. She answers on the first ring.

"Hello, Eliza speaking."

"Hey, Eliza. It's Ashley." I quickly correct myself. "I mean Vivienne."

"Hello, dear."

"Eliza, I know I left you in the lurch last week, but I was wondering if I could possibly ask for my job back, please?"

She stays silent as she thinks.

"I'm so sorry. I got this new boyfriend and I was trying to please him. I made a stupid decision and now he's left me anyway," I blurt out.

"Oh, Ash." She sighs. "Why on earth would you let a man dictate your job?"

"I don't know," I murmur sadly. "Stupidity, I guess."

She thinks for a moment and I close my eyes. I need this job. "Please..." I beg.

"Alright, come in on Thursday night for your normal shift."

I smile sadly. "Thank you."

"Hang on a second, please, Ashley."

I frown as I wait on.

"Ash, I've just checked the roster and we've already filled your shift for Thursday night."

"Oh." I sigh.

"Maybe you could be on the door or something?"

I bite my bottom lip.

"It's just one night and then you can go back to the bar."

I stay silent.

"I really need someone who is flexible, Ashley."

Shit.

"Can you help me out on Thursday night or not?" she asks.

Fuck, I screw up my face.

"Yeah, that's fine," I eventually answer.

"Great, see you at ten."

I smile. "Thanks, Eliza. I really appreciate it."

It's 6.10pm and Owen and I are sitting in waiting room of the medical centre as we wait for Cameron. Of course he's late. He's timed it perfectly so he doesn't have to talk to us.

My heart is in my throat, but Owen is happy enough, playing with his car on the seat.

The door opens and I look up. Cameron's eyes meet mine and he nods once in acknowledgment. "Hello," he offers coldly.

"Hello." I fake a smile and I look to Owen. "Say hello to Cameron, Owie."

Owen glances up. "Hello, Cameron." He smiles cheekily.

Pain crosses Cameron's face as he sees him and forces a smile to his face. "Hello, Owen."

He sits down opposite us in the waiting room and drops his elbows to his knees, clenching his hands in front of him.

He's nervous.

I take out my phone and pretend to scroll through it—anything to not see him go through this. Owen drops to his knees and drives his little tuck across the floor as he makes a tractor sound. Cameron's eyes lift and he watches him in silence. The office door opens and a man comes out in a white coat. "Cameron Stanton?" He smiles.

Cameron stands, fakes a smile, and holds his arm out. "This is Ashley," he introduces me.

"Hi." I gesture to Owen. "This is Owen."

He smiles. "Hello, Owen. That's a great car you have there."

Owen smiles. "It's a truck. Cars don't have diggers on the front."

"Oh, yes, I see now." He chuckles.

"Please, come in."

The three of us stand and walk awkwardly into the office. Cameron and I sit next to each other. Owen climbs onto my lap and he holds his car up to show Cameron. "It's blue."

Cameron smirks. "I can see that."

"So, we are here today for DNA Paternity testing, yes?" the man asks.

"Yes," Cameron immediately answers.

"We will need some hair and saliva sample from both of you, and then we will run it through the computer."

"How long will it take for the results?" Cameron asks.

"We will have the results in a few hours and they will be emailed to you both tonight."

Cameron frowns and I roll my lips as my eyes find him. He looks like he's about to vomit.

The doctor hands Cameron a swab. "If you can just brush it around the inside of your mouth, please."

Cameron nods and takes the swab from him.

"Here, Owen, watch what Cameron does. You're next," I tell him.

Owen concentrates as Cameron brushes it around the inside of his mouth and hands it to the technician.

The man smiles and passes me the swab. Owen laughs suddenly aware that everyone is watching him and he is the centre of attention.

"Owen, open your mouth, please," Cameron says.

My eyes flick to Cameron. *Don't tell my son what to do.*

Cut it out, I correct myself. This is hard.

Owen opens his mouth and chuckles loudly and I hold back tears. If only he knew the significance of this test and how it's going to change everything for him.

"Ahh." He giggles.

My nerves get the better of me. "Don't be silly, Owen. I need you to do this, please."

He lets me swipe the swab around his mouth and I hand it over, watching as the man bags it in a plastic bag.

"Now a snip of hair from you both."

Cameron rolls his lips as he watches the floor. I watch as the technician snips a piece of hair and then pulls out a few strands and places it in the bag. He then moves on and does the same to Owen as he fiddles with his truck.

Cameron inhales deeply as he watches the man. "How accurate is this testing?" he asks.

"If it's over a 95% match it is classed as a positive match. If it is over a 80% match it is a family match, but not necessarily a positive match to this member of that family and further testing will be required."

I nod as nerves begin to flutter deep inside my stomach.

"Is there a chance that this is another family member's child?" the man asks.

"No," Cameron snaps, annoyed at the insinuation, and I shake my head immediately.

"It's a positive match," I whisper and Cameron frowns as he watches Owen.

"Alright then. It's all finished. You'll receive an email in approximately three hours from now."

Cameron stands immediately and I clutch Owen tight in my arms as I look up at him. He glances down. "Goodbye, Owen," he pushes out.

"Bye." Owen smiles happily.

He nods my way and leaves the room in a rush. My eyes tear up. He can't even look at me, so I glance back at the technician. He smiles sympathetically, knowing exactly what's going on here. "These situations are never easy."

I nod and kiss Owen's forehead. "No," I murmur sadly.

"Time makes a difference."

I nod again and stand, placing Owen down on the floor. "Thank you for coming in late for this." I smile.

He shakes my hand and smiles kindly. "Best of luck."

Cameron

Joshua fills my glass with Scotch and ice, and then goes on to fill Adrian's and his own. We're sitting around my desk in my office. I don't care for them to be here, but Murph made Joshua come in from Willowvale to wait for the results.

"It's negative. I know it's negative," I murmur, almost to myself.

"It's positive," Adrian replies. "She wouldn't have lied about this."

Joshua looks at Adrian, deadpan. "At what point did you miss part of this conversation, idiot? Cam knew nothing about this."

"Not telling is not the same as lying," Adrian says calmly.

"Bull-fucking-shit," I snap.

"Agreed," Joshua adds. "I'm with Cam."

I refresh my email again. Still nothing. "What's taking so long?" I snap. "It's been four hours."

The email pings and I close my eyes. This is it. My nerves hit an all-time high.

I open the email.

Subject: Results
From: Testing
To: Cameron Stanton

DNA Match results.   99.9% match.
POSITIVE match result.

Owen Jack Tucker is the biological child of Cameron Stanton.

I close my eyes in physical pain.

The room falls silent as we all process the information.

Tears threaten to fall and the lump in my throat hurts. This isn't how I wanted to become a father. I'm supposed to fall in love, have a wedding and a wife that I love and go through trying to conceive and then the pregnancy... the birth. I'm supposed to know my own child.

Suddenly, what I've missed out on becomes unbearable

I stand without saying anything and head to my bedroom, closing the door behind me.

I need to be alone.

Ashley

I walk into Club Exotic just before my shift at ten. This is the longest day in history. I've checked my phone every ten minutes since the results came through last night. Cameron hasn't called. I didn't see him at all today because he was in his office with appointments. I don't know what I'm expecting, but it was more than this.

Does he even accept the test results?

This is the last place on Earth I want to be.

"Vivienne," my friend the bouncer calls. "Where have you been? They told me you left?"

I smile, grateful to see a familiar, friendly face. "Hey." I roll my eyes. "I wish I left, but I need the damn money." I sigh.

He frowns. "You okay? You seem on edge."

I slam my handbag down on the bar. "I've had the worst week of my life."

"What happened?"

"I found the father of my kid and told him he was his, and he's now my boss and he hates me… and I'm totally, totally fucked," I blurt out in a rush.

His face falls. "Hell. That's hectic."

"I know, right?" I smirk.

"You want me to make you a drink?"

I glance over to the bar. It's a long shift and I do need to unwind. "Yes, please. Actually, make it a double."

He smiles brightly. "Coming right up, babe."

"I'm going to put my stuff out the back. Do you know where I am tonight?"

"I think on the door for a bit and then maybe dancing."

"What?" I snap as I screw up my face. "I don't dance, she knows this." I pick my bag up and throw it over my shoulder. "I swear to God, I do not need this shit job." I growl.

He laughs. "How about I make you a triple?"

I nod. "How about it." I walk toward the backroom. "And keep them coming."

An hour later, I'm greeting men at the door and I'm on my fourth drink. These things are like rocket fuel and I need to stop soon if I plan to drive in eight hours.

"Hello, welcome to Club Exotic." I smile as the men all start to file in. It's a busy night and I can hardly keep up with the large groups of men arriving.

The sexy music starts and another girl comes to the doors to greet along with me.

"Why is it so busy?" I call over the music.

"God, I don't know. Everyone's horny tonight," he replies dryly.

My little friend arrives with another two drinks for us and I shake my head. "No more. I'm seriously getting drunk here."

"But your relaxed, right?" He laughs loudly.

I giggle. "Yes, I do have to admit that I'm relaxed for the first time in a long time."

He winks. "My job here is done."

He disappears down to the Escape girls, and Stephanie walks over to us. "Vivienne, I'm going to need you picking up glasses."

"Sure." I smile. My favorite job.

"You're going to have to wear a dancing uniform, though."

"What?" I ask.

She shrugs. "We don't have enough staff on to cover all these men. If they see more of us around, they're less likely to throw a tantrum."

I glance around at the other girls in their sheer tops and their little hotpants.

"I'm going to get the girls behind the bar to change as well. It just makes it look better if they think there are a lot of dancers on," she adds.

"I'm not changing."

"You can go and tell Eliza in the office then because she's the one who told me to tell you."

I blow out a breath and roll my eyes. "Fine!" I snap. I swear to God, I'm looking for another job tomorrow.

I storm out the back and change into a skimpy pair of hot pants and remove my leather top, throwing on an organza short top in its place.

I turn and check myself out in the mirror and smirk. I do look better in this uniform, to be honest. My bouncer friend comes out with another two drinks and my eyes nearly pop from their sockets.

"You're going to have to drive me home." I laugh.

He smiles cheekily. "Deal."

I pick up one of my drinks and put it onto my tray and begin to walk around picking up glasses from the club. The music is loud and the women are sexy. With the warmth of the alcohol in my blood, I start to smile as I walk around and get on with my job.

I do like it here.

I bend to pick up a glass from a table, but when I glance up, I freeze on the spot.

Cameron is standing with a large group of men, a drink and cigar in each hand, laughing loudly and having fun.

I stand up as the room begins to spin around me.

He's in the Escape Lounge, roped off section. Holy shit... and he thinks I left.

I walk back out the back and throw down my sixth drink as my fury begins to rise.

Who the hell does he think he is? He demands I leave this job, yet he's here to fuck someone else just four days after he left me.

I'm here broken hearted and he's here to orgasm with some random stranger.

I've never been so furious in my life. I storm back out into the club and I feel a hand on my behind. "Hey, Vivienne."

I slap the hand off my ass and turn like the devil has touched me. "Don't fucking touch me." I growl.

"Hey, what's with you tonight, hell cat?"

It's the dipshit that tried to tip me the night in the Escape Lounge. "Don't touch me," I snap.

"I'll do more than touch you. I'm going to fuck you hard." He grabs my hand and tries to pull me down to the Escape Lounge.

I rip my arm from his clutches. "Get your hands off me, asshole!" I snap.

He leans in and tries to bite me, and I slap him hard across the face. He staggers back. I push him hard in the chest. "I wouldn't have sex with you if you were the last man on this Earth," I yell.

He lifts his chin in defiance. "Is that so." He growls.

The bouncers arrive and pull him off me. I weave through the crowd to escape as my heart churns adrenaline through my body at double speed. Shit, I hate that guy.

I pick up my tray and turn just in time to see Cameron take a seat in the lap-dancing bay on a leather couch. He sits back in his expensive suit, drinking his blue label Scotch, waiting for a half-naked girl to rub her body up against his.

Spoiled fucking brat that he is.

Something snaps deep inside. I put my tray down on the nearest table and walk over to stand behind him. I swear to God, I could become Jack the ripper and cut his throat if I had the chance. The song *Yeah* by Usher comes on, and I don't know if it's the alcohol, the adrenaline, or the sheer bad luck from seeing him, but he's going to pay for hurting me.

I slowly walk around, kneel in front of him, and our eyes lock. His jaw clenches in anger, yet his dark eyes blaze with arousal. He licks his bottom lip and I feel my insides clench.

For five minutes, he's mine and he's going pay for the week he's put me through. I climb up onto is lap and spread my legs over his body, then I lean in and take his ear between my teeth and I bite down hard. He inhales sharply.

His cock hardens instantly underneath me. I reach down and grab it through his suit pants.

Rock hard and ready to fuck.

His jaw clenches again and I bend down to rub my breasts all over his face as I grab his hands and place them on my ass. He grabs me hard as I move my hips to the sexy beat.

"Fucking hell," he whispers.

I circle my hips and he grabs me, slamming me down onto his cock. I moan and arch my back, and his mouth drops open as he watches me lean back as though I'm coming. His two hands slide underneath my top and he cups my breasts in his hand, lifting my top to take my nipple in his mouth.

I watch him as my sex begins to throb. I need him. I need to fuck him.

I begin to writhe uncontrollably, and he begins to lift his hips to grind me harder.

"Kiss me." He growls.

I bend down, and as my hair tickles our faces, my tongue slides up against his.

He moans into my mouth and our kiss turns frantic, his hands grabbing my behind with bruising force.

He's going to come.

No.

I break the kiss and stand immediately, smiling sarcastically as I wipe the hair back from my perspiring face.

"Blow your load on someone else, asshole." I sneer.

He snaps suddenly and stands to grab me by the arm. He drags me outside, and next thing I know, he is pulling me across the road to his car.

"Get in the car," he yells. "I told you to leave this fucking place!"

"And you told me you were cancelling your membership."

"Ashley, get in the fucking car."

"No! You don't get to tell me what to do!"

"The hell I don't," he yells. "You are the mother of my child. You will do what I fucking say."

The bouncers come out and run across the road to help me. "Vivienne, come back inside," one of them calls.

"Get in the fucking car, Ashley, or I swear to God."

My eyes flicker between the bouncers and Cameron, and I know that if I do what he says now, I will always end up doing what he tells me....and he will treat me like dirt forever.

This is a power play... and Cameron Stanton just lost.

I turn and walk back in the direction of the club.

"Ashley," he yells.

I turn and give him the bird, and he turns and punches the windshield of his *Aston Martin*. It crackles as it smashes into a spider web of broken glass art.

I walk through the doors of the club with my adrenaline at an all time high.

Holy fuck.

What just happened?

20

I STAND in the hall of the hospital and close my eyes in horror as I get an image of myself writhing on Cameron's lap last night.

Blow your load on someone else, I said. What kind of gutter trash woman says that? Oh God, I've hit an all time low.

Those drinks were just strong enough to take away my brain-to-mouth filter.

I shouldn't have given him the lap dance. I should never have said that to him.

I've stooped to his level and I acted just like a dirty stripper last night.

Regret hangs heavily on my shoulders as I wait for him to arrive.

Would he have slept with someone in the Escape Lounge if I wasn't there?

Nausea rolls my stomach as my mind races a million miles a minute. I don't even know what to think of myself anymore.

The elevator opens and he appears and my eyes slowly rise to meet his.

He looks like shit. Has he even slept?

His hair is unruly, he has bags under his eyes, and his skin is pale. He approaches the group. "Good morning, everyone."

"Good morning," everyone calls back.

I watch him as he takes out the first folder for the morning rounds and he winces. I frown and glance down at his hand. It's the size of a baseball mitt and a nice shade of purple.

Shit, he broke his hand last night when he punched the windshield.

Oh God, I need to do something. "Dr. Stanton, can I see you in the office for a moment, please?" I ask.

His eyes rise to meet mine and after a pause, he answers, "Yes." He looks around at the other interns. "We'll start the rounds in ten minutes, guys. If you want to grab a coffee, go ahead."

He gestures to his office. I follow him in and he closes the door behind us.

"Your hand is broken," I whisper as I pick his hand up and inspect it. "You need some x-rays."

"I'm fine."

I gently turn his hand over so it's palm up. I inspect it carefully. It looks like a rubber glove that has been blown up. "You are *not* fine." I sigh.

"My hand is the least of my worries."

My eyes search his. "Cam, we need to talk." I sigh.

He nods as he watches his hand. He can't even look at me. "Have you slept at all?"

"Not for a few days," he murmurs.

My heart aches for him, and I want to just pull him close and hold him and tell him everything is going to be alright, but I just don't know if it's going to be.

"Are you okay?" I ask.

He frowns at the floor. "I have no idea."

Empathy wins. This is a lot for him to get his head around. "Can we have lunch today?" I ask.

"I'm going to the children's hospital after my rounds. I have a patient over there to see."

"Can I come? We could maybe stop for coffee?" I smile hopefully.

"Ashley, we have nothing to say to each other until you quit working at the club. I can't stand it. I can't handle the thought of you being there with other men."

"Were you going to have sex with someone else last night?" I frown.

He screws up his face. "No. Of course not. Another woman is the last fucking thing on my mind."

"What were you doing there then?"

"I was drinking with friends and just about to leave." He shakes his head as he tries to articulate his thoughts. "I thought I'd get a lap dance to put me in the mood so I could jack off and release some tension when I got home."
I watch him.

"I didn't expect you to be there, Ash," he replies shamefully.

I pick up his broken hand and inspect it again. I rub my fingers softly over his swollen skin and he frowns.

My poor, beautiful man is in pain and the overwhelming urge to fix him takes over.

"I miss you," I whisper as my eyes search his.

He closes his eyes in pain. "Please… don't."

"Cam." I lift his hand and kiss it gently. "You need some x-rays. Let me look after you."
A knock sounds at the door and we jump back from each other. I quickly pick up a file from the desk as a prop.

"Come in," he calls.

Dr. Jameson pops his head around the door. "Cam, do you have a minute?" He smiles when he sees me. "Hello, Ashley."

"Hello." I smile. I hand Cameron the file and go to leave the room.

"Ashley?" Cameron calls.

I turn. "Yes."

"Don't forget it's your turn to come to the children's hospital with me after my rounds this morning."

I smile softly. "Okay." I turn and leave.

Finally, we get to talk.

I follow Cameron out to his car in silence.

I'm not sure how this coffee date is going to go. I'm feeling vulnerable and needy and I know I need to cut this shit out. I should be furious, but I just miss him so much. I want to hold him and tell him I love him. I want to beg him to accept us both.

But I won't. I could never be that woman. My pride would never let me.

My phone pings with a text and I stop to read it.

Hi, Ashley. It's Natasha.
Can we have lunch today?
Don't tell Cameron!

My eyes widen. Shit.

"What time will we be back, Cam?" I ask him as he walks up in front.

He shrugs. "A couple of hours. Why?"

"Will we back here for lunch?"

"Yes. I'm in my office for appointments this afternoon from twelve so I will drop you back here about quarter to."

I smile. This might work out because I can pretend I'm still with him when he goes to the office and get back here at one. I text back.

That would be lovely.
I can meet you at 12?
There is a café called Zooms on Harris Street?

A text bounces straight back.

Great.
See you then
x

We approach his car and I look at the smashed windshield. It's still intact, but totally destroyed. He rolls his eyes and gets in, annoyed.

I get in and slam the door. "What would possess you to punch the windshield?" I ask as I put my seatbelt on.

He clenches his jaw as he pulls out of the parking lot. "It was either the windshield or the bouncers."

Hell, that *would* have been bad.

We pull into the traffic. "You're not going back to that job, Ashley."

I frown as I watch him and screw up my face. "I hate that job, Cameron. Stop making it sound like it's a choice"

"Then why do it?" he barks.

"Why do it? I'll tell you why I do it... to put a roof over your son's head, that's why I fucking do it!"

He glares at me.

"I moved Jenna here from New York to babysit Owen while I work, on the condition that I will pay the rent so she can study from home."

He clenches his jaw as he watches the road.

"I support three people, Cameron, and I'm on a trainee's wage. My salary covers rent and food only. No bills, no car expenses, no preschool fees."

He frowns at me.

I shake my head in exasperation. "I don't have a two-hundred-thousand-dollar car. I don't own a multi-million-dollar property investment portfolio. I live week to week."

He goes to turn the wheel and hits his hand, quickly wincing in pain.

"You need to get x-rays," I snap.

"Stop changing the fucking subject," he yells.

"Stop screaming at me like I'm a child. You need to get used to the fact that I work, and until I find another job, I'm staying where I am."

He shakes his head as he drives. "You don't go back there or there will be hell to pay."

I narrow my eyes and shake my head. "Is this your idea of a conversation? Is it? Because this is my idea of you being a complete brat and demanding that I bow down to your every command."

His angry eyes flicker to me. "Brat?" he yells. "You are a mother and you work in a brothel."

I shake my head. "And you're an idiot. Don't bother going for coffee. We have nothing to talk about."

"Oh, yes we do," he huffs as he pulls the car into a parking lot.

I fold my arms in front of me in anger. This fucking man infuriates me.

"Get out." He growls as he climbs out of the car and slams the door.

I sit for a moment and then he rips my door open. "Get. Out."

I narrow my eyes and climb out of the car and he slams the door behind me and storms into a coffee shop. He goes to the counter and orders our coffee while I take a seat at the back of the café.

I blow out a breath as I try to calm myself down. Calm down. Calm down. My heart rate is through the roof.

Nobody on Earth has the ability to boil my blood like Cameron Stanton.

He sits down opposite me, and his hand hits the table as his jaw ticks in anger.

What must we look like? Him in an expensive three- piece suit and a broken hand the size of a football, and me, a firecracker about to explode.

"Did you get me cake?"

"Yes, bitch pie." He snaps back. "With added arsenic."

I bite my bottom lip to hide my smirk.

He remembers something. "Oh." He fumbles around in his suit pocket and brings out a piece of paper and hands it over. "I printed this out this morning. I need your signature."

I read the piece of paper and I frown.

Births, Deaths and Marriages
Application for name change.

"What's this?" I ask.

"I want his name changed," he replies flatly.

"What?" I screw up my face. "Is that all you're worried about? That he carries the Stanton name?" I push the piece of paper back to him aggressively across the table. "How about you worry about getting to know him?"

"About that." He smiles on cue at the waitress as our coffees arrive. She shakily puts them down on the table. "Thank you," we both murmur. She then returns with my piece of cake.

"I will pick him up tomorrow morning," he tells me.
I frown. "What for?"

He widens his eyes. "To sell him on the black market. What do you think?"

I roll my eyes and pick up my coffee.

"I'm taking him to Willowvale to Joshua's for the weekend."

"What?" I shake my head. "Oh no, you're not." I widen my eyes. He's on crack if he thinks that's happening.

He leans forward like he's the devil himself. "I'll do what I want. He's my son and you can't stop me seeing him."

My blood boils over. That's it. "You are not taking him anywhere with the Stanton children yet. They are strong willed and domineering. They will eat him alive, and in a strange house, he just won't cope."

He screws up his face in disgust. "What do you mean?"

315

"He's an only child, Cameron. He's soft and sweet and gentle, while those kids..." I shake my head and stop to get my wording right. "They're beautiful kids, but the first time you meet him is not the time to put him into a situation where he will be uncomfortable."

"He'll be fine."

I slam my hand down on the table. "And that's exactly why you're not having him. This *he'll be fine* attitude is not how you parent."

"And working in a brothel is?"

"Cut the fucking shit," I snap as I look at the tables around us.

He leans in so that nobody else can hear. "Let me tell you one thing, Ashley fucking Tucker. You brought him into my life. You lied to me about it and you..." He pauses as he sits back in his chair. "Will have no say in how I bring him up."

"The hell I won't." I shake my head. "If you want to get dirty, Cameron, you won't fucking see him at all."

He narrows his eyes in contempt. "I dare you to try and stop me."

I sit back in my seat as a fission of fear crosses over me. For the first time in Owen's life, someone else is fighting for him.

I don't like it.

I don't like it at all.

I think on it for a moment as we sit in silence. "You can come to my house tomorrow and spend time with him."

He glares at me.

"You don't have a backseat in your car, so you can't drive him anywhere, anyway." I sigh.

"I'm telling him," he says.

"Telling him what?" I ask.

"That I'm his father."

"What?" I snap. "He thinks he has a father."

"That's a man you dated. It's not his fucking father." He sneers.

I sit back in my seat and blow out a breath. God, what a mess?

"Fine. Tell him, but I want to be there."

My phone rings and I glance at the screen to see it's Owen's preschool.

"Hang on a minute. It's Owen's preschool," I murmur as I answer. "Hello."

"Hello, Ashley, it's Katrina from the Preschool."

"Hello, Katrina. Is something wrong?" I ask.

"No, everything is fine."

I put my hand on my chest in relief as Cameron watches on.

"I just noticed this morning that when you filled out your emergency contacts, you only put yourself and Jenna."

"Yes, is that okay?" My eyes look up at Cameron and he frowns.

"We need four emergency contacts. It's accreditation policy."

Shit. "You need four emergency contacts?" My eyes are still on Cameron. "Can you hang on a minute, Katrina? I will just grab the numbers."

I put the phone down and cover it. "I need two emergency contacts for the preschool. Who will I put? I only know Jenna in town," I whisper.

"Me."

I watch him think for a moment.

"And Adrian," he adds.

"Are you sure?"

"Yes," he snaps, annoyed. He brings the numbers up on his phone and passes it to me. I blow out a breath and go back to Katrina.

"Um, can I add Cameron Stanton, please?" I ask.

"Yes, sure. What is his relationship to the child?"

I close my eyes as my stomach turns. "He's his father."

Cameron sits back in his chair as the enormity of that statement hits us both, and my eyes rise to the ceiling.

"Next one?" she asks.

"Um." I pause for a moment. "Adrian..." Shit, what's his last name?

"Murphy," Cameron whispers.

"Murphy," I add.

"And what's his relationship to the child?"

I close my eyes and blow out a deflated breath. "Family friend," I reply meekly.

I give her the numbers and then hang up.

I feel like I just lost a round with Mike Tyson. I have effectively lost control of this situation and I feel like packing up and running away in the middle of the night.

I sit and eat my cake in silence and Cameron seems deep in thought, just like me.

"When is his birthday?" Cameron asks.

I smile softly. "January fifth."

His eyes hold mine. "He's turning five?"

I nod.

"He starts school next year?"

"Yes."

He frowns. "He's not enrolled in school yet?"

"There's plenty of time for that. It's only June." I reply as I sip my coffee.

"Not the school that he will be going to. He should have been enrolled at birth."

"He's going to a public school, Cameron." I frown.

His face drops in horror. "No, he's not. Over my dead body is he going to a public school."

"Why not?"

"I'm paying for it, so what's it to you where he goes?"

"I don't want a spoiled brat of a kid."

"It's an education, Ashley."

"With a bad fucking attitude if his father is anything to go by."

He glares at me as his jaw ticks. "Listen to me, Ashley, and listen good. This is a warning. Do not go back to that club. You are bringing up my child. The fathers of Owen's future friends go to that club, and I will not have you disgrace our family."

I sit back, shocked at his audacity. I watch him for a moment and finally reply, "You go there, Cameron."

He glares at me.

Tears fill my eyes. "This is why I don't want my son anywhere near your rich boy culture. In my world, you stay loyal to your wife," I whisper. "You love your wife with your whole heart."

His eyes hold mine. "When I meet her, that's what I intend to do."

Pain slices through my heart.

If he hit me with an axe, it would have hurt less. I stare at his blurred face through tears.

I've got nothing.

I stand and push my chair in. "Let's go." I murmur sadly.

There's no comeback for that, there's nothing I can say that makes that comment from him hurt less.

I need to get away from him.

He's destroying me blow by low blow.

I walk nervously out into the sunny courtyard of Zooms; the place I have arranged to meet Natasha. I don't know if she comes in peace or with a weapon, but I'm hoping since she asked me not to tell Cameron, it may be in peace.

I look around at the busy tables and I see an arm fly up. I glance over to see Natasha and Adrian sitting in the corner.

Shit. Adrian's here. My heart starts to beat at double speed and I walk over to the table. "Hello." I smile as I pull out the chair.

Adrian smiles and stands and kisses my cheek. Natasha gets up and comes around to my side of the table to hug me.

I close my eyes against her shoulder and my stupid eyes tear up. Damn it. Don't be nice to me, I'm on the edge.

I sit down, embarrassed, and wipe my tears as they both look on in sympathy.

"I'm... I'm sorry," I stammer. "I'm ridiculously fragile today."

Adrian smiles and reaches out to take my hand in his. I squeeze it and feel like howling to the moon.

"Are you alright?" Tash whispers, concerned.

I wipe my eyes again. "I am until someone is nice to me." I laugh. "So stop being nice."

Adrian smiles cheekily. "Okay, what's up bitch?" he asks and we laugh.

"Oh God." I shake my head. "You two must think I'm a piece of work." I sigh.

"Not at all," Tash replies. "But we are wondering what the hell is going on?"

I shrug. "Basically, my life is one big fuck up." I sigh and the waitress brings over three Diet *Cokes*.

"Oh, we ordered a salad for you. Is that okay?" Natasha asks, concerned. "We knew you would have to get back to work quick."

"Thank you." I smile and I look between the both of them. "I don't know where to start..."

"At the beginning." Adrian smiles as he continues to hold my hand in his.

I blow out a breath. "Okay, so I met Cameron in Vegas."

"Yes, I was there. I met you that night," Adrian replies.

I nod and smile. "He walked by when this sleazy guy was trying to hit on me, so I grabbed Cameron and introduced him to this man as my husband just to get rid of him." My eyes flick between them as they both listen on. "That started some kind of fun game between us. He was calling me his wife and he was putting bets on what he could make me do. He told me he was a mechanic and I was calling him grease monkey. Stupid shit like that."

"Oh God." Natasha rolls her eyes.

I laugh. "He was fun and we hit it off instantly. I was a total slut and ended up back at his room having wild sex all night."

They both look at me blankly.

"In my defence, I hadn't had sex in two years and... and he was the drought breaker," I stammer.

The both laugh.

"Anyway, we were speaking to each other in French and German, and we just had this instant connection. He took my number and we arranged to meet the following weekend." I pick up my drink and sip it. "But he never called —"

"He lost his phone," Adrian interrupts.

"I didn't know this until just last week," I reply.

They keep listening.

"Anyway, sixteen weeks later, I was feeling really weak and my stomach was swollen. I just felt like shit so I went to the doctor."

Their eyes meet.

"Turned out I was pregnant and seeing as I hadn't had sex with anyone for two years before Cameron or since, a condom must have broken and I knew it was his baby. Only thing was... I didn't even know his real name."

"Oh God, Ash," Natasha whispers. "And you didn't find out until sixteen weeks?"

I shake my head. "So I had to have the child. There was no other option."

Adrian frowns as he listens.

"I was a second year med student and I had all these hopes and dreams." Saying this out loud is making me all emotional and I tear up. "And then this little angel came into my life. Owen."

Adrian smiles. "Do you have a photo?"

"Yes." I smile excitedly and open a photo on my phone and pass it over. Adrian puts his hand over his mouth. "Oh my God, he *is* like Cameron." He gasps as he passes the phone to Tash, and she smiles as she studies it.

"He is. He's like him in nature, too. He's cheeky and intelligent. Gentle."

Natasha smiles through her tears but stays silent.

"Anyway, my family were mortified that I was pregnant by a man I didn't even know the name of."

Adrian's face falls.

"You have no idea of the shame I have felt for five years, knowing that one day I would have to tell my son that I'm a slut."

"You are not a slut." Natasha gasps.

I shrug. "The proof was in the pudding, Tash. I had no name."

Adrian rolls his eyes because he knows it's true.

"Fast forward five years, I got offered an internship on the other side of the country with this brilliant young gun surgeon, and I had no idea how I was going to take it. I organized for my best friend to come with me so she could mind Owen for me while I work, and in exchange I would pay for our rent and food so she could study full time from home."

"What a great idea." Tash grins.

"Jenna is great." I smile. "She's been with me for years before Owen came along and she loves him like he's her own."

Our food arrives and we all take a bite of our salad.

"We moved here and I needed a part time job, so I applied at a bar."

They both frown as they listen and eat.

"Only when I got the job I found out it was Club Exotic." Adrian's face falls.

"What's that?" Tash asks.

"High class brothel," Adrian murmurs.

"I... I just work behind the bar," I stammer. "Nothing more."

Natasha puts her hand on her chest in relief, and Adrian fake wipes his forehead.

"I make seven-hundred dollars a week for two shifts and Owen doesn't even know I've gone. I start at ten and get home before he wakes up."

"So, you do this *and* you work at the hospital?" Adrian frowns.

"Yes." I take another bite. "Anyway, on my first day at the hospital I had to fill out forms and I didn't want to be judged for being a single mom."

"And they would of judged," Natasha adds.

"Yes, you know what's its like. I just wanted to be treated equal, you know?"

She nods. "Definitely."

I frown. "You can imagine my shock when I am introduced to Cameron as the surgeon I'm interning for."

Adrian shakes his head in disbelief. "What are the chances?"

I throw my hands up in the air. "Beats me."

Natasha picks up her drink and sips it. "This is an interesting story."

I smirk. "So then I did something really stupid."

"What?" Adrian frowns.

"I panicked. I freaked out that I had just lied on all of my forms and said I had no children. That's when I heard Cameron say to a colleague that he hated kids."

Natasha frowns. "Cameron loves kids."

"He said that condoms were the greatest ever invention."

Adrian rolls his eyes. "He would say that. That's such a Cameron thing to say."

I blow out a breath. "And then I made the biggest regret of all time. I pretended I didn't remember him."

"Why?" Natasha whispers.

I shrug. "I have no idea. He was gorgeous and happy, and I felt like this loser who he never rang. I wasn't going to turn up with his child."

Adrian grabs my hand again.

"How do you say that to a man? Oh, and by the way, I know we haven't seen each other in five years, but... we have a kid?"

"Shit," Natasha whispers.

"And then it got worse," I add. "I was trying to work out how to tell him. He started messaging me and pursuing me and we weren't allowed to see each other because I'm his intern."

"Why is that?" Adrian asks.

"Hospital policy," Natasha interrupts.

"How did you get together?" Adrian frowns.

I roll my eyes. "Honestly, when I say this story out loud it's cringe worthy. I was at the club and guess who goes there?"

"Who?" Natasha frowns in horror. "Your other boss?"

"Cameron." Adrian sighs. "I know he goes there."

Natasha looks at him in horror. "Does fucking Joshua go there?"

He screws up his face. "No, he likes his balls too much for that."

She smirks and holds up her knife and pretends to cut them off.

I continue. "Cameron turns up at the place, sees me, loses his shit and then demands a lap dance."

"Nooo," Natasha whispers. "Get the fuck out of here."

Adrian's eyes widen in horror. "This really is an interesting story," he whispers. "What did you do?"

I slap my hands over my face. "I gave him one."

"What?"

I nod.

"Oh my fuck," Natasha whispers.

"I've never done anything like that in my life, and then Jenna had to go home because her mom was sick and Owen went to my mom's for twelve days so I could keep working."

"Okay." Natasha frowns as she listens.

"My next shift at the club, Cameron turns up and the chemistry between us is ridiculous. We make out and he rushes me out of the club, back to his house, and we have crazy stupid sex all night."

They both sit wide-eyed as they listen to the story.

"So I keep thinking to myself, I will tell him in the morning, but he springs it on me that he's taking me to New York for the weekend because he wants his weekend that he missed out on five years ago."

Natasha smiles and elbows Adrian. "That's kind of romantic. You have to admit."

I shake my head. "So I make an internal decision to spend the weekend with him and tell him when we get back. Only thing is, he's crazy sweet all weekend and he takes me to the library and shows me the advertisement that he put in the classifieds five years ago when he was trying to find me."

Adrian raises his eyebrows as he sips his drink. "Now that's romantic." He nods.

I blow out a breath. "Every day it got harder to tell him, and every day I was panicking because we just..." I pause as I think of the wording.

"You fell in love," Adrian finishes for me.

My eyes rise to meet his. "I did."

"He did, too. He told me he was in love with you."

I frown. "When?"

"On the Monday after we got back for San Fran. His exact words were *I'm in love with this girl.*"

I put my head into my hands as the sadness takes over.

They both sit in silence as they watch me. "What happened then?" Natasha finally asks.

"I told him I had a son and he threw the biggest tantrum you have ever seen. He smashed a glass up against the wall and left before I could even tell him that the child was his."

"Bloody hell." Adrian sighs. "This is a mess."

"And then he somehow found out and came around the house the next night losing his ever-living shit."

"Margaret told him," Natasha whispers.

My eyes snap to her. "Oh no, how did she know?" I gasp.

"Look at him." Natasha shakes her head. "He's the image of Cameron."

I blow out a deflated breath and shake my head. "Last night I begged for my job back."

"Hang on, when did you leave?"

"Cameron made me leave last week, so I did."

Adrian frowns.

"But the reality is that I need the money. I'm supporting three people. So I went back last night and guess who was there?"

Natasha narrows her eyes. "That fucking snake."

"My thoughts exactly. Only, I was tipsy because I was drinking and I was so mad that he was there for other women... I did something really stupid."

"What?" They both gasp.

"I did a lap dance for him again and then he went crazy and dragged me outside. When I wouldn't get in his car, he punched the windshield of his *Aston Martin* and smashed it and broke his hand."

Adrian's eyes nearly pop out in horror. "His hand is broken?" He gasps.

I nod. "And I have just spent the morning with him screaming and threatening me if I don't give up my second job there will be hell to pay. He's made all kinds of demands about Owen."

Adrian puts his head in his hands and Natasha shakes her head in disbelief.

"I have no words," Adrian whispers.

"I do," Natasha replies. "Holy fucking shit."

I put my head into my hands in despair and Adrian rubs my back. "He's just coming to terms with it."

"Joshua and Cameron have an issue with paternity situations," Natasha replies, her and Adrian exchanging looks. "This is a huge trigger for them and I'm sure it will get better."

I sip my drink sadly as I contemplate my weekend.

"He's coming around to see Owen tomorrow."

Adrian and Tash smile at each other and then at me. "Good luck. You're going to need it."

I watch the *Aston Martin* pull into the driveway.
   He's here.
   "Owen?" I call. "You have a visitor."

21

Cameron

I TURN the engine off and look up at the house. God, this is my worst nightmare.

How do you tell a kid that you're his father when you don't believe it yourself?

I know it's true, I have the proof, and yet somehow, I feel like I'm in a bad dream and any minute Ashley is going to laugh and tell me it's all a joke. Then I can go back to having her in my arms and being happy.

I can stop resenting her so much.

I don't want to resent her… but I can't help it. How could she have hidden this from me?

I take out my phone and scroll through it, hoping to find an urgent message from the hospital saying I'm needed—that I have to be somewhere. I want to be anywhere but here. I grip the steering wheel in my hands as I imagine how this is going to go. How would I have felt if some stranger turned up and announced that he was my father? What would I have thought of him?

Poor kid. What a fucked up start to his life.

Right, that's it. I need to make this right.

With renewed determination, I climb out of the car and head to the door and knock. I glance up the street as a man starts to mow his lawn and I look around. At least this is a nice neighborhood they're living in.

The door opens in a rush and Ashley stands before me. Her hair is in a high ponytail and she has no makeup on. My heart somersaults in my chest. She's so fucking beautiful.

"Hey," I push out.

She smiles and it kicks me right in the gut. "Hi, Cam. Thanks for coming. Please come in."

God, she smells good.

I follow her into the house and glance around. It seems so strange being here without her on my mind. When I was here before, I was so focused on her I don't remember much about the house. It's homey, nice and clean, and I know she said she moved with bare essentials and put the rest of her stuff in storage back in New York. She walks into the kitchen and I follow her, unsure what to do.

"Would you like a cup of coffee?" she asks.

"Please." I frown as I take a seat on a stool at the kitchen counter.

She fusses about and I sit silently, uncomfortable. I feel myself begin to perspire.

She turns and hands me my coffee. "Do you still want to tell him today?"

"Yes." I sip my coffee. "I'm not starting our relationship with lies."

Her eyes hold mine. "Like we did, you mean?"

I raise my eyebrow and sip my coffee. "No comment," I murmur.

She blows out a breath. "I'm sorry, I don't mean to be snarky and I know you are doing the best you can."

I purse my lips as I watch a small spot on the kitchen counter. I need to focus on anything but looking in her eyes.

She reaches out and puts her hand on my forearm. "I've had five years to adjust to this situation, Cam and you haven't. It's a lot to process. It will get easier, I promise."

I nod. "I hope so."

She smiles awkwardly and shrugs. "I thought maybe we could tell him and then, if you want some privacy, I could go out for a couple of hours and leave you two here alone?"

I frown and nod. I feel my nerves flutter.

Don't leave me alone with him.

"Okay," I mumble, distracted.

"What are you going to say?"

"When?"

"When you tell him?"

I shrug. "I don't know. I've run though every possible scenario in my head all night. I think I'm just going to blurt out with it."

"He's very in tune, Cameron, and he's really intelligent. If he picks up on the fact that you're sad about it, he will latch onto that."

My eyes rise to meet hers. "Do you think I'm sad about this?"

She shrugs. "You're acting like you are."

I frown. "I'm not sad I have a child with you. I'm upset with the way it happened, that I've missed out on so much. I'm furious that I found out from my mother and not you. You have no idea how that made me feel."

She closes her eyes in regret. "I'm so sorry the way things transpired, Cameron, and I know you don't believe me, but I can't regret the week I spent with you. We would never have gotten to have that if you'd known earlier. You would have dismissed me as the psycho who turned up here with your kid in a heartbeat."

Her eyes search mine and I don't know what to think... or how to feel?

Blinding betrayal is all that comes through.

I drop my head. I don't want to have this conversation. I can't deal with it.

"Can you get him, please?" I ask.

Her eyes hold mine for an extended moment. I know she wants to finish this conversation, but I can't.

I can't go there. "Please?" I urge.

"Sure." She walks out of the kitchen and calls upstairs. "Owen, you have a visitor."

"Who?" he calls and I hear him run up the hall before he comes bouncing down the stairs. "Who is it?" he asks as he follows her into the kitchen.

"Cameron." She smiles calmly.

Fuck... I wish I felt calm.

His face falls, and then he forces a smile when he sees me.

"Hello, mate." I smile.

"Hi," he replies.

"We're having coffee. Would you like me to make you a hot chocolate?" Ashley asks him.

"Okay." He smiles.

I pull out a stool next to me. "Why don't you sit here?" I tap the stool.

He climbs up and sits at the counter.

His dark hair is unruly and curly like mine. He has the same olive skin and the cheekiest smile I have ever seen. He brings a smile to my face.

"What have you been up to?" I ask.

"You sound funny." He smirks.

"Owen, use your manners, please." Ashley frowns.

"What do you mean?" I ask.

"Your voice is different."

I smile. "That's my accent. I'm Australian."

He frowns as he thinks.

"Can you say Australia?" I ask.

"Australia," he repeats as clear as day. "What is it?" he asks.

"It's a country, my home." I smile.

Owen frowns and his curious eyes rise to Ashley.

"You know, Owen, kangaroos come from Australia," Ashley tells him.

"Oh." He thinks for a moment. "Do you have a kangaroo?"

I smile. "No."

Ashley hands him his hot chocolate. "Thank you." He smiles as he takes it from the counter.

Ashley pulls a stool around to the other side and takes a seat. I inhale.

Just do it.

"So… Owen." I pause. Fuck. "I… I wanted to talk to you today." He sips his chocolate and watches me intently.

"It seems that…" I frown. Fuck, this is hard. "It seems that when you were born, there was a bit of a mix up."
Owen frowns.

I glance at Ashley and she looks to have turned a pale shade of green.

"Yeah," I continue. "There was a mix up and we only just found out about it."

He sips his chocolate as he listens.

"You see, I'm your dad, Owen."
He frowns and I can see the information swirling around in his little head. "But I already have a dad," he says.

"I know. You have two dads."

He frowns and looks over to Ashley, and then back to me. "My other dad's just busy, that's all. He's coming back."

Ashley's eyes fill with tears and she bites her bottom lip.

"I know." I smile sadly. "But I thought maybe you and I could hang out a bit?"

He frowns.
"Would that be alright?" I ask.

"But how did that happen?" he asks.

"Well." I pause. Fuck, what do I say here? "Erm." Fucking hell. "So, your mom had an egg." I poke his little chest. "Which was you and I had the seed and together we made a little baby."

He frowns as he thinks. "How did the egg get the seed?"
I glance up and see Ashley is smirking.

"I…" I shake my head as I try to think of an answer. "When I kissed her. I gave her the seed when I kissed her."

His face falls in disgust. "You kissed my mom?"
I nod. "She's very pretty and I couldn't help myself." I glance up and

Ashley is close to tears again. "And she spoke French," I whisper with a smirk as I rub the top of his head. "Do you know any French, Owen?" I ask.

He shakes his head and thinks for a moment. "I know French fries."

I smile broadly and Ashley laughs.

"Yes, like that, Owie." Ashley smiles. "Just like French fries."

He drinks his hot chocolate and thinks on it for a moment.

"I thought today you could show me around here, because Mom's got some things to do. Is that okay?" I ask.

He frowns and his eyes flicker to Ashley.

She smiles softly. "Cameron is my friend, Owen. He's a lovely man. You're going to have so much fun together. You're very lucky that you get to have him for a daddy."

I get a lump in my throat and Ashley must be able to sense it because she grabs my hand on the counter and I find myself squeezing it as a silent thank you.

"Okay." He shrugs.

I frown. "Okay?" I ask, surprised. Surely it's not going to be that easy...

"Wait, what do I call you?" Owen asks.

I smile softly. "Dad. You call me Dad."

I sit on the lounge room floor and watch Owen play with his *Lego*. It's freaking me out watching a little version of myself making sense of the world.

I've been watching him for two hours. I could watch him all day. "Do you want to go for a bike ride?" I ask.

"I don't have a bike."

I frown. "You don't have a bike?"

"No, because it's dangerous on the roads."

"Oh," I reply. "Shall we go for a skateboard?"

"What's a skateboard?"

Oh God, it gets worse.

"Okay, let's go up to your room and you can get your mitt and we can play catch."

He looks at me blankly. "I don't think I know how to play catch."

I frown. "Where's your ball and mitt?"

He shrugs.

I stand. "Can you show me your bedroom?"

He stands and walks upstairs with me following. He opens the door and holds his hand out. I walk in and look around.

"This is a nice room." I smile.

"It is." He lies on the bed.

I walk over to his bookshelves and go through all the books he has. "You have lots of books."

"Mom reads to me every night."

I smile. "Does she? Is she a good reader?"

He shrugs. "Okay, I guess."

I smile and open his toy box to look inside. It's filled with soft toys and baby crap. "So... where are all your balls and bats?"

He shrugs. "Santa didn't bring me those."

I smile sadly. "Oh."

I frown as I look around. This is the most fucking boring kids room I have ever been in. "Do you want to go for a walk?"

"Yes." He smiles as he jumps down from the bed.

"Get your shoes."

He opens his wardrobe and I peer in from behind him. Two lonely little pairs of shoes sit at the bottom. I glance at the shelves and they are only half full.

He has hardly any clothes.

"Where are your other shoes, Owen?"

"This is it." He smiles. "These are my good shoes for going out." He points to a brown pair of dress shoes. "And these are my shoes I wear on walks."

I smile. "Oh, good. That makes sense." I rub his head. "Grab the walking shoes."

He takes them out and passes them to me.

I frown. "Can you put these on?" I ask.

He shrugs.

"You don't know how to do your laces yet?" I ask.

He shakes his head.

I smile. "Sit on the bed and I will do it." I look around. "Where are your socks?"

"In my top drawer."

I open his top drawer to find three little pairs of socks and a few pairs of underpants.

Guilt hits me like a freight train. She does have it tough.

Suddenly, I feel like the biggest fucking asshole that ever drew breath. I shake my head and put his shoes and socks on before we head downstairs.

"Where does Mommy put her letters from the postman?" I ask.

Owen frowns as he thinks for a moment. "On the side table in the drawer."

"Why don't you head out the back yard and I will meet you there?" I ask.

"Okay." He runs out the back door and I go to the side table and pull out the drawer to flick through the mail. Fuck, I need a rental receipt. I keep flicking... Nothing.

I go over to the counter where there's a basket of letters and things. I flick through those, but still there's nothing. Shit. I glance around and see a folder on top of the kitchen top cupboards. I pull it down and bingo. Bills all put into a paid and non-paid sections. I flick through until I find a rental one. I take it out and stuff it my pocket.

"Dad?" A little husky voice calls from outside.

I stop and frown as a myriad of emotions run over me.

One word has never sounded more frightening; yet more wonderful at the same time.

Shit just got real.

Ashley

I sit and read to Gloria in my lunchbreak.

It's Monday and the weekend went surprisingly well.

Owen was happy when I returned home on Saturday and Cameron seemed to survive it.

They made an arrangement to see each other again on Wednesday. Apparently Cameron is taking the afternoon off work.

Wonders never cease.

Today, at work, we have been amicable, too. Maybe we can do this co-parenting thing. He's gone to his office now and then he's in office all day Tuesday, so I won't see him again until then.

A little voice inside of me wishes he was coming to see me, but I know that's not going to happen now. It is what it is.

Dr. Anderson pops his head around the corner. "Ashley, if you have a minute, could I see you when you're finished, please?"

I smile and nod, shit. Dr. Anderson is Cameron's cute doctor friend. They constantly talk and laugh together, and I know they have a friendship outside of work.

He must have told him.

"Gloria, we might need to leave it there today, honey." I smile.

"Okay, dear. Thank you. That was wonderful. Will you be back tomorrow?"

I smile. Give her an inch and she will take a mile. I take her hand in mine. "Of course." I walk out into the corridor to where Dr. Anderson is waiting in the hallway. With his handsome good looks, I can imagine he's also dating half the nurses in this place. "Just come in here, Ashley," he says as he ushers me into an office.

I frown. "What's this about?" I turn to face him.

He smiles sexily. "Now forgive me for being blunt, and I hope you don't take this the wrong way..."

My face falls. He's going to give me a lecture about Cameron.

"I'm Seb." He holds out his hand to shake mine and I smile and shake his hand.

"Seb?" I ask.

"Sebastian."

I smile. "Nice to formally meet you, Sebastian." I widen my eyes in jest. "I'm Ashley."

"I know who you are." He smiles sexily.

I frown. Okay, this is weird. "How can I help you, Seb?"

"Would you like to go out Saturday night?"

What? God, that was the most unexpected thing I have heard in forever.

"Go out?" I frown.

"Yes. On a date... with me?"

I scratch my head awkwardly. "I'm away this weekend. I'm sorry. I can't," I lie.

Jesus... just say no.

He smiles and nods. "Okay."

He holds my eyes with his. He *is* very cute. "Some other time?"

I smile.

"Sure," he replies. "I hope I haven't overstepped the mark by asking?"

"Not at all." I smile. Quite the opposite. He's just given me a much needed confidence boost.

"So..." He hesitates. "I guess I'll wait for you to ask me out next time." He smiles.

I chuckle. "Okay. You do that."

"Because I wouldn't want to seem pushy and all." He smirks.

"Good." I nod.

"But, just so you know, I am an excellent dancer," he adds.

His cheeky smile rubs off on me and I find myself beaming like an idiot. "That's good to know."

"And I know the all best restaurants."

I smirk.

"And I'm free every night," he adds cheekily.

I shake my head. "Goodbye, Seb." I grin as I leave the office.

"Call me," he shouts in a fake girl's voice as I leave the office and laugh out loud.

That just made my day.

I pull into the parking lot just before 5pm on Wednesday night. I'm here to pay our rent and pick up a few groceries for lunches tomorrow. My phone rings. It's Jenna.

"Hi, babe." I smile as I answer.

"Oh... My... Fucking... God," She stammers in a whisper.

"What?" I frown.

"Cameron turned up this afternoon with a brand new black *SUV Audi*, fitted with a car seat in the back seat."

"What?" I shake my head. "You're joking?"

"Nope. He told Owen he bought it so they could go to his house sometimes."

"Shit," I whisper as I try to cross the road in the busy traffic.

"And get this, then he and Owen went outside just now and they're bringing in bags and bags of shopping and taking it up to Owen's room."

I screw up face. "Shopping? What food?"

"No. Clothes for Owen."

"What?" I shriek. "What do you mean?"

"He's bought him half the shop," she whispers.

"Why? Has he gone mad?"

"I don't know, but it's expensive shit, too."

Oh God, he infuriates me. "Trust him to try and bribe Owen with money. He's such a fucking idiot."

A lady walking past frowns and shakes her head at my language. "I'm sorry." I wince.

"He's just trying to be nice, probably," Jenna whispers.

I shake my head in disgust. "He's spoiling him. He's going to turn out to be a spoiled brat, just like Cameron is." I shake my head. I approach the real estate. "I'll be home soon," I reply.

"Don't tell him I told you. Owen is really excited so be nice. This is his father, remember."

I blow out a breath and close my eyes. "Yeah." I sigh, deflated. "Thanks for the warning. See you soon."

For fuck's sake, what a nightmare. I walk into the Real Estate office and see the nice receptionist. "Hello, can I pay my rent, please?" I smile as I take out my wallet.

She smiles. "Sure, it's Bellevue isn't it?"

"Yes," I reply as I stand with my card in my hand.

She types and then frowns. "Oh, your rent is paid up until the end of your lease."

"What?" I frown.

She shrugs and turns the computer screen so I can see it. "It was paid in full on Monday." She points to the payment on the screen.

"By who?"

"Erm..." She types in a few more things. "Stanton Holdings."

I glare at her, and if she wasn't so bloody nice, I would just love to punch her in the face, simply for being the bearer of bad news. "Really?" I snap.

She smiles and widens her eyes. "Awesome." She does sparkle fingers. "Surprise."

I glare at her, don't mess with me bitch or you will go down today, too.

I turn and storm to the car. I'm furious.

I don't remember getting home. I don't remember driving at all because I am so fuming mad right now that I can't see straight. I pull up in the driveway next to the fancy *Audi* and my blood starts to boil.

I'm going to kill him. I'm going to actually kill him. I walk in the house and see Jenna as she comes running out and drags me back with her to the kitchen.

"He's paid the rent for twelve months," I whisper.

Her mouth falls open. "Oh my God, Ash, that's Awesome."

I screw up my face. "No, its not. This is his way of making everything alright."

"Ashley, stop it. He can afford it."

"It isn't about the money. It's about him assuming he can do it. He didn't ask."

"Calm down," she whispers.

"I will not calm down!" I yell.

She puts her hand over my mouth. "Now is not the time to discuss this. Owen is so excited."

I put my head into my hands. "Oh my God, Jen, this is out of control."

"He will settle down. He's just trying to be nice, Ashley. Let him."

I blow out a breath and rub my hands though my hair. I know on some level she's right. "Yeah, okay."

Shit. I take a seat at the table to try and relax a little.

For ten minutes I sit there, until finally I know I have to make a move.

"I should go up and say hello," I murmur.

"You should probably kiss him, too. He's fucking gorgeous."

I roll my eyes and fake a smile. "So funny." I widen my eyes. "He's also a fucking asshole," I mouth.

She giggles and blows me a kiss.

I creep up the stairs and I can hear them talking and laughing, then I hear Owen shriek in glee.

"Higher." Cameron chuckles.

"I can't go any higher." I hear Owen laugh.

"Don't be a chicken. Yes, you can," Cameron assures him.

What the hell are they doing? I open the door to find Cameron lying on the floor and Owen jumping nearly to the fucking roof on his bed.

"What the hell?" I shriek. "Owen, stop it. Do not jump on your bed!"

"Uh oh." Cameron laughs. "Party pooper's home."

My mouth drops open in horror and Owen stops bouncing, sensing my oncoming meltdown.

"Hi, Momma." He smiles and points to Cameron. "Dad's here."

I glare at Cameron and he smiles cheekily, raising his brows.

"Hello," I greet him dryly. "Owen, you are not to jump on the bed. It's dangerous."

Cameron shakes his head with a broad smile and climbs off the floor.

"You should know better," I snap.

"What else has he got to do?"

My insides begin to spark like petrol on a fire. "Read some books," I snap. "You know, like a human."

"Momma, Dad bought me some new clothes." Owen smiles excitedly.

"Did he?"

Owen runs to the wardrobe and swings the doors open and starts pulling out sweaters and jeans. They're the most beautiful clothes I have ever seen.

"And shoes!" he shrieks. He runs over and grabs three boxes and pulls out a pair of black *Nike* high tops, and another two expensive pairs of runners.

I stare at him as my brain freezes. Owen is so excited, and who am I to take this away from him? "That's nice, baby," I push out. "You're a lucky boy."

Owen remembers something else. "Oh!" he yells. "And I got a cap." He runs over to the bed and puts on a Lakers cap and beams. "Because Dad said we go for the Lakers now."

His cuteness gets me this time and I smile. "Did you say thank you, baby?"

"Thank you." He smiles as he swings his arms goofily beside him.

"You're welcome, buddy." Cameron smiles.

I stand for a moment with my arms folded and look between the two of them. "Whose car is that?" I ask.

"Mine. Well… ours. I bought it to stay with Owen."

I frown. "What?'

"Well, you can have the car when you have Owen, and I will have the car when I have Owen."

I stare at him as time stands still. How often does he think he's going to have him?

"Oh." I have no words. "What's wrong with my car?"

"Your car's a bomb, Mom," Owen interrupts.

I glare at him. "My car is a good car. There is nothing wrong with my car and cut the entitled business, mister," I snap.

Owen withers and Cameron frowns.

"I had to buy a car anyway, and I won't be driving it when I don't have Owen so you can have it."

I nod and I know I should say thank you, but I can't. I can't bring myself to say it.

"That won't be necessary. Owen and I will be driving in my car," I reply coldly. I turn and walk toward the door. "I'll be downstairs." I turn and face them. "And no jumping on the bed."

"Can you come over to my house for ten minutes with Owen?" Cameron asks.

I frown.

"If… if you don't want to come, you don't have to, but I just wanted to show Owen my house."

I stare at him. He has a car now. He can take him when he wants. "Yes, I will come," I reply. He's not going there without me. No way in hell.

We pull up in the driveway of Cameron's house.

"This is it." He smiles into the rear view mirror at Owen.

On cue, Owen gasps, and I roll my eyes. Oh, please, this is pathetic. This new car scent has heightened his excitability.

"This is your house?" Owen whispers in awe.

"Yep. Pretty cool, huh?"

We park the car and walk in, feeling like a party pooper for real. Owen is so excited, he is bouncing around, and Cameron is proud of himself and playing the happy host.

I should be happy, too. I should be happy that they have an instant connection, but I hate to admit that I'm I'm a bit jealous.

Owen could at least act loyal to me.

We walk in and my heart sinks. Last time we were here together I was falling in love, and I can understand exactly how Owen feels.

Cameron is fun and he makes you feel fun.

Owen has Cameron for life and I don't. Is that a selfish thing for me to be feeling?

God, yes. I know it is, but I can't help it. I internally kick myself for being a childish fool. Cameron takes Owen by the hand and leads him through the house one room at a time. I follow them, unimpressed. I didn't get this good of a tour.

He then takes us upstairs. "This is my room." He smiles to Owen and then glances over at me and my eyes drop to the floor.

I spent some of the happiest nights of my life in this room.

"And this is your room." He opens the door and my heart sinks. This is the room I came into before, only now it's painted navy blue and has a single bed and children's furniture in it. He's had it done already.

The linen is all expensive denim with little red, white, and blue flags hanging over the window. The same red, white, and blue cushions are on the window seat. A large, red, circular mat is on the floor near the desk.

It's gorgeous.

Owen's eyes nearly pop out of his head. "This is my room?" he whispers excitedly.

"Do you like it?" Cameron asks, his voice filled with hope.

I can't take this. My eyes tear up and I leave the room in a rush and walk downstairs into Cameron's study.

"Stop it, stop it, stop it," I whisper. I close my eyes as I try to stop my tears from falling, but they won't.

After a few minutes Cameron walks in and closes the door behind him softly.

"What's wrong?" he whispers, concerned.

I scrunch up my face in pain. "It's just so hard watching you give him everything I always wanted to but couldn't," I whisper.

His face falls and he pulls me into an embrace. "Ashley, this isn't a competition." He holds me tight against his chest and lets me cry.

"I know," I whisper. "But it sure feels like it."

He blows out a breath. "It's not."

I pull out of his grip. "Why did you pay my rent, Cameron?"

"So you don't have to go back to the club."

"What?" I frown, that's not the answer I was expecting.

"You're not going back, Ashley. " He replies coldly. "Over my dead body are you stepping foot back in that place."

Suddenly his motive is crystal clear: He wants to control me. He wants control over Owen *and* me.

I step back from him as uneasiness rolls through me. "You don't get to tell me what to do, Cameron. You lost that right when you ended it between us."

His jaw clenches and his cold eyes hold mine. "The hell I don't."

22

Ashley

I FLINCH. "What do you mean *the hell you don't?*" I step back from him angrily. "I'm telling you straight up, I left that job last week to please you because I thought we had a future, but now that it's quite clear that we don't. You don't have a say in my life."

He glares at me. "Yes, I do."

"You don't." I snap. "I'm giving you half a son. That's all I'm giving you."

"Well, let me tell you one thing. My job as a father is to make sure my son's mother is in line."

"In line?" I yell.

"Yes. In fucking line." He growls.

"I'm not a circus animal, Cameron."

"Then stop acting like one!"

I shake my head. "You selfish son of a bitch. This is all about you and your pathetic image."

He narrows his eyes.

"Guess what, Cameron? I work a bar job and if I want, I can work in the Escape Lounge, too. It's none of your goddamn business what I choose to do."

"Isn't it?"

"No, it's not. So butt out!"

"I'm warning you, Ashley. If you go back, there will be fucking hell to pay."

"Go fuck yourself," I snap and then I walk out the door to find Owen standing in the hallway, wide-eyed and listening.

My face falls in horror. "Oh, hi, baby."
Cameron walks out behind me, closes his eyes then shakes his head in regret. "Don't worry about us, mate. We're just being silly. Sometimes grownups are ridiculous." He walks past us and back into the kitchen.

Oh shit. What a nightmare. Owen shouldn't have heard that. What the hell am I doing? I need to be the bigger person in front of him and pretend everything is okay. I walk out and sit at the counter next to Cameron. My heart is slamming hard against my chest in fury.

"Can you make us a hot chocolate, please, Dad?" I ask Cameron flatly.

His angry eyes flash my way. "Sure, Momma." He sneers sarcastically.

I fake a smile at Owen and his little eyes glance between the two of us. Cameron starts making the hot chocolate, and I think I'd better watch closely in case he puts rat poison in mine.

He hands us the hot chocolate and we drink them as Owen chats happily, soon forgetting all about what just happened. Half an hour later, when I'm sure there is no issue, I turn to Owen. "We better get going, baby."

"Okay." He jumps down of the stool and smiles up at Cameron.

"I will pick you up on Saturday." Cameron smiles down at him.

Owen nods an over the top nod with a huge smile on his face, and Cameron goes and retrieves the keys to the new car. He returns holding them up in the air.

I narrow my eyes and snatch them out of his hands. He smirks.

"Can you give Mom a spoonful of honey before she goes to bed tonight, Owen?" he asks.

I shake my head, of all the nerve.

"What for?" Owen asks.

"Sweeten her up a bit." He smiles and throws me a wink, and it's all I can do to not scratch his eyes out.

"Goodbye, Cameron," I snap.

"Bye. Dad." Owen waves as we walk down the driveway.

That man is a pig.

I don't know what's more annoying: the fact that Cameron gets to me or the fact that he knows that he gets to me and plays on it.

We are sitting in the cafeteria while I watch every damn slutty nurse in this god-forsaken hospital make fuck me eyes at him.

One of them is going down real soon and he's going to end up in the ER.

There isn't a doubt in my mind.

He sits with his legs crossed in a fancy suit with everyone hanging off his every word, being all witty and charismatic. I sit on the other side of the table drinking my coffee while I imagine nailing his head to the table. Either that or having sex with someone else on his desk, just to piss him off.

He probably wouldn't even care, to be honest, but it's nice to imagine I could get to him as much as he gets to me.

I'm supposed to be working tonight, and although I have no desire to go—and now that my rent is paid, I technically don't need to—I'm going anyway.

I will leave on my terms and when I'm good and ready. I already called this week and begged for my job back, so I'm not turning around and leaving in the same week. It's bloody embarrassing.

I'll give it another four or five shifts and then I'll scratch it.

However, if they try to make me wear that stupid lap dancing uniform again, I'm walking straight out on the spot.

Screw that, bar work only. A text beeps through and I open my phone to read it. Speak of the devil. It's Eliza.

Hi, Ashley,
I keep forgetting to message you.
I'm taking all of the girls out for dinner on Sunday night for a staff meeting and as a bit of a thank you.
I would love for you to join us.
See you tonight with the details.
Eliza x

I click out of the message and look up to see a nurse leaning over Cameron's chair talking to him and being all seductive. He's listening to what she is saying and being super attentive.

Stupid slut.

My blood begins to boil and I smirk. Imagine if Cameron knew I was mixing socially with the Exotic girls. He would flip his frigging lid.

I should go just to piss him off.

I glance back up and the brunette nurse laughs out loud. "Oh you are so funny Dr. Stanton. You kill me." She laughs.

I look at them, deadpan. He's a complete fucking twat. I go back to my phone and I reply.

I would love to come, Eliza.
See you tonight.
Ashley.

I smirk. That will teach him to try and piss me off... because that *is* what he's trying to do. It's blatantly obvious.

Well, it's not working, asshole. I can piss you off more...

Just watch me.

I pull into the Club Exotic parking lot at 9.45pm and sit in the car in the dark. God, I don't feel like this shit tonight. I pull down the sun visor and stare at my reflection in the mirror for a moment. I run my fingers under my eyes to neaten up my mascara and I take out my phone and check my messages. There's nothing important.

I reapply my lip gloss and sit for a moment. I wonder what Cam's doing now? I get a vision of him cooking someone dinner like he used to do for me.

And laughing.

He has the most beautiful, intoxicating laugh in the world. So wild and carefree. He has this almost childlike happiness... or at least he did when we were together. He still has it with everyone else, just not me anymore. It's depressing.

I blow out a sad breath. This time two weeks ago I was resigning because I thought we had a future and we were about to go away with his family to San Fran for the gala ball.

Now I'm just the mother of his son.

The one he wants to control.

The more time that ticks by, the more I face the reality of what it is I'm really sad about it. I miss him.

I would have loved for him to have fought for me, but I knew he wouldn't. I knew everything would change once he found about Owen. Much to my disappointment, I was right.

He's a great dad, though, and I guess I should be grateful for that. It's been raining on and off all day and the roads are wet and crisp. I climb out of my car and cross the busy road. I'm walking down to the club when I stop on the spot and frown as uneasiness fills me.

Two cars sit down from the entrance and I see the dreaded *Aston Martin*. The windshield is fixed and Cameron is leaning against the car with his ass. Wearing his customary expensive suit, he is still in his work clothes.

His arms are folded in front of him as he watches me walk down the road.

His face is expressionless, but I can feel the animosity from here.

He's not here to come to the club. He's here for the sole purpose to see if I'm coming to work.

And here I am.

"Hello." I swallow nervously and I glance at the door to see the two bouncers on high alert from my last shift when Cameron dragged me out.

He raises an eyebrow in return.

I walk closer towards him. "What are you doing here?"

He tilts his head. "I could ask you the same thing."

My stomach flutters with butterflies. "Cameron, I'm here to work. I can't just leave without notice."
"You did last week."

"And last week I thought you were in love with me."

His eyes hold mine.

"And this week you want nothing but to control me. I'm not your puppet, Cameron."

His eyes hold mine, yet he gives nothing away. Why is he being so calm? It's freaking me out.

Why can't he just tell me that he wants us to work on things? Promise that we can try again?

Why is he treating me like nothing but his child's mother? *A fucking incubator.*

I thought we had something. How could I have been so wrong?

Sadness fills me, and I close my eyes as I work up the courage to walk past him and disappear into the club.

Just give me a sign. Just give me a sign that there is even a flicker of a chance that there will be hope for us, and I promise you, I won't go in.

My eyes search his. *Cameron… please…*

"Is that it?" I whisper. "Is that all you have to say?"

His eyes continue to hold mine. "I've asked you not to work here and I told you why."

"Because of Owen…" I say in a strained voice, pushing through the lump in my throat. *Don't let him see that he's getting to you.*

"Yes," he replies coldly. "Don't mistake my softness for weakness, Ashley. It will be your undoing."

I screw up my face as my anger takes control. "What the hell does that mean, Cameron?" I shake my head. "Are you threatening me? Is that what this is?"

"Yes." He leans back, puts his hands in his pants pockets, and crosses his legs at the ankle in front of him.

"Threatening me with what?"

He shrugs.

I've had enough of this shit. "Go home, Cameron." I shake my head in disgust. "Why don't you go and bang one of your slutty nurses and tell her what to do? Unlike me, I'm sure she will love it."

His jaw clenches in anger and his eyes flicker with anger.

That's it. I'm done. I walk past him and through the doors of the club with my heart beating hard in my chest. I head straight down to the back room. I'm grabbed from behind on my way through the crowd, and I turn to slap the hand from my behind.

I look up to see him. It's the same stupid asshole that's been hitting on me for weeks. "Go away." I growl.

"No." He smiles as if I just challenged him.

I shake my head and Eliza comes over immediately. "Is there a problem here?" she asks me.

"He won't stop groping me. I'm going to leave because of it," I snap.

Give me a reason to walk out right now. I fucking dare you.

Eliza glares at him. "Do not approach Vivienne again or you will have your membership terminated, Judy."

He curls up his top lip in disgust. "You wouldn't terminate my membership. I have too much pull here."

Eliza smiles. "Oh, yes I would. Just watch me."

He looks between the two of us before he finally replies, "She's not worth it." He sneers. He looks me up and down and then disappears through the crowd.

"Are you okay, dear?" she asks as she runs her hand up my upper arm.

I shake my head, because in all honesty I'm not. "That guy freaks me out. He won't leave me alone. He's been hassling me every shift."

She watches him as he walks through the crowd. "Ignore Judy. He's on my list and I'm watching him. He's harassing another girl as well. I'm sorry the bouncers haven't done their job protecting you."

I frown after him.

"Let me know if he bothers you again, okay?"

I nod and smile. "Thank you."

I blow out a breath and head out the back. Time to get to work on *my* terms.

The alarm rings out. It only seems to wake me five minutes after I crawled into bed this morning. Owen is sound asleep beside me. I didn't get home until 4am. It's now 6.15am and already time to get up.

I'm delirious.

I crawl out of bed and open my blinds. I'm so tired and I feel like shit.

Just have a shower and go to work and then you have the whole weekend to sleep, I remind myself.

Thank God it's the weekend. I really need some me time.

It's been a long, hard week.

I trudge to the bathroom and shower to get myself ready for my day. I can't do this for much longer. I am going to resign. This is bullshit, putting myself through Hell to prove a point.

I hate that he wins.

I'm sitting at the kitchen table eating my breakfast when Owie comes down for his morning cuddle in my lap.

"Good morning, baby." I smile as he climbs up.

"Morning, Momma." He smiles as he wraps his little arms around me.

"You have preschool today." I smile. He's not really liking it, but we are trying our hardest to get him excited about going.

"I might stay with Jenna today," he announces.

My eyes rise up to Jenna across the table and she smirks while holding her coffee cup.

"No, remember you have to go to get ready for big school."

He frowns. "But I don't like it."

I smile. "You'll like it if you give it a chance. Just hang in there. Plus, your friend Alison is going today."

His eyes widen. "Alison is going today?" he asks in wonder.

I nod and smile. "Aha, and she is your friend." I giggle as I tickle his chest. "You can play with her all day long."

He smiles as he bites his cute little bottom lip.

"You've got to get going, Ash," Jen murmurs. "You're going to be late."

I blow out a breath. "At least it's Friday."

"I have assessments due. Yay! Go me," she mutters with an eye roll.

I smile as I stand and kiss them both. "Twelve months from now, this shit will be finished with."

"Hallelujah," she replies dryly.

I grab my lunch from the fridge and go take my phone off charge only to notice that in last night delirious state, I didn't turn the power on.

"Damn it," I snap, annoyed with myself.

Jen rolls her eyes knowing what I've done.

"Just ring me at the hospital if you need me," I murmur as I grab my bag. "I'll get Owen this afternoon on my way home so you can get your assessments done. Let's get pizza for dinner."

"Pizza, yay." Owen laughs as he puts his arms in the air.

"Sounds good," she calls from behind me. "Love you. Have a great day."

I hotfoot it across the parking lot to my car. It's been a bloody hectic day to say the least. Cameron had two emergency surgeries and I didn't get to speak to him all day, although the look he threw me from across the room was scary enough. He went to his surgery this afternoon and I know he's going to growl me out about going to work last night as soon as he gets the chance. I glance at my watch. 4.15pm. Shit, the bloody preschool closes at 5pm. I need to hurry. I pick up my pace and start to power walk.

Thank God. Pizza, wine, and bed tonight. I'm so excited to get home. It's been such a long week. I walk up toward my car and notice that someone is parked behind me, just pulled up in the middle of the parking lot behind my car. I go over to the car and it is all locked up.

I frown. What the hell?

I look around for the driver. Where are they? I don't have time for this shit.

I walk up and down the parking lot to try and locate the owner. Who the hell parks their car in the middle of a parking lot behind someone?

For fuck's sake!

I see a man approaching. Oh great, this is him... but he gets into another car parked a few cars down. I run over. "Excuse me, do you know whose car this is?" I ask.

He shakes his head. "No, I don't. Sorry."

I keep searching for the owner with no luck.

Bloody hell. I run down to the office. "Excuse me, there is a car blocking my car in and I can't get out," I splutter in a panic.

The bored attendant looks up form his gaming magazine. Man, this guy is such a dipshit.

"Hmm, go back into the hospital and have them page the number plates," he replies flatly.

"What? I don't have time for this. I have to be at the preschool to pick up my son in..." I glance at my watch. "Fifteen minutes." Ah, shit.

"Sorry, sweetheart, there's nothing I can do. We can call a tow truck, but they usually take over an hour to get here."

"Fine," I snap as I run back to my car. I hate this hellish car park. I'm going to have to ring Jenna to go get him. Bloody hell. I wanted to give her the afternoon off.

I'm not in the mood for this.

I take out my phone and dial Jenna's number. My phone lights up and then goes dead.

My eyes widen in horror.

No.

Oh my God... oh my God. I begin to panic and I run to the cab bay, nearly hyperventilate. 4.55pm. The preschool closes in five minutes and nobody will be there to pick him up.

I get a vision of his little face waiting for me and my eyes tear up. The cab line is ten people long. "Please, let me go first," I beg. "I have to get my son from preschool before five and someone has blocked my car in. This... this is an emergency," I stammer. "Please."

"Of course." The kind people all smile.

"Thank you so much," I splutter as I take my place at the front of the line. "Please hurry. Please hurry," I whisper again and again.

The cab doesn't arrive until 5.10 pm. "Where are all the cabs?" I panic, and the woman next to me rubs my arm sympathetically. "Have you rung them?" she asks.

"My phone is dead," I whisper through my tears. Owen is there waiting and I can't get to him. I feel sick knowing that he is the last little kid on his own waiting for me. How must he feel?

"Do you want to use mine?" she asks.

"Oh, please." I take the phone from her and quickly Google the preschool's number and dial them up. It rings and then I get a message.

Hello, you have reached ABC Learning center.
We are currently closed right now.
Please call back during the operating hours of 8am to 5pm, Monday to Friday.

My eyes widen in horror. "Oh my God, it's the answering machine," I cry.

The lady in the line behind me speaks up. "Do you want me to ring my daughter to go and get him. Where is it?" she asks, concerned.

"This is a nightmare. They wouldn't let her get him anyway."

We wait and we wait, and I can't even ring Jenna because I don't know her number by heart. Why the hell didn't I charge my phone properly?

A cab finally pulls into the parking lot and everyone sighs in relief. "Thank you so much for letting me go first," I thank them as I climb in.

"ABC learning Centre... on... on Russel Street," I stammer. "And please drive fast. I'm so late."

The driver nods and pulls out into the traffic and I glance at my watch again. I'm now thirty-five minutes late.

I'm a terrible mother. How could I have let this happen?

After the longest ten minutes of my life, the cab pulls up at Owen's kindergarten. "Wait here, please," I tell the driver as run up the driveway just as the woman is locking the front door.

"Oh my... God," I pant. "I'm so sorry. My car got blocked in and couldn't get here."

She looks at me, unimpressed. "He tried to call you but your phone was turned off. Owen's father came and got him."

My eyes widen in horror. "What?"

"We called his father and he came and got him. You know what time we close." She looks at her watch. "Forty-five minutes ago."

"Yes. I... I apologize about that..." I stammer. I turn and run back to the cab and shuffle through my purse to dig out Cameron's address on a piece of paper. I hand it over. "Take me here, please."

The car pulls up outside Cameron's house and I gingerly climb out. "Just wait a moment, please. I need to see if he's here," I tell the driver.

I go over to the gates and push the doorbell. The security guard comes out. "Is Cameron home with Owen yet?" I ask.

"Yes, Ashley. He got home about half an hour ago." He smiles.

"Thank you." I smile awkwardly, then I turn and pay the cab driver, not hanging around to watch him as he drives off into the distance.

Cameron's going to lose his shit, and I close my eyes because I know I deserve it.

I walk up the front steps and knock on the door. Owen bounces in to view through the glass. "Hi, Momma." He waves.

I smile as relief fills me. He's safe. Thank God, he's safe.

Cameron opens the door and glares at me.

"Hello." I smile as I bend and take Owen into my arms. "I'm so sorry. I got blocked in and I couldn't get a cab."

Cameron holds his arm out for me to come inside, and I walk in sheepishly.

"Momma, Dad picked me up and I made him a painting today." He smiles happily as he leads me through to the kitchen and shows me his painting in its prime position on the fridge.

Cameron is in navy suit pants and a white shirt. His tie and suit jacket have been discarded, and my eyes fall to his biceps and shoulders that I can see through his shirt.

Why does he have to be so fucking gorgeous?

Owen is drinking hot chocolate and there's cartoons on the television.

"Can I talk to you for a minute?" I ask.

Cameron glances at Owen.

"Alone," I add.

He points to the stairs. "Let's go upstairs."

I gulp. Shit. "Okay." I turn to Owen. "I'm just going to talk to Daddy for a moment, darling. Watch your cartoons and then we will get going, okay?"

"Alright," he calls, distracted by the television.

Cameron walks upstairs and I follow him like a naughty child.

Fuck's sake.

He walks to his bedroom and I follow him in as he closes the door behind me.

"Cameron, it was a nightmare. I got blocked in by some inconsiderate asshole, and then my bloody phone was dead and I couldn't get a cab. I didn't know anyone's number by heart."

He glares at me. "Do you have any fucking idea how angry I am with you?"

"I know." I shake my head. "I'm angry with myself."

"He was there by himself. You should have seen his face. He was so worried."

My face falls.

"Why was your phone dead?"

"Because I plugged it in and forgot to turn the power point on."

"Because you haven't slept," he says, his tone eerily calm. "How the hell, do you expect to parent when you're not sleeping?"

My eyes fill with tears. "It was just a mistake."

"No, Ashley. It wasn't a fucking mistake. It was a choice to go to the club last night and get naked for other men. It was a fucking choice to neglect Owen today."

"This has nothing to do with last night."

"It has everything to do with last night!" he yells, making me jump.

My eyes narrow as tears form — guilty tears.

He puts his hands on his hips and drops his head as he tries to calm himself down. "I don't know what the fuck is going on with you." He sneers. "But you better get your fucking act together real quick."

He leaves the room in a rush and I stand still as the weight of his words swirl around me.

I hate that this happened. I hate that I let this happen.

I slowly walk downstairs and back out to the kitchen to see Cameron pick up Owen off the sofa and put him on his hip. "Come on, mate. I'm going to drive you both home. Mom's not fit to drive tonight."

My eyes close with regret because he's right... I'm not.

Cameron

"What days do you go to preschool, Owie?" I ask as my eyes find his in the rear-view mirror. It's Saturday morning and I have just picked him up for the day.

Ashley's greeting was as icy as ever, but I don't care. I'm off her. She fucking shits me. She can hate me all she wants.

"Tuesdays and Thursdays," he replies as he looks out the window. "But I don't really like it."

"Why not?" I ask.

"Ryan is mean to me."

I frown as I watch him. "What do you mean?"

He shrugs. "He takes my toys and won't let me play chase."

"Well, you just tell him you're playing."

"Yesterday he told me he was going to punch me in the dick."

What the hell? "What?" I snap. "When did he say that?"

"Alison said I could play chase, and then he said if I did he was going to punch me."

"And what did you do?"

He shrugs as he looks out the window. "I just went away."

"What did Mom say?" I ask.

"She said..." He hesitates as he tries to remember. "She said to stay away from mean people."

"Has he been doing this for long?" I ask.

He nods as he stares out the window.

"Owen, I want you to do something for me," I say as my eyes flicker between him and the road.

"What?"

"Next time he says he's going to hit you, I want you to do this." I hold my hand up and then make a fist. "You do this with your hand and you tuck your thumb around the outside."

He frowns.

"Can you do that for me? Show me how you do your hand?"

He makes a fist.

"Now, tuck your thumb around the front of your fist."

He does it.

"Next time he says he's going to hit you, you hit him first. You pull your arm back and hit him straight in the nose as hard as you can with your fist."

He frowns.

"Bullies will only pick on you if they know you won't fight back, Owen."

He frowns at me.

"You don't put up with crap, mate. If someone's going to hit you, you show them you're not scared, and they won't be mean anymore."

He watches me.

"Next time he says something, you do that, and I promise you he won't be mean again."

A trace of a smile crosses his face. "I might get into trouble."

"It doesn't matter." I smirk. "It's better than putting up with crap." I pull the car into the parking lot. "Now, let's go and buy our new skateboards."

His eyes widen with excitement.

"You and me are learning how to skateboard this morning. How does that sound, buddy?"

"Good." He smiles cheekily and makes a fist at me.

I smile broadly and hold my fist over to the back seat and he hits it with his.

Game over. This kid's got me already.

It's 2pm when the doorbell rings. Owen and I have been skateboarding up and down the driveway for hours. He's actually pretty good and has natural balance.

It's time for my family to meet my son, and it feels weird to be honest.

"That's them, Owie." I smile.

His little hands wring in front of him nervously and I smile to reassure him. Ashley was right, he is timid. We head to the front door and find Joshua, Tash, and their five kids. The kids are bouncing balls and the two younger boys are wrestling, as always.

Joshua has wild kids and I guess I didn't realise how wild until I met Owen. I thought all kids were the same. My mother and Murph are with them and I open the door in a rush.

"Hello," they all yell and Owen cowers behind my leg.

"Hello." I smile as I pull Owen out from behind me. "This is Owen." I present him.

Joshua and Natasha's faces fall when they see him, and Joshua instantly chokes up. The resemblance Owen has to me is uncanny. "Say hello, Owen." I smile.

He forces a scared smile as he clings to my hand for dear life. "This is Uncle Joshua and Aunty Natasha, and this is Grandma, and this is Murphy," I introduce.

They all step forward and shake his hand one at a time.

"You look like your dad." Joshua smiles with a cheeky wink. "You poor thing."

Mom bends and grabs him into an embrace and kisses him. "Oh, he's beautiful, Cameron." She smiles happily. "I'm so happy to meet you, little man."

Owen wriggles out of her grip and comes immediately back to my side, grabbing my hand for reassurance.

Natasha smiles and puts her hand on her chest as she gets teary. "You're gentle like your dad, Owen." She smiles.

"We're not gentle, are we? We're tough." I smirk as I swing his hand in mine.

"These are your cousins. Jordy, Ellie, Blake, Joel, and Jackson." The kids all stand in a row as they sum up their new cousin.

"Hello." They smile and Owen cowers deeper behind my leg.

"Come in. We've got lunch ready, haven't we?" I smile down at him.

Owen stays silent as the kids all run off like maniacs through the house. It's going to take him a while to get used to all this action. My family is full on.

It's just gone 5pm and Joshua and I are sitting at the fire pit drinking a beer. Tash is inside with Murph, while Mom and the kids are all playing chase in the yard around us.

I shake my head. "She was there after I told her not to go."

Joshua sips his beer with a murderous look on his face. "So, let me get this straight. You paid her rent for a year and told her not to go back to the club and she went anyway?"

I roll my lips in contempt. "Yep."

He frowns. "What was her reasoning?"

"I swear, she just wants to piss me off." I shake my head. "I don't know. She probably worked in the Escape Lounge that night and fucked someone. How would I fucking know?"

He narrows his eyes. "She's a hooker?"

I shake my head. "No." I hate the thought of her being with anyone else and I blow out a deep breath. "But I don't want her there. Simple as that."

"But you told me you were in love with her only two weeks ago?" He frowns. "You said she was the one."

"I thought she was, but then she springs this on me and she lied about it. How am I supposed to feel?"

He blows out a deep breath as he watches the fire. "Fuck, man."

Mom walks out onto the back patio and calls the children and our eyes flick up to her. "What's Mom said about it?" Joshua asks.

I shake my head. "She's hating Ashley's guts."

Joshua smirks. "She hated her before she knew any of this."

I smile as I sip my drink. "Mom would hate anyone I dated, true, but..." I hesitate and smirk. "Well, she has a good reason with Ash now."

We sit for a moment as the fire dances in front of us.

"And get this, yesterday she forgot to pick Owen up from preschool. I got an emergency call saying she hadn't shown up and her phone was off."

Joshua screws up his face. "What the hell?"

"I know, right? She was shattered from the night before and forgot she was picking him up."

Joshua glares at the fire as it crackles in front of us.

"I need to pull her in line," I murmur as I feel the fury I felt bubble under the surface.

"Yeah, you do. I wouldn't be taking that shit with my kids," he replies.

The children all come running over with marshmallows that Mom has just given them to toast on the fire. Blake picks up a drink can and throws it into the flame.

We all jump back from the fire in fear it may explode.

"What the hell are you doing? Blake, what the frigging hell are you doing that for?" Joshua growls as he stands abruptly. "You do not throw things in the fire. Do you hear me?" he yells at the top of his voice.

The kids all stop for a moment and Blake nods "Sorry," he murmurs.

They then carry on as if this is a normal occurrence, and when we know it's safe, they carry on toasting marshmallows. Out of the corner of my eye, I see Owen standing back. His eyes are filled with tears and his little hands are clenched tightly up in front of his chest. I stand and scoop him up into my arms.

"Hey, what's wrong, Owen?"

His tears fall free and roll down his face as he clings to me, terrified.

"Did Joshua scare you?" I ask softly as I pick him up.

He nods through his tears, and I pull him close to kiss the top of his head. "Oh, baby. It's okay. Don't cry."

He puts his head down on my chest and I can feel him shaking with fear.

"Stan, stop being a big gorilla, scaring my kid," I snap with a shake of my head.

Joshua comes over and rubs Owen's hair. "Sorry, mate, but sometimes I just lose it at Blake. Pay me no attention. He's naughty and drives me mad."

I sit back down in my position by the fire with my son on my lap, clinging to me for dear life, and for the first time in my life, I feel my protective instincts kick in.

Owen comes first. I need to protect him at all costs.

I stare into the dancing flames...

Whatever it takes.

23

Ashley

I SIT at the table and laugh for the first time in two weeks. I'm out with the girls from Club Exotic, and to be honest, this is exactly what I needed. We've been out to dinner, and while some of the girls headed home early, a few of us are now drinking cocktails in a bar. I need to head off soon, though. I'm working tomorrow.

A group of guys have been lingering around us all night and we even just had a dance with some of them. They seem harmless enough.

"I need to get going, guys." I smile. "I have to work tomorrow."

"Stay for another round." The tall guy says as the girls all shake their heads in protest.

I laugh and get off my stool. "Thanks, but no thanks." I wobble on my feet as I stand up. Holy shit, I feel drunk.

"Those cocktails you got us are toxic," I murmur with a laugh. The girls all continue to talk, but I really do have to go. "See you later, guys," I murmur, distracted by how drunk I feel.

"Let me walk you out," the tall guy offers.

"No, you stay with me," one of the girl's purrs as she links her arm with his. His eyes light up in delight.

He's in.

I smile and walk out the front doors and onto the sidewalk as a rush of color mixed with inebriation fills me. Christ, I'm so drunk.

I totter down the street in my heels as I look for a cab. All the cars sound so loud, as if the noise has been magnified.

I look up the street one way, and then the other way as things begin to lose focus. I step back to try and gain my footing.

My God, I need to get home. How did I get this drunk? I continue to walk down the street and I stagger as I nearly lose my footing.

What the hell? I haven't been this drunk for years.

I make it to the cab rank and hold onto the sign as I try to hold myself up. A young girl comes over to me, concerned. "Are you alright, Miss?"

I frown as my vision starts to tunnel and I shake my head. "No, I'm not," I slur.

I hear her muffled voice in the distance as my sight blacks out, and I feel the earth move from underneath me. A huge head spin hits me and I fall, smacking my head on the ground.

Confusion.

Pain.

Darkness.

Cameron

My phone rings and I glance at the clock. 10.45am. Shit, I bet it's Gloria. I pick up my phone and the hospitals number is flashing on the screen. Here we go.

"Hello," I answer.

"Dr. Stanton?" a strange voice asks.

"Yes, who is this?'

"This is Melissa from the Emergency Room."

"Melissa." That's weird. Emergency never ring me.

"Sorry to ring so late, doctor, but we have had someone just bought in by ambulance, and one of the nurses thinks she recognized them as one of your interns."

I sit up in bed. "What's happened?"

"Suspected drug overdose."

I rub my hand down my face. Shit.

"We don't have any contact details and we're trying to get in touch with the family," she continues.

"Of course, I can search through their records. What's the name?" I ask.

"Umm." She hesitates as she reads the licence. "Ashley Tucker."

My eyes widen. What the fuck? "Is... Is she alright?" I stammer.

"She's unconscious at this stage."

"I'll be right there."

I pace at the end of the bed. I'm frantic.

Ashley has been out cold for six hours. The toxicology reports have come back as her having drugs in her system, but they're unsure as to what exactly they are just yet. The sun is rising outside and I can hear the nurses beginning to do their rounds for changeover.

This has been the longest night of my life.

I take her hand in mine. "Please be alright," I whisper so only she can hear me. I lean down and kiss her forehead. "Please be alright, Ash. Baby, can you hear me?" I ask hopefully.

God, how did it come to this? I had no idea she was into drugs.

Why was she alone when she collapsed and who the hell was she with?

There is this whole other side to her that I don't know and I hate it. A text comes through. It's Jenna.

Any news?

I blow out a breath and text back.

None yet.
I will message you the moment she wakes up.

A text bounces back.

Thank you for staying with her.
It means a lot
xx

I blow out a breath and take Ash's hand back in mine. *Please be alright, baby. Please, please, please.* What if she dies? What if she hit her head so hard that there's permanent damage?

I close my eyes in pain. How did it come to this? How does the love of my life go from an angel to a drug-addicted stripper in two weeks?

How could I have been so wrong about her?

An insidious, sick feeling sinks in as I think of poor little Owen. He loves his mother dearly. What if something happens to her? How could I ever tell him that his mom didn't love him enough and she took an overdose?

I hold her hand in mine and sit in the darkness as another nightmare hour passes.

She frowns and I sit up, hopeful. "Ash?" I wipe the hair back from her forehead. "Are you okay, baby? I love you, come back to me, please," I whisper.

This is torture. How long is she going to be under?

She screws up her eyes, her face scrunching tight. "C-Cam?" she whispers in the silent room.

I close my eyes and bend to kiss her cheek and hold her close to me.

"Oh my God, Bloss, I thought you were going to die on me." I hold her tight for a long time and eventually kiss her softly on the lips.

Why do I love this woman so much when she is so obviously running such a different race to me?

"What happened?" She frowns.

"What did you take?" I whisper as I brush the hair from her forehead.

"What?" She frowns.

"You took a drug overdose."

She screws up her face as though trying to remember.

"Who were you with?" I ask.

"Some of my friends from the club," she whispers.

I sit up, disgusted. "What?" She has friends that work there? She mixes with these women by choice?

"We had drinks with some men." She frowns as she tries to remember.

"What drugs did you take, Ashley?" I repeat as my anger starts to bubble.

"Some of the girls had something." She shakes her head. "But I didn't. I swear I didn't."

"Who were the men?" I ask.

"I don't know," she whispers as she drifts back to sleep. "I... don't know."

Adrian.

I walk into Joshua's office to find him seated at his desk. Cameron is staring out the window, deep in thought.

"What's up?" I ask. "How come you're not at work?" I ask Cameron. With both of them in their suits and looking solemn, they are the epitome of power.

Joshua just buzzed for me to come up from level two to see them.

Cameron turns to me. "Ashley took a drug overdose last night."

My face falls in horror. "Oh my God. Is she… is she alright?" I splutter.

He nods and Joshua swings on his chair from side to side with his eyes fixed firmly on Cameron.

"What happened?" I ask.

Cameron's jaw clenches in anger. "She was out with the girls from the Escape Club and took some drugs, although she's denying it."

Joshua runs his tongue over his front teeth in contempt.

I swallow the lump in my throat as my eyes flicker between them. "Is she okay?"

"They discharged her this morning," he replies coldly.

"Who has Owen?" I frown.

"Jenna, her friend."

"Don't you think you should go and help out?" I ask.

Cameron's eyes meet Joshua's. "Yes. That's exactly what I think I should do."

I frown as I get an uncomfortable feeling sweeping over me. "What's going on?" I ask.

"He has to protect his son. That's what's going on," Joshua snaps.

Cameron walks back over to the window and stares out over the city, deep in thought.

"What choice do you have, Cameron? She's out of fucking control. Working in a strip club, forgetting to pick him up… Overdosing."

I frown as my brain catches up with what these two are thinking.

Oh my God, no…"Cameron, wait. You can't do that. She will never forgive you," I say in a panic.

He turns and lifts his chin defiantly. "This isn't about Ashley anymore, Murph. It's about Owen. I need to do what's best for him."

"But you love her," I whisper, horrified.

"I'm a father first," he pushes out, clearly pained.

My eyes flash to Joshua. "You can't let him do this." I have to ring Natasha.

Joshua drops his head as he contemplates the repercussions. "Just say the word, Cam," Joshua says flatly.

Cameron puts his hands into his suit pockets as he stares into space.

How long have they been here together, contemplating this?

"What the hell are you two thinking?" I ask. "Stop it, whatever you're thinking, just stop it."

Cameron's eyes meet Joshua's. "She's given me no choice."

"I know," Joshua replies sadly.

"Let's do it." Cam sighs.

Joshua picks up the phone and rings someone, while I stand still in horror as I watch on. "Hello, Max?" Joshua frowns and then listens for a moment.

"Get four guards over to Ashley Tucker's house to watch Owen, please."

He listens for a moment.

"Don't let him out of your sight."

He listens again.

"Around the clock."

He hangs up.

Cameron hangs his head and exhales deeply.

Joshua rings another number. "Amanda?"

He listens for a moment.

"Send the legal team up to my office immediately."

Ashley

I lie on the lounge in a semi-conscious state as Jenna sits by my feet. "And you don't remember anything?" She frowns.

"I don't know." I shake my head as I try my hardest to remember. "I don't know if it was one of the girls who slipped something in my drink or one of the men."

I frown as the dull ache of my headache pumps through me.

"You are so lucky. You hit the concrete so damn hard. You could have died, Ash," Jen whispers.

I screw up my face. "I know." I shake my head. "Oh God, Jen, what a nightmare."

"Cameron was so worried." Jenna replies.

I smile softly. "He was beautiful. He was kissing me and holding me. He didn't think I heard him tell me he loved me before I woke up."

Jen frowns. "He told you he loved you?"

I smile softly and nod. "He must have thought I was going to die or something."

"You two need to work this shit out." She shakes her head.

"I know, I'm going to talk to him. I'm just grateful that he came when I needed him the most."

Knock, knock, knock.

Jen frowns, gets up and answers it. "Hello."

"Hello, is Ashley Tucker here?" a male voice asks.

"Yes." Jenna frowns. "Can I help you?"

"I have some papers to serve her."

I frown and sit up before I slowly walk to the door. "I'm Ashley. What's this about?" I ask.

"Can you sign here, please?" He points to the dotted line and I sign. He hands me an envelope and I glance out to see two men standing on our front lawn, and another two in a car. Who are they?

The man leaves and I walk out front. "Can I help you?" I ask the man standing on the edge of my lawn.

The man nods and smiles as he approaches. "We're here to watch over Owen Stanton."

I frown. "What for?"

"His father has requested it. We won't bother you, ma'am." What the hell? That's weird. I walk back inside and open the envelope as uneasiness fills me.

Court Subpoena

Cameron Stanton *verses* Ashley Tucker.
Cameron Stanton seeks full custody of Owen Tucker.

He wants full custody.
Oh my God.

24

I FROWN as I stare down at the piece of paper in front of me.
"What is it?" Jenna asks.
"I…" I whisper in horror.
"What is it?" she asks again.
I read it out loud to make sure I'm not imagining this.

Cameron Stanton seeks full custody of Owen Tucker

Temporary emergency injunction requested.

Los Angeles Courthouse on the 8th at 10:00 .a.m.

Closed courtroom application granted.

Legal representation not required as per temporary order requirements to enable time to prepare for full case.

Full custody hearing to be heard in twenty-eight days.

"He wants custody," I whisper in horror.

"What do you mean?" Jenna snatches the papers from my hand and reads them.

I drop to a seated position on the couch in shock.

"What the hell?" Jenna growls. "Is he a fucking idiot? You were obviously drugged. You don't do drugs!" she yells in an outrage.

I hold my chest in pain as the thought that he actually thinks Owen is unsafe with me hits home.

How could he do this?

My head drops to my hands in dismay.

"Oh shit, Ash, that's tomorrow. The court case is tomorrow," Jenna gasps.

I glance up at her. I don't even know what to think. What the hell is going on?

Jenna goes over to the window and stares out at the men surrounding the property. "These men are here to make sure that you don't run with Owen."

"What?" I frown, I stand and go over and peer out through the curtains. "Are you serious?"

"Why else would they be here?"

"I don't believe this," I whisper.

"Get the fucker on the phone." Jenna growls as she runs to find my phone.

I drop back onto the sofa; this is the warning. This is what he was warning me about if I didn't leave the club. I knew he wasn't a man to be crossed, but *this*?

She passes me my phone and I stare at it in my hand. "I'm not ringing him. I'm going over there."

Hell hath no fury like a mother scorned.

I've hit an all-time low.

Who the hell does he think he is?

I buzz his doorbell at the gates of his house, and they open immediately.

He's expecting me.

I march up to the front doors and he waits with the door open. I storm past him into the house.

"Please, do come in," he mutters sarcastically.

"What the hell is this?" I cry as I hold the court papers up to him.

"Calm down."

"Calm down?" I scream. "You have been a father for five fucking minutes and you think you can look after him better than me?"

He glares at me. "I'm not out doing drugs, Ashley."

"Neither am I!" I scream.

"The proof is in the pudding. Where did you spend last night? Where?" he yells.

I stare at him through angry tears.

"I sat at your bedside in the hospital all night, praying that you survived. Praying to God that I never have to tell my son that his mother died from an overdose."

"I was drugged," I whisper.

"Because you put yourself in that position!" he yells. "Who the fuck were you with last night?"

"Some girls from the club."

"Who were the men?" He growls. "Were they clients?"

I wince at the accusation. "What?" I shake my head. "They were men we just met out. It was nothing. Some of the girls were partying with them."

"With drugs?"

"They dropped some coke."

"Did you?" He growls.

"No, Cameron. I swear to you, I didn't." I shake my head in anger. "Don't tell me you have a perfect history, either, because I know you haven't."

"I would never take cocaine if I knew I had a kid at home waiting for me."

"That's the difference between us..." I scream. "For the last five years you've been out partying and screwing everyone you want with a clear conscience, while I've been at home

377

struggling to able to afford to live while looking after *your* baby!"

"I didn't know about him, Ashley, or I would have helped you," he yells.

"Help me now, Cameron!" I cry. "This isn't about you versus me."

"Don't make it like that then. You set the rules here."

"How?" I shake my head. "By not doing what you say? Is that it? Is that what this is about? Do you honestly think that you can tell me what to do?"

"I don't want where you work to come back to haunt Owen later in life," he snaps.

I step back in disgust. "You double standard, rich bastard." He narrows his eyes in contempt.

"You go to that club." I poke him hard in the chest. "You have fucked girls in that club and you have the balls to judge them as if they are nothing." I sneer, and I push him again in the chest, but he catches my hand mid-air.

"Don't push me, Ashley, or I'll fucking push you back."

"Is that another threat, little rich boy?" I sneer.

He squeezes my hand in his and steps forward, forcing me to step back. "Don't push me, Ashley. You won't win." He growls.

My eyes tear up. His power scares me.

He scares me.

"You said you loved me in the hospital," I whisper.

He steps back and drops his head.

"Is that true, Cameron? Do you love me?"

His eyes meet mine and he swallows slowly. "You know I do," he breathes.

"Then don't do this." Tears fall slowly down my cheeks. "Don't take him away from me."

Softness crosses his features, and he steps forward to cup my face in his hands.

"It's temporary, Ash." His eyes search mine. "Just until you get yourself sorted."

I stare at him through my tears.

"I promise you." I pause as I try to get my wording right. "It's just been a bad week. He's not in danger." I wince from the heartache. "I'm a good mom, Cam."

He pulls me into an embrace and holds me as my body shakes from the tears.

"We can work this out," I whisper against his shoulder.

"I have to do this, Ash."

I frown and pull out of his grip as I step back. "What?"

"I have to take precautions to protect him."

"You're really going ahead with this?"

His eyes hold mine. "He has to come first."

"He does, Cameron. He has always come first for me."

"It's temporary," he repeats.

I step back in horror. He's going to do this whether he loves me or not.

I shake my head. "Cameron, I swear, if you do this to me, I will never forgive you."

"Don't say that," he whispers as pain crosses his face.

"Then don't *do this!*" I cry, panicked.

"Ashley, I have to," he snaps, and with renewed determination, he walks to the door and opens it. "Now… You need to leave."

I shake my head as my tears roll down my face. "Cameron. No. I'm begging you. Please."

He closes his eyes as he tries to block me out.

"Cameron, listen to me," I whisper. "We can work this out. We can share custody."

"Ashley. Leave. Now." He gestures to the doorway.

I stare at him. *Who is this man?*

"I will see you in court tomorrow," he says without emotion.

"Is that why you have guards on Owen?" I ask.

His eyes meet mine.

"Do you honestly think I'd take him?" I whisper as the tears roll down my face.

He drops his head in shame.

"*Do you?*"

"I don't know what you would do anymore. The last week has shown me that. You've lied to me all along. From that first day in the hospital, you have done nothing but lie to me. I don't know who you are, I don't know what to think, I don't know what to believe anymore."

Pain crosses my face. I need to get away from him right now. I can't take this hurt any longer.

My eyes hold his. "Believe this, Cameron," I whisper. "I will never forgive you as long as I live."

I turn and walk out the door with my broken heart shattered deep in my chest.

"All rise," the clerk calls.

As we all stand, I feel like I'm having an out of body experience.

I'm in a small courtroom in LA. Cameron stands on the other side of the room.

We're both alone. This is a closed hearing and neither of us have legal representation. The big case is in a month and I will be prepared for that one.

I'm not giving up without a fight. But if I do lose, I *will* run.

I will not lose my son.

The only people here are two secretaries and a security guard.

I glance over as we wait for the judge to arrive, and Cameron's eyes are fixed firmly on the floor. He can't even bring himself to look at me.

He feels guilty, and so he should. This is a cowardly act if ever I saw one.

I bring up his child and this is how he repays me.

The door opens, the judge comes into view, and the floor sways beneath me. I know that face.

It's the man from the club.

Judy.

I frown. That's why they call him Judy. Judge Judy.

He's a judge.

My angry eyes flash to Cameron and he drops his head even lower and blows out a deep breath. He knows that he goes to the club. He knows that I hate him.

I'm going to lose.

My heart starts to race.

Tears instantly fill my eyes as I contemplate what's about to happen.

The judge sits down and reads the papers and then glances up and does a double take when he sees me. His eyes travel over to Cameron and he frowns.

He knows that Cameron spent the night with me in the Escape Lounge. Hell, he even bid against him for the honor.

I close my eyes as I sit quietly while he reads the papers in front of him.

"What's going on here?" he finally asks.

We both stay silent.

"Mr. Stanton, address the court," he orders.

Cameron stands. "I'm applying for temporary custody of my son, your Honor."

"Why?"

"Read the paperwork," Cameron replies, his hatred for this man shining through.

"I have and I want to hear it from you. Need I remind you that you're in *my* courtroom?"

This man is so rude.

Cameron pauses and his eyes find mine. "I feel that his mother is going through a hard time at the moment and that it is in the best interests of the child if he stays with me for a while. It's temporary," he adds.

"I see." The judge watches him carefully and then his eyes travel to me.

"You took an overdose this week, Ashley?"

"I was drugged, your Honor," I reply. "I didn't knowingly take drugs. I would never do that."

His eyes assess me for a moment.

"You are involved in prostitution?" As if he doesn't know… snake.

You screw girls there every night behind your family's back.

"No," I reply flatly. "I work at the bar in a club that has prostitutes working in another area of the club. It's by association that I have been accused of this," I answer firmly.

He raises an eyebrow in question. I would dearly love for it to go on the record that he is a client if he wants me to elaborate.

A fucking aggressive, sleazebag of a client.

He inhales deeply as he flicks through the paperwork. "What do you request of the court, Mr. Stanton?"

"Temporary custody until I am reassured of Miss Tucker's state of mind," Cameron answers.

"There is nothing wrong with my mind," I hiss.

The judge peers over his glasses at me. "You're a medical student, Ashley?"

"I am."

"Do you know the consequences of your future if you are charged with prostitution?"

I drop my eyes to the floor in shame. "I do."

"Your Honor, I have offered Ashley financial support so she can stop working at the bar, but she has, so far, refused," Cameron interrupts.

The judge's beady eyes peer up over those glasses again. "Is that true, Miss Tucker?"

I pause for a moment. "Yes, your Honor."

He frowns and flicks through the paperwork again and then rests his eyes up on us both intermittently.

"In light of this week's events with Miss Tucker overdosing, I feel I have no choice but to grant twenty-eight days temporary custody to Mr. Stanton in the interest of the child's safety. Ashley, you are to attend drug counseling before the next court hearing."

I frown.

He bangs the gavel. "Court adjourned." Judy snaps his folder and stands to leave the room.

I swallow the lump in my throat and concentrate on the carpet in front of me.

No.

No.

No.

This can't be happening.

I feel Cameron's hand on my shoulder. He squeezes it as an offer of sympathy.

I brush it off and stand defiantly. "Don't you ever touch me," I whisper. "I hate you."

Cameron

I sit at the kitchen counter, thinking about today's court case. Ashley was beyond devastated and, even though I know I should be happy I won, that I can guarantee Owen's safety...

I feel like shit.

The front door opens in a rush and I hear Natasha's and Adrian's voices. I instantly roll my eyes.

Here we go.

Stan is with me already. He came here straight from work after the court case at midday. He knows how low I am.

Natasha comes into view and her face falls when she sees me. "Is it true?" she asks, her voice filled with horror.

I stare at her as Joshua walks into the room behind her. He kisses her on the cheek, but her attention stays firmly fixed on me.

"Answer me, Cameron," she snaps.

"Tell me you didn't go through with it," Murph begs.

I drop my head in shame.

"What the *fuck*, Cameron?" Natasha yells. "What the hell do you think you are doing?"

"He's protecting his child," Joshua interjects.

"He doesn't need to!" she yells. "Ashley is a fantastic mother."

"She's forgetting to pick him up. She's working in a strip club one minute and overdosing the next. What am I supposed to do?" I reply in my defence.

"You are supposed to support her."

"*You* never forget *your* kids."

Her eyes widen in disbelief. She's looking at me like I'm stupid. "I have three nannies, Cameron. I have security around the clock and I have never paid a damn bill since I've been with your brother." Joshua and I stay silent.

"Have you two honestly lost your minds?"

I drop my head.

"She's doing the best that she can. She works in that damn strip club to pay for Owen's food, and I can tell you right now, if I had no money and no support, I wouldn't think twice about any job that provided stability for my kids."

"You wouldn't work there," Joshua grumbles.

Natasha turns on him like a crazy person. "I would sleep with the fucking devil to give my kids a home, and you should know that every decent mother on the planet would do the same," she yells as she slams her hand down on the counter. "Have you two deviated so far from reality with your privileged life that you have lost all compassion?"

"Obviously, they have," Murph mutters under his breath.

"Shut up, Murph," I say firmly.

"No, I won't. This is fucking ridiculous, Cameron," he snaps. "I can't believe you are going through with it."

"What am I supposed to do?" I yell. "You tell me what I'm supposed to do when I know for a fact that Ashley is driving around with Owen in the car, surviving on only two hours sleep, twice a week."

They all stay silent.

"If he gets killed in a car accident from her falling asleep behind the wheel and I knew that I could have stopped it... I could never live with myself," I cry.

Natasha drops her head to her hands. "Cam," she whispers.

"I don't know how to stop her working there. I don't have any choice," I reply sadly. "This is out of my control. I didn't want to do this."

"You are doing the right thing, Cam." Joshua sighs sadly.

Natasha screws up her face. "Would you turn on me like this?" she asks Joshua in disgust.

"If I knew you for one week and you had lied to me the whole time and you tried this shit on with my child... Fucking truth, I would." He growls.

"Then you're an asshole, too," she screams. "That's it, I'm leaving." She storms toward the front door. "Adrian?" she calls out.

Joshua rolls his eyes, knowing he's now in the shit, too.

"Coming," Adrian calls back. "Cam, I'm telling you now, if you do this, Ashley is gone for good. You can kiss her goodbye. She will *never* forgive you." With one last lingering look, he disappears after Natasha and the front door slams behind them both.

Fear rises in my chest.

The house falls silent and I am left alone with my brother, each of us lost, deep in thought.

"I have to do this," I murmur sadly.

He puts his hand on my shoulder. "I know you do, mate. I would do the same."

Ashley

It's just turning six in the evening — the time Cameron said he is coming to get Owen. The guards are out the front, surrounding the house.

The house is silent and sad.

I pack the last of the things in Owen's suitcase as I try to pretend I'm happy that he's going on a holiday.

Jenna is in her room crying. We've both been distraught all day.

She can't even face Owen.

I need to be the bigger person and not let my son be scared by what's happening.

He's only a baby.

"Where's my cap?" Owen asks.

"I already put it into your suitcase," I whisper. I take his favorite ten books and put them into the suitcase on top of his clothes.

"Will you come and get me tomorrow?" Owen asks. "I don't think I want to sleep there, either. Can you sleep over, too?"

I swallow the lump in my throat. "No, baby. Mommy can't come."

He thinks for a moment. "But where will I sleep." Tears fill my eyes. "You will sleep with Daddy."

"But he might not let me sleep with him." He frowns, concerned.

"He will." I smile. "He told me that it's okay," I assure him as I keep packing.

Owen frowns. "I'm not going to go. I want to stay here with you."

"You need to go, baby. It's going to be so much fun," I whisper.

I see the black *Audi* pull up and I wince as I try to hide my emotions.

Oh my God. I can't do this.

I close my eyes as I try to gain the strength that I need to get through this. I want to scream and fight and cry and beg him not to take him, but I know that's only going to upset Owen. I can't do that to my little man.

Cameron sits in the car and I slowly seal the suitcase shut. "Dad's here," I whisper.

Owen jumps off the bed and peers out the window, smiling brightly.

"Dad!" he calls, and he takes off out of the bedroom, runs downstairs, out the front and up to the car. Cameron gets out and picks Owen up to hold him in his arms.

I watch from the upstairs window as the tears stream down my face.

Cameron glances up and sees me. His face falls and he drops his head to kiss Owen's temple.

I wheel the suitcase downstairs and out onto the porch. I can't help it now. The tears won't stop.

Owen runs up to me, and his face falls when he sees my distress. "What's wrong, Momma?" He frowns.

"I'm just going to miss you, baby." I smile as I bend and take him in my arms.

I hold him tight to my chest as I scrunch up my face from the pain. Cameron watches on in silence.

I fake a smile. "You be a good boy for daddy." I straighten his shirt and his pants.

I turn to Cameron. "He needs to sleep with you... In your bed," I whisper. "He gets scared on his own."

Cameron's haunted eyes hold mine.

"Promise me he can sleep with you," I push out through my tears.

Cameron nods. "I promise," he whispers.

I squeeze Owen and hold him tight until, finally, I know I have to let him go.

"Go with Daddy, baby," I whisper.

I grab him once more. This is unbearable.

Cameron takes the suitcase from me and I bite my bottom lip to stop myself from sobbing loudly. He takes Owen's hand and leads him out to the car.

I watch on as my heart hurts and the tears run down my face.

He opens the car and lifts Owen into the seat and straps him in. I feel like I've just been shot. I start to cry, hard and uncontrolled, and I know I need to get inside before Owen sees me. I stagger back and make it through the door only to fall into the fetal position on the sofa where I let myself sob.

No, no, no. This can't be happening. He took him.

He took my baby.

I cry out as the pain becomes unbearable. "No," I cry as I shake my head violently. "No, no, no."

I feel Jenna's hands on my shaking shoulders. "It's okay, Ash. It's going to be okay, baby. We'll get him back. I promise you, we will get him back."

The screen door bangs and we both look up to see Cameron standing in the foyer.

"Change of plans," he whispers through haunted eyes. "Owen will stay here now. I'll come and get him at the weekend."

My face falls.

Cameron clenches his hands at his sides, unsure what to say next. Without further word, he turns and leaves, just as Owen comes in the front door.

I stare at Owen for a moment, completely in shock. What just happened?

I smile awkwardly through my tears. "Baby, you're back already?" I run and scoop him up into my arms and sob with relief.

Thank heavens.

25

T HEY SAY that time heals all wounds.
They lied.

It's been six weeks since Cameron tried to take my son from me.

It's been six weeks since I lost all faith in humanity.

I resigned from my internship, and Dr. Jameson stepped in and offered me a placement with him. He knows the full, sordid story.

I hardly see Cameron at work now. We are civil and share custody with Owen. Cameron dropped the court proceedings, but I still have to attend drug counselling once a week from the court orders.

Owen is blossoming before my eyes and he loves his father with all of his heart.

Cameron is good for him. I have no doubt in my mind about that.

Whereas once before I was jealous and nervous around Cameron... now I only have contempt for him.

The gentle, funny man I was in love with has been replaced by the power hungry millionaire he's shown me to be.

The Stanton family is a tight circle. If you're on the inside, they're loyal to each other to the death. But they're a nightmare if they declare war against you.

Sadly, money wins all battles.

I'm scared for my son—scared for the man he is going to turn into.

He will be one of them, I can already see it. Cameron changed his name legally to Stanton a month ago and he added his name as Owen's father on his birth certificate.

He is now Owen Stanton with a hefty trust fund and a rich daddy.

I say that like I despise it, and I don't. I don't mean to be negative. All those years when I didn't know who Owen's father was, I just dreamed of a man who would protect him with all of his heart—who would love him as much as I do.

And he does. Cameron loves Owen. It's undeniable. The bond they share is natural and strong. It's everything I ever hoped for.

Natasha has been wonderful and I've seen her at least once a week since everything happened. We seem to have formed a friendship out of all of this.

She understands my point of view, but she also understands Cameron's. I get it, I really do. All hell broke loose when she found out what Cameron had done. I can't help but wish that she could have talked sense into Cameron before he ruined everything between us.

Part of me is grateful that I know Cameron will fight for what he thinks is best for Owen.

My life has become easier. I don't work at the club anymore. I have three days where I'm childless every week. I joined a gym and I'm reading books for fun again.

I should be happy. My rent is paid. My son is content.

But I feel like an empty vessel—like my heart has been ripped out and put into the blender on high speed.

I don't want to feel like this anymore. I don't want to hate him. I just want to stop hurting over what he did.

I need to get over it. It's all in the past.

Just like my love for him.

It's midnight and I am sitting up alone watching a rerun of *Friends*. Joey can always make me laugh, no matter what.

Jenna has started quite the love affair with her new friend, and she stays over there more times than she stays with me now. I'm happy for her. She deserves someone nice, and he is beautiful.

I check my phone and blow out a deflated breath.

No messages.

I stand up, turn the television off, and head up to bed.

Tomorrow I will feel better. I know I will. Mornings always seem so much brighter.

Sadly, I know that at this time tomorrow night I will feel exactly the same as I do now.

Empty and alone.

Cameron

The phone rings in the middle of the night and I get up to answer it. I knew this call was coming.

"Hello." I sigh.

"Hello, Dr. Stanton. This is Maria."

I rub my eyes as I try to focus. "Hello, Maria." Maria is the head nurse from the cardiology wing.

"Gloria is in her last stages, sir. I know you wanted to be told when it got to this point."

"I did," I reply sadly. "I'm going to come in."

"See you soon."

I hang up, get dressed, and arrive at the hospital half an hour later. It's three in the morning and it's cold.

It's always sad saying goodbye to a patient, but tonight it seems especially lonely.

With no children, and her husband and family all deceased, Gloria is totally alone.

She has been in hospital for fourteen weeks without a single visitor.

I can't imagine not having family around me when it all ends. I park my car and take the elevator

with a heavy heart. Gloria knows she's dying. She will know that I'm coming to say goodbye.

I walk up the hall toward her room and approach the door with a frown on my face when I see someone else in the room.

Ashley is with her, and I stop and stand by the door for a moment as I listen to them talk.

"I don't want to die alone," Gloria whispers.

"You won't." Ashley smiles as she leans over her and brushes the hair back from her face. "I won't leave you. I will stay until the end."

Gloria's sad eyes hold Ashley's. "Do you promise?" she whispers.

Ashley smiles and kisses the back of Gloria's hand. "I promise."

I frown at the floor as I listen.

"You will get to see your husband soon, Gloria," Ashley whispers.

Gloria smiles. "How wonderful." Her face falls. "It's been twenty-two years since I've seen him."

"What was he like? Tell me about him," Ashley encourages, genuinely intrigued.

"He was the crankiest bastard that ever drew breath."

I smile as I listen.

"But I loved him," she whispers. "From the day I met him when I was fifteen, I loved him with all of my heart."

"You are so blessed to have found your one," Ashley says through a soft sigh, and I have to really listen to hear her gentle voice.

"You will find yours," Gloria tells her.

There is a pause. "I already found him."

"You did? This is great news," Gloria whispers.

"Not really, Gloria. My story didn't turn out so well. I'm afraid I won't get my happy ending."

I swallow as I listen. Is she talking about me?

"Why not?" Gloria asks.

I frown as I listen.

"He didn't love me like I loved him." She pauses. "It's okay. I *will* get my happy ending with someone. It just won't be with *my one*."

My stomach drops. She feels how I feel. Regret hangs heavily in my heart over what I have done to us.

"There are lots of handsome men out there, Ashley."

Ashley giggles. "I know. I'm going to find one really soon. I may even go on a date."

"You are?" Gloria gasps. "Oh, I wish I would be here to hear about it."

There is a pause and I peer around the corner to see Ashley softly pushing the hair back from Gloria's face as she stares down at her lovingly. "I'm so happy to have met you, Gloria," she whispers. "You have brightened my days here."

I get a lump in my throat and I close my eyes.

"Will you read to me, dear?" Gloria whispers.

"I would be honored."

"Can you read my favorite part?"

"Of course."

I steel myself and walk into the room. Gloria's eyes light up.

"Ah." I smile as I take her hand in mine. "My two favorite girls here together. I'm a lucky man tonight."

Ashley looks up from her book, and for the first time in a long time, I see relief in her eyes when she sees me.

I pick up Gloria's hand and I kiss the back of it as I smile down at her. My gaze travels over to my beautiful Ashley sitting with the book in her hand. I pull up a chair on the other side of the bed and hold Gloria's hand, listening to the words as Ashley reads through unshed tears.

After a short pause, Darcy added. "You are too generous to trifle with me. If your feelings are still the same as they were last April, tell me at once. My affections and wishes are unchanged, but one word from you will silence me forever.
I love you, most ardently."

Ashley finishes reading and we both glance up.
Gloria has gone in silence.
"Rest in peace, angel," I whisper.
Ashley drops her head and silently weeps.
Death is so hard.

Ashley

"Oh my God," Amber whispers as we walk down the hall to the cafeteria. "So, get this. We went back to his house and we are fooling around, and he asks me if I am feeling playful."

Amber is filling me in on her latest fling with the hospital security guard. She's grown on me. She really is the only fun thing around here and her stories keep me amused for hours.

I watch her as I walk with my folder in my arms. "Yeah?"

"Then he goes to the cupboard and brings out this life size blow-up doll."

"No?" I whisper.

"I know, right?" She hits me as we walk. "He lays her on the bed next to me and tells me he wants to have a threesome with the two of us."

My mouth drops open. "I have no words." I shake my head as we get to the cafeteria and order our coffees. I notice Cameron is sitting with Seb in the corner, and I wave as we take our seats at a table. Cameron glances over and I make myself look away.

"What happened then?" I ask.

"You won't believe it."

I bubble up a giggle. "Probably not."

"He goes downtown on me."

I laugh and then shake my head. "Eww, I'm getting a visual," I murmur, distracted.

She rolls her eyes.

"And?" I ask against my coffee cup.

"This is where it gets fucked up."

I laugh in surprise. "You are in bed with a man and blow up, chick. This is already fucked up, Amber."

"He starts going down on the doll."

I laugh and slap my hand over my mouth to shut myself up. I glance around and see Cameron and Seb looking over at us.

"I have no words," I whisper.

"Then he starts with this role play shit, telling me I have to wait my turn for his tongue, that he has other pussy's to take care of."

I hoot with laughter. "What the actual hell? What did you do?"

She shrugs. "I was so shocked that I just laid there and watched him growl out a fucking plastic doll."

My mouth drops open and I shake my head.

"This is where it gets really bad..." she whispers as she looks around guiltily.

I laugh again. "I can't believe this story."

"He starts lining himself up to fuck the doll."

I frown. "What? He's going to fuck the doll before he fucks you?"

She nods. "Yes, he thinks I'm getting sloppy seconds."

I cannot control my laughter. "Honestly, this is hilarious."

She sips her coffee and looks around unimpressed.

"What did you do?" I ask.

"I lose my shit and somehow fall into this fucked role play, and now I'm demanding he fucks me first before the plastic chick."

My mouth drops open and my eyes are wide. "I can't believe this."

"So he's fucking me and then he starts talking to the doll while we are doing it, saying *I won't be long, baby. I'm saving some come for you. Play with yourself until I get there.*"

"What the hell?" I giggle again and cover my mouth with my hand. "This is priceless."

"Ashley?" Seb smiles as he leans on the back of my chair. The two of us sit back guiltily. I glance up and see Cameron and Seb standing over us.

I turn in my chair. "Hey." I smile up at him.

"Hello." Amber smiles.

Cameron smiles uncomfortably and nods.

"How come you haven't called me yet for our date?" Seb smiles playfully down at me.

Cameron's face falls instantly, and he frowns as he looks between us.

Oh shit. This is uncomfortable. "I told you, I'm not calling you," I answer. "You ask me the same question every day, Seb." I give him a subtle shake of my head.

"One of these days, Miss Tucker, I'll be painting the town red with you."

I laugh and my eyes peer over at Cameron. His jaw ticks as he glares at Seb.

"Whatever you say." I smirk. "I wouldn't hold your breath, though."

Cameron turns and marches off and Seb takes off after him until I see them disappear up the corridor.

"Please explain to me why you won't go out with him." Amber frowns. "Are you sick? He's frigging gorgeous." She puts her hand to my forehead to feel for a temperature.

"Get back to blow-up pussy chick," I snap dryly as I swat her hand away.

She clears her throat and drinks her coffee. "So, he fucks me and it's really good and then when we are finished he wants to go downtown and lick me up."

I frown. "After you've finished?"

"Uh-huh."

I cringe.

"He's going back down when he starts dirty talking at the doll again."

I'm howling, hooting loud laughter. "What did you do?"

"He then went on to screw the doll and I was..." She pauses and shakes her head in disgust at herself. "Seriously turned on by it."

My face falls.

"I watched him fuck the doll and it was hot. He was kissing me while he had sex with doll, and I'm telling you, it was the hottest experience of my life."

I frown. "What are you going to do? Are you meeting him again?" I whisper in horror.

She looks around so that nobody can hear. "He rang me before to tell me that he ordered me a man doll today so I can have a threesome with the two of them."

My mouth drops open. "I'm officially in shock," I whisper.

"Me, too. He said he got the huge cock one so I could really ride it out."

I laugh in surprise again. "Is he going to go sloppy seconds to that?"

She shrugs and sips her coffee. "Who cares? This blow up plastic threesome shit is hot. I'm so into it."

"Oh, Amber... you kill me." I giggle.

Cameron

I walk down the corridor, deep in thought. Seb's been asking Ashley out.

I'm rattled.

She's mine.

He catches up with me. "Hey, so you want to go out on Saturday night?" he asks.

"I thought you had a date with Ashley," I reply flatly as I sign a form at the nurse's station.

"Nah, not yet. I will soon, though. She's warming up to me."

I glance up at him from the notes I'm reading. "What makes you think that?"

He smiles cheekily. "The way she looks at me. She's begging for it. She's smoking hot," he whispers.

I close my eyes as I try to remain in control

Ignore him. Ignore him.

"I think Ashley has a boyfriend," I mutter.

"No, she broke up with him."

My eyes meet his. "How do you know that?"

"She told me. Apparently he was a real douche. Did a real number on her."

I inhale deeply as my fury starts to become transparent. "I've got to get back to work." I storm up to my office, go in, and lean on the closed door as I stare at the wall.

Being around her is hard.

Being around her when she is with someone else will be unbearable.

The car pulls out of my driveway and I watch the black *Audi* disappear. Ashley and Owen have just dropped me back home and taken the car.

I glance up at the house in front of me—my home—and I hate this feeling. I hate this empty feeling I have inside.

I get it every time they leave me.

My heart is living with them at their house, and yet my body lives here alone.

I can't stand the silence when Owen's not here.

I can't stand my empty bed that Ashley's not in.

I can't stand the fact that I'm only happy three days a week, and even then it's only partial because I don't have her.

I know I need to move on, but I just don't know how.

This emptiness is poisoning me, day by day.

I walk in and head straight to my bar, make myself a Scotch, and go sit in the dark by my pool. I hit my playlist of depressing heartbreak songs and a personal favorite by Kaleo comes on. Way down we go.

Father tell me, we get what we deserve.
And way down we go
Way down we go.

The tantric blues music rings out on repeat and I drink myself stupid.

I'm down, alright. I have no idea how to get myself back up.

Way down we go.

Ashley

I pull up in Cameron's driveway.

It's late afternoon on Saturday and I'm dropping them home for the weekend in the car. They've been skateboarding in our street all day long.

Cameron's eyes glance to me from the passenger seat, and he pauses as if he wants to say something. He's been doing this lately—lingering after we finish speaking as if he has more to say. He holds the keys to the house up to Owen in the backseat. "Go and unlock the house, Owie. I'll be there in a minute."

Owen snatches the keys from his hand and leans over to kiss me. "Bye, Mom." He smiles as he jumps out of the car.

"Bye, baby. Have fun." I smile after him.

I sit with my hands on the wheel, my bottom lip firmly caught between my teeth.

Cameron watches me and my eyes eventually find his. "Do you want to come in and have dinner with us?" he asks, sounding hopeful. "I can make your favorite."

I fake a smile. "No, but thank you."

He watches me for a moment before he sighs softly. "How long are you going to hate me for, Ash?"

"I don't hate you."

He frowns. "But you don't like me."

I exhale deeply. "I just don't want to play happy families, Cam." I shake my head. "Just leave it. Please."

"Can't we even be friends?"

"Sure," I reply flatly as I stare out through the windshield.

He frowns. "What do you mean *sure*? Is that to shut me up?"

"I mean, sure, get out of the car. I'm not having this conversation with you. I'm done. You are not my friend, Cameron. You're my son's father and nothing else now. We have been over this a million times. Stop bringing this up."

He stares out the front window. "Wow," he mouths sarcastically.

I swallow the lump in my throat and stare straight ahead. "What do you want me to say, Cam?" I whisper.

"I want you to scream at me. I want you to punch me. Anything is better than this ice queen treatment you're giving me. I can't stand it."

I nod as I purse my lips, and I turn to him. "I would do all of those things if I still cared."

His sad eyes hold mine.

"I don't, Cam. I'm sorry, I just don't. Move on. I have."

"Hello, Ash," Cameron's deep voice travels down the phone. It's Wednesday, around lunchtime.

"Hi, Cam." I smile.

"I have a problem."

I frown. "What's that?"

"Abigail just rang me and she can't work this week because her husband is sick."

Cameron has a nanny the days he has Owen because he leaves so early in the morning. Abigail gets Owen up and ready for the day and drops him at preschool. She then picks him up and watches him until Cameron gets home.

We interviewed for her together and she's a really nice middle-aged lady with her own grownup children. Owen adores her and it's working out well.

"That's okay. We can just leave this week then and you can pick up next week."

"No," he replies quickly. "That means I won't see him until the weekend," he answers in a panic.

I widen my eyes. "So what do you want to do?"

"Well, I was thinking if I could just have him at night and then come over to your house and tuck him into bed, and then he can sleep at your house so Jenna is there."

I frown. "Yeah, I guess. That shouldn't be a problem."
"Good. I'll pick him up about five and then we will be back about eight? Is that okay?"

"Yeah, fine. See you then."

I'm lying on the sofa in my flannelette pyjamas when they come bursting through the door. Owen is on Cameron's shoulders and they are laughing and wrestling.

"Hello?" I call from my relaxed position. Jenna is out for dinner with her boyfriend.

"Hey, Mom." Owen laughs as he leans down and tries to eye gouge Cameron.

"That's it." Cameron laughs as he flips him over onto the couch.

Owen squeals in delight and wrestles harder.

I frown as I try to watch the show on television. "Can you two go away?" I sigh with a shake of my head. "What happened to my nice, quiet son? Where did he go?" I ask myself.

"He was a wuss," Cameron teases.

"You're a wuss." Owen screams as he launches himself at Cameron again.

They wrestle into the kitchen, and then I hear a bang as the bin knocks over.

"That's it!" Owen screams. "I'm getting you bad now."

"Oh, yeah, tough guy. Bring it." Cameron laughs in delight.

They both growl as they wrestle.

"Cut it out," I yell over the television.

I swear to God, he's turned him into an animal.

All this testosterone is bloody noisy. "Owen, it's nearly bed time," I call out.

"Okay," he calls back.

"Dad's reading to you tonight," I add. Ha, sucked in. It is his night, after all.

"I'm reading Diary of a Wimpy kid," Cameron calls.

"You're a wimpy kid!" Owen yells.

"I'll give you wimpy kid." Cameron growls and Owen squeals in delight.

I roll my eyes as I turn the television up louder so I can't hear them.

They wrestle up the stairs, and moments later I hear the shower turn on and peace is finally restored.

I have a cup of tea and finally, when I think the book reading is over, I head upstairs to say goodnight. Owen's door is closed and I stand outside, leaning against it as I listen to the two of them talk.

"I'm going to try and jump tomorrow," Owen says.

I frown as I listen.

"Yeah, you can do it. I told you that," Cameron replies. It sounds like Cameron is walking around tidying up as he talks.

I smirk. What the hell are they talking about?

"Hey, Dad, play our song," Owen says.

"What... now?"

"Please?" Owen begs.

"Okay, just one last time."

I narrow my eyes as I listen to them and then I hear a song play on Cameron's phone. I've heard it before on the radio. It's Justin Beiber singing a song in Spanish with another man.

Cameron's voice rings out as he starts to sing to the words in Spanish, then Owen joins in and their combined voices ring out happily.

Despacito.

I lean my head up against the wall in the semi-lit hallway as I listen. How many times have they sung this song together?

I smile softly in the darkness as their husky voices ring out.

They know the words and it's in Spanish.

This is it. Everything that I dreamed of Owen having is right here.

Cameron loves him. With all of his heart he loves him.

Even after everything I have been through, it's insignificant and means nothing because my son is finally happy.

Really, really happy.

As I listen to them sing together with tears in my eyes, I'm grateful for the relationship that they have.

This is how it was always meant to be.

26

T HE PHONE rings. It's a Friday night, and Cameron was supposed to be here ten minutes ago to pick Owen up for the weekend.

He called in sick today and he had surgery scheduled that had to be cancelled. So he's either really sick or something else is going on. I wanted to call him, but I stopped myself. It's none of my business.

I glance at the screen and the name Cameron lights it up. I frown as I answer.

"Hello."

"Hi, Ash," his groggy voice whispers.

"What's wrong?" I immediately ask.

"Nothing." He pauses. "I'm just not well."

"Are you okay?"

"Yeah." He hesitates. "I can't come and get Owen, though. Please apologize to him for me."

I frown, this is weird. He's never missed a visit.

"What's wrong with you?" I ask.

"I'm guessing a virus. I'll be fine."

"You sound really sick."

"Sorry, I know you had plans for tonight," he says.

For the first time in a long time, Jenna and I were going to dinner and a late movie tonight. Damn it. "That's okay." I sigh. "Do you need anything?"

"No, I'm good." He pauses as if wanting to say something and I wait on the line.

Is he ok?

"I'll... I'll call you later," he murmurs and then he hangs up.

I stare at the phone in my hand for a moment. That was weird.

"We can't go tonight, Jen. Cam is sick," I announce as I walk into the kitchen.

"Fuck it," she whispers under her breath.

"Go and have hot sex. That's what I'd be doing if I was you," I mutter dryly as I open the fridge. I now have to find something to cook. Bloody hell. I really needed a nice night out with lots of wine.

"Ugh, that sucks."

"We can go next week." I sigh.

"Yeah, okay." She smirks as she watches me study the contents of the fridge. "What are you going to have for dinner?"

I frown as I continue to look inside the depressing fridge. "I might take Owen out for pizza actually." I shrug. "I'm not in the mood to cook."

"Do you want me to come with you?" she asks.

"Nah, that's okay." I smile and kiss her on the cheek. "Go do your thing. We'll make our own fun."

An hour and a half and a huge stomach full of pizza later, I find myself pulling up in Cameron's driveway with Owen in the car.

I can't stop thinking that something is wrong. His call was off and has left me feeling uneasy.

Part of my job as Owen's mother is to make sure his father is safe, I justify to myself.

There is nothing weird about me checking on him. I'm just being a responsible mother.

"What are we doing?" Owen calls from the back seat.

"Umm, I just want to check on Dad. He's sick and I want to make sure he's alright."

He smiles, unbuckles his seatbelt, and is out of the car before I even turn off the engine. The guard opens the gates on sight and I walk through and up to the front door. Owen has already gone in. The door must have been unlocked.

"Dad," Owen calls as he runs into the kitchen and I take the stairs two at a time.

Something is definitely off here.

I find him in bed, shaking, covered in a layer of sweat.

"What the hell, Cam?" I whisper as I go to him.

He closes his eyes. "What are you doing here?" he croaks.

I put my hand on his forehead and he is burning up with a raging temperature. "Checking on you. Why didn't you call me?" I snap.

"I'm fine." He shivers.

"You are not fine. We need to get this temp down. Get up."

"I'm fine." He snaps.

I disappear into his bathroom and turn the shower onto a cool tepid stream. I walk back into his room as Owen bounces through the door. "Dad." He smiles excitedly.

Cameron frowns in horror that his son is seeing him like this.

"Dad's sick, baby. He needs to cool down," I tell him. Owen's face falls as he watches his father shiver in bed.

"Come on, help me get him up." I grab Cameron's arm and pull him. "Cam. You need to have a shower and we need to get this temp down," I urge. "Have you had any medication?" I ask.

He shakes his head.

"I thought you were a doctor." I frown with a shake of my head. "Where is your medicine cabinet?"

"In the cupboard, downstairs." He sighs.

I turn to Owen. "Where does Dad keep the band aids?" I ask.

"In the kitchen."

"Can you show me?"

Owen scoots downstairs and I follow him and retrieve the Tylenol as well as a glass of water.

I return upstairs and force feed them to Cameron, and then get him up and lead him to the bathroom. Shit, I think I'm going to have to take him to emergency. He's so sick. What kind of virus is this?

"Owie, go and put some cartoons on. We'll stay here for a while."

"Yay!" Owen calls as he disappears downstairs and I hear the television turn on in the distance.

I put my hand under the shower and I turn to Cameron and grab his face as I look into his eyes. He's near delirious. "Cameron, are you alright?" I ask.

He nods.

"Get in the shower."

He puts his hand out to the shower screen to steady himself on his feet.

Shit, is he going to faint?

"Cameron," I repeat. "Are you going to fall?"

He drops his head as he tries to stay upright and holds the wall for support.

"In the shower," I snap. Damn it. I bend and slide his boxer shorts down his legs and lead him into the shower until he's under the cool water. He stands as he holds the tiles.

"Just stay under there for a while," I tell him as I fuss around grabbing towels. I would tell him to sit down, but I don't think I will be able to get him back up.

I take a seat on the edge of the bath as I watch him standing beneath the water.

He's naked, and for the first time since I've known him, completely vulnerable. For twenty minutes, I sit quietly as he stands under the water. I change the sheets on his bed, and eventually, I walk over to the shower and feel his forehead again.

"How do you feel?" I ask as I check his face temp with the backs of my fingers.

"I'm okay," he answers quietly.

"How long have you been like this?" I ask.

He shakes his head. "I woke up last night, throwing up. That's stopped, but the temperature has gotten higher."

"Cam." I shake my head. "You know this is dangerous. Why didn't you call me?"

He closes his eyes, as though embarrassed. "I'm fine."

"You are not fine. If I can't get this temperature down, I'm taking you to hospital."

He nods as he concedes defeat.

"Come on, back to bed." I hold a towel out for him and he exits the shower. I wrap him in it and he drops his head to my shoulder in desperate need of comfort.

I close my eyes as I hold him and the sick feeling of protectiveness fills me.

Stop it.

I pull out of his arms and dry him, lead him back to bed, and lie him down. His eyes immediately close.

Gosh, he's so sick.

I pull the sheet over him and sit on the edge of the bed to watch him for a while. I feel his forehead and his temperature seems to be dropping.

He has a virus, by the looks of it, but he needs some water. He's dehydrated.

Over the next three hours, I sit with him and give him water every ten minutes as he dozes in and out of a sleepy consciousness.

Who knows what would have happened if I hadn't checked on him when I did? After I'm positive he's better and hydrated, I eventually head downstairs. I find Owen on the couch in his underpants, laughing out loud at cartoons and eating ice cream straight from the tub.

I smile to myself, is this what they do in this bachelor pad?

Owen's eyes rise to me. "Is Dad feeling better?" he asks.

"Yes, he's sleeping." I smile and sit down next to him, placing my arm around his shoulders. "We might stay here tonight, though, I think... just to make sure."

He smiles and punches the air. "Yes!"

Cameron

I hear Ashley's voice drift from the kitchen. "Owen. Do you want a hot chocolate? I'm making tea."

I can hear Owen's little voice from downstairs, too, although I have no idea what he's saying.

The setting sun is just peeking through the side of the blinds, and I lean over to pick up my phone.

Sunday. 5:00 .p.m.

Fuck.

Where did the weekend go?

Ashley and Owen have stayed by my side, never leaving me for a minute. Ash has looked after me and I have no doubt I would have been hospitalized for dehydration if she hadn't shown up when she did.

I inhale as I stare at the ceiling above. God, she's seen me at my worst now.

Naked, soft, and shivering while covered in sweat.

I hear Owen's laugh ring out and I smile as I listen. Ashley is chasing him and they are screaming and laughing through the house.

What a fucking awesome sound.

I get up slowly, go to the bathroom to shower, and then I head downstairs to find them sitting on the floor with their backs up against the sofa drinking hot chocolate and tea, engrossed in an animal documentary.

"Hey." I smile bashfully.

"Well, here he is!" Ashley smiles as she looks over at me. "You survived?"

My eyes hold hers and my heart skips a beat. That's the first genuine smile she has given me in over two months.

"Dad," Owen calls and jumps up to cuddle my leg.

"Hey, mate." I rub my hand roughly through his hair. "Sorry to wreck your weekend."

He smiles and takes a seat back on the floor next to his mom.

My eyes hold hers. "Thanks, Ash." I pause. "You don't know how much I appreciate you staying."

She smiles and sips her tea. "That's okay. I'm sending you to the pharmacy next month to buy my *Tampax* as pay back."

I smirk.

"What's *Tampax*?" Owen asks as his eyes roam between us.

I raise my eyebrows. "Weird girl things," I reply dryly as I lie on the sofa behind the two of them. "What are we watching?" I ask.

"Meerkats," Owen replies. "But this girl's been a naughty one and the mother is getting angry. It's a big family fight," he explains as he points to one of the meerkats who is circling another.

I smirk as I watch the screen. I don't care what we are watching, or whose family is attacking each other.

As long as it's not mine.

The reflection of the fire lanterns flickers across the pool. The sun has set and the cocktail waiters are circling. I'm at Carson's house at a party.

I'm here with my friends and Joshua, although he's leaving around nine to go and have drinks with Tash and Murph who are out at dinner.

He doesn't stay long at these parties anymore. He hasn't since he settled down with Tash.

It's funny, you know. I could never understand why he would rush home to be with her when he sees her everyday—why he couldn't stand to be away from her for more than a few hours at a time. It only got worse when he had kids, and for a long time, he went nowhere without them.

I get it now.

Since Owen came into my life—and Ashley—these parties hold no interest for me anymore.

Beautiful women are approaching me every ten minutes, and all I can do is keep looking at my watch to make sure I don't miss ringing my son to say goodnight at eight o'clock.

What the hell has happened to me?

"Hey, Cam," a voice calls from behind me, and I turn to see Celeste in a tight, smoking hot gold dress. She's smiling sexily up at me.

"Hi." I smile and bend to kiss her cheek as a greeting.

"Hi, Stan." She smiles at Joshua.

He nods and smiles politely. "Hello."

"Do you want to come inside for a drink? It's been months since we spent any time together," she asks hopefully.

I smirk, knowing that was code for *it's been months since we fucked*.

I narrow my eyes as I contemplate the offer. "Ah, yeah. Maybe later. I'm staying out here for a while."

She smiles. "Come looking for me when you're ready to catch up."

I raise an eyebrow. "You know I will."

She walks off and Stan's eyes and mine follow her as she glides through the crowd.

"She's fucking hot," he murmurs.

I exhale. "Yeah, she's okay," I reply, bored as my eyes glance around at the crowd.

He narrows his eyes as he watches me. "What's up with you lately?"

"What do you mean?" I frown.

He sips his beer. "Well..." He purses his lips as he thinks. "I haven't seen you hook up with a girl in months."

I shrug as I take a drink. "That's because I haven't."

He frowns. "Since when?"

"Since Ashley."

He widens his eyes, shocked. "You haven't had sex with anyone since Ashley?"

"Nope," I reply with a shake of my head.

"Why not?"

I shrug. "Nobody's doing it for me."

"Is that a record for you?"

I nod. "Yep. Biggest dry spell since I started having sex."

His eyes hold mine. "What's going on with you and Ashley, anyway?"

I run my fingers through my two-day growth. "I don't know. I think she tolerates me."

"Does that bother you?"

"Fucking truth it does."

"I thought you were getting along?"

I shrug. "She's being nice to me for Owen's sake. Although, last weekend was a little different."

"What happened last weekend?"

"I was sick and she came to my house and looked after me for the weekend."

He listens as he watches me.

"I think I've officially been friend-zoned for the first time in my life." I widen my eyes as I sip my beer.

He chuckles and shakes his head. "You didn't make her clean up your vomit, did you?"

I laugh. "Practically." I shake my head. "Fuck. It was mortifying."

"What are you going to do about it?"

"There's nothing I can do."

He thinks for a moment. "Look, I don't know how it is with you, and you know mine and Tash's story, I loved her from afar for years... But nobody could fill the void that she left."

I blow out a sad breath. "That's what I'm afraid of. What if I never feel the way she makes me feel with anyone else? What if I was supposed to be with Ashley for real and I fucked it all up?"

He watches me for a moment, silent.

"She doesn't trust me." I pause and shrug. "And why would she?"

"But you didn't know her then. You were trying to do what was best for your son."

"We know that, but she doesn't."

He frowns as he thinks.

"And the worse thing is, what if I push for her to forgive me and she can't?" I ask.

"What do you mean?"

"What if I just end up pushing her further away?" I shrug. "At the moment, I would rather be in a room with Ashley while she ignores me than be in a bed with three of the hottest chicks in this party. Another woman is not even an option. I can't think of anything worse."

He purses his lips and stares at me.

I shake my head in disgust. "I seriously messed up so bad and I have no idea how to fix it." I sigh. "If I make a move, I'm fucked. If I don't make a move, I'm fucked."

"Have you tried to talk to her?" He frowns.

"Yep. She shuts me down every time, and it's only since I stopped trying that she has even given me the time of day."

"Fuck." He exhales deeply. "I don't know, man."

I sip my beer. "Maybe I just need to screw her out of my system. Be happy with co-parenting with her while banging everyone else?"

Joshua nods. "Maybe? What about when she meets someone else?

Could you watch her go on and marry someone else and have kids with him?"

I frown as the hairs on the back of my neck stand on end. "I couldn't bear it," I whisper.

He shakes his head in disgust. "Then get your fucking game on and get her back," he barks.

"It's complicated. There's a kid… a kid of ours. I can't wreck the friendship. I can't even risk wrecking the friendship. It's taken her two months just to make eye contact with me."

"There is nothing complicated about it. Either you want her or you don't. Simple as that."

I watch him.

"She's gorgeous, Cam. Another fuckwit is going to swoop in and steal her from right under your nose."

I clench my jaw in anger at the very thought.

Fuck… I couldn't stand it.

"She's with Natasha and Adrian now, you know," he mutters.

I frown. "What? She's out tonight? With them?"

"Yes." He smiles and nods at someone walking past us. "I'm meeting them in an hour."

I watch him as my mind begins to tick.

"So, as I see it, you kinda have two choices," he continues.

"Which are?"

"You can stay here and fuck some random hot chick."

I raise my eyebrows at option one.

"Or you come with me and fight for the woman you really want."

My eyes hold his as I contemplate his two choices.

"What's it going to be?"

Ashley

The sound of the sexy beat echoes through the bar, and I glance at the security that line the wall. What must it be like to be Natasha or Adrian and constantly be followed by security? It's Saturday night and Adrian, Tash and I have just had a nice Italian meal and are now in a cocktail bar.

"I'm just telling you this." Natasha smiles tipsily at me as she sips her Margarita. "You need to get back on the horse and start dating again."

I roll my eyes. "I'm off men forever." I glance at Adrian. "No offence, Adrian, but you don't count." I smirk.

He smirks and clinks our glasses. "I know, I'm like the anti-man man."

I giggle into my drink. I've just told them that Seb has been asking me out and they are urging me to go on a date with him.

I shake my head in disgust. I'm probably way too drunk to be having this conversation. "Cameron has ruined me for life. How can I ever trust another man?"

Natasha cringes. "Cameron is a good man. He's just a strong man who doesn't back down."

I roll my eyes as I sip my drink.

"If he and Joshua honestly think they're in the right, they will fight to the death to prove it," she adds.

"Remember that time you and Cameron had that big fall out?" Adrian asks Natasha.

I frown, confused. Cameron and Natasha always seem so tight, I can't ever imagine that happening.

"We did." She nods. "We've had lots of arguments in the past. He didn't speak to me for a long time because of the way I treated Joshua."

"How did you treat Joshua?"

She widens her eyes and exhales deeply. "God, where do I start? Joshua and I had the most unconventional start to our relationship, and he was a dominating ass."

"Like Cameron," I mutter dryly.

"Yes." She raises her glass. "Exactly like Cameron. Anyway, we broke up and Joshua was heartbroken. Cameron took exception to it and decided he was against me, too."

I frown.

"The thing is with these two, Ash, is that they'll be loyal to each other till the death. You couldn't get two brothers closer than they are. Unfortunately for us, they are also strong, dominant men."

I sip my drink as I watch her.

"If they think with all of their hearts that they're right, they won't give up. They'll fight to get what they want, and God help the person who stands in their way."

"How is taking my child the right thing to do?" I ask with a shake of my head.

"Well, they didn't really know you." Adrian frowns. "Cameron had said that if something ever happened to Owen and he had been neglectful, he would never have been able to forgive himself."

"Why didn't he just ask me if I was alright?"

Natasha narrows her eyes as she thinks. "They have a big trigger with paternity."

"Why?" I frown.

She shrugs. "Ask Cameron about it, it's not my place to say. But when it all came out that you'd lied about Owen's paternity, it set alarm bells ringing for the two of them. You're not completely innocent in this, either."

"And don't forget about TC," Adrian adds.

"Oh God, yes." Natasha shakes her head in disgust. "Joshua was bribed once with footage of him and a prostitute for millions of dollars."

My eyes widen. "What?" I shriek.

She shakes her head. "That's why he couldn't stand the thought of you being put into that same sleazy basket at the club. He couldn't stand the thought of Owen ever going through that shame as a teenager if it came out later."

416

"Why didn't he just say that?" I practically shout.

"Because he's a proud man. He's not going to bring up his insecurities," she answers.

I shake my head as I sip my drink.

"Cameron is a good man, Ashley," Natasha replies. "No matter what he's done in the past, he honestly thought he was looking out for Owen's best interests at the time."

I sit for a moment as I think about what they've said.

"Speak of the devil." Adrian smiles.

I look up and see Joshua walking through the crowd with Cameron following behind him.

Our eyes lock.

The look he gives me sends shivers down my spine.

I want you, I'm taking you, and I'm going to fuck you into submission. Is what it's silently screaming.

Goosebumps scatter. He hasn't looked at me that way for a long time, and I had honestly forgotten its power.

I swallow the lump in my throat as I watch him approach us through the crowds.

Dear God, Cameron Stanton is here, and the way he is looking at me tells me that I'm in trouble.

Big. Fucking. Trouble.

27

J OSHUA WALKS up to us and kisses Natasha, slaps Adrian on the back, and then kisses me on the cheek. "Hello." He smiles politely before taking a seat next to Natasha.

"Hi." I smile back awkwardly. I pick up my drink to distract myself from Cameron's smouldering gaze.

Cameron finally moves and kisses Tash, shakes Adrian's hand and then moves behind me to lean over and kiss my cheek. "Hey, Bloss," he whispers into my ear so nobody else can hear.

Shit. Don't call me that.

"Hi." I smile awkwardly. He stays behind me with his two hands on my bare shoulders. The heat from his fingers pressing on my skin is searing, and he subtly squeezes my shoulder muscles in between his hands, causing more goosebumps to scatter.

Bloody hell.

He pulls up a stool, sits beside me, and smirks knowingly at my body's reaction to his touch.

Cut it out, goosebumps, you traitorous bastards.

"How was the pussy party?" Tash asks as she sips her drink.

I look at Cameron. "A pussy party?" I frown.

He laughs out loud — that carefree beautiful laugh — and I feel my stomach flip at the sound.

"It was okay." He smirks as his drink arrives. "Thank you," he says as he takes it from the waiter.

"Boring. I would much rather be here with you lot," Joshua mutters as he picks up his beer.

"That goes without saying." Adrian grins.

"Why does this surprise you?" Tash adds.

"What the hell is a pussy party?" I frown.

"Pussy on demand," Adrian says, rolling his eyes.

I shake my head and frown. I've heard it all now.

Cameron laughs. "Very poor quality pussy, though."

My mouth drops open. "How and why do I even know you?" I splutter.

"We have a child together. Remember?" He smiles cheekily. "He's four years old and he's insanely good looking... just like his father?"

I smirk. "That was all by chance."

His eyes dance in delight. "You should have known when you met me that I would have super human sperm."
The table laughs.

"Now I've heard it all," Adrian grumbles.

"You have super human sperm?" I repeat. "Please? Give me a break."

He sips his drink. "Yep. It must have tentacles, smashing anything that gets in it's way like some kind of Ninja Turtle."
"That would mean you have hundreds of Ninja Turtle sperm children everywhere then?" I smirk.

His face falls, and he fakes a shiver. "No. Just the one. My ninja powers were saved for you and you alone."

"Nice save," Joshua says though a small laugh.
I smile as Cameron's eyes linger on mine a little too long.

419

Joshua, Tash, and Adrian start talking about something else as Cameron's eyes drop to my little black dress.

"You look gorgeous, by the way," he whispers as his eyes drop down my body and he reaches over to adjust the spaghetti strap on my shoulder.

My cheeks heat as he continues to gaze at me.

"Owen's tucked in bed, fast asleep," he says as he picks up his drink and takes a sip.

"Did you ring him?"

"Yeah, he was just going to bed. I rang to say goodnight." Our eyes stay fixed on each other. I really need to stop drinking. It's giving me asshole amnesia.

I glance over and see Joshua relaying a story to the other two, and Natasha's eyes dance with delight as she looks over at me. I frown in question. What are they talking about?

"How about I spin you around that dance floor?" Cameron smiles sexily.

"No, thanks," I say quickly. There's no way in hell he is holding me in his arms.

"You know, I'm a ten in the dancing category."

I smirk. "You don't have a rating system anymore, Cam."

"I don't?"

"Nope."

His face falls. "Why not?"

"Do you even have to ask?" I reply, deadpan.

His face falls serious as he watches me for a moment. He pauses, as if contemplating which direction to take the conversation. "Are you ready yet?"

"Ready for what?" I frown.

"To talk to me."

"Cam..." I sigh.

"Don't *Cam* me." He puts his hand on my thigh beneath the table. "I want to address the elephant in the room, Ash. It's been here for two months and it needs to be discussed."

"Cam." I close my eyes. "Just leave it. Nothing needs to be said because I don't want to hear any of it."

"We're heading out of here." Natasha smiles.

"Oh." My face falls as my eyes go to them.

Adrian, Joshua, Tash are all standing, and I see Joshua throw Cam a wink. I frown as I turn to watch Cameron.

"I'll get Ash home safe," Cam says as he sips his drink.

Tash and Adrian come around to kiss me, and before I can even mutter a word, they are walking through the crowd until they're completely out of sight.

"That was sudden. What happened there?"

"I asked Joshua to leave me alone with you."

"What?" I frown. "Why?"

"Because I wanted you all to myself."

My eyes hold his. "What's going on here?"

He picks up my hand in my lap. "I want another chance."

I scowl. What the fuck?

"I want you to give me another chance, Ash." He leans forward and gently kisses my lips. "We are so good together, Bloss."

I pull back quickly. "No, Cam." I shake my head. "What the hell are you doing?"

"I'm trying my best to get a kiss." His eyes search mine.

"It's not happening, Cameron."

"Why not?"

"Because I don't trust you."

His face falls and he picks up my fingers to kiss the backs of them. "Please don't say that," he whispers.

I watch him kissing me slowly, and I shake my head. "I can't just turn my feelings back on like a tap when it suits you."

His eyes hold mine.

"The damage you've done is irreversible, Cameron," I reply sadly. "There is no hope for us to ever work it out now. I warned you back then. Now... I don't have the same feelings for you that I used to."

His face falls and he drops his head. Feeling guilty, I squeeze his hand in mine.

"I honestly thought I was doing the right thing, Ash," he whispers.

"I know you did," I reply sadly.

His eyes rise to meet mine, and he stays silent.

"But I can't be with someone who bases their decisions on power."

He frowns.

"You tried to take Owen from me to show me who was the boss."

His eyes hold mine. "It wasn't about the drugs."

"I know it wasn't. It was always about me working at the club."

"I couldn't stand the thought of Owen having to deal with the consequences of that."

"So then you talk to me. You tell me what your feelings are and you ask me to leave in an adult fashion."

He frowns as he listens.

"You don't give me warnings to leave *or else*. You don't just do whatever it takes to get your own way. That is not the way to handle things, Cameron. I know you are a strong man who always gets his way — "

"I don't," he interrupts.

I frown. *Oh please.* "Cam, you've had a blessed life. You have brains and you got into med school. You have good looks so you get the women. You have money so you never have to worry. You are in control of everything, and that's just how you operate."

He scowls.

I smile sadly. "And that's great for you." I swallow the lump in my throat. "But if we ever got back together, I know you would use that power again to control me eventually."

"I wouldn't."

"You would." I nod. "You don't even know how you are."

He shakes his head in disgust. "What are you talking about? How am I?

"You're entitled."

He sits back, clearly annoyed at my presumption. "That's ridiculous. I am not."

"Aren't' you?" I smile sarcastically. "What about right now, Cameron? You have decided that we should try again and you feel you are entitled to a second chance."

His eyes hold mine.

"I don't like that part of you, Cam. I will never like that part of you. It's not how I'm going to live my life."

He sits back as he watches me, inhaling slowly. He's angry and wants to fight back, I can tell, but he's using everything he can to not snap at me.

"You lied to me, too, Ashley. You didn't tell me about Owen."

"I was trying to get to know you first," I whisper.

"I couldn't trust you. You broke the trust first," he whispers, annoyed. "And then you wouldn't leave the club, even after I paid for your rent and offered you money..."

I watch him.

"What was I supposed to think?" he asks.

"Oh, I don't know? Maybe that you can't order everyone around and tell them what to do. How about *I will let her leave in her own time if that's what she wants*?"

"This isn't all about you, Ashley. I did that for Owen. Have you honestly stopped to think about the consequences if he grew up and it came out you had worked there?"
I frown.

"Think about it. Think long and hard. I did everything to protect Owen in the future, and I'm sorry I hurt you, but it was the only thing I could do that got you to leave immediately."

I continue to watch him.

"You were starting to mix with these girls and asshole men who spike your drinks. What's next? You slip a little coke to get through your next shift?"

I roll my eyes.

"Honestly, how long until they slipped some coke into your drink and talked you into one night in the Escape Lounge, and then another, and then another, and before you know it, you're a full on, high class hooker?"

"It was never getting to that."

"Every working girl says that in the beginning."

"I did two lap dances, Cameron, and they were both for you."

His hard eyes hold mine. "How did they get you into the lap dance uniform in the first place, before I even got there, Ashley?"

I frown harder.

"They convinced you it was a good idea. Just wear this for this shift and it will be fine. It's how these clubs operate. They push you a little at a time. Without realizing it, your boundaries are being pushed further and further out, and because your co-worker friends are all doing it, it becomes the new norm."

My stomach drops. He's right, they did push my boundaries and I hadn't even realized it. I swore I would never do half the things they got me to do.

"You go there, Cameron. You go there for the women. Do you know how it feels to be judged by you when you were going there for sex?"

He shakes his head and cups my face. "I cancelled my membership before the court case. I knew what a hypocrite I was being, but I had to do what I did to protect Owen." He leans in and kisses my lips softly. "And I know you don't see it like this, but I thought I was protecting you, too," he whispers as his eyes search mine.

I stare at him through tears as a clusterfuck of emotions roll around in my messed up head.

"I didn't take Owen, Ash. I admit that I was going to let him stay with me for a week, just to teach you a lesson. To teach you that there is more than yourself to consider."

I frown.

"But I couldn't do it..." he whispers.

My eyes hold his.

"I need you to forgive me and I fucking need you in my life," he breathes. "I want you back."

I swallow the lump in my throat.

"I haven't been with anyone since you, Ash. I can't stand the thought of being with another woman."

My eyes search his. Oh God, I so want to believe him.

"How could I be with another woman when I left my heart with you?"

I close my eyes, and just like that he has broken down all my defences.

"Cameron," I whisper.

He pulls my head to his and kisses my forehead.

"I just want a chance to make this right. I fucked up by not being there for you both when Owen was born. I know you've had it tough, Bloss. I know you resent me for not being around. And hell, you've done an amazing job with him on your own. He's perfect."

I can hardly see him through my tears, and I swallow down the painful lump in my throat.

"But, I'm the one who resents myself for every single day I missed out on Owen. I can't get that time back no matter what I do."

I wipe the tears from my eyes.

"And maybe that's the reason I went batshit crazy, lost my mind and took it all the way to court." He shrugs. "Maybe I resented the power that you had over my son. Maybe I resented the fact that I had absolutely no say in anything in his life thus far."

God, what a mess.

"Cam." I pause as I try to articulate my thoughts. "I can't just jump back into a relationship with you." I shake my head.

"I don't want you to."

My eyes search his. "Then what do you want?"

"I want you to forgive me. I want to be able to look you in the eye and not see you drag your eyes away from mine in disgust. I want us to start again fresh."

I drop my head as his proposal runs through my mind.

He leans in and kisses my cheek, lifting my chin with his finger so that our eyes meet.

"I can't promise you anything," I whisper as my eyes search his.

"Just your forgiveness is enough, and at the end of it all, if we have nothing but friendship, that'll be okay because at least we tried. I just can't stand you hating me."

He squeezes his hand in mine and his eyes glow softly. All I can do is nod and offer him a sad smile.

"So do you want to go back to my house and fuck now?" he asks matter-of-factly as he reaches to take a sip of his beer.

I choke on my drink. "Cameron," I splutter. "You just completely wrecked that beautiful speech."

He laughs and holds both of his hands up. "I'm joking. I'm joking."

"You were not joking!" I hit him on the thigh.

He narrows his eyes. "You do have to admit that it would be fucking awesome, though. I've forgotten what sex feels like."

I laugh out loud and shake my head.

"There will be no sex, Cameron." I lift my drink in a toast and he puts his bottle of beer to meet my glass. "To friendship," I say.

His eyes hold mine and he smiles that beautiful, cheeky smile. "To friendship, forgiveness, and new beginnings."

Our eyes linger on each other's, and it's as if I am seeing the old Cameron for the first time in a long time.

I sip my cocktail as he tips his head back to drink his beer, his eyes never leaving mine. I can feel the smoulder from his gaze.

Dear God, he's just so hot. Why does he have to be so hot? It's not fair.

And he hasn't had sex since me, nine weeks ago. Holy hell, that's going to be one hell of a sex session when it finally happens.

I wonder if he's hard under the table right now?

Stop it, you sex maniac.

Maybe I should go...

Yes.

I should go and not be such a damn push over.

I'm not jumping back into his arms or his bed. I'm just moving forward, that's all, and it doesn't mean that we are automatically going to pick up where we left off. It just means that I'm not going to imagine ways of torturing him with various forms of pain now.

I point to the door with my thumb. "I should..." I pause. Jeez, I really don't want to go, but I need to get away from him before he has me undressed and on my back in his bed. I already know that he will if I stay here and continue drinking with him. It's a done deal.

My vagina would be completely ruined.

Hmm, wouldn't that be something, though?

I get a vision of him above me, naked and hard, and I feel a throb of arousal between my legs. His eyes drop to my lips and I know he's imagining the same thing as me.

"Why do you want to go, Bloss?" he whispers darkly.

My breath catches. *Stop looking at me like that.* I shrug as any form of intelligent reply escapes me.

"I... I should probably..." My voice trails off as I watch his tongue dart out to lick his bottom lip.

"You don't trust yourself with me? Is that it?" he asks seductively.

I force myself to smile. "You, Cameron Stanton, have an inflated ego."

He smirks.

"Do you really think I will beg to suck your cock?" I whisper.

He closes his eyes, puts his head back to the heavens, and groans. "Don't even say that to me. I swear I'm about to blow."

"Cameron." I smirk. "We're going home."

He stands and raises an eyebrow. "Now you're talking."

"I mean... I'm going to *my* house."

"That works. We can go there."

"Cameron," I sputter. "You are not coming to my house."

He smiles sexily as he takes my hand in his, picks it up, and kisses the back of it, his eyes holding mine. "Let's go." He leads me through the crowd and out of the club where he raises his hand at a passing cab. By some miracle, it stops.

I turn to him and smile. "See you later."

"Goodbye," he whispers.

"Hello." I smile as I climb in the backseat. "Can you take me to Rosemont, please?"

"Sure." The cab driver smiles.

I close the door behind me and before I can even glance out the window at Cameron to wave goodbye, he's climbing in the other side of the car.

My eyes widen. "Cameron," I whisper.

"I'm just making sure you get home okay."

"I can get home by myself," I snap.

"Just be quiet, please." He smiles and watches the road as the cab pulls out into the traffic.

Ten minutes later, we pull into my driveway and I nervously glance across at Cameron.

"Can you just wait here for a moment? I'm just going to walk her in," he asks the driver.

I walk up the driveway nervously with him hot on my heels.

I put the key into the door and he stands behind me. Way too close... so close that I can feel his breath on my neck and it feels so... jeez. No. Stop.

I open the door and turn to face him. He steps forward and I step back. He keeps walking forward and I keep walking backwards until I'm pinned up against the nearest wall.

"Kiss goodnight, Bloss?"

His hard body has me pinned, and I can feel every damn hard inch of what he's got to offer.

I stare up at him as all the air leaves my lungs.

"Cameron..." I whisper.

His eyes hold mine. "I'm not leaving until I get a fucking kiss," he whispers darkly.

I frown as my eyes drop to his lips. "Why do you have to be so bossy?" I whisper.

He grabs a handful of my hair and pulls it so that my face is tilted to his.

In slow motion, I watch as his mouth drops to mine. His tongue sweeps softly through my open lips, and his eyes close in pleasure.

Holy shit.

Then he's on me. His hips drive me back against the wall as his tongue delves deeper. His hard cock has me pinned. The grip he has on my hair tightens and is near painful, and I feel every single dormant cell in my body reignite.

With my head pulled back, he leans down and runs his tongue up the length of my neck and along my jaw.

Dear God...

His lips suck mine, and I swear it's the kiss of the devil.

Pure sin.

My body quivers in need of the domination he wants to give. He smirks sexily and licks his lips as he looks down at me. "Goodnight then, Bloss. I'll pick you and Owen up at ten in the morning. Be ready."

He turns and casually walks down the path before he jumps into the cab.

I watch him drive away into the darkness with my heart beating hard in my chest.

Holy fuck.

So much for restraint.

I'm totally screwed.

28

"DAD'S HERE," Owen calls excitedly from his place at the window.

"Okay," I call back as my heart goes into epileptic fit mode. Good God, what on earth's going to happen today? We're going shopping for new clothes for Owen. He's had a growth spurt and nothing fits him. Then we're having lunch before going to the Stantons' tonight for a family dinner to celebrate Jordana's birthday.

A full day with him.

Cameron Stanton overload.

And a full day of me pretending not to want him. Even though I know I shouldn't want him ...

It's official. He's a bona fide sex god. I felt his lips on mine for hours after I went to bed last night, and that was after I stared at the mirror for an hour smiling goofily at my reflection.

I've been thinking on this all night, and as I see it, I have three choices. Either, I can fall hopelessly into his arms and declare undying love for him and become his doormat for life. Or, I could completely reject his advances and cut all ties other than Owen, and maybe try to move on with someone else. But, to be honest, isn't that just cutting off my nose to spite my face? Isn't the ultimate goal to try and work it out so that maybe we could be a united, happy family one day?

Or, three... I could try to play it cool, make him sweat for a while, and hopefully regain some trust, then maybe just... I don't know... see how it goes?

I race to the mirror in my bathroom and take another look at myself. I got up early and straightened my honey golden hair so it hangs just below my shoulders. I'm wearing a chunky, cream woollen dress that has short cap sleeves. It's straight and fitted, falling to mid shin length. It fits nice and I think it looks sexy without trying too hard. An annoying little voice from deep inside reminds me that this is his favorite dress.

Hell, why am I wearing it when he knows that I know that this is his favorite dress?

I'm pathetic.

Damn it, I should have worn something he hates. I close my eyes in disgust at my inability to play it cool already. I blow out a breath and reapply my lip gloss before I head downstairs. I find Cameron and Owen standing near the front door, waiting for me. Cameron's eyes glance up and glow with affection when he sees me coming down the stairs

He's wearing army green cargo pants and a black V-neck T-shirt with a puffy sports kind of vest unzipped. His usual expensive trendy get up. His dark hair is a mass of unruly, messy curls and his big lips are an appealing shade of come fuck me.

I smile nervously. "Good morning."

His eyes hold mine. "Momma's looking beautiful today, Owie, isn't she?" He smiles sexily.

Owen smiles an over-the-top smile and nods. I get to the bottom of the steps and Cameron walks over and picks up my hand. His eyes don't leave mine as he softly kisses the back of my hand.

Oh really? He's just so...

I glance down at Owen and he frowns slightly as his eyes flick between us in surprise.

What is the appropriate parent etiquette for this kind of thing? How much is too much, and can you flirt in front of your child without it being weird? I'm quite sure Cameron is going overboard here.

I pull my hand out of Cameron's grip. "Let's go. Wouldn't want to creep out Owen, would we?"

I widen my eyes at Cameron and he smiles cheekily and throws me a wink.

The thing about shopping with boys is… it completely sucks.

"How about this?" I hold up a shirt and Cameron and Owen both shake their heads and turn up their noses.

I roll my eyes. "Why don't you like anything I pick?" I ask.

Owen shrugs as he sits in the shopping cart his father is pushing around the department store. We've been here for over an hour and only picked out one sweater.

"Because you're picking out the daggiest clothes in history." Cameron sighs. "That shirt is guaranteed social suicide."

"It is not." I rearrange the collar of the shirt I am holding and smile as I hold it up to Owen. "Look how cute you look, baby?"

Cam screws up his face in disgust. Owen rolls his eyes and shakes his head.

I slam it back onto the rack in disgust. "Well, you two pick something," I snap. "I'm sick of my choices being rejected."

"Alright." Cameron frowns. He takes his task seriously and pushes his cart off into the distance as he looks around. Owen, too, begins to scan the clothes racks from his cart seat.

I follow them, distracted by my stomach rumbling.

"I'm starving," I announce.

"I've got something you can eat," Cameron says, distracted.

I stare at him, deadpan, and he glances over his shoulder and smirks.

"Dirty bastard," I mouth.

He winks and keeps looking. "What about this?" he says as he takes a sweater from the shelf and holds it up.

I look at it and my face falls in horror. It's a black hoodie and has a large white eye on the front. The pupil is filled with bright colours. It's a long, skinny fit.

"Yeah, Dad!" Owen calls excitedly. "That's totally sick."

"I know, right?" Cam smiles. He holds up his fist and Owen punches it with his closed fist.

Oh God. I roll my eyes in disgust. This boys club thing they have going on is really getting out of hand.
"Yes, Owen, it does look sick. Like somebody vomited on it, sick," I mutter.

"Can I have it, Dad?" Owen begs.

"Sure thing, buddy." Cameron throws it into the cart.

I look at him, deadpan. "You do know he's four, right?"

"Yes, so why are you dressing him like he's eighty?" Cam mutters, distracted as he spots a pair of army green skinny jeans. He smiles and holds them up for Owen and Owen's eyes nearly pop from the sockets.

"Yeah, baby." Cameron smiles as he puts them into the cart. "You could wear these with your black high tops," Cameron instructs.

"Yes!" Owen exclaims excitedly. "With the eyeball sweater?"

"That *is* sick," Cam agrees.

"So cool." Owie smiles.

"Oh my God," I mutter in disgust. "I'm not taking you anywhere in this outfit."

"We could wear this when we go to the skate park," Cameron replies.

"Yeah," Owen yells.

I frown. "You take him to the skate park?"

"Of course."

"We go down the half pipe." Owen smiles proudly.

My eyes widen. "*You go down the half pipe?*" I shriek.

Cameron flicks the peak on Owen's cap. "I told you not to tell her that," he whispers.

My mouth drops open in shock. "You tell him to not tell me stuff?"

"Yeah, but I didn't tell her we skate on the road, Dad," Owen adds.

"Cameron Stanton!" I snap. "What the hell? You skate on the road?"

Cameron flicks the peak of his hat again. "Big mouth."

After half an hour and a cart full of clothes that are suitable for a trendy designer fashion show, we make our way to the fitting rooms. Cameron lifts Owen out and shows him in and organizes the outfits he is to try on together.

I smirk as I stand back. It's so nice having someone else to help me with Owen. Jenna is fantastic, but I always try and take over because I feel guilty that she does too much.

With Cameron, I can let him go as much as he wants and feel no guilt whatsoever.

We are in the fitting rooms and Cam pops his head around the curtain to speak to Owen. "Try these pants on first mate with this top." He pauses for a minute as he watches him. "Do you want me to help?"

"I can do it," Owie replies.

"Alright, alright." Cam nods as he comes back out of the curtain. "What is it with the not wanting help thing?" he asks.

I shrug. "He does it to me as well."

My phone rings and Andrew's name lights up the screen. Shit. I hope his mom is okay. I haven't had time to go and see her yet. "It's Andrew."

Cameron frowns. "Your ex?"

I nod as I answer it. "Hello, Andrew."

"Hi, Ash. How are you?"

I smile. "I'm good. Is your mom okay?" I glance over at Cam as he listens intently.

"She's alright." He pauses. "She's running out of time."

My face falls. "I'm so sorry." I sigh.

"She's asking for you, Ash. She wants to see you and Owen."

I blow out a breath and my eyes rise up to Cameron. "Yes, of course. I can come to New York next weekend," I reply

Cameron frowns.

"Dad. I'm finished," Owen yells.

Cameron sticks the new pair of pants through the curtain without even looking in Owen's direction. His eyes are glued on me.

"That would be great." Andrew sighs relieved.

"You can arrange for us to see her on the Saturday, if that's okay." I think for a moment. "We can fly down on Friday night."

"Thanks, Ash," he replies. "It'll be nice to see you."

Cameron is watching me like a hawk. "It will." I smile as I try to act casual. "See you then."

"Dad, I'm finished," Owen calls.

Cameron flicks the curtain back and looks in. "Excellent, we're definitely getting those. Now try on the jeans, too," he mutters, distracted.

"I have to go to New York next weekend," I announce.

"Is his mom alright?" Cameron asks.

I shake my head. "She's asking to see me and Owen."

He nods as he thinks for a moment. "Okay, so we go to New York next weekend."

I frown. "What do you mean *we*?"

"Well, you don't honestly think I'm letting my family go to New York without me, do you?"

I only heard one thing in that sentence: *My family.*

"Cameron." I frown.

He walks forward, effectively pushing me back into the dressing room. "I could help out with Owen." He tucks a piece of my hair behind my ear.

I frown as my brain stops working because of his close proximity.

"We could get a family suite with a couple of bedrooms," he adds to sweeten the deal. "You won't even have to share a bedroom with me."

I fold my arms in front of me as he tries to talk me into it.

"We could go Friday night, you can go and see them on Saturday, and then on Sunday we could go to the zoo or something. Just the three of us." He smiles hopefully

I smirk as I look up at him. "You would do that?" I ask.

He smiles and takes my face in his hands. "Of course I would. You're my girl. I would do anything for my girl." He bends and takes my lips in his as he holds my face. The kiss is tender, sweet, and lingering. I feel my feet lift off the floor.

"Are you making another baby?" Owen asks, interrupting our moment.

We both look up to find Owen watching us in his underpants.

"Yes, we are," Cameron grumbles, annoyed. "Why are you out here half naked?"

"Because you didn't bring the clothes in," he says as he puts his little hand on his hip with attitude. "You need to concentrate, Dad, you know."

I giggle at the sight of a four-year-old telling his father off. Cameron rolls his eyes and disappears back into the fitting room to continue his duties.

"Let me think about it," I call behind him.

I already know my answer and I smile to myself. It looks like we're all going to New York... together.

Later that afternoon, we walk into Natasha and Joshua's house for Jordana's birthday dinner. We've had a fun day. We went out for lunch and then back to Cam's house this afternoon. I had a nap on the couch while they skateboarded together on the road. I've lost that battle already.

Cameron has kissed me three times today. Once in the fitting room, once in the parking lot after lunch after Owen got into the car, and once in his kitchen at home.

That was the best kiss yet and he had to go and hide in the pantry for a while until the evidence of his arousal... calmed down.

I feel like I'm slipping down a steep hill that leads back to him, and no matter how hard I try to hang onto the rocks beneath my feet, I can't stop the gravity that's pulling me down.

He's beautiful—everything about Cameron is beautiful, and I'm not sure how, after just four kisses, I seem to be forgiving him for all the hell he put me through.

How could I forget what he's done?

But then his reasonings last night seemed so heartfelt and I really want to believe that he was trying to do the right thing.

His family.

That's what we would be. If we get past all this and make it through the other side, we *would* be a family. How wonderful.

We get through the usual security and head up to the house. The front door is wide open and the familiar sound of children's laughter rings out. Owen grips Cameron's hand tight. It always takes him ten minutes to warm up until he's off running riot with the other Stanton children.

These kids are amongst the strongest willed children I have ever met, and funnily enough, when Owen is with them he seems to take on some of their power. He fights back now and doesn't put up with nonsense from anyone. I got called up to the preschool this week because apparently Owen punched that bully kid in the nose. I was mortified, yet Cameron saw it as a victory. Funnily enough the kid hasn't gone near him again since.

I think this is how it was when the Stanton boys were young. Joshua is naturally strong willed and Cameron is naturally like Owen, but because he grew up with such strong characters as brothers, he turned out to be a force to be reckoned with, too. Natasha said that Scott, the eldest Stanton, is just like Joshua, while Wilson, the youngest, is just like Cam.

Cameron takes my hand in his, but I pull out of his grip and shake my head subtly.

He frowns in question.

"Not yet," I whisper. I don't want anyone to know what's going on between us when I don't even know what that is myself.

He frowns and subtly shakes his head in annoyance. We walk out into the large kitchen and family room area and everyone comes into view. Adrian, Tash, Josh, Jarvis, Nicholas are all there, as well as... oh no... Margaret. Cameron's mother is sitting on the lounger. I haven't seen her since she told Cameron about Owen being his son.

This should be fun... not!

They smile as they see us. "Hello," everyone calls as their attention all turns to us.

"Mom and Dad are making another baby," Owen announces to the crowd.

My eyes widen. Oh dear God, no. The blood drains from my face.

The room falls silent and Cameron flicks Owen's cap peak. "Big mouth," he mutters. "We kissed, that's all," Cameron tells them all. "Just kissing. Owen, you're going to get it," he snaps.

Joshua shakes his head and the room breaks into laughter and chatter. My eyes flick to Margaret. Her cold, calculating eyes hold mine, and I shrivel under her glare.

Holy shit, this woman is pure evil. She's openly furious.

I feel my nerves flutter, and Cam puts his hand on the small of my back in a silent show of support.

"Come in, come in." Tash smiles as she glides over and embraces me.

438

I nervously walk in and through to the kitchen as everyone goes back to their conversations.

"What's going on?" Tash whispers so that nobody else can hear. She puts her arm around me in excitement.

"Nothing." I shrug. "He apologized last night and we kissed, that's all. I'm not even sure myself," I add.

"Oh my God, I'm so excited. Get some wine. We're celebrating," she whispers as she squeezes my hand in hers.

I smile. I love this girl. She has all the money in the world, yet she's still so damn normal. If I'd just met her on the street today, I would never know she has money except for the huge rock on her finger... and the security guards, of course.

A bang sounds out the back and then the screaming starts.

Blake has crashed his bike into a huge ceramic pot and is now crying. Everyone rushes outside to his aid, so I turn to pour myself a glass of wine.

"What the hell do you think you're doing?" Margaret's cold voice hisses behind me.

What?

I turn to her as my heart starts to thud. "I beg your pardon?"

"Who in the hell do you think you are?" She growls.

"I could ask you the same question."

She steps forward. "Do you really think that trapping my son is the way to go?"

"I haven't trapped anybody."

"That's your plan, isn't it? You little gold digger. You get yourself pregnant and turn up here to demand half of Cameron's empire."

"What?" I frown. "You're delusional. Leave me alone, Margaret. I have nothing to say to you." I turn my back on her because I know if I don't, I'm going to lose my living shit.

"Listen here, you lying little witch," she continues behind me. "You walk out of my son's life right now. He doesn't need a distraction like you and he is not your bank boost or ticket to freedom."

"How dare you?" Cameron growls from behind us, and we both turn in surprise.

Cameron walks over and puts his arm around me. "Don't you ever speak to her like that again. Do you understand me?" he yells.

"She's... she's no good for you, Cam," she stammers nervously. "She's a gold digger. She got pregnant on purpose and then she turns up here, making demands."

Cameron steps closer to her. "Let's get on thing straight here... I'm the one pursuing Ashley. It's not the other way around. I'm the one who fucked up, and if I have it my way, she'll soon be back with me and you will have nothing to fucking do with it." Natasha and Joshua come back inside and frown as they approach all the shouting.

Cameron glares at his mom. "If you dare disrespect Ashley again, you disrespect me and Owen, too, and I'm not going to allow that to happen. You better apologize now." He growls.

"I will do nothing of the sort," she snaps.

"Margaret," Natasha interrupts. "Cut it out. Ashley is my friend, and what was she supposed to do? She had no way of contacting Cameron. How dare you speak to her like this?"

"Natasha, she's fooled you, too. She got pregnant on purpose. This was no accident," Margaret shouts.

"That's enough, Mother." Joshua sneers.

"Apologize," Cameron yells.

"No," she shouts back.

"That's it." Cameron growls. "Get Owen, Ashley. We're leaving. I'm not putting up with this shit."

"No," I say calmly as my eyes hold Margaret's.

The room falls silent.

"I'm not going anywhere."

Margaret narrows her eyes and raises her chin defiantly.

I fold my arms in front of me and smirk. "You misunderstand me, Margaret. I'm a lot of things, but weak isn't one of them."

"How dare you? This is *my* son's house."

I smile sarcastically. "Oh, I dare. This is Owen's family time, and I will stay with my son while he's here. If you don't like it, that's just too bad."

Our eyes are locked.

"You don't have to like me, Margaret," I say calmly. "But, as my son's grandmother, I will try my best to like you……. although you are making that increasingly difficult." I glance over and Natasha smirks.

"Now, if you don't mind cutting down on your dramatics, I'm here for Jordana's birthday. Go and make a scene somewhere else."

The room falls silent and I turn to Cameron and kiss him on the lips quickly. "I'll be out the back, baby." Then I turn and head out the door.

"Hell, yeah," I hear Joshua mutter as Natasha giggles.

I smirk and head outside without looking back.

Fuck off, you old mole. I'm not taking your shit and I'm not backing down.

I do things my way.

29

I READ the text from Cameron and smirk.

It's Thursday lunchtime now. We've been flirting all week and, other than the quick kisses he gave me when he dropped Owen off, we haven't been alone at all. The Sunday family dinner at Natasha's cemented that we are officially trying again. We went back to his house and had a big talk after dinner and I agreed to try and give things a go. We snuggled on the couch while Owen watched television. Cameron didn't push for anything because he knew I wasn't ready. Things are good between us and I think I'm finally ready to move on. He can sense it.

I missed you last night.

I glance up at him across the cafeteria table and our eyes lock. He's sitting with Amber, listening to her babble, yet he's messaging me. I text back.

You getting soppy on me, Stanton?

He smirks and texts back.

Totally.
What are you going to do about it?

I text back.

That depends.

An answer fires straight back.

On what?

I read his reply and write back.

On what you want me to do about it?

He glances at me and texts back.

Since we both know I'm about to die from a massive sperm overload, I think you already know what I need.

I bite my bottom lip to stifle my smile. Jeez, this is highly inappropriate cafeteria behaviour, but he's just so fun to sext. I write back.

Tell me what you want?
I want the details. All the sordid details.

He raises an eyebrow and his dark eyes drop to my lips before he replies.

I want to start with you on your back, naked, your legs wide open for me.
I want to inhale every inch of you with my tongue.
You have no idea how badly I need to taste you.

How badly I need to be inside of you...

That will do. I look up to see the desire dancing like fire in his eyes, and my body starts to tingle with arousal. When he looks at me this way, it's like I can already feel his touch on my skin. Another text bounces back.

Get Jenna to mind Owen tonight
Come over.
Spend the night with me.

I smirk and write back.

Come over or come under?

He smiles sexily.

You will come under and then you will come over.
I need you.

Good God. I get a vision of riding that beautiful, big cock. God, it's been so long.
Nine weeks.
Nine weeks without him touching me feels like a lifetime. I text back.

I will see what I can do.
xoxo

It's after nine when I knock on Cameron's door.
I waited until I got Owen to bed before I came over. If he knew I was coming here without him, there would have been hell to pay. Cameron answers the door in his boxer shorts and

nothing else. He smiles down on me. I didn't tell him I was definitely coming, but I'm pretty sure he's happy that I did. My eyes drop to his broad, muscular chest and the chiselled abs.

My heart somersaults in my chest. He's just so perfect.

"Miss Tucker," he breathes as he steps forward and takes my face between his hands. His eyes hold mine as he bends and kisses me. He's all suction and domination.

I smile against his lips as his hips grind against me, and I feel my sex clench in appreciation of his hard body. He grabs my hand and rips me roughly into the house, slamming the door shut behind us.

He walks through to the kitchen and sits me up on the counter. He spreads my legs in my dress and runs his hands up my bare thighs.

Goosebumps scatter my skin as he looks at me. "Do you have any idea how badly I need you?" he whispers.

I swallow the lump in my throat and nod. For the first time in nine weeks, we're alone. This could be dangerous.

He grabs my hair in his hand, pulls my head back, and kisses me. His tongue slides through my open mouth and I sigh against his lips.

My eyes shut and I moan. Oh God, I need this.

I need him.

His mouth drops to my neck where he bites and sucks me so hard I think I'll be marked tomorrow, but I don't care. I want him to mark me.

I want him to claim me.

His mouth drops to my breast and he bites my nipple through my dress. I cry out. "Ouch, Cam," I whisper as I hold the back of his head.

"Don't touch me, Bloss. Not tonight," he whispers against my breast. "I need it hard and deep. There is no ouch tonight."

Bloody hell. Let's get straight to it then.

My stomach flutters with fear because I know he means it. Just as he said, he kisses me hard and deep. His lips run feverishly over my collarbone and chest. He pushes me back over the counter and the things go flying. Ah, shit. Can we have a glass of wine first, at least?

I lay back as he lifts my dress and removes my panties. He can't wait one second longer. I hold my breath as I stare up at the ceiling. This seems so damn intimate when he looks at me like this. He parts me with his fingers, slowly bending so his tongue sweeps through my flesh.

Holy shit. "Ohh," I cry

His eyes close and he starts to eat me for dear life – long, hard sucks and nibbles. All I can do is hold onto his broad shoulders. "Jesus Christ, Cameron, can we not get to the bed first?"

He moans a guttural sound and… Oh shit, I'm going to come already.

He holds me apart as his tongue tears down the last of my defences. I cry out as I shudder and come in his mouth.

His eyes darken as he licks up my cream, and my back arches off the kitchen counter.

Holy fuck. Holy fucking fuck.

He bites my inner thigh and I nearly jump off the counter. "I need my cock in your mouth, Bloss." He growls.

"Bloody hell, Cam, get us to the bedroom. You're a sex maniac. Hello, by the way," I breathe.

"You knew this all along." He smirks. "And hello." He grabs my hand and pulls me to my feet. Before I know it, he is dragging me up the stairs and into his bedroom.

He pulls my dress over my shoulders, and his eyes drop to my body. He smiles in appreciation. "You are just so fucking beautiful."

I smile because he makes me feel beautiful.

He slowly removes my bra and then pushes me down onto my knees on the carpet. "Spread your legs." He growls.

I spread my legs as I kneel in front of him, and he smiles as he slides his boxer shorts down.

His huge cock springs free and I gasp as I see the size of him. Bloody hell, how the fuck does he hide that thing?

He grabs the back of my head. "Open," he whispers.

I open my mouth as my eyes search his and he feeds himself into it. He slides deep, and I gag and he throws his head back in pleasure at the feel of my tongue around him. He holds the back of my head as I struggle to take him.

"Relax," he breathes. "You can do this. I need this." His hand dusts tenderly over the back of my head and I nod. He really does need this. I need to calm myself. I relax my jaw and close my eyes as he slowly pulls out, and then slides deep down my throat.

God, I've never been with a man like him before. He's sexually dominant in every way.

The way he takes me.

The way he makes me take him.

He looks down at me and smiles softly as he dusts the backs of his fingers over my cheek.

"Do you know how fucking perfect you look right now?" he breathes.

I close my eyes and moan.

"Oh fuck, yeah." He growls as he pulls out and slides back home.

My sex is throbbing and I need him. I need him to fill me up.

Completely.

With two hands on the back of my head, he gets himself into a rhythm, and I don't know what's hotter: The fact that, in this moment, I own him, or the sight of his beautiful body riding my open mouth. He rides me. His dick goes deeper until I finally feel the jerk of his body as he comes in a rush into my mouth. Oh dear God. I close my eyes to block out the intimacy, and before I know it he's dragged me to my feet and I'm on the bed with my legs wide open.

His finger slowly slip into my sex and I try to swallow my mouth full.

His cock is still hard as he slowly pumps me with his fingers. He uses one at first, then two, then three, and my body

447

shudders at his claiming. When he pushes in four, I grimace in pain, and I know he's only preparing me for what's to come.

"Open," he whispers. "I need you fucking open."

"Cam…" I whisper with fear. "Cam, calm down."

"How can I calm down when this is all I have thought about for two months?" He rises above me, and in one deep thrust, he's in.

My body convulses as it struggles and he pins my legs back against the mattress.

"You will take all of this cock." He slides out and slams into me hard. "All of it. Now." He slams deeper and I cry out.

Holy fuck.

Then he is giving it to me hard. Long, hard, deep thrusts that force me to thrash beneath him as half of me tries to escape his brutality and half of me rides the pleasure wave as it grows.

I've never been fucked like this — so hard, so fast, so fucking perfect.

He holds himself off my body and I can see every muscle in his torso contract. He's covered in perspiration and, oh my God…

This is ridiculously good sex — sex he so desperately needs.

I frown as I try to deal with him.

I can still taste him in my mouth.

He pulls my legs up over his shoulders and lets out a heavy groan.

"Fuck. You feel good." He moans as he thrusts harder.

He bends and takes my nipple into his mouth and bites down. I convulse and come in a rush, and he slams into me, crying out as he ejaculates hard.

We lay still, gasping for breath until his head drops and kisses me tenderly. "I love you, Ashley Tucker," he whispers.

My eyes tear up and I smile against his lips. "I love you more," I whisper back.

We stay in each other's arms in a deep state of sated happiness. We've been making love for hours, and I don't use the term making love loosely after the initial animalistic sex. Cameron has been sweet, gentle, and loving. Above all else, he's been so, so swoony.

This is what it's meant to feel like.

I lie with my head on his bare chest, his lips pressed to my forehead.

"I have to go, babe," I whisper.

He frowns and holds me tighter. "What? Why?"

"I have to be there when Owen wakes up. I'm always there when he wakes up."

I feel him smirk above me. "You're such a good mom, Ash."

I smile.

"How the hell have you forgiven me for being such douche?" he whispers. "I can't stand what I did to you when I look back."

I shrug. If I was a nice person, I would tell him that it's all okay—forgotten. But I'm never going to do that. What he did was not okay. It will never be okay, and while I have forgiven him, I will never forget it.

I just need to move forward.

"Tell me about the situation with your ex?" he asks.

I blow out a breath. "He's a really nice guy. We worked together for ten years and were good friends." I pause as I remember it like it was yesterday. "When I fell pregnant and didn't think I would ever find you, he offered to be Owen's father."

Cameron frowns. "Even before you were dating?"

"He'd always secretly liked me, and when he offered that I finally saw what a genuinely lovely guy he was. I declined at first, but I went on a date with him not long after."

Cameron frowns. "So you were pregnant with my child and sleeping with him."

I screw up my face. "Oh God, no. We just hung out and nothing happened at all between us until the first kiss when Owen was about four months old."

He watches me intently and I know he's never had a friendship like this so he is probably finding it hard to understand.

"We were really just good friends, you know? We should never have started dating." I pause and think on it for a moment. "There was no passion and no burning desire to be with each other. It was just... comfortable."
He stays silent as he listens.

"As Owen got older and Andrew's work picked up, he had less and less time for Owen, and I used to make every damn excuse I could find to not sleep with him. I knew it had to end if I was to ever find true happiness. For both of us, you know?" Cameron runs his fingers through my hair.

"I finally got the courage and left him. It was a really sad time because we genuinely cared for each other." I smile sadly. "It was for the best. We're really just friends. But his mom was beautiful and so, so good to Owen. She accepted him as her own grandchild."

He nods as if he finally gets it.

"I just want to do the right thing and go and see her, spend some time with her and the family before she dies."

"That's what we're doing." He pauses for a moment. "Does Andrew know who I am?"

I shake my head. "No, but I will tell him. He'll be gutted because I know he's always hoped I would go back to him."

I sit up and he curls around me. "I really have to go, Cam." I bend and kiss his open mouth and our lips linger on each other's. We've hit a new level of intimacy tonight.

Fucking, love making, all while making declarations of love to each other. I don't know how many times he's told me how badly he missed me.

Or how badly I needed to hear it.
This is Heaven.
"Okay, we better go then." He sighs as he gets up.

450

"We?" I ask.

He frowns. "Ash… I'm not spending one more night without you in my arms. It's taken me thirty-three years to feel this way about someone and I'm done with sleeping alone. I'll be sleeping with you from now on. Every night."

I smile as I look at his beautiful face and run my fingers through his dark stubble. "Cam." I pause as I try to articulate my thoughts. "I just want to do it right this time."

He frowns as he comes up to rest on his elbow. "What do you mean?"

"We've done everything the wrong way around. We fucked in Vegas before we even exchanged names."

He laughs and pulls me down over him. "That's because you're a sex maniac, Ashley Tucker, my all night fucker." He bites me and I giggle as I try to escape.

I pull out of his arms and sit up to look at him. "I'm serious, Cam. I want to date. I want to get to know you without the constant power struggle between us. I want to have fun like we did in New York. That was the best weekend of my life."

He smiles softly and runs his thumb across my bottom lip. "Did I tell you I loved you today?" he whispers as his eyes search mine.

I smirk. "Only a few thousand times."

He smiles and kisses me quickly. "Let's go home to our son," he breathes as he gets out of bed. "I want my whole family sleeping in the same house."

You know those crazy bitches that look at their boyfriends all doe-eyed and shit?

I'm one of them.

I've officially crossed to the other side.

Owen and I are standing in line as Cameron organizes our luggage at the airport. We're en route to New York to see

Andrew's mother. Cameron is in his navy suit, having come straight from work. With his dark, wavy hair, he is epitome of male perfection. He's cultured, sexy, funny, and such a wonderful father. I mean, what else is there to want in a man?

I've died and gone to playboy heaven and I'm still having trouble believing that he's mine — that he's actually Owen's father — that somehow the fucking universe got its shit together and delivered for once.

Cameron organized the plane tickets and the hotel, He packed Owen's suitcase this morning before he went to work. He hired a car at the other end so that I could drive to Andrew's.

He's thought of everything. Cameron is so capable that it kind of freaks me out. I've always been the adult in my other relationships, but he's automatically taken on that role. I'm like the annoying second kid or something. I don't have to think because I know he's already thought of everything. He ushers us through the line.

"Obtenez votre sac à dos, Owe."

Translation: Get your back pack, Owen.

Owen frowns as he watches Cam, and Cam points to his bag.

"Obtenez votre sac à dos, Owen," Cameron repeats a second time.

Owen finally figures out what he is saying and picks up his backpack, and I smirk. Cam is teaching Owie French, constantly flicking between languages with him, but Owen isn't picking it up as easy as Cam would like. It's funny watching him repeat things up to ten times. We walk through the terminal and then into the lounge. "Let's get a drink at the bar, Bloss," he says as he looks around with his hand on my behind. "Do you want a glass of red?"

I smile. "Okay."

He looks around and then catches me smiling adoringly at him. He frowns in question.

"Thank you so much for organizing everything. You've no idea how much it means to me."

He leans in and kisses me as he holds my jaw in his hand. "Anything for my girl." Our eyes lock and I feel my heart skip a beat.

Oh, I love this man.

"Yuck," Owen groans. "Stop kissing already."

I giggle and Cameron points at him. "Watch your manners." He widens his eyes at his son.

I glance down at Owen and run my fingers through his unruly hair. "Your hair is out of control, mister." I frown.

"Curls get the girls," Owen replies casually.

"What?" I frown.

"Dad said curls get the girls."

I glance up at Cameron and smirk. "Did he now?"

"Yeah, because the lady in the coffee shop likes Dad's hair so he doesn't have to pay for coffee. That's when he told me that curls get the girls."

I smirk and shake my head at Cameron.

Cameron frowns and flicks the peak on Owen's cap. "You have a big mouth."

Owen screws up his face and smiles cheekily at his father.

Cameron rolls his eyes. "I'm getting a double." He heads to the bar.

"Your curls better not get any girls over there," I call after him.

He shakes his head as he disappears.

Cameron

I sit on the sofa next to Owen as he does his mother's hair. She's sitting on the floor in front of him and he's concentrating so hard as he plays hairdresser.

Ashley is screwing up her face in pain at the torturous hairdressing procedures she's enduring, and I smile before I take a sip of my drink.

Who knew this would be my ideal Friday night?

Who had any fucking idea that this would make me happy?

I'm wearing pyjamas, watching the ball game, while my girlfriend gets her hair pulled out by our kid.

I shake my head in surprise. This is the biggest curveball of my life.

Owen struggles with a hair tie as he tries to put it into a ponytail, and Ashley's head gets pulled back again. "Ouch, Owen. You're hurting me," she whimpers as she puts her hand on her hair.

I giggle and wink at Owen before I lean over and grab five strands of hair and tug on them hard.

"Ouuuuch," she cries. "This is getting ridiculous."

Owen giggles and I reach over, grab her hair and yank it again.

"Ahhh. Owen! This is the worst hairdressing salon of all time."

I bite my lip to stop my laugh, and Owen puts his little hand over his mouth as he giggles.

I grab it again and yank hard, and this time she screams and turns quickly, catching me out.

"Cameron!" she shrieks.

I laugh and Owen holds up his closed fist for me to bump it with mine.

Ashley stands and puts her hands on her hips. "That bloody hurt, you know?'

I smile as I look up at her. Two lopsided pig tails sit high on her head.

I raise an eyebrow. "You look like a naughty school girl."

"With a very sore head." She frowns as she rubs her scalp. "Next time Dad's getting his hair done," she murmurs as she disappears into the bathroom.

I lie in bed and read the news on my phone.

Owen is asleep in the other room and Ashley has just gotten out of the shower. I'm dreading her and Owen going out with Andrew for the day tomorrow, but I'm trying to be the bigger person and not let it get to me. She comes around the corner from the bathroom and I drop my phone in awe.

Two sexy, high pigtails hang over her naked shoulders. The only thing she's wearing is my work tie. She looks fucking edible.

"I'm here for detention, sir," she breathes sexily as her eyes hold mine.

I feel my cock twitch with appreciation. "Come in, Ashley, and close the door behind you," I reply calmly. "Lock it."

She smirks and turns to close the door behind her. Once she's locked it, she comes and stands in front of me. She fidgets with her fingers in front of her as she pretends to be nervous.

"You know the consequences of acting up in class?" I ask.

"Yes, sir," she whispers.

"What are they?" I ask.

"I have to let you punish me, sir."

My body starts to buzz. "Do you know what your punishment will be today?"

She shakes her head shyly as she acts along.

I pull the blankets back and show her my hard cock. Her eyes widen as if scared.

I smile darkly. "You need to get up here and ride this cock, Ashley," I whisper.

She widens her eyes as she pretends to be scared.

"That's what happens to naughty girls in my class."

She should probably really be scared, because this is off the charts.

"How will I do that, sir?" she whispers.

"I will show you."

"Will it hurt?" she whispers.

I nod. "For a little while, yes."

She frowns as she thinks. "What are the other options for punishment, sir?"

My eyes hold hers. "You either get on top of me..." I lick my lips as I imagine it. "Or I fuck your ass. The choice is yours."

Her eyes widen and she frowns as she contemplates her decision.

Oh... please let me fuck your ass, baby. My body starts to really come to life at the thought of how hot and tight that would be.

"What will it be?" I ask with a raised brow.

"I'll ride, sir," she whispers.

"Good girl." I smile and pat my lap. "Straddle me now."

She walks over to me.

"Kneel on the bed next to me and throw one leg over."

She slowly does as she's told, and I smile.

"Up on your knees so I can feel you."

She rises onto her knees above me and I run my fingers through her sex.

Dripping wet.

"You're looking forward to this punishment today, Ashley?" I breathe.

I can smell her and I inhale deeply as she intoxicates my bloodstream.

"Yes, sir," she whispers.

Her naked body sits inches away from my mouth, but I hold my tongue and start to slide my fingers through her glistening lips, pushing them into her sex.

"Have you done this before, Ashley?" I insert two fingers and she whimpers. "Has anyone ever touched you here before?" I ask as I look up at her on her knees.

"No, sir," she whispers as her eyes close in pleasure.

I work her hard and the sound of her arousal is the only noise to be heard.

My cock starts to weep in appreciation.

She's so fucking hot.

"We don't have time for a true preparation today. The lunch bell goes in twenty minutes."

"Yes, sir," she whimpers as I pump her hard.

I grab the base of my cock and hold it upright, then I grab her hips and guide her over me.

"Ease yourself down onto it, Ashley," I murmur through my arousal. I'm going to blow so hard playing this game. It's fucking hot.

"Place your hands on my shoulders."

She gently puts her hands onto my shoulders.

"I'm going to slide you down and it's going to hurt for a minute..." I warn.

She nods as she holds my shoulders.

I slowly pull her down and she's so tight. Fuck. My eyes squeeze closed. I have to work my way into her.

"Move side to side to loosen yourself up, Ashley."

She wiggles from side to side and we get in a little farther. Her eyes close and her mouth hangs open. "Is this right, sir? Am I doing it right?"

"Good girl," I breathe. "That's right." I take her nipple into my mouth and suck. "Open your legs a little farther." I moan against her full, perfect chest.

She opens her legs a little farther and I pull her down a little bit more. Her tightness stings and I concentrate on not slamming into her.

I so want to.

I rub my thumb over her clitoris and she closes her eyes.

"This will open you up, Ashley."

She moans softly as her eyes search mine.

"You like that?" I whisper as I look up at her.

She nods and I pick up the pace, circling my thumb over her swollen clit.

Her hips start to move with me and I know she's close to opening up.

"How does that feel, Ashley?"

She moans. "So good, sir." Her hips start to circle faster, her body taking control.

I pull her lips apart so I don't hurt her, and with one hand on her hip, I start to really pull her down onto me with more force.

"Open up, Ashley. Let me in."

She cries out and I pull her down hard to slide home deeper. We stay still as our hearts hammer away in our chests. "Now kiss me, Ashley."

She frowns and leans in and gently takes my lips in hers. I slide her forward on my cock and she shudders.

"You like that, don't you?" I ask as I rock her back and forth.

She smiles against my lips and nods.

"You're such a dirty girl," I whisper.

"Teach me how to fuck, sir," she breathes.

Oh hell, how much can a man take?

"You want to learn how to fuck, baby?" I breathe.

She nods. "Yes, please."

I lift her up and slam her back down onto my cock. She whimpers and her head falls back.

Up and down, I work her hard, all the while watching those beautiful tits bouncing around.

I've never seen anything more perfect.

"Sir," she whimpers with her eyes closed. "You're so deep. Can you feel how deep you are?"

Oh God... I'm close.

"Give it to me, sir. I've been a bad girl. I need to be punished hard before my next class."

That's it.

Restraint gone.

I pick her up, slam her down hard, and she bounces up and down until I can't hold it any longer. I screw up my face as I try, but it's too hard—she's too good.

I slam her down and I shudder as I come deep inside of her, and right on cue, she moans as her own orgasm finally arrives.

We sit for a moment and I shake my head.

"Oh my God," I whisper. "That was smoking hot."

She smiles sexily and gets off me, her mind still in her fantasy role. "I have to get back to class, sir."

I smirk as I watch her. "Good girl, today, Ashley. You took your punishment well."

Her dark eyes hold mine. "I'm going to be naughty in class from now on, sir."

"Then you will be punished in the hardest possible way," I reply flatly.

She smiles. "I'm counting on it." With that she sashays into the bathroom and turns the shower on.

I smile as I fall back onto the bed.

Ashley Tucker, my all night fucker.

Ashley

"I won't be long, I promise." I sigh.

Cameron frowns. "You were with her all afternoon. I don't see why you have to go back tonight."

"She wants me to cook her favorite dinner."
Cameron shakes his head.

After spending the afternoon with Andrew's family, I'm only just dropping Owen back with Cameron. Somehow, I've been coerced into making dinner for his mother tonight. "I felt like I couldn't say no. She bought all the ingredients so I could cook it for her," I add.

"Let me say no for you then," Cameron snaps.
I roll my eyes. "I've got a splitting headache. I don't even want to go."

"So don't." He shakes his head in disgust.

"I just dropped Owen back so you weren't alone tonight. I'll be a few hours. You two go out for dinner and I'll be home for dessert."

"Fine," he snaps. "Where do you want to go for dinner Owie?"

"McDonald's." Owen smiles hopefully.

Cameron screws up his face. "That's not happening. We'll find somewhere else."

I smile and kiss them both on the cheek. "See you both soon."

The sound of a dishwasher is loud and I feel groggy. I look around and frown.

What the hell? Where am I? I sit up to find myself on Andrew's mothers couch with a knitted blanket over me.

Huh?

What the hell?

It's daylight.

Last thing I remember, I was watching a movie after dinner. Hang on a minute.

Horror dawns.

Oh my God.

I jump up. "What... what time is it?" I stammer at Andrew's mother as she walks out of the kitchen.

"Just gone seven, love."

"What? On Sunday?" I shriek. "What the hell? I slept all night?"

Oh my god, oh my fucking god. I hold my head in horror.

"You were so zonked out from the headache tablets I gave you that you went out like a light. I didn't have the heart to wake you."

My mouth drops open. I grab my bag and my keys. "See you later," I scream as I run out the door. I scramble through my bag for my phone and dig it out.

Seventeen missed calls from Cameron, the last one just two hours earlier.

I check and it's on silent.

My eyes close. Oh my God. How could this happen?

He's going to freak. My eyes tear up and I dial his number as I start the car.

My heart is hammering hard in my chest.

I went to my ex-boyfriend's and didn't come home.
This looks so bad.
I get his voicemail.

Hello, you've reached Cameron Stanton. Leave a message.

No, no, no, no.
I drive like a bat out of hell, and when I get to the traffic lights I try again.

Hello, you've reached Cameron Stanton. Leave a message.

My eyes tear up as I imagine him waiting for me when I didn't come home.
What must he think?
I can hardly see the road through my tears and I swipe them away angrily. I drive like a maniac, all while frantically trying to call him.

Hello, you've reached Cameron Stanton. Leave a message.

"Ahh, stupid voicemail," I scream. "Answer your fucking phone."

For half an hour, I battle traffic.
I get to the hotel and park in the loading bay then run through the foyer and push the button on the lift. "Come on, come on, come on," I whisper.
It arrives and I jump in and scrunch up my face as my tears pour free. This is a disaster.
I get to my floor and run down the long corridor, shoving the door open.
My heart sinks.

The room is empty. "Cameron?" I call. "Owen?"

Their stuff is gone. I notice something on the coffee table and I run over.

My lone plane ticket is sitting there alongside a note.

We've flown home early.
You may as well stay here.

30

M Y HANDS go over my mouth. He left.
He left me here in New York.

I've got to try and catch him at the airport. I glance around the room. Annoyingly, I need to get my things together. I just don't have time for this shit. I run around and grab my toiletries and clothes from the bathroom. I pick up my shoes from the floor and throw them into my bag, zipping it up double speed.

I can't believe he left me here...

Damn Andrew's mother. This is all her bloody fault. Why in the hell didn't she wake me up? She knew exactly what she was doing, the old snake. Andrew wasn't even at dinner with us last night. He had an engagement party to go to. I was there alone.

With one last glance around the room, I head out the door and run down the corridor with a deep sense of dread sitting heavily in my stomach.

This might be it for us. This really could be it. I messed up and what's the first thing he does?

Takes off with Owen.

I'm furious with him, too. How dare he take off?

He's such a spoiled brat! Is this how he controls the situation? By cutting me out?

I get into the elevator and I slam the button four times. Who am I kidding? I didn't come home from a date with my ex...

What do you expect, you idiot?

Cameron

Two hours earlier.

I close up our suitcases and place them on top of the bed.

I'm furious.

Like a lovesick puppy, I sat here and waited for her in the hotel room.

Like a lovesick fucking puppy, I waited up all night, worried, thinking she may be dead in a ditch.

She's with him. Her ex.

A man she shares a past with.

I close my eyes at the thought. I can't bear it and I feel sick to my stomach.

I've never been in love before. I've never even been close to feeling what I feel for Ashley.

And this is how she treats me. This is the amount of respect she has for me.

I have absolutely no control over my emotions and I can't stand relying on someone else for my happiness. I've never felt so helpless in my life.

I'm done. She can go to hell.

I won't be here when she gets back.

She can find someone else to be her puppy.

I wake Owen. "Come on, mate. We have to go home to LA."
He frowns as he wakes up. "I thought we were going to the zoo?"
he mumbles.

"Change of plans. I will take you to the zoo another time," I
reply flatly as I pack the last of the things into my overnight case.

I pick up my phone and check it once more. No calls, no
messages.

What if she's been hurt in an accident? The sick, nervous
feeling in my stomach churns again. I go over to the window and
stare out over the city as the sun comes up.

Where are you?

With him, my subconscious replies.

I look back over at Owen as he tries to wake up. It's only
6.30am.

She's fallen asleep after they had sex—it's the only logical
explanation.

I close my eyes in pain. I hate this.

I hate feeling like this. "Owen. Up," I snap.

He goes to the bathroom as I line the bags up near the door and
he gets dressed. I fish out Ashley's plane ticket from my bag and put
it onto the desk. With a heavy heart, I write her a note.

We've flown home early.
You may as well stay here.

I just wish I knew she was safe before I left. What if something
has happened to her?

God, I hate this shit. I put my head into my hands in disgust.

"I'm hungry." Owen yawns.

"We can have breakfast at the airport."

"Where's Mom?" He frowns.

"Um." I try think of an answer. "She's with Andrew. She'll be
home later."

Owen frowns as he processes the information.

I blow out a breath and continue packing until everything is
done. I just wish I had confirmation that she was okay before I left.

What if something has happened to her? My heart asks.

It hasn't, you fool, my head replies.

"Let's go, Owen."

I grab the suitcases and he follows me out and down the corridor. When we get down to the lobby, I hold my phone in my hand and the doorman hails a cab.

We climb in. "Where to?" the driver asks.

"The airport," I reply flatly.

He pulls out into traffic and begins the journey when my phone rings. Ashley.

I frown as I stop myself answering it. I'm not losing my shit at her while Owen is with me.

It goes to voicemail and when it's complete, I listen to it.

"Fucking voicemail," she shrieks in a panic. "Oh my God, Cameron. I'm so sorry. I took some headache tablets and they must have knocked me out. I just woke up on Andrew's mothers couch. I'm so sorry. I'm coming now." She hangs up.

My blood pressure rises. The fury I feel is beyond belief and boils my blood.

Does she think I'm stupid?

"Was that Mom?" Owen asks.

I nod, lost in my thoughts.

"She's going to be very angry that we left without her."

I glance over at him and then back to the road.

"She might not come home. She might stay here." He frowns, speaking with a worried little voice.

I take his hand in mine as I stare out the window. The phone rings again and I let it go to voicemail before I listen to it.

Ashley's voice is frantic. "Oh my God, Cameron, forgive me. I love you. I'm on my way."

I get a lump in my throat as I stare out the window.

Every ounce of my being wants to be as far away from her as possible, yet I know if I go and take Owen, it will be over for us.

"Can't we just wait for Mom?" Owen asks. "She won't be long. You know she's slow all the time."

I stare out the window as my mind goes into overdrive. Do I believe her?

Do I trust her?

I think back to everything we've been through. Despite it all, she's somehow learned to trust me again.

I took her child and she forgave me.

I lean my elbow up against the door as I hold my head, deep in thought.

I don't want to see her...but if I don't go back...

Ashley

The elevator finally opens out into the foyer and I run out, dragging my suitcase behind me when I get to the doorman. "I need a cab, please," I blurt out in a panic.

The doorman frowns as he looks me up and down. "Are you alright?"

I nod, but in all seriousness, I'm on the edge of a complete meltdown.

"Won't be a minute." He goes out onto the street to hail me a cab and I wait in the drop off bay.

What a disaster.

"Come on, come on," I murmur as I look around frantically. "Where are all the bloody cabs?"

Everything was going so well. Why did I mess this up?

A cab pulls up, and low and behold...

Cameron is sitting in the backseat with Owen.

My face falls and he glares at me as he gets out of the cab and slams the door. He walks around to get Owen out.

I smile through my tears.

He came back.

He retrieves the suitcases out of the trunk and I wait on the spot.

He walks over, emotionless. "Get up to the room now before I strangle you in public," he growls in a whisper.

"Oh my God, Cameron, I'm... I'm so sorry," I stammer as the tears break the dam. "I had some headache tablets after dinner and..." I shake my head as I try to get my words out quicker. "And, honestly, I have no idea what happened, but I woke up on the couch this morning."
Cameron looks at me, deadpan.

"And my phone was on silent," I add.

He narrows his eyes and storms over to the elevator. Owen and I run after him like little puppies.

We get in and the elevator attendant stands to the front and looks straight ahead.

Cameron stands at the back and I face him. "You have no idea of the horror I felt when I woke up and realized what had happened." I shake my head. "And then I got here and you were gone," I continue. I grab his hand and he tears it out of mine.

"Stop talking to me. I'm furious with you." Cameron growls.

Owen stands next to the elevator attendant at the front and swings his arms, smiling stupidly up at him. The elevator attendant glances down at Owen and smirks.

"But, Cam... you came back." I smile in relief. "You came back for me. Thank God you came back," I whisper.

Cameron looks at me, deadpan.

I smile broadly through my tears like a crazy person. "This means we've progressed. You really do love me."

"You're getting ahead of yourself. I hate you today."
"Liar." I smirk.

Owen is still smiling goofily up at the elevator attendant as he swings his arms. "My mom and dad are fighting," he announces.

The attendant nods subtly, trying not to be rude to Owen while remaining respectful to us.

"Sometimes they always kiss, but today my dad hates my mom," he continues.

"Owen," Cameron snaps.

"Because my mom went out with my other dad and didn't come home all night."

The attendant drops his head, embarrassed.

"Owen Stanton. Stop telling everyone everything!" Cameron snaps.

Owen widens his eyes. "I think he hates me today, too. He's very cranky, isn't he?" he adds.

The attendant drops his head to hide his smirk.

Cameron shakes his head, exasperated.

I wrap my arms around Cameron and smile against his chest as he stands still with his arms rigid by his sides.

"I love you, Mr. Stanton." I smile up at him as I start to quickly kiss him all over. "And you came back for me and this is progress for us. I think Andrew's mother tried to set me up and I'm so bloody angry with her," I continue.

He moves his face away from me so I don't kiss him, and I know he's going to be furious over this for a while.

It doesn't matter. He came back.

There's hope for us yet.

Trust is earned.

And little by little, Cameron has earned it. I think the turning point for us was when he came back for me in New York.

Furious beyond belief, yet he came back.

He lost his ever-living shit and didn't talk to me for a week. *But he stayed.*

Every night, we stayed together as a family and, although he wasn't talking to me and it was torture, he was in my bed and I felt safe.

That was twelve weeks ago and our little family has gotten into somewhat of a routine now. The nights that Cam would have had Owen, we stay at his house, and the nights that I would have had Owen, we now spend at my house. Cam cooks for all of us and has us in stitches with his sense of humor. Jenna and Cameron are getting along famously and life is surprisingly good. Of course, there is still a power struggle between the two of us at least once a day. I have to admit Cameron usually wins, simply because I can't be bothered fighting with him anymore.

It's funny how things turn out. I've stopped sweating the small stuff.

I sit at the table in the hospital cafeteria with Amber and our intern group.

Cameron comes and sits beside me with Dr. Jameson. He picks up my hand and squeezes it subtly in his own personal greeting. Everyone knows about us now. Cameron went to the hospital board to explain the situation and they have granted permission and wavered the rules.

It seemed weird receiving an email that Cameron sent to all of the interns stating we were dating and that we had a history and shared a child.

He wanted to be the one to tell them. He felt it best he was honest and up front. He didn't want them to hear it from somewhere else as cheap gossip.

It was comical watching Amber's reaction when she read it. Her eyes nearly popped out her head and she punched me hard in the arm. I even had a bruise. She's now in a full on deviant relationship with her security guard and their two blow up bed partners. She gets to sleep with three people while remaining loyal to one. It's a cool kind of set up, and it works for them.

I don't think I could ever watch Cam have sex and orgasm with someone or something else.

I would still be jealous even if they didn't have a pulse.

He even changed his phone number so his past history of beauties can no longer contact him. I never asked him to, he just did it.

Cameron takes me on a date every Friday night. He remembered me saying I wanted to date and get to know each other without just being his child's mother, and he has gone to extreme lengths to give me what I want.

Friday nights are heaven and I get him all to myself. I dress up sexily and we drink cocktails, go to fancy restaurants, dance, laugh, and of course I swoon all over the table. We drop in and out of languages with sarcasm and challenge each other's brain power.

I still think my brain is superior and he still disagrees.

Sometimes Tash, Josh, and Adrian come, but Cam likes it when it's just the two of us.

He's protective of his alone time with me because it's so limited and I love him even more for it.

Saturday mornings I seem to always suffer because I can't drink like he does without suffering the consequences. He and Owen skateboard around the neighborhood and let me sleep in before they eventually return with the morning papers.

Life is good. So good Like... dreamy good.

I still pinch myself every day when I look at him, this beautiful man who is a beautiful father. I can't believe he loves me.

How is this even possible?

One by one the table get up to return to their duties and Cam hangs back. He wants me alone for two minutes, as he always does.

He sips his coffee and smiles across the table like a Cheshire cat.

"What are you smirking at, Stanton?" I smile as I subtly rub his shin through his suit pants with my foot.

His sexy eyes hold mine. "Just this really hot chick who I can't wait to bone tonight."

I snort as I sip coffee. "Bone?" I mouth with a raised brow. "Really? Did you just say bone?"

He nods with a devious smile.

"Well, your high school boning is going to have to wait. I'm working in emergency tonight, remember?" Hospital policy states that all interns do a minimum amount of hours working in emergency. It helps us get experience and helps the hospital with staffing. I've been rostered on tonight.

He frowns and then rolls his eyes. "Uch, that's right." He sips his coffee. "Boning before breakfast it is."

I smile broadly and his face mirrors mine. "You really are intent on keeping that romance score of three, aren't you?" I reply.

He chuckles cheekily. "You wouldn't like me if I was normal."

My eyes drop to his sexy mouth as his tongue darts out to lick his bottom lip.

"Probably not," I whisper. "It's the naughty in you that I love the most." My eyes hold his.

"Ashley Tucker, my all night fucker," he breathes.

I glance around at the tables around us. "Behave yourself, Dr. Stanton. I've got a reputation to uphold."

His eyes hold mine and he raises a brow. "So have I."

I put my hand on his thigh under the table. "Listen, Dr. Love: You keep dreaming how you're going to serve me my breakfast boning, and I'm going to go back to work. See you about three in the morning."

I get up and push my chair back.

"Drive home carefully, Bloss."

I smile and bend to his ear with my hand on his shoulder. "I love you."

He smiles and puts his hand over mine. "What's not to love?"

I shake my head and he laughs out loud — that carefree beautiful laugh that permeates through my bones. "Goodbye, Cameron." I shake my head and go back to work.

It's four in the morning when I pull into his driveway.

The gates are immediately opened on my arrival. I know that security have been waiting for me to get home. I lock up my car and put my fingerprint into the front door scanner. It unlocks and opens. Whoever would have thought I would one day stay in a house where a key isn't required?

The kitchen light is on, and I walk in and throw my handbag down.

A note is sitting on the counter.

Your dinner is in the fridge, hottie,

x

I smile and walk into the laundry, take off my scrubs, and put them straight into the washing machine.

We both do this. It's a habit. As soon as we get home from hospital, our scrubs get washed immediately before the germs can spread throughout the house or anywhere near Owen. After ER shifts, especially. I head back to the kitchen in my robe, put the TV on, and open the fridge. Chicken satay stir fry. Yum. I smile. Cameron's a much better cook than I am. I heat up my dinner and flick through Facebook while I eat in silence to some early morning crap television. I need this half an hour wind down time after being so busy for so long. I'm still buzzing.

Eventually, I head up to our room and find my prince sleeping soundly on his side. I walk over and gently kiss his cheek as I watch him.

His dark hair is splayed across the pillow and his chest rises and falls as he breathes. His big lips are semi parted, and his black, thick eyelashes flutter as he sleeps.

Just looking at him brings a smile to my face. His cheekiness and naughty boy personality is the light of mine and Owen's life. I run my hand through his hair as I watch him, and after a much needed hot shower, I climb into bed behind him and snuggle against his back.

"Hey, Bloss," he whispers sleepily as he pulls my arm around him.

I kiss his back. "Hi, babe," I murmur as I rub my cheek on his skin. No place is more home to me than he is.

"You okay?" he murmurs softly with his eyes still closed.

"Yeah." I kiss his back again. "It was an easy shift tonight."

He worries about me working in emergency. On his first few shifts someone seemed to die every time and it traumatised him for life, I think.

I'm just falling asleep when the pitter patter of tiny feet walk into the room, around to Cameron's side of the bed.

"Dad," Owen says softly.

Without a word Cameron, pulls back the covers and Owen crawls in. Cam kisses the top of his head. "Goodnight, buddy. Go to sleep now," he whispers sleepily.

I smile. Owen almost always goes to Cameron's side of the bed now because he knows that Cam, the big softie, will just let him in. At least I *try* and take him back to his own bed. He doesn't do it every night anymore, though—probably three nights out of seven. It's always around this time, too, and he always goes to Cam and not me.

I lie in the darkness with my arm around Cam, listening to the sound of my two men breathing deeply as they sleep, and I say my daily thank you to the heavens.

I'm finally home.

"Close the door, baby." I watch Owen climb into the back seat of the car. I have the morning off after working late last night, and I'm dropping him at preschool. I pull out of the drive and onto the road when a song I hate comes on the radio. I push the button to change the channel.

"Oh, play mine and Dad's playlist," Owen suggests excitedly.

I frown as my eyes find him in the mirror. "You have a playlist?"

"Yes, number four."

I flick through until I get to playlist number four and hit play.

The sexy beat comes on.

"Oh, this is your song, Momma."

I frown. "What?"

"Dad said this is your song."

I smirk and shake my head. The song playing is *Candy Shop* by Fifty Cent. It was the song that I walked down the catwalk to in the Escape Club that night. How does he even remember that?

I turn the corner as my mind goes back to that night. It seems like a lifetime ago and I get a visual of Cameron uploading the song to his playlist.

I do love that man.

"Yeah, Dad said this is your song because you're really good at sucking lollipops," Owen continues.

My eyes bulge.

Cameron. What the fuck?

Unable to help it, I break out in a broad smile. He does call me Mistress Head on occasion, but to tell our child lollipop information is going a step too far.

I shake my head and start to giggle, then I burst out laughing. This man kills me.

The things that go on in his brain, I will never know.

We drive along and listen to the sexy words and I get an idea. I'll take you to the candy shop, all right, Dr. Stanton...

You'll be cotton candy in my hands.

Friday Night.

Cameron spins me around on the dance floor as he sings the words out loud.

We're in a cocktail bar and have come here after we had a Friday night dinner date in our favorite restaurant.

I smile as I watch him and he frowns as he sings to give it more oomph.

I laugh as he spins me again and I run my fingers through his two-day growth, staring up at him adoringly.

He smiles down at me and kisses me softly. "What are you looking at, Tucker?"

I shake my head. "The worst singer I've ever heard."

"Worst singer?" He cringes. "Well, I'm the best dancer." He twirls me out and I go flying into another couple dancing,

They stagger sideways as I hit.

"Oh my God, I'm... I'm so sorry," Cameron stammers.

The man narrows his eyes at Cameron and turns back to his partner to continue dancing.

Cam pulls me back to him and I giggle against his chest. "Every time we dance, you fly me into someone," I whisper.

He holds me close and looks down at me sexily. "They should get out of my way, I'm a lethal weapon out here." He kisses me.

"À plus d'un titre," I whisper against his lips.

Translation: In more ways than one.

His eyes darken. "Allons à la maison, ma belle bombe Bloss."

Translation. Let's go home, my beautiful Bloss bomb.

I smile as we continue swaying to the music. After a few more dances, he drags me from the dance floor and over to the elevators.

The bell pings and my eyes flicker over to him as he smirks.

Oh no.

"You know, small things amuse small minds," I whisper. The doors open and reveal three people in the elevator. He raises his eyebrow sarcastically.

"I wouldn't know. I don't have either." He holds my hand in his and walks into the elevator and we take our place at the back.

He looks at me for a moment. "You know, we really shouldn't be doing this. You are my children's nanny after all," he announces so that everyone can hear him. The other people in the elevator all drop their heads as they pretend not to listen.

I smirk. Every time. Every damn time we get into a elevator.

"Well, she should have given me that pay rise I asked for," I reply flatly.

His eyes dance with mischief as they hold mine.

"Then I wouldn't have to take my payments into my own hands," I add as I brush my hands over my hips. "I do love it when your wife's away, though. Do I look good in her dress?"

A woman behind me gasps.

He smiles sexily as his eyes drop down my body. "You look good in her dress, but not as good as you will look underneath her husband," he replies darkly

I drop my head to stop myself laughing, and he squeezes my hand in his.

"I'm disgusted," the woman behind us whispers to her husband.

"It's going to be disgusting alright," he mutters under his breath. "Disgustingly dirty."

I squeeze his hand again. Oh my God... what next? Where does he get this shit?

"Oh my goodness," The woman gasps as the door opens and he pulls me out. We both burst out laughing and stumble across the foyer and out onto the street. Then he drags me around the corner and is on me. He has me pinned to an alleyway wall, his lips searing mine, his hard erection promising me bad things — disgustingly dirty things, just like he just told everyone in the elevator.

"One day somebody from an elevator is going to put a picture of you on Facebook with the heading 'Do you know this sleazebag?'"

"Or his nanny." He laughs and dips his head to suck on my lips. His tongue has a certain edge in it tonight. He's in his rough mood — the one I love so much.

"Can we go back to my house before we go to yours?" he breathes as his arousal starts to become uncontrollable.

"Good idea," I murmur as he grinds me hard with his hips.

That's code for *I want to fuck you loud and noisy.*

He turns out onto the street and puts his arm up with renewed determination. "Taxi!"

Twenty minutes later, Cameron is leading me through his house and up the stairs in the darkness. And it just so happens I have my own little surprise waiting for him. I slipped over here this afternoon and got the things ready while he was at my house with Owen. I pretended I needed to get some groceries.

We walk into his bedroom to find a large mirror up against the wall and an armchair in front of it.

He frowns as he looks around the room. "I have a little surprise for you tonight, Dr. Stanton." I smirk.

I lead him to the chair and I sit him down in front of the mirror. "Back in a minute," I whisper with a tender kiss.

I walk into the second wardrobe and close the door behind me. It's filled with my things now and I grab the outfit I need. I got Tiffany to borrow one of the lap dancing uniforms as well as a dark wig from the club. I quickly put them on and then reapply some hot pink lipstick, just like the night I first danced for him.

I find the song on my phone and I giggle at myself in the mirror. Who would have ever thought I would do anything like this?

Cameron Stanton makes me gah gah crazy.

I walk back out and stand in front of him. He inhales sharply. I'm wearing short, leather, caramel hotpants with coffee, knee-high boots and an organza see through top. Not to forget my long, dark wig.

It's just like the two occasions I danced for him in the club, only this time we're alone and he can have whatever he wants from me.

He hisses in approval and sits back, rearranging the erection in his pants. "Fucking yes," he whispers.

I get on my knees in front of him and hit play on my phone. The sexy beat plays out.

His eyes widen.

"Somebody told me that I suck a good lollipop," I whisper.

His eyes widen as he glues the puzzle pieces together. "Owen has a big mouth."

I giggle as I pull him forward in the chair aggressively and spread his legs.

In slow motion, I unzip his pants as my eyes hold his. His mouth hangs open as he watches me and the backs of his fingertips dust my face.

"How can I service you tonight, sir?" I whisper as I kiss his cock.

He flexes it in approval.

I lick the length of him and close my eyes. God, he's so fucking hot.

This beautiful body is all mine, and I intend to take full advantage of it.

I run my tongue over the tip and his eyes never leave me, as if he has to watch every single moment of this to believe it's real.

I continue to tease him with my tongue, doing everything I can to drive him wild except for taking him fully in my mouth.

His breath is catching and he is lifting off the seat toward my mouth. His eyes are flicking between the mirror and me.

I tear his legs farther apart and cup his balls in my hand. Pre-ejaculate is seeping from his end.

God's gift to women.

"Suck me," he eventually moans. "Fucking suck me, Ashley."

I smile against his cock as my eyes search his. "Make me."

The song starts again on repeat.

His eyes flash with delight. He knows I want to be dominated. I want him to take me how he wants me.

He feeds his cock into my mouth and grabs the back of my head, pushing me down onto him. Hmm, tastes so good.

He sits back and watches us in the mirror as he pushes me down onto him before his eyes close from the pleasure. God, he's close already. I can feel it.

I suck as hard as I can, and it would have to be near painful for him. Finally, he moans and throws his head back.

"Putain d'enfer, tu fais si bien, bébé." He moans.

Translation. Fucking hell, you do that so good, baby.

My eyes close. As soon as he starts talking dirty in French, I'm gone.

Mind and body overload.

His hand tenderly stokes my hair as he watches on.

I start to stroke him with my hand as my mouth sucks hard, and he convulses in pleasure as his body lifts off the seat to meet me.

"Ride me." He growls. "Ride my cock now."

Before I can respond, he's lifted me and is ripping my shorts off, tearing my top over my shoulders. He turns me to face the mirror and pulls me back, spreading my legs before he impales me in one swift movement.

We stay still, our eyes locked on each other in the mirror, our breaths quivering as we try to hold off from our orgasms. I'm instantly transported back to the club when I desperately wanted to do this.

His hands take control of my hips and he circles me around him to open me up.

This is so hot, seeing my naked body spread out for his pleasure in the mirror. Seeing his thick cock slide into my body.

I will never get enough of this—get enough of this beautiful man beneath me.

Of this beautiful cock and how close it brings me to him.

He lifts me and brings me back down, forcing me to close my eyes.

"Spread your legs, Bloss. I need it hard, baby." He growls.

I don't know if I will even last two pumps with this visual in front of me. His two hands grab my pelvis and he starts to lift me and bring me back down hard. He bites my neck and I cry out.

He watches over my shoulder in the mirror. This is ridiculously hot.

The sight of us it spurs him on, and he starts to bounce me up and down with force.

"Knees up." He growls.

Oh shit, I don't know if I can take him like that. He's too big.

"Cam…" I whisper.

"Get your fucking knees up, Ashley," he snaps as he grabs my ankles.

I bring my knees up and he circles into me deep. My body shudders and, sensing my oncoming orgasm, he rides me hard. Up, down, in and out, and oh so fucking good.

The friction is shredding me, burning me—his cock is turning me inside out.

I bounce high and he grabs my shoulders from behind to hold me deep. I cry out as my orgasm rips through my body and he tips his head back and moans a guttural sound as his body reaches its own climax.

He turns me and kisses me over my shoulder, softly and tenderly. I smile against him.

Instant perfection.

"Hope you're in the mood for pain, Bloss." He smiles.

I giggle and he lifts me. His body is still in mine when takes me over and bends me over the bed, penetrating me deeper.

His lips drop to my neck. "You're in for a hard night."

I sit with my hand on Cameron's thigh as he sits deep in thought, completing his crossword. Owen is upfront playing with the other kids.

We are on board the Stanton private plane on our way to Vegas with Joshua, Adrian, Natasha, all the kids, and three nannies. Jenna even came at Cameron's insistence; they really do like each other. The boys are going to be busy, so Tash, Jenna, and I are going to go out on the town one of the nights. I wasn't really keen, to be honest, but Tash and Jenna talked me into it. I would rather have stayed home, but they wanted a girl's night out.

Jenna and Tash have gotten to know each other from Tash's visits to our house. They have become firm friends.

10AK NIGHTCLUB

I stand in the crowded club as I wait for Tash and Jenna at the bar. Security is as tight as always. Natasha's guards are never far away. I glance around to see them at their stations against the wall.

"Hey, good looking. Do you want to dance?" a man asks.

I glance around. Shit, where are the girls? "Ah, no thanks." I smile. "I'm just waiting for my friends."

"But you look so hot." He grabs my arm and I pull it out of his grip.

"I said no, thank you," I snap.

"What's your problem?" He sneers.

"No problem. I just don't want to dance." Frigging hell. Buzz off, douche.

Cameron appears. Oh thank God. He stands next to the man and looks between us, sensing my apprehension. "Is there a problem here?" he asks.

"Who are you?" the guy snaps.

I start to look around. Where are the bloody security guards when you need them?

"None of your business," Cameron snaps.

Oh shit. I look around. Security? Hello? You're kind of needed over here.

"Is this dead shit your husband?" He frowns.

Bloody hell. "No, this is my..." I start to reply, but as I turn back to Cameron, I find him crouched down on bended knee with a ring held out in his hands.

My eyes widen.

"I'd like to be your husband for real." He smiles up at me. "This time in Vegas, things will be different."

My world stops.

This is the exact way we met, in the exact same spot. I get instant goosebumps, and his romantic score just skyrocketed through the roof.

Cameron's eyes glow with affection as he looks up at me, waiting and expectant.

I glance over to Natasha and Jenna to see they are standing with Joshua, Adrian, and the group. They're all watching on and smiling broadly. Natasha and Jenna are bouncing up and down on the spot. They so knew about this.

This was all planned.

Is this really happening?

"I should have trusted my gut instincts five years ago and taken you straight to the chapel and married you that night." Cameron smiles hopefully.

I get a lump in my throat as I watch him on bended knee. He is perfect.

This is perfect.

The place we met.

"Will you marry me, Ashley Tucker?"

I nod, laugh, and then bend to kiss him. The crowd cheer around us. Our faces are scrunched together as we kiss and I think my smile is going to crack my cheeks. He stands and slowly slides the ring my finger. I can hardly see it through the happy tears.

It's big—stupid huge, actually—and I hold my hand out to look at it before I glance back up at him.

"You didn't answer me," he whispers as he wraps his arms around me.

I smile against his lips as he starts to kiss me softly.

"Say it out loud," he begs quietly.

"Yes, I'll marry you." I laugh. "You are the best fake husband I could ever have hoped for."

THE END

No matter how hard I tried, I couldn't do this story justice in a two-page glance into the future… so stay tuned.
Follow the next five years in the Dr. Stanton's epilogue novella

Read on for an excerpt of Stanton Adore -Joshua and Natasha and Marx Girl- Bridget

MARX GIRL
Releasing October 2017

1

Kamala

"DON'T LOOK at me like you want me. If you don't," I murmur into the silence.

He sits back and readjusts his length. His dark eyes hold mine, but he doesn't answer.

The water laps around me as I lie on the inflatable mattress, floating around the pool in my white string bikini. The sun is just setting over the horizon and everyone has disappeared to get ready for dinner.

We are alone.

His eyes are locked on mine as he sits in his deck chair around the pool.

He has no right to look at me—to watch me with wanting eyes.

But he does.

And... I still like it.

Ben is my sister's family's bodyguard and the head of their security. Things are... *difficult* between us.

The attraction we have for each other wasn't supposed to be there, but forbidden lust never felt so good.

At six-foot three inches tall, with his sandy hair, honey brown eyes, and his large, muscular physic — a by-product of his ex-military life — Ben Statham is one hell of a man.

The lingering looks caused a clench deep in my sex when he looked at me.

The smouldering fire when he'd sneak into my room late at night.

Our story began six months ago, when my sister Natasha became involved with her then-boyfriend, Joshua Stanton.

I was always with Tash and Ben was always with Josh. We came together through circumstance, mutual acquaintances and nothing more.

He was the strong man at the back of the crowd watching over everyone.

I was busy watching him.

While the rest of the world was concentrating on my beloved sister and Joshua's blossoming relationship, I was concentrating on fighting the attraction. The pull I felt towards him only grew day by day.

Laughter turned to conversation. Conversation progressed to lingering looks. Lingering looks turned to goosebumps, and then one day in the kitchen pantry it happened.

He kissed me.

It was the most perfect kiss I'd ever had.

It was sweet, sexy, and it opened up a world of passion that I'd never even known existed.

For three weeks we snuck a kiss in whenever we could, until during one moment of foggy passion, I asked him to come to my room after everyone else had gone to sleep that night.

He did.

We made love… storybook love.

Our perfection carried on for six weeks until tragedy struck our family. As the head of security, Ben blamed himself for what happened and he pulled away from me.

When I needed him the most, he was nowhere to offer support.

And now we're here, on a family holiday in Kamala, Thailand.

My feelings for him haven't changed.

He's still the head of security.

I'm still his boss' sister-in-law.

But he left me when I needed him the most and I won't forget that in a hurry.

Our eyes are locked.

"Why do you think I don't want you?" he whispers in his heavy South African accent.

I frown, unsure how to answer. Eventually, I reply, "Do you want me?"

He sips his beer, taking his time to answer.

I run my fingers through the water beneath me as I try to articulate my own thoughts.

I don't know what's going on with us, but I do know I can't stand feeling the way I do.

I can't go on without the answers that I need. He's a strong man who doesn't show his true feelings, but what the hell happened to us? How do you go from passionate lovers to nothing without even having a conversation about it?

There was no fight, no discussion. Just silence.

Still, he waits, not answering my question. His jaw clenches as his eyes hold mine.

My eyes search his.

What the fuck is going on with him?

Does he want me to beg?

I climb off the inflatable mattress and make my way over to the pool steps. I want to be the one who ends the conversation, not for it to be the other way around.

Who am I kidding?

I'm the only one *in* this conversation. I slowly walk out of the pool, watching as his hungry eyes drop down my body. I bend and pick up my towel, wrapping it around my waist. With one last lingering look, I walk inside.

His refusal to address our issues infuriates me.

It hurts and makes me wonder if everything we shared was some kind of delusion.

I know he's strong, I know he's not a talker, but the nights spent in his arms were filled with tenderness and love.

Where is that man?

I want him back.

I lie in the darkness. It's one in the morning. The sound of the ocean is drifting through the room and the soft breeze rolls over my body. As usual, I'm torturing myself with thoughts of Ben Statham and his beautiful body. *Where is he now? Is he asleep?*

The last time we were together I told him I loved him. I never meant to, but I couldn't help it. I was all soft and emotional from my orgasm high and it just slipped out.

Is that why he ran?

I blow out a deep breath and stare at the ceiling as I go over that last night we had together for the ten thousandth time.

If I knew it was going to be our last night together, I would have done more. I would have said more.

I'd have done anything to make him stay.

The door slowly opens and I roll over. My heart catches in my chest.

"Ben..." I whisper.

He walks in and closes the door behind him. His hands clench at his sides, he seems nervous.

I frown into the darkness as I watch him.

"I wanted to see you," he whispers."

I lie still and quiet. He can talk this time.

"I look at you like I want you..." He pauses and takes a breath. "Because I do."

I frown.

"You have no idea how badly I want you Bridget or how hard it is to stay away."

"Then don't. Why are you doing this to us?" I whisper.

He sits on the side of the bed and cups my face in the palm of his hand. His eyes search mine in the moonlit room and his thumb gently dusts over my bottom lip. He hesitates and frowns, clearly pained. "I'm not who you think I am."

I sit up onto my elbow and frown as I watch him. "Are you married?" I whisper. Oh no. My heart starts to beat furiously. He has a whole other life in South Africa, doesn't he? I have no idea what's going on at home for him.

He shakes his head and a soft smile crosses his face. "No, my love. I'm not married." He leans in to kiss me softly. "But I am unavailable to give you my heart."

Tears fill my eyes.

"Please know that I love you, Bridget."

"Ben," I whisper. "What's going on? Talk to me."

He leans in and sweeps his tongue gently through my mouth. I can't help it... I screw up my face up as the tears fall.

It's there again... the urge to tell him that I love him.

This man makes me so weak.

I sit up and wrap my arms around his broad shoulders. We kiss slowly and I feel my arousal start to rise.

"I've come to say goodbye," he whispers against my lips.

"What?" My eyes search his. "But you said—"

He cuts me off. "I can't be who you want me to be, Bridget."

"Yes, you can, Ben. *You* are who I want," I whisper angrily. Damn it, I hate this sneaking around shit. I can't even raise my voice.

He runs his thumb over my cheekbone as he studies my face. "I have a past, my love—one that I don't want to ever catch up with you. I won't bring that into your life."

I shake my head. "What are you talking about? We all have pasts. We can work it out together, Ben."

"Goodbye, Bridget," he whispers sadly. As he goes to stand, I grab his wrist.

"No. Don't go," I beg as I lose control. "Don't leave me. I love you."

He bends and kisses me gently. "Remember me with love, angel."

I stare at him through my tears.

"I love you," he whispers.

With one last lingering kiss, he breaks from me and stands to leave my room without looking back.

I curl into a ball. My heart physically hurts in my chest, and I weep.

Five years later

I smile at my beloved sister and I squeeze her hand in mine across the backseat. "God, it's so good to see you."

Tash screws up her face. "It really is."

"How long has it been since we were in the states?" Abbie frowns as she thinks.

"Five months." Natasha sighs as she blows out a deep breath. "But remember you are coming over for Thanksgiving."

"Try and stop us." Abbie smiles as she reapplies her lip gloss in her compact mirror.

We're in the back of a hire car on our way to a cocktail bar to meet the boys. Natasha, my sister, has lived in the US with her husband Joshua and their children for five years. Now she's finally come home to Sydney, Australia for a family wedding tomorrow. I've been so excited to have her home; I haven't been able to sleep all week.

Our best friend Abbie is with us, as well as Natasha's two security guards in the front. Max is driving and Anton is in the passenger seat. Joshua, Natasha's husband is an app developer who's hit the big time. Security is ridiculously high around her and their kids after everything they have been through.

Tash holds her hands up in the air in an exaggerated gesture. "Oh my God, tell me everything. What have I missed?"

I shrug. "Well..." I glance at Abbey. "I don't know?"

"I can't wait to meet your new boyfriend, Didge."

I smile. Everyone calls me Didge. It's short for Bridget.

"I can't wait for you to meet him, either. He's coming to the wedding tomorrow." I smile proudly.

"Great." Tash beams.

"Eric is a dick." Abbey smirks.

My mouth drops open, but I can't fight my smirk. "He is not." Bloody Abbey and her unfiltered, honest opinions.

"Is too," Abbey snaps. "He thinks he's Starsky or Hutch or some shit."

Natasha's eyes flick to me in question.

"He's not that bad." I laugh. "And yes, he's a cop. He's smoking hot though. Keep your opinions to yourself, Abbs. Please remember you're dating a gorilla on steroids. You can't exactly judge me and my choices."

Natasha and Abbey laugh, and I glance up and see Max smirk in the rear view mirror.

"Yeah, well, that gorilla is an animal in the bedroom. I'm down with gorillas."

Tasha and I both giggle. Abbey is a slut—a bona fide, self-confessed slut. She loves men and sex and is enjoying every perk of being a super attractive, single woman. Her hair is long and golden, and she has a kicking body that she shows off unashamedly.

Every man she meets ends up eating out of her hand.

Her mantra is no boyfriends, no ties, just fun.

And boy, does she stick to it.

We pull up, climb out of the car, and make our way to the bar where we're all meeting.

Joshua, Cameron, Scott, and Adrian are all sitting at a table. We make our way over. "Didge," Cameron calls as he grabs me and pulls me into a headlock. I laugh, scurry free and make my way around the table to kiss them all on the cheek. "Oh, it's so good to see you all. I'm getting a drink first and then I will be right back." I smile.

I walk to the bar, completely buzzing. My family are home and it feels so damn good.

We are in for a great weekend. They'll get to meet Eric tomorrow and I'm so excited.

"Hello, Bridget," a familiar voice says calmly behind me.

I turn around in a rush.

Dear God. The blood drains from my face.

"Ben," I whisper. He towers over everyone around him. My body recognises the strength in his, immediately weakening my legs.

My heart starts to hammer in my chest.

"What…?" I shake my head. I have no words. "What are you doing here?"

His hungry eyes drop down my body. "I'm here for you."

STANTON ADORE
Excerpt.

Available now – full series completed.

"YES I'LL have a tall latte, double shot," he smiles. "I'll have a skim cap please." The waitress scribbles on her pad and leaves us alone.

He rests his elbows on the table and links his hands together under his chin, waiting for me to speak first. His eyes have a mischievous glow to them.

"So Josh, tell me about your life?"

He shrugs his shoulders. "What do you want to know?"

"I hear you're wealthy."

He smiles, "In some things."

I tilt my head on the side, "What do you mean?"

"Well, I have money. It depends on your definition of wealthy."

Oh, I suppose. What's your definition?" I ask, surprised.

He shrugs again. "Happily married, healthy kids."

The waitress returns with our order.

Smiling, I rest my chin on one hand while I find myself swooning at his feet. "Are you dating?" I ask.

He scrunches up his nose, "Hell no." Our drinks arrive and the waitress's eyes linger a little long on Mr Orgasmic here. I narrow my eyes at her. Ok, enough, buzz off.

"You," I frown.

"Huh?"

"Are you dating?" I ask.

"No, nothing like that. Mum told me you had a boyfriend."

I nod a little embarrassed. "Um, ex-boyfriend," I murmur.

"What happened? Why did you break up?"

I smile. He smiles, "I see you're still a shit liar."

"I hoped you hadn't heard about that," I wince.

"What? Heard that some poor bastard asked you to marry him and you knocked him back and dumped his sorry ass?"

I put my hand over my face in embarrassment. "It sounds cold when you put it like that." I peek out from behind my hands to see him smirking at me.

"What happened?" He asks.

"We were never going to work out. I've never been so shocked in my life as the day he proposed. It was awful." His thumb is under his chin and he is wiping the side of his pointer across his lips as he listens, his gaze locked on mine.

"Why wouldn't you have worked out?"

"We weren't …compatible."

He raises his eyebrows. "Compatible," he repeats.

Why did I say that?

"You mean sexually?" His eyes darken with an emotion I'm familiar with. Arousal.

"Among other things," I quickly add. I suddenly feel very uncomfortable. "Why aren't you married?" I blurt out.

He smiles a slow sexy smile. "I haven't found anyone who fits the job description."

"What's the job description?" I breathe.

His eyes bore into mine with an intensity that heats my blood. "Someone who fucks like a slut, with the morals of a nun."

I choke on my coffee. Of all the things I thought he would say, that was definitely not it. I feel a frisson of uneasiness creeping up on me.

"You can't be serious?" I gasp.

494

"Absolutely," He nods as he takes a sip of his latte, his eyes not leaving mine.

"You want to marry a slut?"

He nods again. "It depends what your definition of a slut is. What do you think a slut is?" he asks.

"Someone who will sleep with anyone," I reply.

He nods and takes another sip of his latte. "You see I think a slut is a woman who loves to fuck."

I swallow the large lump in my throat. His voice has dropped to a low husky sound, one that is screaming to my subconscious. He continues, "I couldn't be with a mousy woman who doesn't love to fuck as much as I do. I have an insatiable appetite for sex," He licks his lips. "High maintenance so to speak." His eyes burn into me once again, silently daring me to say something. His eyes drop to my lips and want pools in my stomach. "The woman I marry will have to endure hours and hours of being tied to our bed, legs spread wide while I pleasure her with my tongue and fuck her with my hands. Then put up with me continually driving into her tight cunt with my cock so hard that she won't know where I end and she begins. Constantly. She would have to love taking me orally, vaginally and anally…. repeatedly." He gazes at me again and steeples his hands under his chin.

For the love of god, my mouth has gone dry.

"Can I take your order, love?" I jump, oh shit did she just hear that?

"Um, bacon and eggs please, and an orange juice." I'm embarrassed and put my head down to hide my blush.

"I'll have the same." He smirks a sexy smile at me.

Bloody hell.

Ok, my brain has fried. I can't even speak as I visualize exactly what he has explained to me. Orally, vaginally and anally……shit. That sounds exactly what I want to do today. Is he trying to drive me out of my frigging head? He's not playing fair.

"So, precious." My eyes snap up at the nickname he used to call me. "Do you know anyone that you could put up for an interview?"

I scowl at him. He's playing with me, the bastard. He knows exactly what he's doing.

"Yes, I do actually, "I reply. Actually no I don't. Only me. I would rather cut of my left arm than put someone else up for that position. I scan my empty head for a comeback. Nope nothing, a 2am regret coming up.

"Are you purposely trying to turn me on?" I whisper.

"Is that what I'm doing?" His gaze bores into me, burning holes with its heat.

"Yes," I whisper. "You know you are."

He inhales a deep breath through his nose as he leans back in his chair and rearranges his cock unashamedly in his pants. My eyes drop down to between his legs and I swallow a golf ball in my throat. Ok, if he gets away from me today without giving me what I need, I'm going to need sectioning tonight.

"I'm always hard when I talk about what I need in a wife."

"You have this conversation often?" I'm offended.

"No, first time," He smiles.

I narrow my eyes. "Bastard," I whisper. "Stop playing with me."

Printed in Poland
by Amazon Fulfillment
Poland Sp. z o.o., Wrocław

53408616R10296